D1409888

DEC 0 8 2010

A Suitor for Jenny

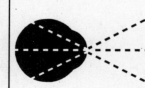

This Large Print Book carries the
Seal of Approval of N.A.V.H.

A SUITOR FOR JENNY

MARGARET BROWNLEY

THORNDIKE PRESS
A part of Gale, Cengage Learning

GALE
CENGAGE Learning·

Detroit • New York • San Francisco • New Haven, Conn • Waterville, Maine • London

GALE
CENGAGE Learning™

LIBRARY OF CONGRESS CATALOGING-IN-PUBLICATION DATA

Brownley, Margaret.
   A suitor for Jenny : a Rocky Creek romance / by Margaret Brownley.
     p. cm. — (Thorndike Press large print Christian romance)
(A Rocky Creek romance ; v 2)
   ISBN-13: 978-1-4104-3270-4
   ISBN-10: 1-4104-3270-X
   1. Women—Fiction. 2. Middle West—History—19th century—Fiction.
3. Large type books. I. Title.
PS3602.R745S88 2010b
813'.6—dc22   2010036318

Published in 2010 by arrangement with Thomas Nelson, Inc.

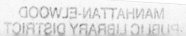

For Lee Duran
Friend, sister, mentor
The world is a brighter place
because of you.

When looking for a husband, it's best to go where the odds are in your favor.

— *The Compleat and Authoritative Manual for Attracting and Procuring a Husband,* MISS ABIGAIL JENKINS, 1875

ONE

A good man is like a good corset.
He will always be supportive and
never leave you hanging.
— MISS ABIGAIL JENKINS, 1875

Rocky Creek, Texas
1881
Old man Hank Applegate should have
known trouble was brewing the moment the
stagecoach thundered into town one week
and two days late.

Not that anyone cared. Actually, no one
but Hank so much as noticed the stagecoach, late or otherwise. He might not have
noticed either, had it not been for the
astounding amount of luggage tied to the
roof and back of the coach. Few people of
any importance or interest ever came to
town on the Wells Fargo stagecoach anymore. Nowadays, most folks preferred to
travel by train. And who in tarnation would

9

travel with *that* much luggage?

A gust of wind followed the stage, kicking up a whirlwind as it traveled through town. Hats blew off like popping corks. Emma Hogg's skirt flapped like the sails of a storm-tossed ship. Not that Hank was interested in the old spinster's skirts or anything else about her for that matter.

The horses hitched in front of Jake's Saloon pawed the ground, and the bat-wing doors swung to and fro.

The stage came to a halt in front of the weathered two-story Grand Hotel. Its driver scrambled to the ground like a man trying to escape an angry mob.

His curiosity stoked, Hank rose from his rocking chair for a closer look, his bony legs creaking like a dried-out saddle.

Squinting beneath the brim of his leather hat, he spat a dark stream of tobacco juice over the railing of Fairbanks General Merchandise and clamped down on his jaw, letting his toothless gums rub against each other.

The door of the stage flew open, and he caught a glimpse of a dainty slipper and a slim, feminine ankle. Thinking he was seeing things, he leaned forward until the rickety railing wobbled beneath his weight. Not that he noticed. He was too busy watching a pretty miss emerge from inside the coach.

By thunder! If she wasn't a sight for sore eyes! Dressed in fancy blue garb trimmed with black lace, and a hat with feathers enough to tar a mountain, she tugged at her fitted jacket and gave her blue parasol a determined shake.

Still, he didn't suspect a thing, not a thing. Any thought that the town and its male inhabitants were in mortal danger was the furthest thing from his mind. Then two *more* women stepped out of the coach behind her, all dressed in kind and chattering like nervous young hens.

The blonde woman in blue appeared to be the leader of the petticoat troop, and the others referred to her as Jenny. With skirts awhirl, she ordered the driver to unhitch the luggage. Pointing here and pointing there with the tip of her parasol, she issued one command after another, never so much as stopping for air.

"Be careful with this," Jenny instructed. "Be careful with that." At one point she grabbed a bandbox from the driver and carried it to the porch of the hotel herself, muttering under her breath.

Hank could hardly take his eyes off her. That Jenny woman was something, all right.

Bold, brash, and as subtle as a grizzly with a sore backside. Even the wind knew not to mess with her, the air as still as an old battlefield.

She turned to scold one of her charges, who had done nothing but gripe since disembarking. "Hush up, Mary Lou. You haven't stopped complaining since we left Haswell. How do you expect me to find you a husband when you never stop talking?"

Hank scratched his whiskered chin and inched his way down the warped wooden steps to make sure he'd heard right. Did she say *husband?*

The girl called Mary Lou pushed out her lips in a childish pout, blew a wisp of blonde hair away from her face, and fanned herself furiously. "You think you're going to find me a husband in this awful town?" She looked around with obvious distaste.

"Absolutely." Jenny lifted her chin, her eyes bright with determination. "By the time I'm finished with this town, both of you will have kind and loving husbands."

Hank blinked. *Both?* As the full implication of what the Jenny woman said took hold, his eyes nearly popped out of his head. It was no secret that from the day they were born, womenfolk devoted themselves to landing husbands. But never had he heard it stated so boldly. And when did the female population start searching for husbands in packs?

That's when it hit him like a ton of spit. Only one conclusion could be drawn from such a flagrant female presence: the town was under siege.

Jenny gave her younger sisters a warning look. She was in no mood for their complaints. She was hot and tired, and every bone in her body ached from the journey.

Traveling to Rocky Creek had been a nightmare. The stagecoach had broken down not once but twice. The driver blamed Jenny's unprecedented amount of baggage for their troubles, but she knew better. It was his reckless driving that caused the axle to break and the wheel to fall off. If only she'd used a little more tact in saying so. Maybe then they wouldn't have had to sit on the side of the road for three days waiting for another stage while he pouted.

Mary Lou heaved an unladylike sigh. "This has got to be the sorriest-looking town I've ever set eyes on."

"Watch what you say," Jenny scolded. "Any man hearing you carry on so is likely to take off in the other direction." She hiked up her skirts just above her ankles. "And

Brenda, for goodness' sake. What are you eating now?"

Brenda was almost twice as wide as Jenny. "Nothing. You laced up my corset so tight I *can't* eat. I can't even breathe. You didn't lace up Mary Lou's corset this tight."

Mary Lou gave her head a jaunty toss. "That's because I come by my figure *naturally*."

"You don't have to act so superior," Brenda said, straightening her shawl and scowling at Mary Lou. "Especially since you are wearing —"

"Oh, hush up," Mary Lou said irritably.

Feeling sorry for Brenda, Jenny gave her youngest sister's cheek a loving pat. Brenda loved to eat and it showed, no matter how tightly Jenny laced her corset. Poor Brenda had been so nervous about making this trip and the prospect of landing a husband, she had practically eaten nonstop during the planning stages and now had a double chin to show for it.

"Stand proud, my dear sister. You are blessed with a loving, generous nature and a sweet disposition," Jenny said.

"What good is that?" Brenda patted the dark sausage curls that bounced beneath her hat. "Men don't care a fiddle about dispositions."

14

"Oh, they'll care. I'll make sure that they do," Jenny said with a determined nod. She'd planned this trip with meticulous care, leaving nothing to chance. If necessary, she would use every last penny from the sale of the family farm to procure husbands for her sisters and secure their futures. Nothing or no one would be allowed to stand in her way.

"Maybe you'll find a husband too," Brenda said softly.

Mary Lou shook her head. "Jenny's too independent to get married. Even Father said so. Besides, she's too old."

"She's only twenty-two," Brenda argued. "That's only old if you're a cow."

"I don't need a husband," Jenny said, giving her sisters a stern look. "I'm perfectly capable of taking care of myself. Now, come along. We have work to do before I can start interviewing the men of this town."

Satisfied that the last of the luggage had been hauled down from the stagecoach, she handed the harried driver a coin, though the fool man didn't deserve a pittance. Her parasol tucked beneath her arm, she clapped her hands twice. With quick, efficient steps, she herded the two younger women toward the double doors of the hotel, issuing orders all the way.

"Stand up tall. Head high. Take little steps. And whatever you do, act like ladies . . ."

At first, Marshal Rhett Armstrong couldn't make heads or tails out of Hank's ranting and ravings. The marshal lifted his booted feet from his desk and sat forward.

Had he heard right? Did Hank say something about the town being under siege?

"I'm a-tellin' ya, Marshal, we got ourselves a peck o' trouble."

Hank looked so distressed Rhett jumped up from his desk and tore open the door of his office. Stepping outside, he glanced up and down the narrow dirt road running through town. It was midday with not a soul in sight.

He slammed the door shut. "What are you carrying on about? No one's out there."

"That's because they're at the hotel."

"That makes sense," Rhett said, trying to tease the old man out of his ramblings. He took his place behind the desk again. "Strangers generally like to take a bath and rest before attacking a town."

"You're right." Hank made a face and grunted in disgust. "I wouldn't put it past them to get all gussied up before they confront us. I'm a-tellin' you, Marshal, not a man alive can defend hisself from the likes of that Jenny woman."

That got Rhett's attention. "Did you say *woman?*"

"That's what I'm tryin' to tell ya. We've been taken over by three womenfolk. The colonel's name is Jenny."

"Colonel?" Rhett studied Hank. As far as he could tell, Hank hadn't been drinking, at least not any more than usual. "Let me get this straight. Three women want to take over this town?" The idea was so absurd it was all he could do to keep from laughing.

Hank, however, remained serious. "Now you're ropin' the calf."

Rhett rubbed his chin. "Why would these women want to do such a thing?"

Hank's eyebrows disappeared beneath the brim of his hat. " 'Cuz they want to catch themselves husbands, that's why. Heard it with me own two ears."

Rhett sat back in disbelief. "They came *here* to hunt for husbands?" Any woman aiming to find eligible men in Rocky Creek was either desperate or ill-advised.

"I'm a-tellin' you, Marshal, it was that crazy war. Nothing ain't ever been the same since. When that Lincoln fellow freed the slaves, he opened up a whole can of worms. Now womenfolk think they got rights too.

17

And I'll tell you somethin' else . . ."

Rhett stifled a groan. Once the old man got on his soapbox, there was no stopping him. The War Between the States had been over for a good many years, but folks still blamed everything that happened, good, bad, and otherwise, on the war. It was the bane of Rhett's existence. If people would stop talking about the war, maybe he could stop thinking about it — thinking about what happened there.

"I'm telling you trouble's a-brewin'," Hank continued. He studied Rhett with obvious misgivings. "So what are you aimin' to do about it?"

Rhett twiddled his thumbs. "It's not against the law for women to look for husbands. If it were, I'd be obliged to put Miss Emma Hogg in jail." It was common knowledge that the spinster's marital lasso was aimed straight at Redd Reeder, owner of the Rocky Creek Café and Chinese Laundry.

"If you ask me, that's where the fool woman belongs." Hank gave an emphatic nod. "It's your duty to protect the citizens of this here town from sneaky, connivin' scoundrels." He stabbed the desk with a tobacco-stained finger for emphasis. "And I'm a-tellin' you, that Jenny woman is 'bout as connivin' as they come."

"All right, if it'll make you feel any better, I'll keep an eye on things." Rhett rose and walked around his desk, hoping Hank would take the hint and leave. "If they cause any trouble, they'll have to deal with me."

Hank looked him over from head to toe, doubt written on his weathered face. "I ain't got nothin' ag'inst you personally, Marshal. I know you can outdraw, outride, and outsmart practically every man in Texas. I also know you've captured your fair share of crim'nals since you took over for that Briggs fellow. But this is different. This woman's out to find husbands. I'm a-tellin' ya, them's the worst kind."

Rhett reached for the doorknob and swung the door open. "I appreciate your concern, Hank, but I've never met a woman I couldn't handle."

Hank made a face. "That's 'cuz you ain't never met the likes of Colonel Jenny. We're in for trouble, Marshal, and you better be ready." Without another word, Hank left the office and Rhett closed the door after him.

Rhett sat down at his desk and chuckled. Imagine thinking the town was under siege by three women. What a ridiculous notion. Nothing of the kind was going to happen on his watch. Since taking over as marshal a year earlier, he had single-handedly turned Rocky Creek into a law-abiding town. Any outlaw who was fool enough to show his face soon saw the error of his ways.

Rhett liked to think of himself as tough but fair. A straight-shooting man who questioned God's will but never His existence.

People respected him. Outlaws feared him. Nobody ever got close to him. He didn't let them get close.

He had every reason to believe he could handle whatever came his way.

Even a bunch of husband-hunting petticoats.

Two

The way to a man's heart is through his stomach, but never underestimate the power of a generous dowry.
— MISS ABIGAIL JENKINS, 1875

Jenny marched from building to building. She stopped only long enough to hammer a hand-printed billboard onto a door, wooden post, or siding with the heel of a high-button shoe before moving on. The notice read:

WANTED: HUSBANDS

**ONLY MEN WITH GOOD CHARACTER
NEED APPLY
INTERESTED PARTIES ARE TO MEET
AT THE GRAND HOTEL
10 A.M. TO 4 P.M.
MUST PROVIDE PROOF OF
FINANCIAL SECURITY**

The pounding of heel upon nail brought

men running out of saloons. Others hurried from across the street to read the notices, their curiosity stoked by Jenny's presence. Those unable to read insisted the announcements be read aloud.

For the most part, Jenny ignored the townsfolk — mostly men — milling around in the late afternoon except for a polite greeting and nod. Most showed little regard for good manners. Some didn't even know enough to lift a hat when greeting a woman. One man actually splattered a stream of tobacco juice in her path, forcing her to lift her skirt and walk around it. Another stood scratching himself like a flea-ridden dog.

What few women she passed looked down their noses with obvious disapproval after reading the notices, then hurried away.

It wasn't just the uncouth citizens that worried her. The town was in a shocking state of decay and disrepair. Never had she seen a more sorrowful hotel. Grand indeed! The room Jenny shared with her sisters was sparsely furnished with only a lumpy bed, a desk, a small bureau, and a washstand. There was no place to hang their clothes, and she had to pay double to get clean linens.

She wasn't certain the town had a school or library, and it had only one eating establishment. The Rocky Creek Café and Chinese Laundry stood between two saloons like a slim book flanked by two oversized tomes.

Even the church on the hill tilted to one side as if looking for a place to fall.

The town certainly was not what she had expected.

It wasn't by chance that she traveled to Rocky Creek. An article in the *Lone Star Tribune* stated that Rocky Creek had the highest number of rich bachelors per capita than any other place in Texas due to the recent cattle boom. Not that money was everything, of course, but an honorable man was an honorable man regardless of his bank account. For that reason, she saw nothing wrong in limiting the field to men with substantial financial means.

If what the newspaper said was true — and she was beginning to have serious doubts about the legitimacy of the claim — they were also the least civil-minded men imaginable. Not one penny had gone to improve the condition of the town.

Eager to finish hanging the remainder of her handbills and return to the hotel before dark, she hastened her step, but the feeling she'd made a terrible mistake in coming to Rocky Creek continued to haunt her for the rest of the night.

The following morning, Jenny rushed around the hotel room in a whirlwind. "Do hurry," she called, her voice thick with impatience. Her sisters' futures were at stake; this was not the time to dawdle.

She spent the better part of the morning supervising their toilettes, leaving nothing, not so much as the smallest detail, to chance. Every shiny hair on their pretty heads was perfectly coiffed, every fold of their dresses meticulously arranged, every piece of jewelry artfully chosen.

Already potential suitors lined up in front of the hotel in response to the handwritten notices Jenny had plastered around town the day before. Their rough, sometimes querulous voices drifted through the open window.

The town was a disappointment. Still, she couldn't help but feel encouraged by the number of men waiting outside.

"It's hot," Mary Lou complained. She paced the room restlessly, fanning herself.

"How many times do I have to tell you? You must fan yourself gracefully." Jenny took the silk fan from her sister and, with a gentle wave of the arm, demonstrated. "See?"

Mary Lou grabbed her fan away and defiantly fanned herself with the same quick flicks of the wrist as before. Jenny sighed. Her younger sister could be as ornery as a three-legged mule. Though Mary Lou sometimes pushed her to the limits, Jenny secretly loved her spirit and hated having to put a damper on it.

Jenny threw up her hands. "Mary Lou, how will I ever marry you off if you fight me all the way?"

Mary Lou's eyes blazed. "If finding a husband means I have to watch everything I say and do, then I'm not sure it's worth all the bother."

Brenda entered the fray. "Why can't we be like you? I don't see you putting yourself out to snare a husband."

"I don't need a husband," Jenny said with as much regret as bitterness. The burdens of her past weighed heavily on her shoulders. At times she resented her sisters, resented the choices she'd made to provide for them after their father died. She loved them both dearly, of course. Still, it was hard not to resent the circumstances that had forced her to relinquish her own dreams of marriage. No decent man would ever want her as a wife, not after what she had done.

She pushed the thoughts away. This was no time to count regrets. "I'm perfectly capable of taking care of myself. Whereas you —" She reached out to straighten one of Brenda's dark curls. "You're like our dear sweet mama. You need a man to love and cherish you."

Brenda wrinkled her forehead. "Yes, but Mama was lucky. She had Papa, and there aren't many men like Papa."

"I know." Pain squeezed Jenny's heart. Many, including her grandfather on her mother's side, considered their father a ne'er-do-well. Papa had chased the current boom like a dog chasing its tail. His dreams of hitting it big in his youth took him to the California goldfields and Colorado silver mines. Not even marriage or children prevented him from falling for the great Nevada diamond hoax or chasing after the booming wheat business in the Panhandle, though he had no knowledge of farming and even less of business. His faults were as big as his dreams, but as a father none could compare. He lavished his daughters with love and never once tried to change them or make them behave in a way that went against their natures.

No doubt he would be appalled if he knew what she had put her sisters through these last few months, but then he didn't understand that their mother came by her grace and beauty naturally. Most women had to work to achieve such desirable attributes.

Pushing such thoughts away, she glanced about the room. Much to her dismay, her sisters looked close to tears. Even after seven years, any mention of their parents caused grief.

Fearing their faces would get all red and splotchy, Jenny broke the solemn silence that filled the small hotel room with a no-nonsense voice meant to distance them from the past. "Brenda, shoulders back. And Mary Lou, mercy me. What have you done to yourself?"

"She's wearing bosom pads," Brenda said.

Jenny leveled a sharp look at her sister. "Is that true?"

"What if it is?" Looking as defiant as ever, Mary Lou wiggled her shoulders and purposely arranged the neckline of her yellow gingham dress to show as much cleavage as possible. "You said it yourself. What the good Lord doesn't give us naturally, we have to give ourselves."

"I was talking about grace and charm, not body parts." Jenny held out her hand. "Give them to me."

"I will not!"

"You'll hand them over, young lady, or I'll take them myself."

"Ohhh!" Mary Lou reached into her dress, pulled out the Zephyr Bosom Pads, and tossed them on the floor. "There! Are you happy now?"

Jenny heaved a sigh. "You're beautiful, Mary Lou, just the way you are." It was true, every word. Her heart-shaped face and delicate pink complexion provided the perfect canvas for her lively blue eyes and ever-changing expressions.

Brenda, apparently feeling guilty for snitching on Mary Lou, slipped an arm around her shoulder. "Anyone can see how beautiful you are. I'd give anything to have your small waist."

"See?" Jenny said, approvingly. "What more assurance do you need?"

If landing a husband for Mary Lou depended on appearances alone, Jenny would have no trouble. Unfortunately, a man drawn to her obvious beauty would have to be hard of hearing to put up with her constant complaints.

Voices drifted up from the street below. Jenny peered through the window and gave a satisfied nod. The crowd just kept growing. At least fifty, maybe even a hundred, men gathered below. The line snaked from the hotel all the way to the Wells Fargo bank at the other end of town.

Jenny smiled. This was going to be easier than she'd thought. It was entirely possible that she would achieve her goal and round up two prospective husbands before the day was over.

Feeling greatly encouraged, she gathered up her satchel and gave her sisters one last inspection. Mary Lou looked perfect in every way, but Brenda — oh dear, what was she going to do with Brenda?

Jenny used every possible trick she could think of to draw attention away from Brenda's full figure. Ruffles and ruching added bulk that could either be attractive or unflattering, depending on the size and shape of one's form. For this reason, Jenny chose the plainest dress possible for Brenda, a brown, long-sleeved gown with only the slightest bustle in back, and a matching shawl. It was amazing how much a shawl could hide when draped properly.

By the sound of rising voices, the crowd outside was growing restless. "Time to go. Ladies, your gloves."

While her sisters donned their gloves, Jenny checked her own appearance in the beveled glass mirror over the dresser.

She hadn't fussed much with herself other

than to pull her thick blonde hair into a no-nonsense bun at the nape of her neck. Her blue gown was almost as plain as Brenda's, but not for the same reason. Her slender form might have benefited from a ruffle or two, and her hat had seen better days, but the excitement of seeing her dreams for her sisters about to materialize put a shine in her eyes and brought a blush to her cheeks.

If she was successful in her quest for suitable husbands, her sisters would never want for anything again. Maybe then she could put the past behind her.

Maybe then she might even be able to forgive herself.

She clapped her hands. "Remember, now. Smile and act like ladies."

THREE

Charm and composure must prevail at all times. If a gunfight erupts, exit the scene with grace and serenity.
— MISS ABIGAIL JENKINS, 1875

Marshal Rhett Armstrong should have known trouble was brewing. He'd first spotted those boldly worded posters early that morning when he rode into town. How could he miss them? They were plastered everywhere, even on the door of his office.

Most men would take offense at the tone of the posters, but none did more than he. The nerve of the woman. Did she really think the men of Rocky Creek would stand for such nonsense? Financial proof, indeed!

Who was this woman? And what gave her the right?

She obviously had a thing or two to learn about his town, and he was just the man to teach it to her. He ripped the poster off the

31

door and tossed it into the wastepaper basket. No man in his right mind would fall for such feminine foolishness.

By the time he heard the commotion outside, close to a hundred men had proven him wrong. At least half of them were proving it with their fists.

Rhett ran outside where a brawl was in full swing. He pulled out his pistols, pointed the barrels toward the sky, and fired. The loud pop of gunfire got the brawlers' attention, and for a fleeting moment the rowdy men froze in place, some with their fists midair.

"Get up, all of you," Rhett bellowed. One by one, the men staggered to their feet, some with bloodied lips.

Satisfied that order had been restored, at least temporarily, Rhett holstered his guns and followed the line of men all the way to the hotel. "If there's any more trouble, you'll all find yourselves in jail."

He reached the front of the line, which started at the Grand. Three wide-eyed women stood on the boardwalk in front of the hotel staring at him.

Well, now. He hadn't seen so much feminine finery since he'd last traveled to New Orleans. Womenfolk came to town to shop at Fairbanks General Merchandise and attend Sunday worship service. But since there wasn't much else to do on Main Street but drink and act rowdy, women mostly stayed away.

That's why he was surprised to see several members of the Rocky Creek Quilting Bee in town so early. The show hadn't even begun, and already the women's mouths puckered in disapproval.

Rhett pushed his hat back on his head, leaned against a wooden post, and hooked his thumbs onto the belt of his holster.

At the front of the crowd, a tall woman with hair the color of honey stepped forward and regarded the men with a slow, sweeping glance that registered neither disappointment nor approval.

Her eyes met his with none of the usual feminine fluttering of eyelashes, matching him stare for stare.

Bold as a bull, she was, with flashing blue eyes and a stubborn chin that rose a notch higher as she gazed at him. He sensed her measuring him against standards that he didn't have a prayer of meeting.

She studied him with keen interest before glancing at the shiny marshal's badge on his vest. Her eyes narrowed and an obvious look of dismissal crossed her face before she turned away.

He squinted and tightened his jaw. She knew nothing about him and yet she had clearly judged him and found him lacking. Only two other people had been foolish enough to make that mistake, and both had lived to regret it. He didn't need anyone to tell him that this was the woman old man Applegate called *the colonel.*

Well, she was the prettiest colonel he'd ever set eyes on, that's for sure, even if she did lack tact or the ability to judge a man on more than just appearance and bank account.

She lifted her voice and addressed the crowd with businesslike demeanor. "My name is Miss Jenny Higgins," she said. She held a leather notebook in one hand and wielded a parasol in the other.

You could have heard a pin drop as the men hung onto her every word. Even the Quilting Bee members fell silent.

One by one, Miss Higgins introduced her sisters, pointing out their many accomplishments. Rhett was surprised to see Miss Higgins's gaze soften as she regarded each of her sisters with evident pride. Both young women stepped forward in turn and the crowd went wild. The men shouted approval. They clapped and stomped their feet, tossing their hats in the air.

Brenda Higgins was the plump one with brown hair, unlike her blonde sisters. Dressed more conservatively than her slender siblings, she won the crowd over with her shy smile.

The one named Mary Lou made no such attempt to endear herself. If anything, she looked bored to tears. Not that it seemed to matter. The men were too dazzled by her big blue eyes, blonde hair, and shapely figure to care about anything else. They stomped their feet and called her name.

Mrs. Hitchcock clucked her tongue in disapproval, the feathers on her shiplike hat flying in every direction. "Disgusting," she said, repeating herself.

Next to her, Mrs. Taylor trembled with outrage. "There ought to be a law against women parading around like that."

Both women glared at Rhett as if it were his fault that no such law existed. He shrugged and turned his attention back to Miss Jenny Higgins.

"I love you, Mary Lou," one spectator called out.

Jenny cast a disapproving glance in his direction and the others, taking the hint, fell silent.

Rhett was amazed how quickly *the colonel* could control the crowd. While he sometimes required a gun to manage a mob, her weapon of choice was nothing more than a disapproving glance and the men grew still as tombstones.

Jenny glanced at her sisters as if to offer encouragement. The soft, loving look she gave them came and went so quickly, Rhett wondered if he imagined it.

Her expression now stern, she cleared her throat. "As you know, I'm looking for husbands for my two sisters."

This announcement drew shouts of approval from the men and groans of protests from the women. Mrs. Hitchcock swooned and looked about to faint, but Mrs. Taylor quickly relieved her of that notion with a firm shaking.

Jenny frowned and waited for quiet.

A man whom Rhett recognized as Timber Joe yelled out, "Just let us know where we can sign up."

Men began to push and shove, trying to move closer to the hotel, but Jenny could not be persuaded to rush things.

"Not all of you need sign up," she said, her voice ringing with command. "I shall only consider those of you with adequate financial means."

"Shucks!" Theo Barker moaned. "That leaves me out."

"Better luck next time," someone yelled.

Jenny gave the wooden railing one swift rap with her parasol, commanding silence. "Along with a bank statement proving financial means, I insist that you be of good moral character."

She quickly listed the qualities she sought: honesty, devotion, and kindness. "Vulgar language will not be tolerated, nor will a man who spits in public. And if you have a fondness for whisky or gambling, do not bother filling out an application."

Consulting her notebook, she continued to list her stringent requirements, which included how a man should talk, walk, and dress.

Rhett's eyebrows kept rising. No such man existed. At least he hoped not.

A few men left, but most stayed, including those whom Rhett knew didn't have a gnat's chance in a sandstorm of meeting her strict standards.

"You must also prove you know how to treat a lady," Jenny continued.

"How can we prove *that?*" one man shouted.

Jenny leveled him with eyes cool enough to douse a prairie fire. "If you have to ask, then you're probably not qualified to be a husband."

Turning back to the crowd, she resumed her instructions. "You are not to make contact with my sisters without my express permission. If your application is approved, I shall inform you as to which of my sisters you may court."

Inching his way around the outer circle of the crowd, Marshal Armstrong studied the faces of the men and was stunned by what he saw. Each man hung on to her every word. Indeed, they were practically eating out of her hands.

Traitors! All of them.

What was the matter with these men? A woman couldn't just stand up and announce she was looking for husbands like so many head of cattle. It wasn't right. Such delicate matters should be discussed in parlor rooms, behind closed doors.

The only male growing up in a household that included his mother, grandmother, and three sisters, Rhett had a strong opinion on what constituted proper behavior for a woman, and *Colonel* Jenny clearly failed on all accounts.

"Fill out this application," she said. The men called out and waved their arms as she walked through their ranks, passing out forms.

Rhett shook his head. The way the men

carried on, you'd think she was handing out currency instead of life sentences.

That did it! Someone in this town had to restore order, if not sanity. He waited until she stepped onto the boardwalk in front of the hotel and again faced the men. He then made his move.

Forging a path through the crowd, he charged up the steps and confronted her head-on. Her two sisters moved away, allowing him full rein.

"Now see here, miss," he began. He remained cool on the outside, but inside he seethed. His anger was fueled as much by her earlier dismissal of him as it was by the trouble she caused.

Had he expected her to cower or drop her uppity demeanor, he would have been sorely disappointed. She didn't look the least bit intimidated by him. Not a good thing.

Up close, she was even taller than he supposed, but he still towered over her, forcing her to lift her head to look him in the eye.

She didn't even flinch. "I'm afraid you'll have to get in line and wait your turn like everyone else."

"Wait my —" he sputtered. "I have no desire to —"

"Just write it on the application," she said. She held up a form.

"I'm not filling out your blasted application."

Her gaze locked with his. "How can you expect me to consider you as husband material if you refuse to fill out a simple form?"

"Miss . . ."

"Higgins."

"Miss Higgins, I am here for one reason and one reason alone. I am the town marshal, and you are creating a disturbance."

Her eyes widened in surprise. "I believe you have that wrong, Marshal. *You* are the one creating a disturbance. I am merely trying to do what I came here to do."

He leaned over until his nose practically touched hers. "Well, you're going to have to take your business elsewhere. Me and the boys here don't take kindly to having our finances and morals scrutinized by a stranger."

His combative attitude gave others the courage to voice their own objections.

"You're darn tootin' I don't want my morals scrut'nized," someone called out. "Give a woman an inch and the next thing you know, she'll want to scrut'nize *ev'rythin'*."

Obviously sensing a shift in the men's demeanor, Jenny's eyes blazed. "Now look what you've done, Marshal."

He pulled back, but not far away enough

40

to escape her delicate lavender scent. "What *I've* done? You're the one who came to town and got the men all riled up."

"And as soon as I have finished my business, I shall leave," she assured him.

"If there's any more trouble, you'll be leaving *before* you've conducted your business. You can be certain of that."

"Here's something *you* can be certain of, Marshal. I have no intention of being told what I can and cannot do."

Having his authority questioned in front of all these men was intolerable. All eyes were on him, waiting. Though no one moved, he could almost hear their thoughts. *What are you going to do about it, Marshal?*

He leveled her with cool assessing eyes. "You'll do exactly what I say."

"You can't make me —"

"The last person who said that to me is now cooling his heels in jail." He placed his hand on the handcuffs at his side to show he meant business.

Her mouth dropped open. "You wouldn't!"

He tilted his head back and glowered at her. "Try me."

Mary Lou wanted to die. The horror of it all. Never had she felt so embarrassed in all her born days. All these men ogling her. Now the marshal threatening to put Jenny in jail.

During the escalating argument, the men standing in line seemed to enjoy the spectacle. Some even took bets as to who would emerge the victor. This only added to Mary Lou's misery. If Jenny ended up in jail, Mary Lou would never be able to show her face again.

To make matters worse, she was hot. Though it was only the beginning of June, already it felt like summer. She felt sticky and itchy and just plain miserable. There had to be an easier way to find a husband. Unable to stand another humiliating moment, she picked up her skirts and hurried into the relatively cool hotel lobby, away from prying eyes and unrelenting sun.

Jenny would be furious with her, of course, but Mary Lou didn't care a whit about that. All she wanted to do was leave this awful town. What she would give to go back home to Haswell, but that was no longer possible. Jenny sold their small farm and was determined to use every last penny, if necessary, to find suitable husbands for her and Brenda.

Just as Mary Lou reached the staircase, a male voice rang out behind her.

"Excuse me, miss!"

She turned and stared at the serious face of a man she guessed to be in his late twenties. Never had she seen a man so oddly dressed. His short pants cut to the knees looked like they had been fashioned from a mackinaw blanket the U.S. government issued to Indians. He wore a wide scarlet sash tied around his waist, high leather boots, and a red knitted cap. His rugged, handsome face was bronzed by the sun, his eyes so blue they took her breath away.

"Are you talking to me?" she asked, though there was no one else in the lobby but a droopy-eyed clerk behind the reception desk.

"Yes," he replied, his mouth tilted upward in amusement. Pulling off his cap, he walked toward her with a lazy grace at once intriguing and disturbing. He had brown hair that fell to his collar and a neatly trimmed mustache. "If memory serves me correct, your sister introduced you as Miss Mary Lou Higgins. Is that right, ma'am?"

She eyed him up and down warily. She was sure he didn't mean to harm her. Still, there was something in the way he looked at her that made her nervous. "T–that's correct," she stammered. "W–why do you ask?"

He raised a dark brow as if trying to

decide whether the question deserved an answer. "I need to know what to call you," he said at last.

"Why?" she asked, impatient to escape to her room before Jenny discovered her gone.

"I'm Jeff Trevor." When she made no reply, he added, "Your future husband."

She was barely able to control her gasp of surprise. "Oh, you d–don't understand," she stammered, annoyed to feel her cheeks blaze hot. "You must first fill out an application, and then my sister —"

He discounted her words with a wave of his hand. "I can't fill out a form," he said. "I can't read. Can't write either."

This surprised her. He certainly *looked* educated. His eyes were warm with intelligence, and he held himself with a confidence that implied he was knowledgeable in matters that counted.

"Without schooling, I'm afraid you don't qualify," she said in a kind voice, not wanting to hurt his feelings. She turned toward the stairs. Much to her surprise, he bounded past her and stood on the step in front of her, blocking her way.

"Don't get me wrong, ma'am. I had plenty of schooling," he said. "I just never learned to read. I could never get the letters to stop bouncing around long enough to make head or tails out of them."

Mary Lou had never heard of bouncing letters. Was he serious or just having fun at her expense?

"I–I think you better discuss this with my sister." The frigid tone of her voice would have put most men in their place, but Mr. Trevor didn't seem the least bit discouraged.

"I have no intention of discussing my personal affairs with anyone but you," he said.

Alarmed by his persistence, she glanced over her shoulder at the still-sleeping clerk. "I'm really not interested in your personal affairs, Mr. Trevor."

"If you're not now, you will be," he said. "You'll save us both a lot of time and bother if you do it and get it over with."

She regarded him with open curiosity. "Do what?"

"Why, interview me, of course. Since you're the one I'm going to marry, it makes sense that you be the one to interview me. Come on. Don't be shy. Ask me whatever you like."

Not knowing what to do, she looked him up and down. He stood as straight and tall as a towering pine tree, his legs sturdy as tree trunks. Was it possible for a man built so sturdy to have a weak mind? She didn't think so.

He gave a knowing nod. "You want to know why I'm dressed like this."

Her lashes flew up. "I want to know nothing of the sort." Unable to hide her reddening cheeks, she glared at him.

"No need to feel embarrassed, ma'am. I'm a logger. Work at the Rocky Creek sawmill, I do. I own a small cabin outside of town. Built it with my own two hands. All it needs is a woman's touch to turn it into a real home."

Exasperated, she fanned herself furiously, not caring that she broke ladylike conventions. Obviously bouncing letters was the least of the man's problems.

"As I explained," she said, pronouncing each word precisely so there would be no further misunderstanding. "I have no interest in you. Certainly I have no intention of marrying you."

He stared at her, surprise written all over his face. "How can you be certain? You know nothing about me."

"I know that you are most stubborn."

His face split into a devastating smile that made her heart pound. "I guess you know as much about me as I know about you."

Not certain if he was insulting her or

merely agreeing with her, she drew back. "Yes, well . . . Now if you'll step aside . . ."

"That's it? You don't want a financial statement from me?"

"Certainly not!"

Approval warmed his eyes. "I have to say that speaks mighty well of you, Miss Higgins." He put on his cap and let her pass.

Head held high, she walked up the stairs and tried to ignore the feel of his heated gaze on her back.

Once she reached the second-floor landing, she couldn't resist looking over her shoulder. He stood exactly where she'd left him, casually leaning against the dull brass banister. He looked about as self-assured as a man could possibly look.

"Since there's nothing more you want to know about me, you can consider us engaged," he called after her.

She tried to draw a breath, but the air caught in her chest. Never in her life had she met such a brazen man. "I never —" She was so upset, she actually sputtered.

"So that's all that worries you," he said, looking immensely relieved. "Sounds like you're a fine Christian woman. A man couldn't ask for anything more. Don't you worry. Once we're married, I'll teach you everything you need to know. I have a feeling you're a fast learner. Good day." With that, he hurried down the stairs and through the lobby toward the double doors leading outside.

Cheeks burning, Mary Lou stared after him until he had vanished. "Of all the nerve." She glanced at the desk clerk, but much to her relief, the man was still asleep. No one had witnessed her embarrassing encounter with Mr. Trevor.

She turned and ran down the hall to the room she shared with her sisters, and she locked herself inside.

Shaking, she leaned her head against the closed door until her cheeks no longer burned and her knees finally stopped shaking.

She threw her fan on the bed, pulled off her gloves and hat, and paced the floor. It was all Jenny's fault! Had Jenny not forced them into traveling to this horrid place, she would never have met the likes of Mr. Trevor.

As much as she wanted to confront Jenny, she knew that her oldest sister would only lay the blame on her shoulders for returning to their hotel room unchaperoned.

Not that she had anything to worry about. Not really. No one could marry her without her consent. Not even Jenny could force her to do something she didn't want to do.

Mr. Jeff Trevor was simply having fun at her expense. Bouncing letters, indeed! Chances are she would never set eyes on him again, and that was just how she wanted it.

FOUR

If you don't know whether or not to kiss a
handsome man, give him the benefit of
the doubt.
— MISS ABIGAIL JENKINS, 1875

That night, Jenny sat in their hotel room at
the battered oaken desk, reading through
the stack of applications. An oil lamp
flickered and hissed, casting a yellow glow
across the form in her hand.

This particular application had been filled
out with scrawling handwriting that was difficult to read. Every other word was misspelled and the writer described himself in
such glowing terms, she couldn't help but
laugh. He wrote, *Handsum, edukated, and
lively. I have two dolars under the matres and
there's more where that came frum.*

Sighing, she placed the application on the
fast-growing rejection pile and debated
whether to call it a night.

A stack of reference books took up most of the desk, leaving little room to write. The dog-eared pages addressed everything a proper lady needed to know from fashions to writing letters, from finding a suitable beau to planning the perfect wedding.

Grateful for the cool air that drifted through the open window, she glanced at the bed where her sisters slept, making certain they were adequately covered.

After a full evening listening to their incessant chatter, she welcomed the peace and quiet.

The day had been far more exhausting than she expected — and far less successful. True, an amazing number of men had shown up at the appointed time. But never would she have guessed so many of them could neither read nor write.

More than half of the applications had been left blank or simply signed with a single X. Of the forty-some forms that had been completely filled out, a dozen or more showed real promise. The number was nowhere near what she hoped for, of course, but she would take quality over quantity any day.

She reached for *The Compleat and Authoritative Manual for Attracting and Procuring a Husband* and flipped through the well-marked pages. Using the book as a guide, she fully expected to determine the suitability of each candidate in quick order.

Her major concern at the moment was getting her sisters to cooperate. Unfortunately, the author didn't address that problem. She returned the book to the pile.

She was still furious with Mary Lou for sneaking away. Sometimes she didn't know what got into the girl. Finding a husband was serious business, not to mention hard work. The sooner Mary Lou got that into her thick skull, the better for all of them.

The marshal, now, he was another problem. There was something about the man that made her feel . . . what? Threatened? Vulnerable? Perhaps it was the way he looked at her as if her carefully constructed defenses were nothing more than see-through glass.

He hadn't left her alone for a minute, not until she returned to her hotel room. And later when she'd glanced outside, she saw him standing across the way, no doubt watching her window. It was nerve-wracking. *He* was nerve-wracking. One look into those analytic eyes was enough to send goose bumps down her spine. Not even her closely guarded secrets seemed safe beneath the marshal's scrutiny.

What a pity that such a handsome face was wasted on the likes of him! He had some nerve, threatening to put her in jail if she caused another disturbance. As if it were her fault that the citizens of Rocky Creek didn't know how to behave in the presence of ladies.

Feeling oddly restless, she rose from her desk and paced around the room, careful not to wake her sisters. She paused in front of the window. Surely the marshal wouldn't still be spying on her. Not at this late hour. Still, she couldn't resist looking outside to make certain.

The sound of fiddles, drunken brawls, and an occasional gunshot had kept her on edge for most of the night, but now the town seemed deserted. A full moon cast a silvery glow on the street below.

Then she saw him. The dark form of the marshal on the opposite side of the street in front of the Rocky Creek Café and Chinese Laundry could not be missed. Even in the shadows, he was a formidable presence.

Heart pounding, she spun away from the window. Her back to the wall, she tried to think what to do. Did he plan to stand guard all night long? Unbelievable. He treated her like a criminal. Fuming, she decided to put a stop to such nonsense.

Head held high, shoulders back, she quietly let herself out of the room. With determined steps, she hastened along the dark hall, ran down the stairs, and rushed through the lobby. The thin fabric of her shirtwaist and skirt offered little protection against the cool night air, but she was too angry to care. She charged across the street, ready to confront the marshal face-to-face.

Here she comes.

Somehow Marshal Rhett Armstrong knew she would. Moments earlier he had dropped off his laundry at the Rocky Creek Café and Chinese Laundry across from the hotel. The café was owned by a range cook by the name of Redd Reeder. By night, Lee Wong, a former railroad worker, operated a laundry on its premises. This explained the large vats that took up half the dining room, the bags of laundry piled up on the boardwalk in front, and the clotheslines in back. It also accounted for the strong smell of lye soap that permeated the air, burned the eyes, and tainted the taste of café food.

After leaving his dirty laundry by the door, Rhett happened to look up at the single lit window of the hotel. Somehow he knew it was her room even before he saw her pacing back and forth.

He couldn't help but wonder who or what kept the lady pacing the floor so late at night.

Now he watched her hurtle toward him and chuckled. He couldn't help it. He could practically feel the heat emanating from her like a rampaging bull. He told himself to stay calm. *Don't let her get to you.*

He waited until she had crossed the dirt-packed street and stomped onto the board-walk in front of the café and laundry.

"Is it my turn to be interviewed?" he drawled softly.

"Don't flatter yourself." Hands at her waist, she glared at him. "I wouldn't let you marry either of my sisters if you were the last man on earth! I came to tell you to stop watching my every move."

He could tell her he was there to drop off laundry. It was the truth, and it would put the lady's mind at ease. Instead, he decided it would be more to his advantage to let her think he was, indeed, watching her.

"As long as you persist in this harebrained scheme of yours, you don't give me much choice."

"I am not doing anything illegal," she said.

"And I mean to see that you don't." In the light of the full moon, he imagined he could see stars in her eyes. More likely they

55

were barbs pointed straight at him.

"How do you propose to do that?" she demanded. "Surely you're not going to threaten to lock me up again, are you?"

"Don't tempt me," he said. If she were a man, she'd already be in jail for causing a ruckus that morning in front of the hotel. "As long as you understand I'm in charge of this town, we won't have a problem."

She gave her head a haughty toss. "You may be in charge of the town, Marshal, but you're not in charge of me. In fact, you have no control over me whatsoever."

It was a challenge if he ever heard one. "Are you sure about that, Miss Higgins?"

She paused a moment before answering. "Quite sure!"

He noted her hesitation with satisfaction. Obviously, she wasn't as sure as she'd like him to believe. Finding a chink in her armor, he studied her. She was something, all right. Righteous indignation had never looked so appealing. She stood ready to fight him tooth and nail, but it was the softer, more feminine side that worried him. That was the part that was dangerous.

Strands of unruly hair escaped her bun, softening her sharp features. The full moon cast a silvery light upon her face and added a luster to her eyes that was hard to ignore.

Her gaze could be a lethal weapon one moment and soft as candlelight the next. She sent out so many conflicting signals, he didn't know whether to duck for cover or take her in his arms.

Recalling how she had so easily dismissed him as a prospective husband for her sisters, he felt an almost overpowering need to prove himself. Let her dismiss him because of his badge, but never because she found him wanting as a man.

With this last thought in mind, he stepped forward, grabbed her around the waist, and kissed her soundly on her pretty pink lips. Let that show her who's boss.

The lady didn't even put up a pretense of a struggle. Instead she surprised him by throwing her arms around his neck and kissing him back.

Drat! Her lips were every bit as bold as the lady herself, and every bit as captivating. Her lavender fragrance encircled him, providing a pleasant remedy to the acrid smell of lye that wafted from the nearby laundry. Savoring the smell, feel, and taste of her, he was in dire danger of sinking into his own trap.

Astonished and more than a little intrigued, he hated to let her go, but he was trying to make a point, not a conquest.

Shaken, he pulled away. He towered over her and looked deep into her eyes. "Still think I'm not husband material, Miss Higgins?" His voice low, he watched for the least sign of surrender.

Instead, a knowing smile played at the corner of her mouth. "Still think you can control me?" she countered.

Both questions seemed to hang in midair before falling away unanswered. After a moment's silence, he stepped back and looked her up and down. For a woman who had just been kissed, she looked surprisingly unabashed. He rubbed his temple and turned. Hesitating for a moment, he then walked quickly to his waiting horse.

He mounted and regarded her from astride his saddle. Even now she looked ready to fight him. "Good night, Miss Higgins," he said, touching a finger to his white hat.

"Good night, Marshal," she replied in a stiff voice that clearly stated he had failed in his attempt to show her who was in control.

He galloped away with a sense of unease. The lady held her own, no doubt about that. He hated to admit it, but she got under his skin. Something stirred inside him, something strange yet oddly familiar. Something he didn't dare name. Not feelings.

Dear God, don't let them be feelings. The moment he let himself feel again would be his undoing.

Following the road out of town toward Ma's boardinghouse where he roomed, he considered how best to handle the Higgins woman in the future. He'd have to be a whole lot more careful, that's for sure.

Standing alone on the deserted street, Jenny watched the marshal until he disappeared into the folds of the night. Wolves bayed in the distance and laughter from a late night reveler drifted out from one of the saloons lining the street, but she hardly noticed. Or maybe it was simply that her heart was pounding too hard.

She took a deep breath. Laundry fumes filled her lungs and brought tears to her eyes. She forced herself to calm down. She hadn't counted on the marshal's interference. Nor could she have imagined his unorthodox methods.

Of all the —

She placed her hand on her mouth.

Imagine him thinking he could control her with a kiss. How ridiculous. How outrageous. The marshal's conduct was so outside the realm of normal behavior, she doubted her etiquette books would offer any help in dealing with him.

Her lips trembled beneath her fingertips. Though her body seemed oddly feverish, she shivered. The marshal kissed her. Worse, she kissed him back. For one crazy moment in time she lost control and it scared her. All those years ago she'd lost control of her life, and it almost destroyed her. It took years to fight her way back. When she did, she vowed never again to let a man ruin her.

Kissing the marshal only proved how perilously close she was to resorting to her old ways. What happened tonight must never happen again. Not ever.

She straightened her dress and patted her hair, but no amount of grooming could stop her spinning senses. Arms rigid at her side, hands curled into fists, she forced herself to concentrate on the task at hand. She came here for one reason and one reason alone: to find husbands for her sisters. And no one, not even the marshal, was going to stop her.

It was a long time before she was able to gather her wits enough to trek back to the hotel.

FIVE

Women who fall in love at first sight often wish they'd taken a second look.
— MISS ABIGAIL JENKINS, 1875

Marshal Armstrong rode into town the next morning, surprised to find a long line of disgruntled men outside his office. Tethering his horse, Lincoln, on the hitching post, he rubbed his hand along the gelding's slick neck before walking up the steps to the boardwalk to see what all the fuss was about.

Everyone talked at once. No one made sense.

"Quiet!" he ordered at last, motioning with his arms. Silence followed and he pointed to the man in front. "Silas, what's got you all riled up?"

Silas stepped forward. A tall, skinny man with a long, pointed face, Silas held his slouch hat in his hand. "The boys and me don't take kindly to that . . . that hussy and

61

her hoity-toity ways."

Armstrong grimaced. He didn't even have to ask the woman's name. Jenny was still stirring up trouble. No surprise there. "What has she done this time?"

"She posted the names of the men she wants to interview, along with a time schedule. It's right in front of the hotel for everyone to see."

"That she did," shouted a rough voice.

"Who does she think she is?"

The clamor of voices rose again.

"Quiet," Armstrong said. He waited until he had their attention. "Now listen up. No one is required to be interviewed against his will. Do you understand me? If you don't want to court her sisters, no one's forcing you. It's your choice."

His words were met with stony silence. The men looked at each other with puzzled expressions. Finally, Walt Merritt stepped forward. Widowed twice, he was in his forties and doing an admirable job of raising three children by himself.

"That's just it, Marshal. Our names ain't on the list."

Armstrong blinked. "So what's the problem?"

"The problem is that Miss Higgins ain't givin' us due consideration. She ain't givin' us a choice one way or the other."

"That's exactly right," the town barber said. Kip Barrel was as round as he was tall and had a deep resonant voice. Trained as an opera singer, his stage fright kept him from his dream of pursuing a singing career. "All that matters to that woman is a man's bank account."

Armstrong scratched his head. "If you think you should be considered as prospective husbands, I suggest you approach Miss Higgins directly."

"Oh, we ain't interested in marryin' no one," Merritt said. "It's just the princ'ple of the thing."

"That's right," Silas added. "I don't want no stranger tellin' me I ain't fit to be wed. That's for me to decide."

"Hear, hear!" the men yelled in unison.

Armstrong rubbed his head. It was too early for this. He'd hardly slept a wink last night. It was bad enough having to deal with Jenny Higgins during the day. Now she was interfering with his sleep. Enough!

Ready to get rid of the grumbling men, he hid his own annoyance behind a conciliatory expression. "I don't know what to tell you. As far as I know, no laws have been broken. I admit that Miss Higgins's methods are rather unusual, but as long she stays within the law, there's nothing I can do about it. Now go, get out of here. I've got work to do."

Stomping onto the boardwalk, he walked into his office. A list, eh? So what *kind* of man met with the lady's approval? He peered through the window and waited until the last man left.

Then he barreled toward the hotel to take a look at that confounded list of names for himself.

Mary Lou was worried about Jenny. A stickler for neatness, her oldest sister normally jumped out of bed each morning issuing orders and rushing them through their morning ablutions and chores in whirlwind fashion. "Orderliness and virtue go hand in hand" was Jenny's equivalent to "good morning." She acted like a misplaced shoe or unfolded garment would lead them down the road to iniquity.

On that particular morning, however, Jenny had hardly said a word. She didn't even seem to notice that the bed was still unmade when they left the room.

Even now, as they sat at a window table at the Rocky Creek Café and Chinese Laundry, she was uncommonly silent and hadn't once scolded Mary Lou for her table manners. Instead, she toyed with her food and stared into space. Something was clearly on her mind.

Mary Lou glanced at Brenda, who shook her head. It was obvious that she, too, was worried about Jenny's strange mood.

Maybe Jenny was having second thoughts about coming to this dreadful town in search of husbands. God, please let it be true!

Brenda stared at Jenny with a worried frown. "Jenny, do you feel all right? You've been awfully quiet all morning."

Jenny blinked like someone coming out of a trance. "I feel perfectly fine." She glanced around the room as if it suddenly occurred to her where they were. She then opened up her ever-present notebook and stared at the day's schedule.

"Do hurry and finish your breakfast. I've got work to do."

Her effort to pull herself together didn't fool Mary Lou in the least. Jenny could deny it all she wanted, but something was clearly bothering her.

Jenny frowned. "And you two have to attend to your lessons."

Mary Lou yawned with boredom. She stabbed at the sorrowful excuse for a flapjack on her plate. Every minute of the day

65

was planned with no time left for fun. Not that there was anything to do in this town, but staring at rocks had to be more fun than those horrid, dull books Jenny insisted they read.

Even the food was dull. The bill of fare was an impressive five pages long. But it soon became apparent that everything from roast beef to chicken, scrambled eggs to flapjacks — even the coffee — smelled and tasted like wet linsey-woolsey and lye.

Not that Mary Lou and her sisters had any choice. The Rocky Creek Café and Chinese Laundry was the only eating establishment in town. Other diners didn't seem to mind having to step over piles of laundry on the way in and out of the restaurant, but Mary Lou dreaded the prospect of stepping on someone's grubby long johns.

Equally unappealing was the sign on the wall that read FRESH COFFEE MADE WEEKLY.

The owner sauntered over to their table. His hangdog face was topped by a shock of red hair. His sideburns hugged his temples like parentheses, as if his face was an afterthought.

At the next table, a thin, horse-faced woman fluttered her lashes and tried to catch his attention.

"Be with you in a moment, Miss Hogg," he said politely. His back toward the flirtatious woman, he rolled his eyes. "The old mule won't leave me alone."

Mary Lou giggled, which earned a stern look from Jenny.

Redd wiped his hands on his ankle-length white apron and asked, "Would you ladies like some more Arbuckle's?"

"I think not, Mr. Rivers," Jenny said, still eyeing Mary Lou with disapproval.

"You can call me Redd, ma'am. That's what everyone calls me around here."

After he left, Mary Lou pushed her plate away. "This has got to be the worst food I've ever tasted."

"Shh," Jenny said. "Act like a lady."

Her arms folded on the table, Mary Lou leaned forward. "I don't want to act like a lady. And I don't want a husband. Not if it means being paraded around like a common circus freak."

Jenny looked shocked, then hurt. "You're not being paraded around," she said emphatically. "You're being *formally* presented. That's how it's done in polite society."

Brenda looked up from her plate. "Stephanie Holbrook found her husband in a mail-order catalog."

Jenny grimaced. "I hardly think that

ordering a husband like one orders gloves or a corset is appropriate. Now do hurry, I still have a stack of applications to go through. And you, dear sisters, have to work on your needlepoint."

Mary Lou's stomach knotted at the thought of spending the day at the hotel. She hated sewing, hated the strict regime Jenny had scheduled. One hour for this and one hour for that. Calisthenics, for goodness' sake! Reading aloud. Memorizing poetry. It was enough to make her want to scream.

She stifled another yawn. Her gaze traveled to the window. Jeff Trevor walked past the restaurant looking every bit as tall and handsome as she remembered him.

"Oh!"

Jenny looked up from her notebook. "Oh, what?"

"Nothing." Mary Lou rubbed the front of her shirtwaist with her napkin, pretending she spilled food. Head lowered so Jenny couldn't see her heated cheeks, she waited until Jenny returned to her notes. She then strained her neck to follow Mr. Trevor's progress down the street and practically fell out of her chair.

Jenny lifted her head. "Mary Lou! What is the matter with you? You're acting very strange."

"Nothing," Mary Lou said, remembering to breathe. "I was just thinking, can't we take a walk?" Mr. Trevor had nothing to do with her sudden interest in exploring the town. He didn't! It was simply . . . curiosity. There had to be something more to Rocky Creek than could be seen from the café or hotel. No place could be this boring.

Jenny hesitated. "I told you I have work to do."

"You don't have to come," Mary Lou said.

Even Brenda seemed to brighten at the prospect. "Please," she begged. "We won't be long."

"I don't think it's a good idea," Jenny said.

"You let us go to Haswell unchaperoned," Mary Lou said.

"That was different. We don't know anyone here," Jenny argued.

"We know the marshal," Mary Lou said. "He said he was going to watch everything we do. So how can we possibly get into trouble?"

Jenny hesitated, her face oddly flushed. Maybe she was coming down with something.

"Please," Brenda begged, hands clasped beneath her chin.

"All right," Jenny said, her voice thick with reluctance. "But I expect you back at the hotel in one hour."

Mary Lou wasn't sure she heard right. Jenny gave in? Just like that? That proved it. Jenny was not herself.

Jenny gathered up her notebook. "I'll head back to the hotel. Stay together, and if a man tries to talk to you, refer him to me. And don't forget, one hour." She gave Mary Lou a stern look. "And not one minute more."

Mary Lou couldn't get out of the café fast enough. Leaving Jenny to pay for their meal, she and Brenda rushed out the door like horses escaping a burning barn.

"Act like ladies," Jenny called after them.

Knowing that Jenny watched from the window, Mary Lou forced herself to walk with proper little steps, looking for all the world like a perfect lady. Fortunately, not even Jenny could read her wayward thoughts. *Where is he? And how can I get rid of Brenda?*

It was still relatively cool, and the town buzzed with activity. People rushed to do errands before the heat of the day, cluttering up Main Street with wagons, buckboards, and shays. Despite the early hour, horses were tethered in front of all seven saloons. Laughter and music drifted out of bat-wing doors. From a distance came the sound of a train whistle.

The moment they were out of Jenny's line of vision, Mary Lou ducked into an alley that led to the back of the buildings and Brenda followed her. Wash hung from clotheslines behind the café and laundry, affording ample cover, providing the train stayed in the station until she was finished.

"What are we doing here?" Brenda asked, looking bewildered.

Mary Lou stepped between two rows of drying bedsheets. She dug into her reticule for two knotted lace handkerchiefs and stuffed them one by one into her bodice.

Brenda gasped. "If Jenny knew —"

"Knew what?" Mary Lou asked. "That you have a pocket full of sweets?"

"That's not the same as walking around looking like one of those . . ." She lowered her voice. "Ladies of the night."

Mary Lou shrugged. "There you go again, acting all dramatic."

She adjusted the padding beneath her shirtwaist until she was satisfied no unnatural lumps existed. Knotted handkerchiefs were a poor substitute for Zephyr Bosom Pads, but they would have to do until she could figure out how to get another pair.

She then led the way back out of the alley and glanced up and down the street. Jeff Trevor was nowhere in sight. Not that it mattered, of course.

"Let's check out the general store," Brenda said, sounding amazingly cheerful given the lack of prospects the town offered for entertainment.

Mary Lou frowned. Judging by the display of shovels and other tools propped on either side of the door, she doubted that the store carried anything of interest. Certainly no fashions. "You go. I'll . . . stay here."

Brenda's eyes gleamed with suspicion. "You aren't going to get into trouble, are you?"

"I should be so lucky," Mary Lou muttered. Maybe there was another street to this town.

"Jenny told us to stay together," Brenda said, her brow creased with worry.

"I'm only going to look around." Mary Lou glared at two homely looking men who stopped to stare at them. Brenda was such a worrywart. At times she made Mary Lou want to scream.

She threw her shoulders back and pinched her cheeks for color. "We'll meet here in a half hour. If we're late getting back to the hotel, Jenny will come looking for us."

Brenda started to argue then changed her mind. Tugging at her shawl, she crossed the dirt-packed street to the other side, dodging a wagon. With a quick backward glance, she vanished into the general store, the bells on the door jingling in her wake.

Alone at last, Mary Lou looked up and down the street. No town could possibly be this boring. There had to be something . . .

She walked the length of Main Street, passing various saloons all the way to the Wells Fargo bank.

Any hope that the town might have something of interest to offer faded the moment she reached the end of the boardwalk, which dropped off without warning.

She turned with a sigh and stared in the other direction. What was Jenny thinking to bring them here?

This had to be the sorriest-looking town she ever did see. Even Haswell wasn't this drab. Rocky Creek was every bit as dull and boring as it appeared from their hotel-room window.

As if to read her thoughts, a bay gelding tethered to the hitching post in front of the bank neighed and nodded his head.

She stomped past the bank again.

"Miss Higgins."

Recognizing the smooth resonant voice, her pulse quickened. Willing herself to stay calm, she turned and tried to act surprised. "Mr. Trevor."

Jeff Trevor stepped away from the bank entrance, a smile on his face. "Should I be encouraged that you remember my name?"

"Only if you plan to run for office," she said. Not that women could vote, of course.

He chuckled and looked her up and down, his eyes warm with approval.

"You're looking mighty pretty, ma'am," he said.

Acknowledging the compliment with a gracious smile and nod of the head that even Jenny would approve, she bid him good day and continued on her way.

He fell in step beside her as she knew he would. "The boys and me are planning a little get-together next week. Nothing fancy. A little music, a little dancing, some refreshments. I thought perhaps you and your sisters might like to join us. There aren't many single women around here, and I'm sure the boys would welcome your company."

She stopped and faced him. He was taller than he appeared on the stairs of the hotel. A thrill of excitement coursed through her.

Dancing? Music? Maybe the town wasn't as boring as she thought.

She studied him. In spite of his odd clothes, he really was pleasing to look at. If it were physically possible to drown in a man's eyes, she was in terrible danger of doing so.

"So what do you say, ma'am?" he asked.

She didn't know, really, what to say. If this invitation was his way of apologizing for his brazen behavior yesterday, it would be rude of her to turn him down. On the other hand, she didn't want to do anything to encourage him.

"Next week?" she asked, biding for time.

"That's right, ma'am. I'll be happy to provide transportation for you and your sisters."

She bit down on her lower lip. "I'll have to ask Jenny."

"Of course. Leave a message with the hotel desk clerk. He knows how to contact me." His eyes dark and powerful, he continued to study her.

Since he was more or less blocking the boardwalk, she didn't have much choice but to stare back at him, hoping he'd take the hint and move.

"I better head back to the hotel," she said

at last, indicating the direction she wished to go.

"Of course," he said, stepping to the side.

"Thank you for the invitation." Not knowing what else to say, she brushed past him. Her shoulder rubbed against his arm, and a tingling sensation settled in the pit of her stomach.

"Just one more thing," he called after her.

Her heart jolted. She turned to face him. "Mr. Trevor?"

His steady gaze bored into her. "Do you happen to know your ring size?"

Her breath caught in her lungs. Did she hear him right? "R–ring size?"

"Since we're all gonna be together, I figure it's as good a time as any to make our engagement official."

Her mouth dropped open. Obviously, the man wasn't about to take no for an answer. "Mr. Trevor!"

"Feel free to call me Jeffrey."

His attempt at geniality only annoyed her more. "I do not now nor ever intend to marry you. Nor do I intend to call you by your Christian name." Even she knew that calling a man by his first name was the height of familiarity. Fueled by anger, her voice was steady and firm. "Furthermore, I shall not be attending your dance."

He didn't look the least bit daunted. If anything, he appeared even more confident than before. "Don't you worry none, ma'am," he said. "There'll be plenty of time to announce our engagement. About next week . . . if you change your mind, you know how to reach me." With that, he turned and walked back toward the bank, whistling as if he hadn't a care in the world.

Staring after him, she muttered, "Of all the nerve." She looked around to see if anyone had witnessed the odd exchange. Much to her annoyance, a previously unnoticed old man sat in a rocking chair in front of the general store looking straight at her.

Just then Brenda walked out of the store carrying a small package. Mary Lou motioned for her to hurry. "It's about time," she snapped the moment Brenda joined her.

"What's the hurry?" Brenda tucked the package into her pocket. "It's only been a short while."

Mary Lou said nothing. Instead, she hurried toward the hotel so fast that it was all Brenda could do to keep up.

Six

To a potential suitor, your reputation is all.
It's not how a woman has comported
herself; it's how she is perceived.
— MISS ABIGAIL JENKINS, 1875

"Marshal, come quick. There's trouble at
the *Gazette*." Redd was flushed and out of
breath from running.

Rhett rose from his desk in one swift
movement and grabbed his hat. Brawls and
fistfights were daily occurrences at the
saloons, but the newspaper office? That was
a new one on him.

By the time he reached the office of the
Rocky Creek Gazette, a crowd had gathered
outside. He pushed his way through the
spectators. No robbers or gunmen greeted
him. No drunken troublemakers.

Instead, he found Miss Jenny Higgins
threatening the newspaper editor with her
parasol. Slumped in his chair, Jacoby Barnes

held his arms over his head to ward off any imminent blows.

Though the two of them were screaming at each other, Rhett couldn't make hide nor hair out of what they were yelling about.

"Break it up," he bellowed. Because neither one of them seemed to hear, he rushed around the editor's desk and grabbed the parasol out of Jenny's hand.

The immediate danger to his person no longer an issue, Barnes lowered his arms. Jenny placed her hands on her hips. They both started talking at once.

"This man —"

"This woman —"

The rest of their sentences were so garbled together, they sounded nonsensical.

"Quiet, both of you," Rhett said, growing impatient. "Now, one at a time. Miss Higgins, you go first."

Jenny tossed her head back and shot daggers at the editor. "My sisters and I take great pride in our reputation. But this . . . this despicable man doesn't care a whit about anything but selling" — her eyes flashed — *"newspapers."*

"It was a mistake," Barnes whined.

"It was a mistake, all right," Jenny stormed. Since she looked about to attack the editor physically again, Rhett grabbed

79

her by the arm and pulled her away.

"You stand there, and you" — he pointed to Barnes — "stay right where you are."

Barnes pushed his spectacles up his imposing nose with an ink-stained index finger. Elbows on the desk, he pressed his hands together and regarded Jenny with narrowed eyes, his carefully trimmed mustache twitching up and down like a seesaw. The angry red scar that stretched from brow to chin made his face look lopsided but no less obstinate.

"It was an *honest* mistake," Barnes said.

Jenny scoffed. "Honest? Don't make me laugh."

Accusations flew back and forth, each one growing louder in pitch.

Rhett cut the argument off with gesturing arms. "Calm down, both of you. Now would you kindly explain what's going on here before I haul you both off to jail for disturbing the peace?"

"See for yourself," Jenny said. She snatched a newspaper off the desk and held it up for him to read.

The headline stretched across the width of the page in big bold letters: *The Hussy Sisters Begin Manhunt.*

Rhett blinked. "Hussy sisters?"

"I thought their last name was Hussy.

That's what I heard." Barnes shrugged. "Everywhere I went, I heard about 'those hussy sisters.' Naturally, I assumed that was their name. Like I said, it was an honest mistake."

Jenny glowered. "You wouldn't know honest from a horse's —"

"Quiet!" Rhett ordered. "I can't think with all this racket." He turned to Barnes. "All right, what do you propose to do to rectify your . . . eh . . . mistake?"

"I offered to run a correction in the next edition."

"Not good enough," Jenny snapped. "He doesn't even know when the next edition will be published."

Rhett scratched his head. Neither one looked like they would give an inch. He didn't approve of Jenny's method of finding husbands for her sisters, but he had even less respect for Barnes's journalistic integrity. Any factual statement that made its way into the *Rocky Creek Gazette* was purely by chance.

He could think of only one possible solution. Aware that Jenny was staring at him, he reached into his pocket, counted out several gold coins, and tossed them on the desk.

"I want every newspaper you printed

delivered to my office, pronto."

Barnes stared at the stack of coins and drooled. Jenny's mouth dropped open.

"Some of them may have already sold," Barnes said without taking his eyes off the money.

"Buy them back," Rhett ordered. "I want every last one of them." He glanced at Jenny, and when she offered no objection, he stepped outside.

"Show's over," he said to the lingering crowd gathered there.

Groans of disappointment filled the air. Barnes was not well liked and most of the spectators were rooting for Jenny to clobber him.

Since some men continued to hang around hoping for more action, Rhett waved them away like a farmer chasing chickens. "Scat!"

Everyone took off in different directions and he headed toward his office.

"Marshal."

At the sound of her voice, he stopped and waited for her to catch up to him. She wore a rust-colored skirt and white shirtwaist tied at the neck with a rust-colored ribbon. Unlike last night, every last strand of her blonde hair was in place.

"I'll come to your office later with the

money I owe you," she said. She couldn't have sounded more businesslike had they just finished discussing the financial terms of property or livestock.

He frowned. "You don't owe me a thing."

She tilted her head slightly, but whether in surprise or determination, he couldn't tell. "I owe you for the newspapers," she said.

He shook his head. "I don't want your money."

"And I don't want your —" The look of raw pain that flashed in her eyes was quickly replaced by a hostile glare. "Charity." She spit out the word like someone might spit out rotten food.

Stymied by the hurt in her eyes, it took him a moment to react to the anger. "It's not charity," he assured her. "It's my way of apologizing for my behavior last night."

She stared at him and her cheeks reddened. The eyes that had moments earlier brimmed with anger and pain now shimmered with confusion. Whether she was confused by his actions or her own, he couldn't guess. He didn't even know himself what confused him more.

"You don't have to —"

"I want to," he said.

She took a deep breath and tossed back

her head. "We'll split the cost."

He drew back in an exaggerated gesture. "That sounds like an admittance of guilt."

She observed him through lowered lashes. "My own behavior last night was rather . . . shall we say, unfortunate?"

Her face burned with humiliation, and he couldn't help but feel sorry for her. "On the contrary, Miss Higgins, you did what any red-blooded woman would do had she been accosted by a charming, handsome marshal. You simply lost your head."

Her surprised expression was as good as a white flag of surrender. "I do believe you're right," she said slowly. "Since your charms are so *irresistible,* it seems only fair that you pay the *entire* cost."

She looked immeasurably relieved. A slow smile inched across her face.

"Good day, Marshal," she said, looking remarkably composed for a woman who had just finished negotiating payment for a kiss.

He tipped his hat. "Miss Higgins."

Head held high, she walked away, everything about her in perfect control except for an intriguing flash of petticoat beneath the hem of her skirt.

He had to give her credit. He offered her an out and she jumped on it. A moment of moonlight madness had been dealt with and dismissed, just like that.

Now they could both relax.

The next day, Jenny whisked about their hotel room like a small tornado.

The Hussy sisters, indeed! She was still incensed about the headline. Is that really what the townsfolk called them behind their backs?

But it wasn't the headline or name-calling that kept her in a whirl as much as the mounting suspicion that it was a name she deserved. The memory of kissing the marshal stayed with her like a melody she couldn't stop humming. No matter what she did, she couldn't put it out of her mind.

For two nights now she'd tossed and turned. Her mind had seemingly turned into tumbling dice that always came up with the same memory. In her more irrational moments, she imagined she liked his kiss, liked the feel of his lips on hers. Mostly she saw it for what it was: the kiss meant nothing. It was a game. A dangerous game, as it turned out, but a game nonetheless. Even his attempt at an apology was a game.

Oh, the shame, the shame. Thank goodness her sisters had been asleep at the time and unaware of her reckless behavior.

She must forget it, put it out of her mind,

lock it up with all the other things in her past she didn't want to think about. The marshal apologized. She accepted part of the blame. It was over, finished. She wouldn't give it another thought.

You did what any red-blooded woman would do.

The thought coming from nowhere weakened her resolve and started the sequence of memories all over again. And so it went.

At last she could stand it no longer. She slapped her hand on her chest. *Stop! No more.*

In a desperate attempt to quell her raging thoughts, she stuffed her notes into a leather satchel along with her notebook and interview schedule. The first prospective suitor was to meet her in the lobby in twenty minutes.

She ignored the strange stares from her sisters. They both lay facedown on the bed, *The Prelude* by William Wordsworth open in front of them. When they weren't staring at her, they took turns reading aloud.

She rifled through her satchel to make sure she had everything she needed. She'd forgotten to include *The Compleat and Authoritative Manual for Attracting and Procuring a Husband.* She had bookmarked the Potential Husband Aptitude Test (PHAT) at the back of the book. No candidate would be allowed to court her sisters without passing the test.

After slipping the hefty tome into her satchel, she checked her hair one last time in the beveled looking glass. Satisfied that not one unsightly strand escaped from the tightly wound bun at the back of her head, she turned to her sisters.

"This could be your lucky day, my dear sisters," she said, managing to sound more cheerful than she felt.

Predictably, Mary Lou made a face and groaned. Brenda looked disinterested. Jenny shook her head. "Don't just lie there," she scolded. "Keep reading."

"I hate this book," Mary Lou complained. "It's got to be the dullest book I ever read."

"It's a beautifully written story of a man's life," Jenny said.

"All eighty years of it," Mary Lou moaned.

"All eighty *boring* years of it," Brenda concurred.

"Wait till you get to the French Revolution," Jenny said, though at the rate they were going, she doubted they ever would.

Without another word, she grabbed her satchel by the leather handle and left the room, hurrying down the stairs to the lobby.

Marshal Armstrong sat sprawled on the

horsehair settee in front of the fireplace, his hat on the cushion next to him. His arms stretched along the back, he nodded. "Miss Higgins."

Surprised to see him, her heart hammered against her ribs and it was all she could do to pretend indifference. "Don't tell me it's against the law to conduct interviews in the lobby."

"Not that I know of," he said. "Better here than . . . in your hotel room."

Was that innuendo in his voice? She searched his handsome square face for confirmation, but his still expression gave nothing away.

"How nice to know I'm not breaking any laws." She felt self-conscious beneath his steady gaze but nonetheless managed to keep her voice light. Why he affected her so, she couldn't imagine. Certainly it had nothing to do with that ridiculous kiss.

The kiss. Now why did she have to go and think about that again?

Irritated at herself, she briskly arranged her paperwork on the small table in front of the stone fireplace. Act busy. Don't stop to think or, heaven forbid, remember. Never look back. Keep to the schedule. Stick to the plan. Her motto had served her well these last few years. No reason it wouldn't serve her now.

When he refused to take the hint and leave, she asked, "So why *are* you here?"

His mouth quirked with humor. "Maybe I came to be interviewed."

"Sorry," she said lightly, "but your name is not on the list."

She pulled out a chair and sat. She tried to maintain calm, to act like nothing improper had happened between them. Judging by the knowing look he gave her, she was doing a poor job.

The marshal rose from the settee and sat down opposite her. Elbows on the table, he folded his hands together. The only other person in the lobby was the sleepy clerk behind the reception desk.

"I thought it might relieve you to know that every newspaper has been accounted for and destroyed."

"Excellent," she said crisply. So far, so good. Message delivered and received. No reason for him to hang around.

Only that's exactly what he continued to do.

He watched her with a puzzled frown.

"Would that be all, Marshal?" she asked.

"That's all," he said, though he still made no motion to leave. "Just out of curiosity, what made you come *here* to look for husbands?"

"Rocky Creek has the most eligible bachelors per capita than any other Texas town," she explained. "And the most financially secure."

His brows quirked upward. "Whatever gave you that idea?"

"An article in the *Lone Star Tribune*." She leaned forward, hand on her chest, and lowered her voice. "Although I must say, by the looks of this town, the men around here certainly hold a tight purse."

"If what you say is true, they also have tight lips, because it's the first I ever heard of it." He tapped his fingers on the table. "So how do you interview a prospective husband?"

She stole a slanted glance at him. "Every man will have to pass a test."

He knitted his brows together. "A test?"

She nodded. "It's called the Potential Husband Aptitude Test. PHAT for short."

He scratched his temple. "I never heard of such a thing." He squinted. "What kind of questions are on the test?"

She shrugged. "Questions about a man's background and occupation. His past."

"And a man's financial status," he said, his voice edged with disapproval.

"Yes, that too," she said evenly.

90

After a moment, he asked, "May I see the test?"

She didn't want to show it to him. He would only criticize or deride it. Still, she couldn't think of a way to turn down his request without seeming rude. Reluctantly, she pushed the open book across the table.

He read the questions in silence, his eyebrows inching upward as he progressed down the page. Finally, he shook his head and pushed the book toward her.

"It sure does seem like a strange way to pick a husband." He sounded more puzzled than critical.

"A woman can't be too careful," she replied. Nothing was more detrimental to a woman's well-being than an ill-chosen mate.

"Is that all you'd ask a prospective groom? Where he lives, went to school, plans for the future?"

"What else is there?" She eyed him with curiosity. "What would *you* ask a prospective bride?"

He looked straight at her. "I would ask if she believed in God."

His answer given without hesitation or justification surprised her. Shocked her, really. The PHAT covered many aspects of a man's life but failed to consider his religious beliefs. She hadn't thought to ask the question herself, and this worried her. Obviously, she'd grown more distant from God than she knew.

"I plan to ask additional questions," she said defensively.

Anxious to show that her methods were prudent if not altogether conventional, she said, "Let's say for the sake of argument that you qualified as a suitor — which, of course, you don't — which Higgins would you choose for a wife?"

"Sorry, not interested," he said.

"But if you were?" she pressed.

He looked her straight in the eye. "*If* I were interested, I'd choose the oldest one," he said.

His answer restored her confidence and she could barely contain her delight. "Which proves my point, exactly. Without asking proper questions, I'm likely to choose unsuitable mates for my sisters, as you just did." She folded her arms. "Mary Lou is definitely *not* your type."

"Mary —" He stopped himself.

He looked momentarily surprised, and she could easily guess why. "Some people think Brenda's the oldest, but Mary Lou is." At nineteen, Mary Lou was one year older than Brenda. "Do you still want to stay with your first choice?"

He gave a distracted nod. "So why do you think . . . eh . . . Mary Lou isn't my type?"

"For one thing, she's stubborn."

"Stubborn, eh?" No longer scowling in disapproval, his eyes twinkled as if he were privy to some joke. "I would never have guessed it."

"And single-minded," she added. "Once she gets something into her head, there's no changing it."

"I seem to have noticed that," he said, lightly.

"And she tends to set unrealistic goals."

He drew back, hand on his chest in an exaggerated gesture. "No-o-o."

"Don't get me wrong," she hastened to add. "She is very attractive, as I'm sure you've noticed —"

"Absolutely," he said.

"And she can be very sweet and loving —"

"Excellent qualities," he said. "The question is, can she cook?"

"I'll have you know, all us Higginses are excellent cooks," she replied with more than a little pride. She had personally made certain her sisters were well versed in running a household.

He splayed his hands. "I'm sure she'll make some man a fine wife."

"But not you," she said.

"Definitely not me." He looked so relieved she couldn't help but laugh.

He grinned back at her. "Ah, so you *can* laugh?"

She snapped her mouth shut and resumed her usual businesslike demeanor. "And what is that supposed to mean?"

"Nothing. Except you're always so serious." He pointed to her notes and lists. "I doubt you do anything without first committing it to paper."

"I've been known to be spontaneous," she said.

"Ah, yes, I seem to remember a . . . certain incident." His gaze swept across her reddening cheeks, and he gave a knowing smile.

It irritated her that the kiss that had caused her so much grief did nothing more than amuse him.

"Yes, well . . ." Spotting her first interviewee walking through the lobby door, she stood, grateful for the interruption. "Sorry, I have no more time for this."

The marshal glanced at the man standing next to the counter and nodded with approval. "I know Harold Hampton. Nothing tight-lipped about him. He has money and isn't afraid to let it be known." He stood, walked around the table and whispered in her ear, his warm breath caressing her neck.

"He could teach Mary Lou a lesson or two in single-mindedness."

He straightened and greeted the man in a loud, cheery voice and an equally exuberant handshake.

"I'll leave you two alone," he said as if doing them a favor. He scooped his hat off the settee, placed it on his head, and stalked away.

Mr. Hampton greeted her with a nod. "I apologize for being late."

She wouldn't have known he was late had he not mentioned it. Normally his failure to arrive on time would go against him, but she could ill afford to dismiss the most promising candidate the town had to offer.

"Mr. Hampton. Please take a seat."

She glanced over her shoulder. The marshal had already left the hotel, but thoughts of him continued to plague her. So he was interested in Mary Lou, was he? Rhett Armstrong and Mary Lou. What a disastrous combination. A woman would have to be strong willed to stand up to the likes of Rhett Armstrong. Jenny couldn't imagine him giving into her sister's whiny complaints or passion for fashion.

She might have continued her reverie indefinitely had Mr. Hampton not given a discreet cough.

She covered her inattention with a quick shuffle of notes then regarded him with a critical eye. He was a compact man with a round face, brown hair, and brown eyes. Though he had no distinguishing features, he was pleasant enough to look at.

According to his application, he was a rancher. Dressed in pin-striped trousers and vest, his hair and sideburns neatly trimmed, he looked more like a banker.

She liked that he had taken the interview seriously enough to dress for the occasion. She started with the first question on her list. "Exactly what are your intentions?"

"My intentions are to be a good and loyal husband," he said with perfect ease. "And, if the good Lord is willing, to raise a family."

Encouraged and somewhat relieved that he had alleviated the need to broach the subject of God, she bombarded him with one question after another. His answers were quick, honest, and precise, earning a full five points each. He was nothing like that annoying marshal who thought this all a big joke.

By the end of the interview, she was convinced that she had found the perfect match for Mary Lou, and his financial statement supported her opinion.

She stood and offered him her hand. "Would you be available to meet my sister tonight, say, at seven?"

"I'm afraid I have to travel out of town on business. Would you mind if I meet her next week instead? Perhaps you would allow me to take her on a carriage ride."

"I'm sure she would find that most pleasurable."

They settled on a date and time. He then took her offered hand and raised it to his lips. He donned his hat and she watched him walk away, noting for the first time the stylish carriage parked in front. Smiling to herself, she sat down, convinced that she had taken a very important step in securing a long and happy future for Mary Lou. Now she could concentrate on finding a suitable match for Brenda.

She glanced down at her notes. The next man to be interviewed was Timber Joe, a strange name to be sure. She wasn't even certain why she chose this particular man except that he seemed fairly educated and described himself as a man with a cause. What that cause was, she had no idea.

"Ma'am?"

Startled, she looked up from her notes. "I'm sorry, you must be —"

"Timber Joe," he said. He pulled out a chair and sat down, his wooden leg extended straight out. The barrel of his rifle on the floor, he leaned on the wooden stock.

Jenny's heart sank. Though the War Between the States had been over for fifteen years, he was dressed in a Rebel outfit that should have been retired several battles ago. He wore a kepi hat, sported a beard, and his long hair was tied behind his neck.

"Go ahead, ma'am. Ask your questions. A man who's got nothin' has nothin' to hide."

She cleared her voice, not sure where to start. "I'm not clear about your occupation."

"Nothin' to be clear about, ma'am. I'm a Rebel soldier."

"Still?" Her gaze traveled down his threadbare gray jacket. "But the war is over."

"That's what they want you to think, ma'am." He glanced around as if to look for spies. He then lowered his voice. "But don't you believe it for a second."

Jenny studied his earnest face and tried to think of a tactful way to end the interview.

"No need to worry, ma'am. When they attack, I'll be ready. I'll defend hearth and home till my dying day." For emphasis, he raised his rifle and thumped it against the floor. The thud startled the sleeping hotel clerk, who opened his eyes, looked around, and then promptly fell back in his chair.

"That's . . . very nice to hear." Not wanting to hurt Timber Joe's feelings, she went through the motions of questioning him. She took care to write his answers down, no matter how ridiculous or absurd. At last she stood, indicating the interview was over.

"Thank you for coming . . . Mr. —"

"Just call me Timber Joe," he said. Taking her cue, he stood and saluted her. He then walked away, his wooden leg pounding the wood plank floor like a hammer.

Jenny sat down with a sigh. She'd only conducted two interviews but already she felt exhausted. The last interview was almost as laughable as Rhett thinking he and Mary Lou would be a match.

Pushing the thought out of her mind, she rose to greet the next candidate.

SEVEN

No marriage-minded woman should
engage in rowdy behavior, coarse
language, or gossip. Such disagreeable
habits can only be broken with
unyielding vigilance.
— MISS ABIGAIL JENKINS, 1875

That Sunday, Jenny pulled up in front of
the white clapboard Rocky Creek church in
a carriage rented from the livery stable. The
church stood on a hill overlooking the town.
The building listed to the side like a slow-
sinking ship. The clapboards were warped
and the edges of the tin roof curled upward.
Still, with all its faults, the church was in
better shape than any of the buildings in
town.

According to the sign out front, it had
been built shortly after Texas became a state
in 1845. Behind the church was a cemetery
surrounded by woods.

100

"I still don't see why we have to go to worship," Mary Lou complained. "We never went to church in Haswell."

"Haswell didn't have a church," Jenny said. What Haswell had was a circuit preacher who rode into town every six months with a Bible in one hand and a six-shooter in the other.

The explanation did nothing to relieve her guilt. She couldn't remember the last time she prayed or read the Bible. After that terrible winter when she and her sisters practically starved to death, everything changed, even her relationship with God.

Especially her relationship with God.

She waited for her sisters to climb out of the wagon.

"Save me a seat," she called. With a click of her tongue, she snapped the reins and drove off to find a place to park.

Ignoring the stares of other churchgoers, Jenny followed the narrow footpath toward the double doors. A knot started in her stomach and worked its way upward until it felt like a rock in her throat.

She wasn't even certain she belonged here. She swallowed hard. Dressed in her finest attire, she looked like a lady but felt like a hypocrite. *How did things go so terribly wrong?*

Surprised to find herself shaking, she took a deep breath. She couldn't do this. Not yet. Maybe never. She whirled about and started back toward the carriage.

Without warning, she was accosted from behind.

Startled, she turned to find herself staring down into the sunny, bright face of an adorable little girl whom she guessed was around two. Clinging to Jenny's skirt, the child stared up at her, her eyes rounded in surprise. Apparently, she had mistaken Jenny for her mother.

The little girl pulled away and started to run off again, but spying a woman she suspected to be the child's mother, Jenny caught the little girl around the waist and held on to her.

From a short distance away, a woman hobbled down the path toward them, one hand on her protruding belly.

"Elizabeth Wells, I'm gonna tan your hide," the woman called, the loving smile on her face contradicting her words. She was still smiling when she reached them, though terribly out of breath.

She held out her hand. "I'm Sarah Wells, the preacher's wife. You must be one of the sisters I heard so much 'bout."

"Jenny Higgins." Keeping one hand on

the squirming toddler, she shook Sarah's hand with the other. The woman's hair, red as a hen's comb, was almost the same color as her well-worn boots. Giving no heed to fashion, she wore her hair loose down her back beneath a man's felt hat.

"This here is Elizabeth," Sarah said, taking her young daughter by the hand. "Say hello to the nice lady."

Elizabeth gave Jenny a shy smile but said nothing.

Jenny smiled back. "I'm pleased to meet you, Elizabeth." She was a pretty little girl with long blonde hair and fringe bangs. Though the mother was rather plainly dressed, there was nothing plain about Elizabeth's outfit. Her navy blue knee-length dress was edged in lace and tied in back with a full bow.

Old man Applegate glared at Jenny as he ambled past them, but he smiled at Sarah. "I see you're still wearin' your bustle in front," he called.

Sarah laughed. " 'Fraid it's gonna stay that way till September," she called after him.

"Is that when your baby's due?" Jenny asked. "September?"

"Sure as shootin' is. Only three more months to go." Sarah looked Jenny square in the face. "It's hard walkin' into a new church and all. But you'll find us friendly as a swarm of bees."

Jenny wasn't sure if Sarah meant that in a good or bad way, but she couldn't help but smile. The preacher's wife was as plain talking and straightforward as her dress. "It's been a while."

Sarah regarded her with clear blue eyes. "Before I met Justin . . . Reverend Wells . . . I hadn't stepped foot inside a church for sixteen years." She glanced at the building, a fond look on her face. "Didn't think I belonged here either."

Jenny stared at her. "I didn't say I didn't belong here."

"You may not have said it, but you sure do look it," Sarah said.

From inside the church came the sound of a piano. The tin roof vibrated, sending a hapless raven into the air, screeching in protest.

"Come with me." Sarah linked her free arm around Jenny's, giving her no choice but to comply. Without another word, she walked Jenny into the church like she had every right to be there.

All eyes were on the two women as they made their way down the center aisle. Gloved hands muffled whispered voices, but no amount of feathers, veils, or plumes could hide the disapproving stares from Rocky Creek's small but opinionated female population.

Jenny took her place next to Mary Lou. Sarah and Elizabeth sat on the other side of her.

"It's about time you got here," Mary Lou said, sounding strangely flustered. Next to her, Brenda gave a shushing sound.

Jenny glanced at Mary Lou's red face. Was it possible that her sister felt as awkward at coming to church as she did? But why? What did Mary Lou have to worry about? It wasn't as if *she* had done anything wrong.

After a few moments of silence, the pianist pounded the ivory keys again, and the choir stood. The choir consisted of a motley group of men. Most of them didn't seem to know a high C from a cow's moo. One singer, however, saved the day, his resonant voice rising above and eventually drowning out the other voices.

Jenny recognized the prominent singer. If she recalled correctly, his name was Mr. Barrel. He had presented himself as a potential suitor and was one of the few men whose writing skills met her criteria. However, his unfortunate choice of a profession disqualified him, as did his finances. With a voice like that, he should have been a singer rather than a barber. His bank account couldn't have suffered any worse.

After the singing stopped, Reverend Justin Wells took his place behind the podium. He was a tall, handsome man who managed to combine a commanding air with a humble countenance.

"Welcome on this glorious day the Lord has made," he began. "I see some new faces out there." He looked straight at Jenny. "Strangers to the town, but not to God. No one is a stranger to God."

Jenny's face grew hot. Was she that easy to read? Both the pastor and his wife were able to accurately guess her discomfort. What else could they guess? Were her secrets not safe?

Feeling exposed, Jenny glanced around. Her gaze inadvertently locked with the marshal seated on the other side of the aisle. He acknowledged her with a slight nod as if he, too, guessed the reasons for her reluctance to be there.

Cheeks burning, she quickly pulled her gaze away. For the rest of the service, she focused on Reverend Wells, looking neither left nor right.

After church Sarah introduced Jenny to her preacher husband.

"Welcome to Rocky Creek," Reverend

Wells said, taking her hand in both of his. Elizabeth ran off and Sarah chased after her, leaving the pastor and Jenny alone.

He released her hand but continued to study her. "Do you plan to make this your permanent home?"

The question surprised her. She hadn't even considered staying in town. "No, I'm here for only a short while," she said. She had no idea what she would do once her sisters were married. "I may have need of your services in the near future."

"For a wedding?" he asked.

"Weddings," she said. "I have *two* sisters."

"Ah." He lifted his gaze to watch his wife and daughter in the distance. The glow in his eyes brought a pang of envy that surprised her with its intensity. She would give anything to have a man look at her like Reverend Wells gazed at his wife.

Maybe, with a little luck and careful selections, her sisters would one day soon come to know that kind of love. She never would, of course. Couldn't.

"Are you okay?" the preacher asked, cupping her elbow with his hand.

"I'm sorry," she said, feeling off balance. Lately, her mind kept wandering and it was so unlike her. What was it about Rocky Creek that made her dwell on the past?

"You were talking about your sisters," he prompted.

"Yes, of course. How do I go about booking weddings at your church?"

He dropped his hand to his side. "I will have to meet with all parties concerned. Marriage is a serious proposition."

"I know," she said. "That's why I'm taking such pains to find my sisters perfect matches."

He rubbed his chin as if the very idea amused him. "Where men and women are concerned, there's no such thing as a perfect match," he said. "There's only a *God* match."

"A God match?"

He nodded. "Sometimes God brings couples together for His own purpose."

Why God would concern Himself with matchmaking, she couldn't imagine, but it didn't seem proper to argue with a man of the cloth, so she said nothing.

Sarah joined them. "If you have need for weddin' gowns, those ladies over there can turn any garment into a bridal dress." She pointed to a group of women whispering among themselves. "They made Elizabeth's dress."

"It's beautiful," Jenny said.

Justin picked up his little girl and jostled

her up and down. "I'll be happy to talk to your sisters any time." He stared straight at her. "If there's anything *you* would like to talk about, I'm at your service," he said.

Unnerved, she thanked him and was relieved when he turned to his wife and the two walked off together.

Someone clapped. She knew even before she turned that she'd find Marshal Armstrong watching her. He leaned against a tree and folded his arms across his chest. A slight breeze ruffled his brown hair. Nothing seemed to ruffle the rest of him.

"Congratulations, Miss Higgins. You've planned the wedding gowns and the church. You've only been in town for what? Four, five days? And already your sisters are two-thirds married. All you need are the grooms. From what I hear, you've even got that under control."

Not wishing to discuss her plans with him, she started toward the carriage where her sisters waited. Much to her dismay, he fell in step next to her.

"Have you nothing better to do with your time, Marshal?" she asked.

"I reckon keeping you out of trouble is about as good a use of time as any."

She glanced at him from the corner of her

eye. "I don't need you watching everything I do."

He shrugged. "I guess you could say we have a difference of opinion in that regard." He stopped her with a touch to the arm.

The heat of his hand blazed through the sleeve of her shirtwaist. His sudden change of expression surprised her. He went from flippant to serious in a single heartbeat.

"I noticed that Timber Joe was on your list of men to be interviewed."

Now she really was curious. For a man who claimed his only concern was to keep her out of trouble, he seemed to take an inordinate amount of interest in her match-making affairs.

"I spoke to Mr. . . . Timber Joe," she said.

"Already?" he asked, clearly alarmed.

"He was originally scheduled for next week, but I had an unexpected opening and he agreed to come in early." She was forever changing times and days to accommodate various work schedules.

He frowned. "Timber Joe has . . ." He hesitated as if searching for the right words. "He's a good man, but . . ."

"He has a soldier's heart," she finished for him.

"You know?" He looked surprised if not altogether astonished.

"Isn't it obvious?" she asked.

He studied her. "Most folks around here think he's just plain *loco*."

"Haswell lost many young men in the war," she explained. "The few who came back were never the same. Sometimes . . . things happen that change a person forever." The war certainly did that, but other things did too.

"Timber Joe had a twin brother." Armstrong stared into the distance, his face a stony mask. She sensed that whatever he saw in his mind's eye, he didn't much like. The man was obviously having as much trouble running from the past as she was.

"What happened to Timber Joe's brother?" she asked. *What happened to you?*

"They went off to war together. Vowed to take care of each other." His gaze locked with hers. "Only one came back." His voice drifted away along with eye contact.

"That poor man," she said softly. What would she have done had Brenda died during that long-ago winter? Clamping down on the memory, she studied him. The usual teasing lights were gone. Instead, she saw a glimpse of despair.

"As long as he keeps playing soldier, he can pretend his brother is still alive," he said.

She hadn't thought about that possibility,

111

but it made perfect sense. Surprised by Rhett's insightful perception, she asked, "How do you know so much about a soldier's heart?"

He hesitated. "The same way you do, I guess." His voice was husky, distant. Without so much as a farewell nod, he walked away.

Surprised and more than a little disconcerted by his abrupt departure, she called after him. "You needn't concern yourself with Timber Joe. I'll let him down easy."

The marshal kept going and never looked back.

Brenda waited impatiently for her sister to finish stuffing her bodice with knotted handkerchiefs. It had become a daily routine. As usual, they hid behind the Rocky Creek Café and Chinese Laundry. Bedsheets, flour-sack towels, and men's trousers flapped in the breeze.

The smell of lye soap and wet wool did little to mask the reek of decaying garbage. Not only did the stench make Brenda sick to her stomach, she was in danger of being crushed to death by her double-hip corset.

"I can't stand this thing another moment," she cried, shaking her arms. "You've got to do something."

Mary Lou straightened her square neckline, but no matter how many handkerchiefs she stuffed inside, it remained perfectly chaste. "Not again."

"Please," Brenda begged. "I'm suffocating."

"Oh, all right. Turn around."

Brenda grimaced from the pain. "I don't know why they invented these horrid things, anyway."

Mary Lou unbuttoned Brenda's bodice in back. "To make men happy and women miserable." She loosened the lacings. "There you go."

Brenda gasped for air but her relief was only temporary. Now that she could breathe freely, the stench of the alley hit her full force. "Hurry or I'm going to be sick."

"Hold still," Mary Lou grumbled. She tugged and pulled and finally threw up her hands in frustration. "I can't button the last two buttons."

Brenda wanted to cry. No matter how much she tried to control her eating, she couldn't. The gnawing emptiness inside never seemed to go away, no matter how much food she stuffed in her mouth.

"Don't worry about it," Mary Lou said. "The opening is hidden by your hair. Come on, let's get out of here." She led the way down the alley.

They reached Main, and Mary Lou gazed up and down the street.

Brenda took gasping breaths, filling her lungs to full capacity. The air smelled of dust and heat and horse dung, but she didn't care. At last she could breathe.

"Who are you looking for?" Brenda asked. Mary Lou had been acting even stranger than usual lately and had stopped confiding in her. That was always a bad sign. Mary Lou seldom held her tongue unless she was up to mischief.

"I'm not looking for anyone," Mary Lou said in a tone that clearly stated the opposite. She waggled her fingers. "Run along. I'll meet you in a half hour."

Brenda eyed her with suspicion and more than a bit of envy. Mary Lou never worried about propriety. She did pretty much what she wanted to do, fighting Jenny all the way.

"You seem awfully anxious to get rid of me," she said.

Mary Lou scoffed. "Don't be ridiculous. I know you can't wait to get to the general store to buy more candies. Would you see if their new shipment of dime novels has arrived?"

"If Jenny finds out you're reading those novels, she'll have a fit," Brenda said. Jenny called them potboilers and had forbidden them both to read them.

Mary Lou gave an unconcerned shrug. "I don't care. Anything's better than Mr. Wordsworth. I'd much rather read about Indian wives and detectives than boring clouds and hills."

Brenda couldn't argue with her there, though she did think the poet had a lovely way with words. "I'm not going to the store. If you insist upon reading those melodramatic novels, you'll have to purchase them yourself."

"All right, I will."

"Good!" Brenda blew a wisp of hair from her face and one of her small bone buttons popped to the ground. She groaned. That did it. She wouldn't eat another bite until she could button her dress again.

Not wanting Mary Lou to see her tears, she started in the opposite direction. Ignoring the looks of those she passed, she came to the end of the street and kept walking. Up a hill and down she went, huffing and puffing all the way. She didn't know how far she'd walked and didn't much care. She just needed to be by herself, away from Jenny's domineering ways and the town's prying eyes.

She stopped to rest along the babbling creek. Pulling off her shoes and stockings, she soaked her feet in the cool clear waters and watched a minnow swim away.

She stretched out on the grass and closed her eyes. A slight breeze rustled the grass and fanned her face. She imagined the tantalizing aroma of fresh pastry floating on the gentle wind.

Startled, she shook her head. *Mustn't think about food.* She forced herself to absorb the sounds of nature. Birds chattering in the treetops vied with water gurgling over rocks. Both competed with the sound of her rumbling stomach.

Finally, she could stand it no longer.

She sat up and sniffed. It wasn't her imagination. She really did smell something heavenly. Leaving her shoes and stockings behind, she followed her nose to a clapboard house hidden by a clump of trees. The house had a picket fence in front and a barn in back. Horses grazed in the distance and chickens pecked at the ground. A cow stared at her with woeful brown eyes, its jaw moving in circles as it chewed its cud.

Walking closer to the house, she spotted two pies cooling on the windowsill. She closed her eyes and inhaled the delicious smell of warm berries and fresh-baked pastry until she felt dizzy. What she wouldn't do for a piece of pie.

"Who's that?" a male voice boomed.

Startled, she backed away, then turned and ran. The man shot out of the house and gave chase. "Wait! Don't go."

Brenda ran as fast as her bare feet would allow, but it wasn't fast enough.

The man grabbed her by the arm. Thrown off balance, she tripped, pulling him with her, and the two rolled down a grassy knoll.

They were both winded by the time they reached bottom. His eyes wide in alarm, he quickly pulled away.

"I'm sorry, ma'am," he said, blushing. He offered his hand and pulled her to her feet. "Are . . . are you all right?"

She nodded, though she was a mess. Her skirt covered in grass and dirt, she was certain she'd popped even more buttons. Her unbuttoned bodice had slipped down her arm, revealing a bare shoulder and a ruffled corset strap.

She looked up to find him staring at her, but he quickly averted his eyes. Blushing, she rearranged the front of her dress but nothing could be done about her gaping back or bare feet.

"You can look now," she said.

Soft brown eyes met hers. "I'm sorry, ma'am. I didn't mean you any harm. I saw you looking at the pies and I wanted to offer you some."

He sounded so apologetic, she smiled at him. "That's very kind of you."

He was a big bear of a man whose rotund body more than justified his deep booming voice. Recognition crossed his face. "You're one of the three sisters," he said. "I'm sorry, I don't remember your name. Hus—"

"Higgins," she replied quickly. "Brenda *Higgins.*" She waited, but when he made no move to introduce himself, she prodded, "And you are?"

"Oh, sorry." He looked flustered or confused, maybe both. "Kip . . . Kip Barrel."

She peered at the man through lowered lashes. "I wasn't going to steal the pies, honest."

"If you were, you wouldn't be the first." He reached out to pull a blade of grass from her hair. His hand brushed her face, bringing an unexpected jolt to her senses. Looking embarrassed, he pulled his hand away and held his arms tight by his side.

"You were in church Sunday. I don't know if you remember me, but I sing in the choir."

Now that she had a closer look at him, she recognized him too. "I remember. You're a beautiful singer." Shyly, she bit her lip. "Some of the other voices are rather . . ." Not wanting to sound unkind, she quickly added, "What I meant to say was I wish you would sing solo."

Her enthusiasm for his singing seemed to break the tension, and he visibly relaxed. His face split into a wide grin that outshined the sun. He had a nice face, a gentle face. Round and full, it was like the sea with its ever-changing moods.

A wistful look wiped his smile away. "I'm afraid singing solo is not possible."

"Why not?" she asked.

"Whenever I sing solo in front of an audience, I sound like a screech owl."

"I don't believe that," she said. Not after what she heard in church.

"It's true. I wanted to be an opera singer, but I couldn't get over my stage fright. I dreamed about being the Barber of Seville. Instead, I'm the barber of Rocky Creek." He made a face and imitated a pair of scissors with his fingers to demonstrate.

She couldn't help but laugh, though he didn't join her.

Fearing she might have offended him, she quickly grew serious. "It seems like such a waste of talent," she said. She would give anything to sing as well as he did. To do something, anything, that well.

He gazed off into the distance as if looking at something outside his reach. "Life doesn't always go the way we plan." He studied her a moment and suddenly brightened. "Stay here. I'll be right back."

Before she could say a word, he ran up the hill and disappeared among the trees, showing remarkable agility for someone his size. She quickly checked her dress. She managed to button one of the buttons in back, but not enough to close the gap.

She patted down her hair and brushed off her sleeves. After putting on her shoes and stockings, she sank to the ground, her back to a willow to hide her unfastened dress. He returned a short time later carrying a pie with both hands.

"Siebel gathered flowers and placed them at Marguerite's door. Me? I have nothing to offer thee but pie."

She gasped in delight and clapped her hands together. "Please tell me you didn't steal that. And who is Siebel?"

He grinned and pulled two forks out of his pocket. "I didn't steal the pie, honest. And Siebel is a young lad in the opera *Faust*."

She'd never heard of Faust and knew nothing about opera, but she liked the way his eyes sparkled when he spoke of it. "Is that your house?" she asked.

"That's Ma's boardinghouse, and I live

there." He handed her a fork and sat down by her side.

"Did your mother bake the pies?"

He chuckled. "Ma's the name of the proprietress. She's not my mother, but everyone calls her Ma. She acts like a mother sometimes. And yes, she baked them." He motioned toward the pie. "I believe it's customary for ladies to go first."

That's all Brenda needed to hear. She stuck her fork into the pie and lifted a morsel to her mouth. The pastry was flaky and practically melted in her mouth. She leaned her head back and savored the sweet, tart taste of fresh berries on her tongue.

"Mmm."

Laughing, he followed her lead.

"What made you want to be an opera singer?" she asked between bites. It struck her as an odd occupation for one to pursue.

"When I was seven, I accompanied my father to Washington on business and he took me to a concert. I'll never forget it. Have you ever heard of Jenny Lind?"

She shook her head.

"She came to America to give a series of concerts sponsored by Mr. P. T. Barnum. I'll never forget her voice and how it touched me here." He placed a hand on his chest next to his heart. "To touch someone like that, to bring tears to their eyes . . . it's a gift from God.

"After that, whenever I was alone and feeling sad, I sang." He shrugged. "Of course, when I announced my decision to pursue a singing career, my family disapproved. It didn't help matters that when I tried singing to my father's cattle, they stampeded."

"Oh, no." She laughed. "So how did you end up here, in Rocky Creek, as a barber?"

"To pay for my singing lessons, I worked in a barbershop. After I failed in my opera debut, I decided to travel back to Texas to join the family cattle business. I'm not cut out for the job, but I didn't know what else to do. While passing through Rocky Creek, my horse suddenly died."

"Oh, no," she gasped. "The poor thing."

"Died just like that." He snapped his fingers. "I took it as a sign from God and decided to stay in Rocky Creek. I taught singing, but that didn't work out too well. The only students who showed up were cattlemen wanting to learn to sing to their cattle."

He laughed and she joined him. She couldn't remember ever having so much fun. On and on he talked. She wasn't sure which of his stories, if any, were true, but she loved hearing them all the same.

He looked surprised when she told him she was originally from Haswell. "My family owns property there," he said. "My cousin often travels there on business."

"Maybe I met him," she said.

"I hope not." Changing the subject, he immediately plunged into another tale, this one about a magical flute.

She forgot all about the time until the sun disappeared behind the distant trees. "Oh!" She jumped to her feet. "I better go." Jenny would kill her if she knew she spent the afternoon eating pie with a near stranger.

He rose and looked genuinely sad to see her go. They stood on either side of an empty pie dish, staring at each other. "When can I see you again?" he asked.

She shook her head. "Jenny would never —" She backed away, then turned and ran.

EIGHT

A woman wishing to win the heart of
a man must refrain from disapproval
or boredom should he engage in
frivolous discourse.
— MISS ABIGAIL JENKINS, 1875

Rhett looked up from his desk and groaned.
Not again.

Hank Applegate was given to making
almost hourly visits to the marshal's office
since Jenny and her sisters had swept into
town. Today was no different. He seemed to
think it his God-given duty to report their
daily comings and goings.

Now he stood in front of Rhett's desk
chomping on his gums and waiting respectfully for the marshal to quit writing.

Rhett took his own sweet time finishing
his report. He then stuck his pen into its
holder and sat back. Soap lather covered
one side of Hank's face. The man couldn't

even finish his shave before barreling in here?

"What is it this time, Hank?"

"Colonel Hussy is at it again."

Rhett sighed. No surprise there. "Her name is Miss *Higgins.*"

"I don't care what her name is, she's going where she ain't got no bus'ness goin'." He pointed to his face. "See this?"

Rhett stared at Hank's half-shaven chin.

"I'm sittin' in the barber chair mindin' me own bus'ness and who should walk in but the colonel. Without so much as a how-do-you-do, she walks up to the man in the chair next to me and demands to know why he missed his interview."

Surprised, Rhett sat back. "James Martin missed his interview?" *After he ran around town bragging that he made Jenny's approval list?*

Hank tilted his head. "How did you know it was Martin?"

"I told you I was keeping an eye on things."

Hank wiped the back of his hand across his lathered chin. "You ain't doin' a very good job. Not if she can walk into a man's domain like nobody's bus'ness. Nothin's sacred anymore. One day a woman walks into a barbershop. The next day, she'll try

125

to turn Texas into Wyomin' terr'tory and demand the right to vote. I'm tellin' you, there ain't gonna be no stoppin' 'em."

"So what do you want me to do about it, Hank?"

"I want you to make certain places off-limits to the colonel and her two husband-chasin' sisters."

"Off-limits?" Rhett shuddered to think what Jenny would say if he were to be so foolish as to restrict her movements. Not that he had any intention of doing so.

"It's a mighty sad day when a man can't get his beard trimmed in peace. Even the preacher's pushy wife knows enough to stay out of the barbershop."

"I'll talk to her, Hank."

"Talkin' ain't gonna do no good. The woman needs to know where she ain't welcome. She needs to know who's the boss."

Rhett rose from his chair and walked Hank to the door, hand on his back. "You go and finish your shave, and I'll take care of Jenny Higgins."

No sooner had he gotten rid of the old man than he headed for the hotel. It was high time that he and Miss Higgins had a heart-to-heart.

Jenny sat at the table in the lobby alone,

writing. She looked up when he approached, then closed her leather notebook. Scattered across the table were notes. He wondered if the woman ever did anything without first writing it down.

"Closing shop?" he asked.

"For the day," she said with a sigh.

He couldn't help but notice that she looked frustrated. In the dim afternoon light, her eyes appeared to be more violet than blue.

"Problems?" he asked.

"None that would interest you." She looked him up and down. "What are you doing here? I don't recall your name on the day's schedule."

He swung a chair around and straddled it. "I thought we both agreed that I fail to meet your qualifications."

"You're right." She studied him a moment. "So why *are* you here?"

He considered how best to broach the subject. "It seems that some men have strong opinions about a . . . woman's place."

She stared straight at him, an indulgent glint in her eyes. "By some men, would you be referring to yourself, Marshal?"

"It's your good fortune that I have a more democratic mind than most."

She sat back, her lips curved upward.

127

"Broad-minded *and* arrogant," she said lightly. "What a winning combination. Perhaps I misjudged you. Perhaps I *should* schedule you for an interview. You couldn't be much worse than some of the other men."

He grinned. He couldn't help it. The lady had a way of disarming him. No question. "That's a mighty generous offer, but I think I'll stop while I'm ahead. Wouldn't want you to change your mind and add me to your eligibility list."

"I doubt things would go that far." She arched a light brow. "You're hardly Mary Lou's kind."

He sat back in surprise. "Mary Lou?"

She gathered up her notes before transferring her gaze to him. "You said if you had a choice it would be the oldest, and that's Mary Lou."

He drummed the back of the chair with the palms of his hands. "You got me there."

She watched with a wary expression. "You still haven't told me what you're doing here."

He chose his words with care, watching for the first sign of objection. "There's been a . . . complaint."

"About me?" she asked.

"About you entering the barbershop." A

warning cloud settled on her face. Obviously, he'd hit a sore spot. "Some people take exception to a woman's presence in a male establishment," he added.

Her eyes blazed. "I can assure you I wasn't there by choice. I was looking for Mr. Martin, whom I was told was getting a haircut."

He leaned forward. "Even so, it would be best if you refrain from entering" — he tried to think of a tactful way of wording it — "certain establishments."

Her lips thinned and her nostrils flared. "Is that an order or a suggestion?" she asked, her voice cold.

"I never found suggestions to be of much use," he said, lightly. "So just for the sake of argument, let's call it a direct order."

"That's ridiculous," she sputtered. "It's a free country." She raged on and on, dragging in every known argument about the unfairness of women's rights — or rather, the lack of them. She did everything but recite the Gettysburg Address.

Well, now. He sure did like watching her rant and rave. Her eyes sparkled, her cheeks grew pink, and an inner fire melted her cool facade.

When she finished — ran out of breath was more like it — he stood. "Just trying to keep the peace, ma'am." He touched a finger to his hat and walked away, chuckling to himself.

Mary Lou didn't think it possible that anyone could be more boring than Mr. William Wordsworth. But if Mr. Hampton didn't exceed the poet in mind-numbing verbiage, he certainly was a close second.

They had been riding along the countryside for more than two hours, during which time Mr. Hampton had managed to talk nonstop about the prickly barbed wire that took over Texas and, in his words, "changed the cattle industry forever."

No matter how hard she tried to look at least halfway interested, her mind wandered. She couldn't seem to stop thinking about Mr. Trevor. She tried to envision the cabin he built that needed a woman's touch. What would it be like to be Mrs. Jeffrey Trevor? The thought blazed through her like a bolt of lightning, yanking her back to the present. Not that she had any interest in Mr. Trevor, of course.

Even if she did, he would never pass Jenny's stringent requirements. Even if he could read and write, his profession disqualified him.

She sighed and forced herself to concentrate on Mr. Hampton's monologue. As far as she could tell, he hadn't missed a beat. His monotone voice threatened to put her to sleep.

The sun had set more than a half hour ago, and stars studded the darkened sky. Though it was still relatively early, no later than eight, she started to nod off. Catching herself, she took a deep breath and sat up straight, forcing her eyes wide-open.

"Really?" she asked, feigning interest. "There are five hundred types of bob wire." She pronounced the word *barbed* the way he did. She stifled a yawn and pulled her wrap tighter to ward off the cool night air. "Who would have guessed?"

Who, for that matter, even cared?

Mr. Hampton was too caught up with his own enthusiasm to notice her bored tone. If anything, the question seemed to delight him.

"I was the first rancher in the area to see the benefits of bob wire," he said without modesty. "Not that I'm taking *all* of the credit. I was lucky enough to meet a bob wire salesman by the name of John Gates. He told me his product was 'light as air, stronger than whiskey, and cheap as dirt.' No truer words have been spoken."

Mary Lou rolled her eyes. The quarter moon hidden behind the trees provided no

131

light, and the small carriage lantern supplied little more. It was too dark to see much of anything beyond the rumps of Mr. Hampton's two fine horses.

The carriage followed the dirt road along the river's edge. Mr. Hampton surprised her by changing the subject. "You can't see it for all the bushes, but there's an old swimming hole over there. Hardly used anymore." He gave her a sideways glance. "Perhaps you and I can take a dip together some day."

Over my dead body, she thought. Out loud she said, "My sister forbids me to swim." That was true if not altogether accurate. What she didn't say was that her sister had forbidden her to swim in the *nude.*

"What a pity," he said.

From across the water came the sound of fiddles playing a lively tune. A bonfire blazed on the opposite embankment.

"That's the sawmill over there," Mr. Hampton said, correctly guessing the object of her interest. "Sounds like Trevor and his men are having themselves a good time."

At mention of Mr. Trevor's name, Mary Lou's heart skipped a beat. "D—do you know Mr. T—Trevor?" she asked, hoping he didn't hear the tremor in her voice.

"I know him all right," he said, showing

132

no signs of noticing her stammer. "He and I stand on the opposite of the fence where bob wire is concerned."

She blinked. Barbed wire again. Was there anyone or anything that didn't involve what Mr. Hampton called "the wire that changed the West"? Nonetheless, her interest was piqued.

"Are you saying that the two of you don't get along?" Not that it surprised her. Jeff Trevor was determined to get his own way and didn't take no for an answer.

Mr. Hampton glanced at her. "Trevor thinks bob wire is inhumane to animals. Calls it the devil's rope."

Her jaw tensed at the very thought of animal injury. "Is . . . is he right?"

Hampton made a derisive sound with his mouth. "If you ask me, Trevor's more concerned about his bankroll than cowhide. A bob wire fence is horse high and bull strong. You can't say the same for a wood fence. That's not something a sawmill worker wants to hear."

The road straightened and veered away from the river's edge. He clicked his tongue, snapped the reins, and the horses picked up speed.

Mary Lou couldn't resist a backward glance at the small dot of fire on the opposite shore.

The sawmill. Heart pounding, she sat back in her seat.

The boys and me are planning a little get-together . . .

A mental picture of herself dancing in Jeff Trevor's arms came to mind. She sighed a deep sigh and blinked, but the vision remained with her all the way back to town.

If Mr. Hampton noticed her silence, he gave no indication. If anything, he seemed to enjoy talking without interruption. "I'm telling you, bob wire is what's taming the West, not the railroads. And I'll tell you another thing —"

By the time Mr. Hampton pulled up in front of the hotel, Mary Lou had a headache.

He scrambled to the ground and helped her from the carriage. Bowing, he held her hand. "Perhaps you would do me the honor of your company in the near future."

Mary Lou forced a smile, but all she said was, "Good night, Mr. Hampton." She turned and hurried into the hotel, through the empty lobby, and up the stairs.

Jeff Trevor stepped out of the shadows at the landing.

Startled, she jumped back, heart pounding. "You nearly scared me to death," she gasped.

Offering no apology, he greeted her with a half smile. "If your rush to escape is any indication, I'd say you found Mr. Hampton as much of a bore as I do."

Not wanting to give him the satisfaction of knowing her evening was a dismal failure, she leveled a steady gaze at him. "What are you doing here?"

"I was just curious to know how my *fiancée* enjoyed her little carriage ride," he said.

Her mouth dropped open. His brazen behavior never failed to amaze her. "I am *not* your fiancée, and it's none of your business."

She started past him, but he grabbed her by the arm. The flesh beneath his touch prickled, sending streaks of warmth throughout her body, but she would not be intimidated by him.

"That bad, eh?" he drawled, his head close to hers, his breath hot against her already heated face. "I'm sure you'll find an outing with me much more to your liking."

Trembling, she pulled her arm away. "I–If you know what's good for you, you'll leave before my sister finds you here."

He studied her intently. "Very well, but I'll be back."

He lifted his fingers to her cheek. Shocked by his impertinent persistence, she slapped his hand away, but the heat of his touch remained. He winked and stepped aside, allowing her to pass.

Hand on her burning face, she hurried down the hall, his low warm laughter trailing after her.

Fumbling for the door handle, she glanced over her shoulder. He stood looking at her, his eyes blazing with intensity. Her mouth dry, she slipped into the room, closing the door quietly but firmly behind her.

Jenny looked up from the desk with a bright smile. "Mr. Hampton brought you home on time as promised. He really is a gentleman. I do hope you expressed your gratitude."

Mary Lou pulled off her shawl and tossed it on a chair.

"Do tell us everything," Brenda cried. She sat cross-legged on the bed, bouncing up and down in eager anticipation. Dressed in a muslin nightgown, her hair hung down her back in a single long braid.

"There's not much to tell," Mary Lou said. "Unless you're interested in *bob* wire."

"Barbed wire?" Brenda frowned. "Is that what Mr. Hampton talked about?"

"And talked about and talked about and

talked about." Mary Lou whirled across the room in circles until she was close enough to the window to peer outside without seeming obvious. Mr. Trevor walked across the street with easy strides and mounted his horse. He glanced up at her window and she quickly drew back. After a long moment, she chanced another look and he was gone.

"Surely he must have talked about something else," Brenda pressed.

"The man is a bore," Mary Lou said. "I would rather have spent the evening with a lamppost." *Or Mr. Trevor.* The unbidden thought left her breathless and she flopped down on the bed.

"I found Mr. Hampton to be a very interesting and intelligent man," Jenny said.

"Then *you* go out with him!" With that, Mary Lou promptly burst into tears for no good reason.

"Oh, dear." Jenny hurried to her side. Pulling a handkerchief from her sleeve, she dabbed at Mary Lou's cheeks and hovered over her like an old mother hen.

The moment her tears subsided, Jenny questioned her, an anxious look on her face. "Did Mr. Hampton . . . do something?"

Mary Lou shook her head. "No, he was a perfect g–g–gentleman," she said. "Just like you said."

Jenny smoothed her hair away from her face. "Are you sure? You would tell me if he wasn't, wouldn't you? If he tried to —"

Mary Lou pushed Jenny's hand away. "I told you, he was a gentleman."

Brenda bounced up and down again. "Maybe *that's* the problem."

"That just shows how little you know," Mary Lou said, sticking her tongue out.

Jenny stood back, hands at her waist. "So what *is* the problem?"

"I told you he's a bore, and I don't want to ever see him again! He even makes Mr. Wordsworth seem interesting."

Jenny sighed. "It would be a shame to waste such a strong candidate. There doesn't seem to be as many eligible men here as that newspaper article suggested. Perhaps" — she turned to look at Brenda — "Mr. Hampton would consider courting you."

Brenda paled, but Jenny didn't seem to notice. Instead, she hastened to the desk — a woman clearly on a mission — and pulled a sheet of stationery from the drawer.

She thought for a moment then checked both *The Compleat and Authoritative Manual to Attracting and Procuring a Husband* and *The Worcester Letter Writer.*

Mary Lou raised her eyes to the water-stained ceiling. It was never a good sign when Jenny consulted her reference books.

"Dear Mr. Hampton . . ." Jenny said aloud, putting pen to paper. "I shall forever be in your debt for the kind attention you've shown my sister, Mary Lou. However, I believe it would be in both our best interests if you would kindly consider courting Brenda instead."

Brenda's eyes widened in alarm and, for the first time in her life, Mary Lou felt sorry for her.

NINE

A lady, if promenading, must avoid
seeking the attention of the opposite sex.
Looking over one's shoulder to gauge a
man's interest is never permitted.
— MISS ABIGAIL JENKINS, 1875

The following morning, Jenny left the hotel
and headed for the general store. It was still
early but already the air shimmered with
heat. The horse-drawn sprinkler wagon had
passed earlier. Nevertheless, the stage
churned up clouds of dust as it barreled
into town.

The marshal stood in front of his office
talking to Redd Reeder. Neither man paid
her any attention. Bracing herself, she
passed by with nary a glance at Marshal
Armstrong, but no amount of determination could keep her from looking back to
see if he had noticed her.

Had she not been so busy peering over

her shoulder, she might have seen the boy darting out of the general store. As it was, she didn't know what hit her. One moment she was standing properly upright, the next flat on her back, her petticoats in shocking disarray.

Dazed, she stared up at a youth of perhaps eleven or twelve. The hair that fell over his eyes failed to hide the startled look on his young face.

"Ma'am, I —"

Mr. Fairbanks ran out of his shop wielding a broom and yelling, "Why you —"

The boy glanced at the shopkeeper, then back at her. Self-preservation evidently taking precedence over common courtesy, he took off running with the shopkeeper close behind.

Rhett reached her side, followed by Redd, but already she was on her feet.

"Stop!" she called. She started after the shopkeeper but swooned. The marshal caught her in his arms and held her steady.

"Miss Higgins, are you all right? Are you hurt?"

Frustrated at her inability to rush to the boy's defense, she buried her face against his vest. "If he hurts that boy, I'll —"

"Don't worry about Fairbanks," Redd

said. "He yells a lot, but he wouldn't hurt a flea."

"Redd's right." The marshal cupped her chin and tilted her head upward so he could see her face. His eyes were soft with tender concern. "It's you I'm worried about."

Her mouth went dry. It had been a long time since anyone worried about her. "I'm fine," she managed, though her heart beat so fast she could hardly breathe.

She allowed herself the luxury of relaxing in his arms a moment longer before pulling away. Lifting her hand to the back of her head, she felt a small lump. "Ouch."

"Come on, sit down." His arm encircling her waist, he led her to the boardwalk steps. "There you go." He dropped down beside her. "After you've rested awhile I'll take you to see Doc Myers."

"Is that a direct order?" she asked, trying to make light of her mishap.

His gaze locked with hers. "It wouldn't hurt to have the doc check you out," he amended.

"Want me to go and fetch him?" Redd asked.

"Thank you, Redd, but that won't be necessary." She moved her legs and arms. "See? Nothing's broken. I'm sure the doctor has more pressing matters to attend to."

Rhett frowned. "You could have a concussion."

"I'm fine. Really I am."

Redd looked down the street and suddenly turned white. "If I'm not needed here, I just remembered today's the day I make fresh coffee."

Before Jenny could thank him for his concern, he took off running. He barely made his escape before Miss Erma Hogg's buckboard roared down Main and pulled in front of the bank.

Rhett laughed. "Perhaps you could give Miss Hogg some pointers on how to catch her man."

"I could use some pointers myself," she said. She thought her plan to travel to Rocky Creek infallible. Two pretty young women, a town full of eligible men. What could be simpler? Or at least it seemed so at first. But nothing was working out the way she hoped.

He studied her. Something passed between them, a flare of light perhaps. A sudden flame. A physical awareness. Whatever it was, it caught her off guard. A flood of warmth rushed through her body.

"Would you at least allow me to walk you back to the hotel?" he asked.

Before she could reply, Mr. Fairbanks

143

returned, broom in hand. He was breathing hard and sweat beaded his forehead. "I'm telling you that boy will be the death of me yet."

Rhett stood, and the moment, if there had been a moment, was gone.

"What did he do this time?"

"Stole cheese and beef jerky, he did. Right from under my very nose."

Rhett's face grew somber. "I'll take care of it."

Mr. Fairbanks scoffed. "That's what you said last time, Marshal."

"The boy's twelve. What do you want me to do? Put him in jail? You know his situation."

Fairbanks spat out a stream of tobacco juice. "I don't care about no situation. Scooter Maxwell is a thief. And I expect you to do something 'bout it."

Grimacing in disgust, Fairbanks stormed into his store. The bells jingled loudly in the wake of the slamming door. A pickax on display fell over and Rhett stood it upright.

Jenny rose and brushed off her skirt. "Cheese and beef jerky hardly seems like something a boy his age would steal." A twelve-year-old would be more likely to steal sweets or maybe even something off-limits such as alcohol or tobacco. She glanced at him sideways. "Unless he's hungry."

"His father's a drunk." A muscle quivered at his jaw. "He probably took the food to feed himself and his younger brother."

She stared at him in dismay. "You aren't going to punish him, are you?"

"What he did was wrong," he said.

Anger flared inside her. Her father died during tough economic times. Haswell families barely had enough to feed their own, let alone three orphans. Rocky Creek was nowhere near as fiscally sound as the *Lone Star Tribune* indicated, but neither did anyone look like they were doing without.

"What is wrong with this town?" she cried. "The boy is hungry and all you can think about is punishing him!"

"It's my job to maintain law and order," he said.

"And what about your job as a human being!"

He drew back as if she'd physically attacked him. "I told him that when things got bad, to come to me for help."

"He won't ask for help," she said.

The marshal tilted his head slightly and she could see him struggling to understand. "Why not?"

She bit her lip, not knowing how much or

how little to say. After her papa died, her maternal grandfather offered to help her and her sisters, but she turned him down. He thought her father a ne'er-do-well and blamed him for his daughter's death. Partly out of pride but mostly to protect her dear papa, she told everyone that he'd left them financially secure. Not only was it an out-and-out lie, it was the worst mistake she ever made, and she paid dearly for it. Was still paying for it.

Her anger spent, she drew a deep breath. "He doesn't want anyone to know how bad things are." She gave him a beseeching look. "He's protecting his father. It's what children do."

His face clouded in emotion. He shook his head as if chasing away whatever feelings had momentarily overcome him.

"Are you sure you can get back to the hotel okay?"

The back of her head still hurt but otherwise she felt fine. "Quite sure."

He studied her with cool regard. "Then if you'll excuse me, I need to ride out to the Maxwell place." He hesitated. "I'm glad you weren't seriously hurt. Take care of yourself."

Without another word, he walked away. A moment later, he was astride his horse. He gave her one last lingering look before riding out of town as if something or someone gave chase.

The Maxwell cabin was located a mile out of town off the main road. The place looked deserted, and only a slight movement at the window told Rhett someone was home.

Rhett tied his horse to the hitching post, noting the lack of water in the trough. Mrs. Stevens, or Ma as she was fondly called, owner of the boardinghouse where he lived, insisted that the Maxwell cabin had once been a happy home. That was long before he arrived in Rocky Creek. Even so, it was hard to believe.

"When Cynthia Maxwell died, we should have put her husband in the grave right next to her," she'd said. "It would have been the humane thing to do."

Rhett walked up the steps to the porch. Twisted needles from the towering loblolly pines that surrounded the area muted his footsteps. He banged on the door.

"Scooter, open up."

Nothing. He tried the doorknob, and the door sprang open. It took a moment for his eyes to adjust to the dim light inside. He doubted his nose would ever adjust to the unpleasant smell that rose up to greet him.

A young boy stood in the back of the room. It was Scooter's eight-year-old brother, Jason.

The boy looked scared.

Rhett held his hands palms out. "I won't hurt you," he said gently. "Do you know where Scooter is?"

The boy continued to stare at him but said nothing. Stepping inside, Rhett moved slowly so as not to startle him. The log cabin with its clay-chunked walls and rough-hewn wood floors was consistent with dozens of other cabins in the area, but that's where the similarities ended.

Shocked by the condition of the small room, he stopped and stared.

The room was dark and dingy mainly due to the dirty windows. Only the red-and-white oilcloth on the table added a splash of color. Flies circled and buzzed around the dirty dishes stacked on the counter. Cupboard doors stood open, bearing empty shelves. Clothes, trash, and empty whiskey bottles were strewn everywhere. The smell alone was enough to turn his stomach.

"Remember me? I'm the marshal," Rhett said, turning his attention back to the boy. He'd seen Jason in town on occasion but hadn't really gotten to know him. Now he wished he had.

Jason continued to watch him but showed no recognition, though curiosity had replaced the earlier fear in his eyes. His trousers were so threadbare it was a wonder they still held together, and his oversized shirt practically buried him. His hair was long and dull.

Rhett felt sorry for the boy. When was the last time he had a bath? Or a decent meal? When did the child last smile?

"I brought you something," he said, keeping his voice low so as not to frighten Jason any more that he already was. Rhett had stopped at the boardinghouse on the way to the Maxwell cabin to pick up some of Ma's delicious macaroons. Now, he opened the cloth napkin and held it out.

Jason stared at the offering but made no motion toward it.

"I brought them for you," Rhett prodded.

This time, Jason grabbed an almond cookie and stuffed it whole into his mouth.

Rhett nodded approval. "There you go."

Jason wiped the crumbs away with the back of his hand and reached for another one without further invitation. In quick order, he finished off the lot.

"Do you know where your pa is?" Rhett asked.

Jason shook his head but said nothing.

"What about Scooter? Do you know where he is?"

Again the boy failed to respond.

Rhett debated what to do. Matt Maxwell worked odd jobs here and there. He wasn't able to keep a job for very long because of his drinking, so he could just as easily be at one of the saloons in town. Scooter was probably hiding in the woods or down by the river.

A fly buzzed in his ear and he slapped it away. Glancing around the room, he was sickened anew. No one should live like this. Certainly no child.

Things were bad, but there was nothing he could do. It wasn't against the law to live in a messy house. Even the laws that applied to child neglect were vague and, for the most part, unenforceable. The cabin wasn't even in his jurisdiction. It was the county sheriff's problem, not his.

He turned to leave. *And what about your job as a human being!*

He froze. No, he wasn't going to get involved. Couldn't. He'd promised himself years ago not to get too close to anyone. Not to feel. Not to care too deeply. It was the only way he knew to keep from drowning in the murky waters of his guilt.

He glanced back at the boy. Never had he

seen a child look more neglected. Something stirred inside. Sorrow, sadness, and empathy washed over him. Rage surged through him. He cursed his feelings — fought them — but in the end he had no choice but to surrender to them.

Spurred both by anger and the need to breathe fresh air, he threw open the windows. Grabbing a metal pail, he filled it with empty whiskey bottles and carried it outside. In a work shed out back, he found a shovel. The soil was soft and easy to dig, giving little release to the rage inside.

What was the matter with Maxwell? Couldn't he see what he was doing to his sons? Where was God in all this?

And why did God have to let Leonard die?

There it was. He knew it. The moment he started caring about something, it would start. At sixteen, Rhett had fought in that terrible war. Seen things he never thought to see. When his childhood friend Leonard died, Rhett managed to survive by ignoring his feelings and learning to focus on the here and now. It was thinking about the past that got you in trouble. It was giving into feelings that could kill you.

He hid behind his marshal's badge and, for the most part, it worked. But one comment from Jenny and everything changed.

Spurred on by the need to keep his thoughts at bay, he kept digging until the hole was close to six feet deep and almost as wide — the same size as the grave he'd dug all those years ago on a remote battlefield for his friend.

Shaking the memory away, he picked up the pail and dumped the contents. Bottles tumbled and crashed to the bottom of the pit with a clatter. Glass shattered.

He turned to find Jason by his side. The boy studied him with serious eyes. He held two empty bottles by their necks as if holding up a peace offering.

"Good boy," Rhett said, nodding approval.

The boy tossed the bottles one by one into the hole then ran into the house, presumably to gather more.

It took them both several trips before the room was cleared of trash. Leaving Jason with the task of filling the hole with dirt, Rhett pumped water from the well, dumped some into the horse trough, and heated the rest on the wood-burning stove so he could wash the dishes. The food was caked on and it took much scrubbing before the dishes were clean.

Then he swept the floor and porch.

Jason returned to the house and watched

in silence. Rhett tried joking with the boy and singing silly songs, but Jason never said a word. Nor did he smile. It was eerie to see a child that young so grim and silent.

More than an hour later, Rhett stood back and surveyed his work. Not bad. The last of the flies were gone, but the smell of whiskey still lingered. It was as if alcohol had seeped into the very foundation of the house, along with the owner's grief and depression.

He turned to Jason. He had passed the point of no return, and this time he didn't even try to fight the need to help this child. "How would you like to go for a little ride?"

The boy stared at him.

Rhett looked around for paper and pencil to leave a note for Maxwell but found nothing he could write on.

Giving up the search, he led Jason outside to his horse.

"Say hello to Lincoln," he said. The horse gave a low whicker, but the boy remained mute.

Rhett helped Jason onto the saddle then mounted behind him. The sun disappeared behind a veil of dark clouds and lightning zigzagged upon the distant hills. A few drops began to fall, but the full impact of the storm didn't hit until they arrived at the boardinghouse.

Ma, his landlady, greeted him with a buttery smile. She was round as a muffin, her white hair in a neat bun. Her whole face lit up at sight of Jason.

"And who have we here?" she asked, clapping her hands in delight. She blinked. "Not Jason Maxwell. Look how you've grown."

"I invited Jason to have supper with us," Rhett said. "I hope you don't mind."

Ma nodded approval. "I wondered what I was going to do with all that fried chicken and berry pie."

Jason looked all around him, his eyes wide with amazement. Next to the Maxwell's modest cabin, the boy probably thought the boardinghouse looked like a castle.

"This is where I live," Rhett said. "My room's upstairs. If you like, I'll show it to you."

"He doesn't want to see your room," Ma said. "He wants to eat." She took the boy into the kitchen and washed his face and hands, talking nonstop.

Ma was a widow whose husband had been killed years earlier during an Indian uprising. She had a big heart but that didn't make her any less particular about the boarders she took in. The rules were stated plainly in the neatly furnished parlor on a sign that read: *No drinking, no cussing, no smoking, and no courting.*

Only good Christian men were permitted to board there. She did break her own rule once by allowing the pastor's wife Sarah to stay, but that was temporary. Then as now, she had a soft spot for children, and if anyone could win Jason over, it was Ma.

Leaving Jason in those good hands, Rhett hurried back outside to put his horse in the barn out of the storm.

A short time later, Jason sat at the dining room table between Rhett and Kip Barrel. Lee Wong, owner of Rocky Creek's Chinese Laundry sat opposite. Lee Wong didn't speak much English, but he smiled a lot. Many immigrants responded to the anti-Chinese movement sweeping the country by cutting off their queues and dressing more American. Not Lee. Dressed in his native tunic, wide-legged pants, and wooden shoes, his pigtail reached all the way to his waist.

Redd was the only other boarder, but because of his responsibilities at the café, he seldom took his meals at the boardinghouse.

Rhett reached for one of Jason's hands, and Barrel took the other. Ma lowered her head and said grace.

"Our dear heavenly Father, bless this food and everyone at this table." She lifted her head. "Let's eat."

Rain scratched the windows like the claws of angry cats. Lightning flashed, followed by low rumbling sounds.

Jason didn't pay any attention to the rain. Instead, he kept his eyes on his plate as if he feared his food would disappear if he looked elsewhere. Rhett couldn't imagine where the skinny kid put all the food Ma placed in front of him. Then he noticed the boy trying to stuff a chicken leg into his pocket.

He leaned over and touched Jason on the arm. The boy looked up with a guilty frown as if caught doing something wrong. Rhett winked at Jason but addressed his comments to Ma.

"Do you have enough leftover chicken for Jason's brother?"

Ma didn't miss a beat. "Not only do I have enough chicken, but I have some fresh-baked macaroons."

Despite Ma's best efforts, she couldn't get Jason to say a word. She leaned over and whispered in Rhett's ear. "He's protecting his family," she said. "That's why he won't talk."

Her comments came as no surprise. Jenny said much the same thing.

Later, when Rhett helped carry dirty

dishes into the kitchen, Ma turned to him, shaking her head. "I had no idea things had gotten this bad. What are you going to do?"

"I don't know." Rhett had talked to Maxwell on numerous occasions. Locked him up time after time in an effort to dry him out. Nothing got through to the man.

Ma insisted that something had to be done about the boy's clothes. She asked Lee Wong and Kip Barrel to carry kettles of water upstairs for the bath.

She turned her attention to an old trunk. Kneeling on the floor, she rummaged through it. "I may have something that fits him. Yes, yes, look at this." She held up a pair of child's knee-length trousers and a little sailor shirt. "These used to belong to my grandson, Jeff." A wistful look crossed her face. Jeff Trevor now was a grown man working at the sawmill.

She sighed, her eyes veiled with memories. "They grow up so fast."

Barrel announced that the bath was ready, and she snapped out of her reverie. She stood and ran her fingers through Jason's hair. "Let's go and clean you up."

Jason balked. With his arms tight across his bony chest, he took on a mulish look and his lower lip stuck out.

Rhett had never seen such obstinacy in

one so young. For some reason he thought of Jenny. He could well understand why Jason felt the need to protect himself, but why did Jenny? The thought coming out of the blue startled him, though in reality it should have been no surprise. Lately, it seemed like everything reminded him of Jenny.

Something else he tried to fight to no avail.

Ma tried reasoning with Jason. "A bath and clean clothes and you'll be as good as new."

She reached for his hand, but he pulled away and said, "No!"

A delighted smile crossed her face. "Praise the Lord, you *can* talk. I was certain the cat stole your tongue."

The boy cried out. "I ain't takin' no bath!"

Barrel stepped up and sang, lifting his operatic voice to its highest pitch. "I'm not taking a bath!"

Jason stared at him, his eyes rounded, a look of uncertainty on his face. "I won't," he said, his manner hesitant as if testing a new toy.

"I won't," Barrel sang, his strong tenor voice rattling the dishes on the shelf.

Lee Wong slapped his hands over his ears. Despite his discomfort, he grinned.

Jason was clearly intrigued. One by one he shouted negative responses and looked delighted when Kip repeated them in song. The boy was so fascinated, he failed to notice that Kip had gradually led him from the parlor to the hall and, finally, up the stairs.

Rhett and Ma stood at the bottom of the stairs listening to the commotion on the second floor. Jason screamed and cried. Kip sang. There was a splashing sound and then silence.

"Oh, dear," Ma said, hands to her mouth. She and Rhett looked at each other then crept up the stairs to take a look. Before they reached the landing, Jason laughed out loud.

"Do it again," he yelled out. "Blow another bubble."

Kip responded in song, and Ma breathed a sigh of relief. Since Kip had everything under control, Rhett and Ma walked downstairs again.

"God gave Mr. Barrel the greatest talent, but He forgot to give him the courage to use it," she said. "He should be singing on stage."

Rhett smiled. "It looks like God has other plans for Barrel's talents."

Ma nodded. "Like making a scared little boy laugh." She shook her head. "I wish you could have met Jason's mother. She was a beautiful person, inside and out. So kind and loving."

Others had described Jason's mother in much the same way. "What did she ever see in Maxwell?" he asked.

"Not the alcohol. The man never touched a drop until she died. It's like a poison eating up everything good inside him, even his love for his wife."

Rhett balled his hands into fists. "If he loved her so much, why doesn't he take care of their children? That's what she would have wanted."

Ma heaved a sigh. "Grief can do awful things to people," she said. "Guilty grief . . . now, that's the worst kind."

"What's he got to feel guilty about?"

"He blames himself for his wife's death. Said he should have called for the doctor the moment his wife went into labor. By the time the doctor arrived, it was too late for mother and child."

"There's no guarantee that medical intervention would have made a difference," Rhett said.

"We all told him that." She shrugged. "But there's nothing logical about guilt."

"It's only natural to feel guilty under such circumstances," he said, surprised to find himself defending the man. But why wouldn't he? He knew all about guilt. It was a constant companion plaguing him day and night. Everything he did stemmed from guilt.

"There's a big difference between guilt and godly sorrow," she said. "Godly sorrow helps us to grow. Guilt is more likely to destroy us. There's only one cure that I know of, and that's God's grace."

He frowned but said nothing. Thunder boomed and Rhett's stomach tightened. It sounded like cannon fire and he quickly forced away the memories that inevitably followed any thought of the war. Thoughts of Leonard.

Jason walked down the stairs looking like a different child. Behind him, Kip Barrel beamed like a proud father.

Jason's wet hair was parted and combed to the side. The clothes Ma found in her trunk fit as though they'd been made special for him. He smelled of soap and a hint of cedar from the lining of Ma's trunk.

Best of all, a broad smile curved across his freshly scrubbed face.

It was an encouraging sign and Rhett found himself smiling in response. It wasn't too late to save Jason and maybe even Scooter. Maxwell, he wasn't so sure about. All he knew was that he suddenly wanted to help him. His reasons weren't entirely self-less. Maybe by helping Maxwell overcome his guilt, he could help himself.

Show me how, God. Show me how.

TEN

Never engage in boisterous laughter.
If you must show mirth, a polite smile
or titter will suffice.
— MISS ABIGAIL JENKINS, 1875

The storm had passed and stars twinkled between the fast-parting clouds. Puddles dotted Main Street like a merchant's display of hand mirrors. Water dripped from the roofs of false-faced buildings.

Jenny hurried along the boardwalk, the earthy air tickling her nose. She ran into Marshal Armstrong halfway between the hotel and marshal's office.

"I was just coming to see you," he said.

"I was on my way to see you," she said. An unwelcome surge of excitement left her feeling breathless.

"How's your head?" he asked.

"A little sore, but otherwise I'm fine," she replied. His concern wrapped around her like a warm blanket.

They stood gazing at each other in a circle of yellow gaslight. There was something different about him, but she couldn't quite place her finger on what it was.

"You said you were on your way to see me," he probed.

Her mind blank, she impatiently pulled her thoughts together. "Yes, I wanted to know about the boy . . . Scooter."

"I haven't been able to talk to him." He told her about his encounter with Scooter's brother and how the boy had been fed and given new clothes. He seemed pleased with the way things worked out with Jason.

"I just took him home, but his brother wasn't there. His pa didn't know where he was."

"Poor child. He must be scared." She shuddered to think of the boy all alone. Especially during that rainstorm. "Is Scooter his real name?" It seemed like such a strange name to call someone.

He shrugged. "I don't know his real name. Supposedly, he never learned to crawl as an infant. All he could do was scoot along on his backside."

She smiled at the vision his words evoked. Something made her want to get to know the boy. Maybe it was the horror on his face when he stared down on her and saw what he had done. Or maybe she simply identified with a young boy who stole food so that his younger brother might eat.

"I hope he's okay," she said softly.

"He'll be back," the marshal said.

The certainty in his voice surprised her. "How can you be so sure?"

"He won't leave his brother. Not for long, anyway."

It was a comforting thought. "I want to help. I don't have a lot of money, but I can help with food and clothes."

In the dim light, his eyes looked soft as satin. "Right now, the best thing you can do is pray."

The simplicity of his answer both surprised and alarmed her. He had no idea what he was asking. Talking to God didn't come easy. She never quite knew what to say to Him. How did you explain away a period so dark that you didn't even dare mention God's name? Still, praying for Scooter was the least she could do, and she intended to give it her best shot.

She bit her lip. "What I said earlier . . . I didn't mean to criticize you."

"Sure you did," he said.

She opened her mouth to protest but then caught his shadow of a smile. "You're right,

I did," she said lightly.

He shrugged. "I knew it." He shifted his lean form. "So how's the hunting going?"

Grateful that he harbored no ill feelings, she was nonetheless surprised by the sudden change of subject. "You make it sound like I'm trying to bag a deer."

"Deer, husbands, same principle," he said. "Sneak up on your prey, aim, and fire."

She stared at him then burst out laughing. Eyes warm with humor, he grinned back at her. For some odd reason this only made her laugh harder.

"Jenny?"

Mary Lou's voice startled her. Her laughter died as quickly as it came.

Her sisters stepped out of the shadows.

She groaned inwardly. After all her lectures on conducting themselves like ladies, here she was laughing her fool head off. In public, no less. In the company of a man.

"What are you two doing out?" she asked, her voice edged with irritation.

"We wanted to take a walk," Brenda said. "We were tired of sitting in our room."

"It's after dark," Jenny scolded. "Go back to the hotel."

Mary Lou looked about to argue. Instead, she flounced past Jenny and headed for the hotel in a most unladylike manner. Brenda followed close behind with considerably more grace.

Jenny flashed Rhett a look of apology. "I best go. Let me know when you find Scooter."

"Let me know when you find husbands." His tone was teasing, but this time she didn't even crack a smile.

She didn't want to go back to the hotel. She wanted to stay with him, to laugh with him. She let out her breath. Who was she kidding? She didn't want to socialize. She wanted him to hold her, to kiss her, to make the lonely, aching hole inside her go away. She wanted all the things she couldn't have. Could never have.

"Good night," she said, her voice choked.

"Good night, Jenny."

It was the *Jenny* part that made her heart skip a beat as she hurried away.

Brenda couldn't sleep. Even after the raucous laughter and querulous voices outside their window had faded away and Main Street was deserted, she lay staring in the dark.

She didn't want to go out with Mr. Hampton. She couldn't say what scared her most about the man: his fancy clothes or stern, humorless expression. He wasn't at all like

167

that nice Mr. Barrel who shared his pie and winked at her in church when he thought no one noticed. Now *that* was an interesting man.

Next to her, Jenny and Mary Lou slept. Earlier Jenny cried out as if having another one of her bad dreams. Brenda rubbed Jenny's back, as she so often did in the middle of the night, until the nightmare passed. Questioning Jenny about the nightmares that kept her tossing and turning did no good. Either Jenny didn't remember or didn't want to talk about them.

Now Brenda turned on her side ever so slowly so as not to disturb the other two. It wasn't only her troubled thoughts that kept her awake. The room was hot and stuffy. The temperature had dropped a few degrees, but the rain had made the air clammy. To make matters worse, she was hungry, famished. Her stomach churned like rocks tumbling inside her.

Under Jenny's watchful eye, Brenda's supper had consisted of a sliver of roast beef and a generous portion of stringed beans. No bread, no butter or pie. A bird would starve on such a pitiful diet.

Slipping out of bed, she reached beneath the mattress. Her fingers tightened around an empty sweet bag, her last hope. Defeated, she sat on the floor, her back against the bed, and held her head.

She hated this, hated this dependence on food — this obsession. No matter how hard she tried to curb her appetite, she couldn't seem to help herself. Food was the only way she knew to fill the void inside. At times, the hole seemed so big, she imagined herself caving inward like a child's cardboard Easter egg. Sometimes she feared disappearing altogether.

A sound made her look up. She held her breath. There it was again. A sharp tap on the windowpane. Rising to her feet, she ran barefoot across the room and looked out.

Much to her surprise, Mr. Barrel stood in the middle of the street holding a lantern.

The window had been closed earlier to block out the noise from the street below. Now the town looked deserted. She quietly opened the wooden sash and leaned on the sill.

"What are you doing?" she whispered as loud as she dared.

He motioned to her with his arm. "Come," he said softly, though his motions were exaggerated, dramatic. He looked like he was playing the role of a desperate lover on stage. "Come."

He then pretended like he was serenading

her, though he made not a sound.

She placed a hand over her mouth to stifle a giggle.

She hesitated and stared back at the bed. If Jenny woke —

Still, it was hard, if not altogether impossible, to resist his playful invitation. Heart pounding, she left the window open. Feeling her way in the dark, she found her cloak and wrapped it around her shoulders. Then she shoved her feet into her velvet slippers.

She listened, but as far as she could tell, Jenny and Mary Lou hadn't stirred. Hand on the door handle, she was almost overcome by mingled guilt and excitement. What was she doing? Sneaking out in the middle of the night to be with a man! That was something Mary Lou would do, not Brenda, the good girl. The one who felt guilty if an unkind thought so much as crossed her mind.

She closed her eyes. *Dear God, forgive me.*

Quickly letting herself out of the room before she changed her mind, she ran through the dark hall, down the stairs, through the lobby, and into the street.

Barrel greeted her with the widest grin possible. He was the only person she'd met who could smile with his whole body. "I didn't think you'd come," he said, taking her hand in his.

She glanced up at the darkened window over her head. "What would you have done if Jenny or Mary Lou came to the window, instead of me?"

"I would have run for my life," he replied.

She giggled softly. She doubted he could outrun Jenny, but it would be fun to see him try. The smile died on her face. She enjoyed his company but couldn't help worrying.

"I shouldn't be here."

"What? Not be here in this magical place?"

Indeed, it did seem magical. The stars looked like diamonds tossed carelessly across a black velvet sky. The rain had washed away the laundry odors, and the air for once smelled fresh. The glow of his lantern turned paned windows into sparkling jewels.

Laughing, he led her down the street, singing softly in Italian.

"Where are we going?" she asked.

"You'll see," he said with a mysterious air. He stopped in front of the barbershop. Outside stood a six-foot freestanding pillar painted with red-and-white stripes and blue stars. He let go of her hand and threw open the door with a flourish. Bending at the waist, he invited her inside with a gracious wave of his hand.

Oohing and aahing, she glanced around. It was like entering another world. Never had she seen so many candles lit at one time.

The flickering flames danced upon the porcelain shaving mugs lining the shelves on either side of a beveled glass mirror. Each custom-painted mug bore the name of its owner. An array of hair tonics, straight razors, and atomizers were lined up on the counter. The shop smelled of soap, Turkish tonic, and bay rum. But it was another, more tantalizing smell that tickled Brenda's nose.

"I smell —" Surely she was imagining things. It was then that she noticed a small table with two place settings.

Barrel hung the lantern on a metal hook then turned to reach across the table to lift a pan lid.

"Fried chicken," he said with the tone of a man introducing royalty.

Brenda gasped in delight. "My favorite."

Barrel grinned. Like a child lifting the lids off penny-candy jars, he walked around the table picking up metal covers one by one to reveal an appetizing array of mashed potatoes, pan gravy, and butter beans. "And," Mr. Barrel said, saving the best for last,

"Ma's famous berry pie."

Brenda clapped her hands. "It's wonderful but . . . it's the middle of the night."

Barrel pulled his watch from his vest pocket. "It's three fifteen," he said. "But not to worry. Before waking you, I dropped off my laundry and Lee Wong assured me that it's supper time in Hong Kong."

Brenda laughed. What a perfectly fun and intriguing man.

He pulled out a chair and made a production of whisking it clean with a linen napkin. He then gestured with his arm for her to sit. "Madam."

Taking her seat, she folded her hands on her lap and waited. He sat on the chair opposite her and said grace. "Our dear heavenly Father, bless this food and the company." He then sang "Amen." His fine tenor voice rose to a crescendo. He sustained the last note so long he left Brenda gasping for air.

She clapped in appreciation. "How do you do that?"

"The secret is in the breathing," he said. He picked up the tongs and poked around at the chicken. "What part would you like?"

"I'll take a limb," she replied, using the polite term for *leg*.

He laughed. "A *limb* it shall be." Ignoring

her protests, he proceeded to fill her plate. Next he filled her glass with freshly squeezed lemonade.

While they ate, he told her the stories of the operas he had once dreamed of singing onstage. At times, he burst into song, his rich vibrant voice reaching inside her like the warming rays of the sun.

"They all seem so sad," she said, after he had described the stories of several operas. "Someone always dies at the end."

"Comedies were once considered strictly for the lower class," he explained. "A composer wishing to be taken seriously had no choice but to write tragedies. More pie?"

She shook her head. "I don't think I can eat another bite." She glanced outside. The silver light of dawn greeted her. She couldn't believe her eyes.

"Oh, no!" She quickly jumped to her feet. "Please tell me that's not the sun!"

He stood and peered out the window. "So it is," he said. "So it is."

"My sister will kill me."

"Ah," he said lightly. "The perfect scenario for an opera."

Despite her dismay at losing track of time, she couldn't help but laugh as they walked outside. "I had a really good time."

"Me too." He tilted his head. "Are you

sure you don't want to stay for breakfast?"

"I don't think I'll be able to eat another bite for the rest of the day." She laughed.

Her laughter turned into a strangled cry the moment she spotted Jenny charging toward them like a rampaging bull.

"There you are," Jenny stormed. "I've been looking for you everywhere." She scolded Brenda but glared at Barrel.

"I . . . Mr. Barrel —" Brenda began. "We were in the barbershop."

Jenny's gaze bored into her. "How was I supposed to know that?" She gasped. "And please tell me you're not wearing your nightgown."

Brenda pulled her cloak tighter. She'd forgotten she wasn't properly dressed. Though it was still early and no one else was around, she flushed.

Barrel stepped between them. "I didn't mean any harm, ma'am. Your sister and I, we were just —"

Jenny's face hardened. "How dare you ruin my sister's reputation."

"Oh, no, ma'am. I would never do anything like that."

"If you ever come near her again, I'll have you arrested for immoral behavior."

With that, Jenny grabbed Brenda by the

hand and dragged her all the way back to
the hotel.

ELEVEN

Flirting is permitted, but only after mutual
interest is confirmed.
— MISS ABIGAIL JENKINS, 1875

Rhett was late arriving at the office that
morning. Earlier, he rode out to the county
sheriff's office to discuss the Maxwell boys.
Though the American Humane Society had
been founded for the prevention of cruelty
to children and animals four years earlier in
1877, some Texas courts hesitated taking
the young away from their natural parents.

Abe Slacker was the new county sheriff
who had little rapport and even less influence with local and state officials. Rhett
didn't have much hope of either the county
or state doing what needed to be done.

It had been a frustrating morning. Adding
to his bad mood, he still hadn't found
Scooter. No one, not even his father, had
seen the boy since he stole meat and cheese

from Fairbanks General Merchandise.

No sooner had he finished checking his few prisoners than the owner of Jake's Saloon burst into his office. Jake's presence surprised him. Seldom did he see the man when he wasn't behind the bar pouring drinks. Nor had he seen the man look so upset. His heavy frame and drooping mustache quivered, and his already squinty eyes kept getting smaller.

"You gotta do somethin' about that woman. I'm telling you, she came barrelin' into my place like nobody's business."

Rhett sighed. He didn't have to ask the woman's name. "Why would she do that?" As far as he knew, Jenny didn't imbibe.

"Accused me of hiding her sister, that's what. I'm warnin' you, if you don't do somethin' about them Hussy —"

"Higgins."

"— sisters, we're gonna have to take the law into our own hands."

That was the last thing Rhett intended to let happen. "The only thing you're gonna do is calm down so we can get to the bottom of this. Why did Jen . . . eh . . . Miss Higgins think you were hiding her sister?"

"How am I supposed to know?"

"All right, let me look into it and see what I can find out."

Jake didn't look happy, but he agreed not to do anything until Rhett had a chance to investigate.

No sooner had Jake left than Mrs. Hitchcock took his place. Her garish dress, feathered hat, and high-pitched voice were an assault to the eyes and ears at any time but never so much as they were that morning.

"As a member of the Rocky Creek Quilting Bee, Quilting Bee, it is my duty to inform you that our members are feeling threatened by the Hussy sisters —"

"Higgins," he said. "Their name is Higgins."

He had no idea why the quilting bee members were up in arms over Jenny, but he listened respectfully. When he got a chance to get a word in edgewise, he stuck his pen in its holder and sat back to ask, "Threatened, how?"

"The way those women, those women, are carrying on." She stuck up her nose and sniffed. "The available decent women in this town don't have a chance against those . . . those hussies!" She shook so hard that her hat slid down her forehead like a colorful bird swooping from its perch. She readjusted her hat before continuing. "Mrs. Fields's daughter hasn't had a gentleman caller, gentleman caller, since those women traipsed into town."

Cutting her off before she had a chance to repeat herself yet again, he offered assurance. "The fine women in your group have nothing to worry about. Once the novelty wears off, things will go back to normal." At least he hoped so.

"It better," she said.

No sooner had she left than Kip Barrel charged through the door. In one eternally long sentence that only a trained voice could manage on a single breath, he described his middle-of-the-night supper.

Rhett stared at him. Never would he have imagined Kip capable of such outrageous behavior. In one single day, the man had gone from winning a little boy's heart to ruining a young woman's reputation.

"I'm afraid I have to take Jenny's side on this one," Rhett said.

Kip's face crumbled in dismay. "I was a perfect gentleman," he protested. "We talked about opera."

"But enticing a woman out of bed in the middle of the night?"

Kip raised his hand as if taking an oath. "As God is my witness, nothing improper happened."

"I believe you. But if you wish to court

Brenda, it would be to your advantage to go through Jenny . . . eh . . . Miss Higgins, like everyone else."

Kip's mouth dipped. "What chance does someone like me have? I used all my savings to start my business. Do you know how much barber chairs cost? And I have two."

Rhett sympathized. Kip Barrel was a moral and honest man. A woman couldn't go wrong with a husband like him. "I'll put in a good word for you."

Kip looked dubious. "It's going to take a lot more than a good word to calm down Jenny Higgins. You should have heard her. My ears are still ringing." He lifted his arms and fluttered his fingers. "High Cs and Fs all the way. Trust me, Donna Anna has nothing on Brenda's sister."

"Donna Anna?"

"The jilted woman in *Don Giovanni*."

Rhett knew nothing about opera, but he could well imagine Jenny's outrage. Where her sisters were concerned, she was like a mother bear. "You're a good man, Kip. A good Christian. You'd make a fine husband." Rhett tried his best to sound encouraging.

Kip shook his head. "Brenda's sister isn't looking for a good man. She wants a rich man. You'll be wasting your breath."

Rhett felt Kip's frustration. It seemed as if

all Jenny cared about was money. What a pity that such a pretty mouth . . . eh, face . . . was wasted on such a stubborn, mercenary woman. "I'll do the best I can," he said, but he didn't have much hope of changing Jenny's mind.

Kip gave a frustrated sigh. Without another word, he shuffled out of the office, shoulders down, head bent low.

The next one to burst into his office was Hank Applegate, stomping around like a man with itching powder in his boots.

"Now what?" Rhett asked.

Hank could hardly get the words out fast enough. "That colonel woman was seen walkin' in and out of Jake's saloon at the crack of dawn like nobody's business."

"I heard. Jake was here already, complaining."

"He had every right to complain. It's gittin' so a man can't drown his sorrows without a woman's interference."

Rhett shook his head. He didn't have much patience for anyone seeking comfort from a bottle. "She was looking for her sister."

Hank made a face. "She was lookin' for trouble. That's what she was lookin' for."

Rhett's jaw tightened with annoyance. "So what do you want me to do about it, Hank?"

"You ain't gotta do nothin'. I've got everythin' under control." Hank held up a hand-lettered sign. Most of the words were misspelled, but Rhett was able to figure out what it was meant to say: KEEP OUT BY ORDER OF THE SOCIETY FOR THE PROTECTION AND PRESERVATION OF MALE INDEPENDENCE.

Rhett frowned. "You're kidding, right? A society?" That seemed like a highfalutin word for the likes of Hank. "Male independence?"

Hank stuck out his chest. "Me and the boys decided to band togeth'r and fight the colonel."

Rhett grimaced. It sounded like war.

Hank's mouth twisted upward. He stabbed at his sign. "What this here means, Marshal, is that Colonel Jenny is forbidden to step foot in any male establishment. From now on, a man will be able to get himself a shave or liquid refreshm'nt in peace and without feminine interfer'nce. Furthermore, she's not to approach men in the streets, nor is she to glare, glower, or otherwise stare at a man without his perm'ssion." He emphasized his words with a nod of the head.

Rhett tapped his fingers together. "I don't know, Hank. This doesn't sound right. It *is* a free country."

"And I aim to make sure it stays that way. If a man ain't wantin' to get married, that's his perog'tive."

Rhett rubbed his chin. He had a bad feeling about this, but once Hank made up his mind, there was no changing it.

"I don't see why you're so against marriage, Hank."

Hank wiped his nose on his sleeve. "It ain't natural, that's why. Money's not the root of all evil. Marriage is. And I'll tell you another thin' —"

Determined to stop him before he got *both* feet on his soapbox, Rhett waved his hand through the air. "I don't want any trouble."

No one ever told him when he went into law enforcement that his biggest challenge would be mediating the battle of the sexes.

"That's what I'm aimin' to avoid," Hank said. "If you're interested in joinin' our group, our first meeting is tonight at Jake's."

"Thanks for the invitation, but I think I'll pass."

"Suit yourself, Marshal."

Hank wasn't gone but five minutes when Jenny burst into his office like a Texas tornado. She slammed the door shut with such force, the windows shook and his hat fell off its nail. Whirling about in a swish of skirt and petticoats, she glared at him, hands on her waist.

"What kind of town is this? My sister was abducted in the middle of the night, and I want the perpetrator arrested at once."

He should have known she would blow things out of proportion. "It's not abduction if the person goes willingly."

Judging by the stunned look on her face, she didn't want to hear that her sister was equally responsible. "He . . . he had no right."

"That may be, but unless Kip Barrel took your sister at gunpoint or in some way overwhelmed her, my hands are tied."

She straightened but her eyes showed no less fire. "What about the signs posted all over town forbidding women to enter certain establishments?"

He had no idea Hank had already hung his signs. He sure didn't waste any time. "The men of this town value their privacy."

"And I value mine." She tossed her head. "I demand that you protect my sisters and me from these . . . these barbarians!"

Rhett clenched his hands. Now she'd gone too far. Last night she'd looked all soft and concerned about Scooter. Today, she was her usual stern and unrelenting self. Her softness was his undoing. He was far better able to handle this more formal side of her.

"First of all, Kip Barrel is not a barbarian. He is a decent, law-abiding, churchgoing citizen. If that doesn't make him worthy of your sister's attention, then you've got a lot to learn about men."

She looked momentarily disconcerted but quickly regained her composure. "Your idea of decent leaves a lot to be desired."

He rose slowly and leaned forward. Their noses practically met. He could smell her lavender perfume, smell the sunshine in her hair. It was all he could do to block out the memory of their kiss.

"If anything leaves a lot to be desired, it's your ridiculous requirements," he said.

No longer was he thinking about Kip or even Hank. The truth was, he was still smarting at the way she so easily dismissed him the first day they'd met and deemed him unworthy of her consideration. Not that he had any interest in a wife, of course. Certainly, he wasn't interested in her sisters. Nor did he have anything to prove. It just wasn't right to judge a man based solely on his profession or bank account. Not right at all.

She backed away. "I'm only trying to protect my sisters," she huffed.

"Protect them, Miss Higgins? Or shackle them?"

She tossed her head. "If you were doing your job —"

"If you would kindly allow me to."

The stared at each other like two wild animals in a territorial dispute. The standoff might have gone on forever had Timber Joe not rushed into the office, shouting, "The Yankees are coming!"

TWELVE

An inappropriate suitor should be quickly
and thoroughly banished before he wins
the heart of his intended.
— Miss Abigail Jenkins, 1875

Jenny marched back to the hotel looking
neither left nor right. Still shaken from her
meeting with the marshal, she wondered yet
again if coming to Rocky Creek hadn't been
a mistake.

She expected more from the town, more
from its people. Maybe she should leave and
go to Houston or maybe even Boston.

She still couldn't believe that Brenda
would sneak out in the middle of the night
to be with a man. That was something Mary
Lou would do, not dear sweet Brenda.

So deep were her thoughts she would have
walked right by the hotel desk had the clerk
not called to her. "You have a message,
ma'am," he said, yawning.

"Thank you."

Jenny took the message and unfolded it, approving the fine quality of linen stationery. It was from Mr. Hampton, who graciously agreed to meet with Brenda instead of Mary Lou. Jenny couldn't believe her good fortune. After last night, she was more anxious than ever to get Brenda settled into a good marriage before she pulled another scandalous stunt.

Breathing a sigh of relief, she reached into her reticule for a coin, but already the clerk had dozed off again. Never had she seen anyone sleep so much. She left the coin on the counter before turning away.

Her spirits lifted, she walked upstairs only to find the room filled with doom and gloom.

Mary Lou sat on the bed in full pout. Brenda gazed out the window in some sort of trance.

"I've got good news," Jenny announced cheerfully. "Mr. Hampton has graciously agreed to court Brenda."

Mary Lou rolled her eyes. "Lucky Brenda."

Brenda didn't even bother pulling her gaze away from the window.

Jenny walked across the room and stood by Brenda's side. "I'm trying to do what's

189

best for you," she said. "You do understand that, don't you?"

"Kip is what's best for me," Brenda mumbled.

Kip? Brenda called him by his given name? Had things really progressed that far? Oh, dear. It was worse than she thought.

Jenny laid a hand on Brenda's shoulder. She shuddered at the memory of seeing Brenda leaving the barbershop in her nightgown and slippers. Oh, the shame, the shame. Where had she gone wrong? Was it because she had been so lax in seeing to Brenda and Mary Lou's religious training all these years? Was that the problem?

"A man who would entertain a woman in the middle of the night simply isn't to be trusted."

"I trust him," Brenda said, her voice muffled.

"You weren't even dressed. He has no thought or care for your reputation. Brenda, please. All I ask is that you give Mr. Hampton a chance."

Brenda turned away from the window. Her eyes were dull, her face blotchy from crying. "Kip is the only man I'm interested in."

Jenny threw up her hands. "You can't possibly know that. You don't even know any

190

other man."

Brenda gave her a beseeching look. "I know *him*. He's the only one who accepts me for who I am."

"That's ridiculous. I accept you."

"No, you don't!" Brenda cried. "You're always trying to change me. To turn me into something I'm not."

Jenny stepped back as if she'd been slapped. "That's not true, Brenda. It's not." Jenny took her sister's hand. "I just want what's best for you. I don't want you to ever —"

Brenda's gaze sharpened. "Ever what? What don't you want me to do?"

Jenny searched for words. "Go hungry or have to struggle." She glanced at Mary Lou, who sat watching from the bed. Jenny was used to arguing with Mary Lou, but never before had Brenda given her this much trouble.

"Please, Brenda. All I'm asking is that you give Mr. Hampton a chance. What could it hurt?"

In the end, Brenda agreed to go out with him, but Jenny didn't have much hope that she would look upon the man with much favor.

Later that night, Jenny sat brushing her hair when a knock came at the door.

191

She glanced at her sisters. Brenda hadn't spoken to her since their argument and had refused to eat. She now sat at the desk, writing in her diary. Mary Lou gloomily stared out the window.

Since neither one of them showed an inclination to see who was at the door, Jenny laid the brush on the dresser and hurried to open it herself. It was Rhett.

Scooter stood next to him, his head hung low. His face was clean and his hair combed, but his clothes were filthy and his bare feet black with dirt.

Rhett gazed at her as if seeing her for the first time. Something in his eyes made her flush. Feeling strangely vulnerable, she reached up to touch her hair, which hung loose down her back.

"I apologize for disturbing you," he said, "but Scooter has something he wants to say."

"Sorry," the boy mumbled.

Rhett frowned. "Sorry what?"

Without looking up Scooter said, "Sorry I knocked you down."

Jenny's heart went out to him. Looking at him, she saw herself all those years ago. She'd been only a few years older than he was when her father died, leaving her with the care of her two sisters. She would never forget how afraid she was, how alone. How terribly overwhelmed.

"I don't think we've been formally introduced," she said. "My name is Jenny Higgins." She held out her hand and the boy stared at it before raising his own. She shook his hand lightly. "Apology accepted."

Scooter jerked his hand away as if he'd been burned.

Rhett gave him a reassuring pat on the shoulder. "Let's hope Mr. Fairbanks is as forgiving as Miss Higgins."

Rhett bid her good night. His gaze lingered on her a moment longer before he turned to leave. Reaching the top of the stairs, he looked back, but the hall was too dim to read his expression. She waited until he had vanished from sight before closing the door.

She pressed her forehead against the wood and willed the pounding of her heart to stop.

Mary Lou was a nervous wreck. She couldn't take two steps without bumping into that annoying Mr. Trevor. There simply was no getting away from him. No matter how much she protested, he continued his ridiculous charade.

He was not her fiancé! He was nobody. He meant nothing to her.

Still, as outrageous as he was, never did she expect him to bother her in church. Was nothing sacred?

On Sunday he sat directly behind her. She wouldn't have known he was there had he not *deliberately* kicked the back of her chair during prayer.

Startled, she turned around to find him grinning at her. She glared at him from beneath her best flat bonnet. He winked at her and she quickly turned to face the front of the church. Her cheeks aflame, her mouth rounded into a disbelieving *O*.

The nerve of the man!

For the remainder of the service she refused to acknowledge him, though his heated gaze felt like two hot pokers on her back.

Most shocking of all was the way he leaned forward from time to time to whisper in her ear. He cleverly timed each covert murmur so Jenny wouldn't notice.

"Don't forget to tell me your ring size," he said following Reverend Wells's sermon.

Later, while the offering plate worked its way from the front of the church to the back, he leaned forward and whispered, "I don't believe in long betrothals, do you?"

Had Jenny not been so busy glaring at the choir or, rather, at Mr. Barrel, she would surely have noticed and put a stop to Mr. Trevor's outrageous behavior. As it was, Jenny seemed completely oblivious to what was going on beneath her very nose.

He even changed the words in the closing hymn from *carry me* to *marry me.*

That was the final straw. "Stop it," she hissed.

"What am I doing?" Brenda asked.

Jenny, sitting on the other side of Brenda, glared at both of them. *"Shh."*

After church, Mary Lou hastened to their carriage ahead of her sisters, anxious to make her escape. Much to her dismay, Mr. Trevor galloped up on his horse.

"Miss Higgins," he said, tipping his hat. He dismounted. Instead of his normal work clothes, he wore dark pants, a vest, and a white shirt. His usual red cap had been replaced by a more stylish wide-brimmed straw hat. Not only did he look handsome, he was positively dashing.

"You're looking especially beautiful to-day," he said, his gaze traveling the length of her.

She wore a yellow skirt draped in front and ruffled in back, and a matching form-fitting Basque bodice. It had taken three days of begging before Jenny finally broke down and bought it for her. Judging by the look of approval on his face, the outfit had been worth all those extra chores Jenny made her do in return.

Cheeks burning, she glanced over her shoulder, but Jenny was still a distance away, talking to the minister and his wife.

She gritted her teeth. "If you don't leave me alone, I will report you to the marshal."

He seemed more amused than concerned. "There's no law against a man talking to his fiancée," he drawled.

"I'm not your fiancée." She gave her head a haughty toss. "I wouldn't marry you if you were the last man on earth."

"Those are mighty hurtful words, ma'am," he said, though the twinkle in his eyes made him look anything but injured. "I'd sure hate to think you mean them."

She peered at him from beneath a furrowed brow. "I mean them all right."

He feigned a wounded look that didn't fool her in the least. "I would never force you into doing something you didn't want to do," he said.

She almost laughed in his face. "That's exactly what you've been trying to do since the first day we met."

"Let's just say, I've seen the error of my ways."

She studied him from the corner of her

eyes. "Does this mean you will stop harassing me?"

"What it means is that I'm prepared to make a proposition."

Something in his voice — or maybe it was the glint in his eyes — made her uneasy but no less curious. "What . . . kind of proposition?"

A lazy smile inched across his face. "If after kissing me you still feel the same way, we'll call off the engagement and I'll never bother you again."

She stared at him, not sure she'd heard right. "Did . . . did you say k–kiss?"

He made a slight gesture with his hand. "One kiss is all I ask. If I can't change your mind with a kiss, then I don't deserve your hand in marriage."

Her breath caught in her throat, and for a long moment she could do nothing but stare. "That's the most ridiculous thing I've ever heard," she managed at last. Though kissing him didn't seem all that objectionable, it was nonetheless out of the question.

The invitation in his smoldering eyes was rife with challenge. "You aren't afraid, are you?"

She scoffed at the very idea. "Of course not."

He shrugged. "Then what have you got to

lose? It's just one kiss."

Her cheeks burning, she glanced at Jenny, still deep in conversation. She swallowed hard before turning back to meet his gaze. "And . . . and you'll leave me alone?"

"You have my solemn word."

She searched his face for signs he was mocking her. Much to her chagrin, he looked dead serious. Still . . . a kiss. What kind of man would make such a proposition? What kind of woman would agree to it?

As if to accept her silence for compliance, he nodded his head and mounted his horse, the saddle creaking beneath his weight. He stared down at her, reins in hands. The expression in his eyes was hidden beneath the brim of his hat, but his confident smile was all too evident.

"Perhaps we can meet tomorrow night? After your sisters retire? Say around eleven? It shouldn't take but a few minutes for you to make up your mind. I'll be waiting for you outside the hotel."

Giving her no time to answer, he pressed his legs against the side of his horse and galloped away.

The full extent of what he proposed hit her. She would never agree to such a thing. She couldn't. Kissing a man under such circumstances was out of the question. It simply wasn't done. She didn't need Miss Abigail Jenkins's book of proper courtship behavior to know that.

She opened her mouth to call to him, but nothing came out except a strangled sigh. A searing pain filled her chest. Her lungs felt as if they were about to explode. Without realizing it, she had forgotten to breathe. Gasping for air, she leaned against the side of the carriage until she calmed down.

Kiss Mr. Jeff Trevor. Of all the crazy —

She placed a gloved hand to her mouth. Even as she considered the scandalous idea, she giggled then quickly looked around to make sure no one saw her. Kiss Mr. Trevor? A thrill of anticipation raced through her. What could it possibly hurt?

Jenny rushed up to the carriage. "Where is your sister?"

"I don't know," Mary Lou said, her voice husky. "I thought she was with you."

She took a deep breath and willed her heart to stop pounding, but not soon enough to escape Jenny's scrutiny.

"Are you feeling all right?" Jenny asked. "You look flushed and don't sound like yourself. I must say you acted rather strange in church. Are you coming down with something?"

"I'm fine," Mary Lou said, trying to think of an explanation for her behavior. She needn't have bothered. Already Jenny had turned away to search for Brenda.

Brenda ducked into the bushes and glanced back to make sure she couldn't be seen. She shuddered to think what Jenny would do if she found her with Kip again.

Kip had signaled her to join him in the woods next to the church, and she was convinced that Jenny would descend on them at any moment.

"I can't stay long," she whispered.

Kip took both her hands in his. "I didn't think you were coming."

"I wanted so much to see you." She would have come sooner had Mrs. Hitchcock not cornered her and given a detailed description of her sacroiliac problems. Brenda had no idea that such an annoying condition existed.

"I'm sorry to cause you so much trouble with your sister," Kip said, his voice filled with regret.

She smiled up at him. "I had a really good time that night. I think about it all the time."

"Me too," he said. "Me too."

"I love hearing your voice." Indeed, she often imagined his voice at night as she lay awake long after her sisters had fallen asleep. "Hearing you sing is like being hugged," she whispered.

His face softened before turning red. "Hugged by my voice. I like that," he said. "That's the nicest thing anyone's ever said to me."

"It's true, every word."

His eyes brimmed with tenderness. "I just wish we could spend more time together." A look of determination crossed his face. "I'm going to talk to your sister."

Brenda sighed. "It won't do any good."

He looked crushed. "I . . . I can't bear the thought of not seeing you."

She lifted a hand to his cheek, and he held it there. "I don't know what to say. My sister will never let us be together."

"There has to be a way." He studied her for a long moment. "Would it be so awful if you went against your sister's wishes?"

She looked into his kind eyes. "I could never do anything to hurt Jenny," she whispered, fighting back tears. She pulled her hand away. There she was again, the good girl. Doing exactly what everyone expected her to do.

Seeing the despair on his face, she tried to explain. "Jenny took care of us after my parents died."

She shuddered. That horrible December when they almost starved to death continued to haunt her. It was the driving force behind everything that happened since, even Jenny's determination to marry her off to a rich man.

"She saved my life."

"That doesn't give her the right to command it," he said. "Brenda, please!"

"I've got to go," she whispered.

"Wait." He wrapped his arms around her and kissed her gently on the lips. It was the first time Brenda had ever been kissed. Never had she imagined anything as sweet as the feel of his lips on hers.

Shy at first, she worked her arms around his neck. Confidence building, she then kissed him back and her heart filled with the most amazing joy.

Tears sprang to her eyes. Not because it was her first kiss, but because it would be their last. Pulling away, she turned and hurried to join her sisters.

THIRTEEN

A man who presumes to know a young
woman's mind is woefully misguided and
should be scrupulously shunned.
— MISS ABIGAIL JENKINS, 1875

For the rest of the day, Mary Lou was a
nervous wreck.

She hadn't been able to think of anything
but her encounter with Mr. Trevor. Even
the dime novel hidden among the pages of
Mr. Wordsworth's book failed to hold her
interest.

Abandoning her book, she paced around
the hotel room until Jenny finally threw up
her hands in frustration.

"You're going to wear a hole in the carpet
if you don't settle down," Jenny said, as if
one more hole in the threadbare carpet
would make a difference. "What in the
world has gotten into you?"

"Nothing," Mary Lou snapped, glaring at

Brenda for no good reason. Everything and everyone got on her nerves.

One kiss is all I ask . . .

The very thought of kissing Jeff Trevor filled her with so many perplexing emotions she didn't know which way to turn. Her inner turmoil ranged from utter dread to eager anticipation in the course of a single minute. Her mind swirled with indecision.

No sooner had she decided not to play his games than she changed her mind again. If she stayed away, he would continue to harass her. There simply was no choice but to accept his challenge.

The decision brought her no peace of mind. It wasn't as if she'd never been kissed. The Parker boy — what was his name? Thomas? Theodore? Whatever it was, he had tricked her into kissing him the day she turned thirteen. Then, of course, there was that two-timing Jimmy Mason, who smelled of hickory and tobacco and had the annoying habit of humming while he kissed her.

None of her previous experiences left much of an impression. Kissing was definitely overrated. Apparently, it was one of those annoying things that women were required to endure, like tight-laced corsets and rag curlers. Still, if tolerating Mr. Trevor's kiss was all it took to get rid of him, it would be worth a few moments of inconvenience.

The following night, Mary Lou thought her sisters would never fall asleep. At last their even breathing told her it was time to make her move. She climbed out of bed quietly, careful not to disturb the bedding. She tiptoed out of the room, her ankle-length nightgown flapping around her legs.

Fortunately, none of the other hotel guests was around. Judging by the loud snores that the paper-thin walls failed to mute, most, if not all, of the guests were asleep.

Earlier she had hidden her favorite blue gingham skirt and a soft pleated shirtwaist in a linen cabinet at the end of the hall. Now, after gathering her clothes from the hiding place, she quickly slipped into the candlelit water closet to change.

The room was so small that both elbows touched the wooden walls when she lifted her arms to arrange her hair. Still slightly damp from her earlier bath, her hair tumbled down her back in a riot of yellow curls. Earlier Jenny had pleaded for her to get out of the bath lest she catch her death of cold.

The mirror was only wide enough to see one side of her head at a time. Her cheeks were rosy pink and her eyes feverishly bright. Whether her heightened color came from nerves or anticipation she couldn't say, but the effect was most pleasing.

She wished for the luxury of perfume but didn't dare go back to the room to retrieve it for fear of waking Jenny. Other than that lack, she was satisfied with her appearance. She took one last look in the mirror, hid her nightgown in the linen closet, and crept down the stairs to the empty lobby.

Outside the hotel, she stood in the shadows until she got restless. She pulled her father's pocket watch from the little pouch sewn in the waist of her skirt. She moved into the circle of light provided by the kerosene lantern hanging from a hook above her head and checked the time. It was ten minutes to eleven.

She pocketed the watch and stepped back into the shadows to wait.

Maybe he wouldn't show up. She paced back and forth in front of the hotel. Maybe he was watching her.

She stared across the street with narrowed eyes, but as far as she could tell, no one hid in the shadows.

The Rocky Creek Café was still lit. The restaurant sign had been replaced as it was every night with a sign that read LEE WONG'S CHINESE LAUNDRY. A man pulled in front of the laundry in his shay. He flung a sack of dirty clothes in front of the door and drove off.

Music and laughter poured out of various saloons. Somewhere an argument ensued. Sharp voices escalated then faded away.

Someone stumbled out of a saloon singing at the top of his lungs. Two horsemen rode down Main Street and hitched their horses in front of Jake's Saloon.

Where is he?

She had just about decided to return to her room when she spotted a horseman riding toward the hotel. Panicking, she quickly moved away from the light and hid in the shadows.

What was she thinking? Meeting a man under such ridiculous circumstances was just plain foolish. She closed her eyes tight as he drew near, hoping he wouldn't see her. Heart pounding, she held herself perfectly still.

"Miss Higgins."

Flinching at the sound of his voice, she opened her eyes. Her first thought was to run, but her feet refused to move.

He dismounted and tethered his horse to the hitching post in front of the hotel. He walked toward her with long easy strides. "I wasn't sure I'd find you here."

She swallowed hard. He had her trapped, but she was *not* going to make a fool of herself. "You promised to leave me alone if . . . I don't find . . . eh . . . things to my liking."

"I'm a man of my word," he said. "You just relax and let me know when you're ready."

"Ready?"

"For your kiss."

How one got ready for a kiss like this, she had no idea. She was so nervous she could barely think. Her mouth felt like it was stuffed with cotton. She ran her damp hands along the sides of her skirt.

"You aren't nervous, are you?" he asked.

"Of course not," she said a tad too quickly. Fearing he might have heard the quiver in her voice, she added, "If my sister finds us . . ."

"Ah, yes, your sister." He thought for a moment. "If you prefer, we can find another spot. No one will see us in front of the newspaper office or barbershop."

"Y–yes," she stammered, "perhaps that would be . . . best."

They walked side by side, leaving the hotel behind. She was careful to leave as much space between them as the boardwalk allowed, but even so she was keenly aware of his every move.

The streetlights didn't reach this far down Main Street, but gaslights from a nearby saloon provided a soft yellow glow.

Once they reached the darkened office of the *Rocky Creek Gazette,* Mr. Trevor faced her and waited. His fine head was outlined by the light filtering though bat-wing doors across the street. His manly fragrance filled her head with an enticing combination of the great outdoors and freshly cut lumber. She felt all at once vulnerable and safe in his presence.

He moved closer. She stiffened and forced herself to breathe. His fingers circled her arms. Not knowing what else to do, she put her hands on his chest. They stood so close she could feel his sweet breath in her hair, feel the power of him. It was as if all of Texas coiled inside him.

He lowered his head and captured her lips in one easy swoop. With seemingly no effort, he took command of her senses. Nothing else existed but the touch and feel of him. Warm sensations worked down her spine all the way to her toes. It was unlike any kiss she'd ever experienced.

All too soon, it ended. He drew back and dropped his hands to his side.

She shook her head in an effort to think

straight. She was hot — no, cold. Her lips burned. She didn't know what to say, where to look, what to do. Where was Miss Abigail Jenkins and her book of endless rules when you needed it?

"Well?" he asked, as if he sought her opinion on something as mundane as a fence post. "What do you think? Have you changed your mind? Do you want to marry me?"

Shaken, she moistened her lips and flattened her back against the building so he couldn't see her face. She hated that she could so easily be swayed by a man's lips. By *his* lips.

Angrier at herself than with him, she shook her head hard. "No," she said as firmly as she could manage. "Nothing's changed. I have no desire to marry you."

For the longest while he didn't say a word. Silence stretched between them like a flimsy bridge she was too afraid to cross. She wanted to, oh how she wanted to, but something held her back. Flustered, she waited for him to make the next move.

"Very well," he said at last, his voice low. "As were the terms of our agreement, I shall not bother you again." He extended his crooked elbow. "May I escort you back to your hotel?"

She was stunned. That was it? No argument? No attempt to change her mind? He accepted her answer just like that?

"You needn't bother," she said. And because she was about to make a fool of herself by bursting into tears, she picked up her skirts and ran all the way back to the hotel.

FOURTEEN

A woman more knowledgeable than a
man is obliged to hold her tongue and
feign ignorance in all matters except, of
course, childbirth.
— MISS ABIGAIL JENKINS, 1875

On Tuesday morning Jenny walked down
Main Street, seething all the way. Every
window held a sign warning her and her
sisters to keep out. She had no desire to
step foot into a saloon or even the barbershop, but the warning signs irked her nonetheless.

The Society for the Protection and Preservation of Male Independence, indeed! Who
ever heard of such a thing?

The ridiculous signs continued to pop up
like toadstools after a spring rain. She was
about ready to march into the marshal's office and demand that he do something
about the annoying signs when she spotted

Scooter Maxwell. An idea suddenly occurred to her.

"Scooter!" she called.

He stopped in his tracks, but he looked ready to run in the opposite direction. His expression was hidden by the hair that fell in his face; he stiffened as she drew near.

"It's okay," she said, keeping her voice low. "I'm not going to harm you. I just want to talk to you." She reached his side but he didn't look at her. Instead, he kept his head down.

"Would you like to earn some money?"

He looked up, but a wary expression crossed his face. She knew that look, knew that feeling.

"I pay quite well," she said. Her enticement seemed to work. At least he appeared more interested than suspicious.

He scratched his neck and then his arm. His skin reddened beneath his fingers. "What do I have to do?" he asked.

It was a good question and one she should have asked all those years ago, the day she unwittingly accepted a stranger's offer to help. A decision that had changed her life forever.

"Don't worry, it won't be hard." She looked him up and down. Never had she seen such a pitiful sight, but it was the haunting look in his eyes that touched her and made her more determined than ever to help him. She was particularly worried about his skin rash. If he didn't watch out, it could become infected.

"First, I require anyone under my employ to take a bath." Not that she'd ever employed anyone, but he didn't know that.

He shook his head and backed away, waving his hands as if warding off an imminent attack by a wild animal. "I ain't takin' no bath."

Ignoring his protests, she continued, "I also require my employees to have a full meal."

He looked no less obstinate.

"At my expense," she added.

This time, he stopped moving. He brushed the hair away from his face with a quick flick of his wrist. "You're gonna buy me a meal?"

"Anything you want at the Rocky Creek Café." It was the best she could do given her current circumstances. How she wished she could offer him a home-cooked meal instead.

His forehead creased with indecision. He was obviously tempted but no less distrustful. He scratched his chest, then the back of his neck.

"What do I have to do?" he asked again.

She moved another step closer. "See that sign in the window?" She pointed to an offensive notice. "They're all over town. I want you to remove them."

He squinted up at her. "That's all?"

"The trick is to remove them without being seen," she explained. "You may have to wait until after dark."

He studied her with eyes that looked too old and too heavy for his young face to bear. "I can do that," he said at last.

"I'm sure you can." She tilted her head sideways. "Do we have a deal? Dinner, bath, and signs." She ticked off each one on her fingers. She then held out her hand, but he made no move toward it.

"About the bath —" He wrinkled his nose in distaste. "I ain't wantin' no bath."

She shrugged. "It's all or nothing." She tilted her head. Bathing might not altogether cure his skin rash, but it couldn't hurt. "So what's it going to be?"

He hesitated for a beat before shaking her hand. "Deal."

His handshake was as weak as his voice. Fearing he would change his mind, she hustled him quickly into the café and supplied him with the best Redd had to offer.

Never had she known anyone to eat so

215

much at one sitting. She doubted that Redd's cooking had ever been more appreciated.

Getting him to eat was the easy part. Getting him to take a bath was a different story. He cajoled and pleaded with her to reconsider, but she stuck to her guns. No bath, no job.

Now as she stood in the hallway of the hotel with Mary Lou and Brenda waiting for Scooter to finish his bath, she wondered if she would ever get him to come out. Nearly an hour had passed since she and her sisters left the room so he could undress and bathe in privacy.

Mary Lou complained nonstop the entire time. For once, Jenny didn't blame her. A lively poker game was in progress in the hotel lobby, which meant they had no choice but to wait in the hall outside their room. The air was hot and stuffy and smelled of stale cigar smoke.

"What is taking him so long?" Mary Lou whined. She banged on the door once with her fist.

Brenda gave a worried frown. "Maybe he drowned."

Mary Lou rolled her eyes.

"It's possible," Brenda said in a defensive voice. "I doubt that he's had much experience with baths."

What seemed like a ridiculous idea at first began to seem more plausible as time passed. Even Mary Lou began to look more worried than annoyed.

Finally, Jenny knocked lightly. No answer. Fearing the worst, she opened the door a crack and peered inside.

Scooter sat in the tin tub, his back toward her. Wide at one end and narrow at the other, the tub was, unfortunately, shaped like a coffin. Sometimes Jenny and her sisters bathed in cold water rather than pay extra for hot water that had to be ordered in advance. Today, Jenny spared no expense. She even paid double for clean towels. She only wished something could be done about the boy's clothes and shoes.

Lye soap in hand, Scooter scrubbed his arms and chest. He scrubbed so long and so hard it was a wonder he had any skin left.

Memories of her past assailed her. She knew — knew with every essence of her being — that it wasn't dirt he tried to scrub away but something much deeper. That something was a combination of anger and pain that no amount of soap or water or even scrubbing could make go away.

Quietly, sadly, she closed the door.

■ ■ ■ ■

Several hours later, Jenny watched the street below. It was a moonless night, and the kerosene lanterns and gas streetlights did little to penetrate the darkness.

Scooter darted in and out of doorways like a fleeting shadow. He snatched the sign from the window of the Rocky Creek Café and Chinese Laundry directly across from the hotel then bolted to the establishment next door.

Smiling to herself, she craned her neck but already the youth had disappeared into the folds of the night. *Just wait till Mr. Applegate and the members of The Society for the Protection and Preservation of Male Independence find their precious signs missing.*

She glanced at the bed where Mary Lou had finally settled down, engrossed in her book. Mary Lou had taken a great interest in Wordsworth lately. Jenny nodded approval. Maybe there was hope for her sister after all.

The sound of carriage wheels drew her attention back to the window. Mr. Hampton's fine carriage and horses drew up in front of the hotel, right on schedule. He stepped down and helped Brenda alight.

Hidden from view, Jenny kept her gaze focused on the street below, hoping to see some sign of affection or interest between the couple. There was none.

Not wanting to look like she was prying, she pulled away from the window just as Brenda burst through the door.

She flung off her shawl and frantically clawed at her bodice. "You've got to get me out of this thing," she cried.

She turned her back and Jenny started on the row of tiny buttons that ran from her neck to her waist. "Do keep still. How can I unfasten you when you wiggle so?"

The gown fell to Brenda's feet. Jenny loosened the corset lacings. Brenda wiggled out of it and then kicked the offending garment across the room.

Jenny draped a dressing gown around her sister's shoulders. "Did you and Mr. Hampton have a pleasant carriage ride?"

No answer.

Jenny's hopes died. It didn't look promising. The problem was Mr. Hampton was the only man who met the criteria as stated in Miss Jenkins's book. He was also the only one with a perfect PHAT score. "What did you two talk about?"

Brenda let out a bracing breath. "Mr. Hampton talked about barbed wire."

Mary Lou looked up from her book and laughed. "What did I tell you? The man is obsessed."

Jenny gave Mary Lou a warning look. "Mr. Hampton is serious about his occupation. It's only natural he would want to talk about it."

Brenda bristled with indignation. "Kip doesn't talk about razors and haircuts. He talks about interesting things like opera."

"Which proves my point exactly," Jenny said. She pulled several combs from Brenda's hair, and her dark curls tumbled down her back.

"Not only did Mr. Barrel show poor judgment in stealing you away, but his weakness for opera leaves a lot to be desired. Miss Jenkins wrote in her book that a man who likes opera is nothing more than a namby-pamby."

"That's not true!" Brenda pulled away, her eyes ablaze. "There's nothing weak or foolish about him. He's a very gifted singer. He could have been famous had he not suffered stage fright."

Jenny sighed. The foolishness of youth. "You know I only want what's best for you. I don't want either one of you to ever have to worry about your next meal. Mr. Hampton can offer you a wonderful life, if you'll let him."

Brenda wrinkled her nose. "What if I don't want what Mr. Hampton can give me?"

"It's what Papa wanted for you," Jenny said, and that ended the argument.

Their father's last wish on his deathbed was that Jenny take care of her younger sisters. He made Brenda and Mary Lou promise to obey her. His concern for his daughters came too late but had no less of a binding effect. Even Mary Lou loathed going against their father's wishes, still now, seven years after his death, though she continued to fight it.

Jenny won the battle with a sense of uneasiness. She didn't hold much hope that Brenda had found her match.

Mr. Hampton apparently thought otherwise. The very next morning, she was astonished to receive a message from him requesting permission to take Brenda on yet another carriage ride.

Oh, happy, happy days.

Now all she had to do was convince Brenda to give Mr. Hampton another chance. Always quick to recognize another's fine qualities, Brenda was bound to learn to appreciate Mr. Hampton's many virtues.

Jenny glanced at the message again, unable to believe her good fortune. Who would have guessed that Brenda would have a beau before her more outgoing and slender sister?

With this thought in mind, she practically flew up the stairs to break the news.

FIFTEEN

When unjustly incarcerated, a lady must maintain her standards of propriety, even when the brigand in the next cell ogles her charms. Under no circumstances should she bellow, screech, or weep, unless absolutely necessary to gain release, of course.
— MISS ABIGAIL JENKINS, 1875

Trouble started first thing that morning. Rhett left the boardinghouse earlier than usual, but already a crowd waited outside his office when he rode into town. Applegate was clearly the leader.

Drat. What did Jenny do this time? Fighting the urge to keep going, he dismounted and tied his horse to the hitching post. Applegate and the others thundered off the boardwalk to greet him, everyone talking at once.

"Quiet," Rhett ordered. "One at a time."

Applegate was at the head of the line so he spoke first. "If you don't do somethin' 'bout that Maxwell boy, we're gonna have to take the law into our own hands."

Expecting the usual complaints about Jenny, Rhett hooked his thumbs over his belt and waited. He didn't like hearing that Scooter was in trouble again, but he'd rather deal with the boy then have to confront Jenny with another complaint.

"Yeah!"

"You tell him, Applegate."

"Yeah!"

Rhett signaled for quiet. "One at a time."

"I'm tellin' you Marshal, that boy ain't nothin' but trouble," Fairbanks called from the back of the crowd.

"What did he do this time?" Rhett asked. It must have been something big to bring everyone to his door this early in the morning.

"He done gone and stole my signs," Applegate sputtered.

Rhett stared at him. "Are you telling me that all this fuss is about a few cardboard signs?"

"They ain't just cardboard signs," Applegate said, looking offended. "Those were the express property of The Society for the Protection and Preservation of Male

224

Ind'pendence."

"Yeah!" the others yelled, raising their fists.

"No one has the right to steal our property!" a man shouted.

"Ya durn tootin' they don't have no right," Applegate said.

"Right no," Lee Wong said.

Rhett lifted a brow and regarded the Chinese man with open curiosity. "You belong to the group too?"

Wong crossed his arms and slid each hand into the opposite sleeve of his tunic. "Marriage no be good," he said in his singsong voice. "Wife do laundry. No need Lee."

Rhett couldn't argue with him. If he ran a laundry, he'd be against marriage too.

Applegate stared at Rhett with rheumy eyes. "So what do you plan to do about it, Marshal?"

Rhett sighed in frustration. "I'll talk to the boy."

A collective groan filled the air.

"No offense, Marshal, but you've been talkin' to the boy and there ain't nothin' changed. It seems to me that it's time for action, not words."

Rhett considered his options. In the past he'd been lenient with Scooter because of his age and family problems. The boy was only doing what any boy would do under the circumstances: trying to survive in the only way he knew how, by stealing. But this latest escapade was different. That's what worried Rhett. This wasn't about food or other necessities. This was mischief, plain and simple.

As much as he hated to think it, it was time to teach the boy a lesson before he ended up in real trouble.

"So what do you plan to do 'bout it, Marshal?" Applegate persisted.

"Plenty," Rhett said. Without another word, he mounted his horse and rode out of town.

"What?" Jenny looked up from the desk and stared at Mary Lou, certain she'd heard wrong. "What did you say?"

Mary Lou tossed her reticule on the bed. She and Brenda had just returned from their daily walk. "I said Scooter is in jail."

"Jail!" Jenny jabbed her pen into its holder. "That can't be true. He's only twelve years old. He's too young to be in jail. You must be mistaken."

"No mistake," Brenda said. "We saw the marshal ride into town with Scooter on the back of his horse."

"And he was handcuffed," Mary Lou

226

added, her eyes round.

Jenny shook her head in disbelief. What was Rhett thinking? To put a boy that young in jail was criminal. "What did he do? Steal food?"

Brenda shook her head. "Mr. Applegate said Scooter stole his signs."

Jenny's mouth fell open. All this fuss was about a bunch of foolish signs? Signs that she paid Scooter to steal? Shock turned to dismay.

"Rhett . . ." She cleared her voice and started again. "Marshal Armstrong put him in jail for stealing . . . signs?"

"Mr. Applegate said it was private property," Brenda said.

Jenny jumped to her feet. "I don't believe this. Of all the ridiculous . . ." She hit the desk with her fist. Books fell and papers scattered everywhere. "I won't allow this."

Mary Lou and Brenda exchanged worried looks.

"What are you going to do?" Brenda asked.

"What that boy's own father refuses to do. Protect him." She grabbed her parasol and reticule and stormed out of the room, slamming the door so hard the whole hotel seemed to vibrate. She didn't stop until she reached the marshal's office.

Rhett looked as if he'd been expecting her. He leaned back in his chair, arms folded behind his head. "If you came because of Scooter, you can save your breath. He's in jail, where he belongs."

"You can't be serious. He's a child."

"He's a thief."

She took a ragged breath. "He's only twelve."

His eyes darkened. "He's old enough to know better."

She drew back. She needed a moment to think. Hiring Scooter to take down signs seemed like a good idea at the time. She was able to help him without making it seem like charity. In retrospect, she wished she'd found another way. Now she had no choice but to confess.

She swallowed hard and lifted her chin. "He was only doing what I asked him to do."

Rhett sat forward, both hands gripping the edge of his desk. "And what was that?"

"I paid him to steal those signs," she said.

He shot her a penetrating look. "*You* paid him?" He tilted his head sideways, a dubious expression on his face. "If that's true, why didn't he say so?"

"I made him promise not to say a word. That was part of the deal." She cleared her voice and plunged on. "Since I'm responsible, I insist you release him at once."

He shook his head, but whether in disbelief or resistance she couldn't tell.

"I can't do that." He let out an audible breath and grimaced. "He's in jail as much for his own protection as anything else."

Not sure she'd heard right, her mouth dropped open. "His own protection?"

His eyes softened into pools of appeal. "The folks around here tend to be pretty passionate about their possessions."

She stared at him in utter disbelief. "We're talking cardboard signs."

"The boy's out of control and heading for trouble. I aim to see that doesn't happen." He rapped the desk once with his knuckle. "I also hope that as soon as Maxwell finds out his son is in jail, it'll shock him out of his stupor. God knows nothing else has worked."

The door burst open and Redd popped his head inside. "Trouble at Jake's."

Rhett rose with one swift move and plucked his hat off a hook. Glancing at her with a look of apology, he dashed out the door.

Frustrated, Jenny paced the floor waiting for his return. She couldn't stand the thought of that poor boy in jail, and all because of her. There had to be something she could do.

She spun around and stared at the door leading to the jail cells in back. If only . . . The key ring hanging from a hook beckoned her.

"Jenny Higgins, don't you dare!" No sooner were the words out of her mouth than she reached for the keys. It was almost as if her hand had a mind of its own.

Now it shook so much, she could hardly fit the key into the lock. The door sprang open with a squeak of rusty hinges.

She hurried toward the cell. Three men lay on cots, hats covering their faces. Scooter sat on the floor in a corner, his head down. He looked so forlorn her heart went out to him.

"Scooter," she whispered, not wanting to wake the other prisoners.

He raised his head and she motioned him to the barred door. He jumped to his feet and moved toward her. "What — ?"

"Shh." She glanced at the men. One grizzly fellow removed his hat from his face. He lifted his head off the cot to give her a sleepy-eyed look before resuming his nap.

"Listen," she whispered. "Stealing those signs was my idea. I should be in jail, not you." She glanced over her shoulder to make sure Rhett had not returned. "We're going to have to move quickly." Talking softly, she told him what to do.

Frowning, he shook his head. "It's dangerous." He rolled his eyes in the direction of his cell mates. "You could be hurt."

His concern touched her. She glanced at the prone prisoners. They seemed harmless enough.

"I'll be fine," she said. When the stubbornness remained on his face, she added, "Your brother needs you."

At mention of his brother, the worry lines on his forehead deepened and no further discussion was necessary.

Moments later Scooter had fled jail and she had taken his place. During the exchange, the three men jumped to their feet but not fast enough. By the time they realized what happened, Scooter had already locked her inside.

Now that she got a good look at the men, she wished she'd taken Scooter's concern for her safety more seriously. Three of the raunchiest, smelliest men she had ever encountered shared her cell.

"Looky what we got here," one said, scratching his chest. He was the tallest of the three.

"Yeah," said another, leering at her. The

others were bigger, but this one looked meaner, his face flattened and pummeled by numerous brawls.

"Jail just got a lot more interestin'," said the third man with a toothless grin.

They advanced toward her, backing her into a corner.

"You stay right where you are," she warned. She stepped onto a cot and held her parasol in front of her with both hands. "Don't you dare come any closer."

One of the men laughed. "Who's gonna stop us?"

"I am! Leave her alone!" Rhett bellowed, and all three men froze in their tracks. No one had noticed the marshal enter the jailhouse.

Eyes blazing with anger, Rhett stared straight at her. "What do you think you're doing?" he demanded, his voice harsh. "And where's Scooter?"

Flashing a warning look at the prisoners, she stepped off the cot, but she held her parasol out in front to do battle if necessary. "I'm serving my time," she said. Rhett's face grew more menacing, but she continued. "Scooter was acting on my behalf. It's only fair that I'm the one who is punished."

She fell silent and waited. Naturally, she

expected Rhett to see the error of his ways and release her at once. Since he was taking his own sweet time in doing so, she pointed the tip of her parasol toward the keys dropped in the passageway by Scooter.

Jaw clenched, he swooped the keys off the floor and turned away.

Her body stiffened. He wasn't going to leave her here — was he? With these . . . barbarians?

As if he had second thoughts, he stopped. She snapped her mouth shut. Head held high, shoulders back, she assumed as much righteous dignity as she could muster.

He turned. His face as grim and unrelenting as before, he unlocked the cell.

She had no intention of making it easy for him. He was wrong to have jailed Scooter, no matter what his reasons, and the least he could do was admit it. "I'm not leaving!"

Let him beg. Let him fall on his knees and plead with her. She had no intention of leaving until he apologized.

"You got that right." He pointed at the three men who shared her cell. "You, you, and you. You've had enough time to dry out. Get out of here, all of you."

Aghast, she stared at him. Surely he wasn't serious! He wasn't going to hold her there, was he? And let those horrible men go free instead?

The three male prisoners glanced at each other as if they couldn't believe their good fortune, then silently slipped through the open cell door and quickly escaped.

Staring at her, Rhett slammed the steel door shut with a loud clank, locking her inside.

"I hope you're happy," he said. With that he stormed away. The door between the jail cells and his office banged shut with such force that she flinched.

Stunned, she tossed her parasol and reticule on a cot. Grabbing the bars with both hands, her thoughts whirled. Rhett wouldn't . . . he couldn't. Of course he couldn't. She forced herself to calm down and take a deep breath. He was only trying to scare her. He'll be back.

She paced back and forth. Minutes passed. She kicked a wall, then hopped around on one foot till the pain subsided. She cocked her head and listened. Nothing.

"I hope you're enjoying yourself," she called.

Still nothing. An hour passed. Maybe more.

She told herself for the hundredth time that he would be back, but the longer he stayed away, the more she worried.

Growing increasingly anxious by the moment, she glanced around in disbelief. She still couldn't believe he left her in jail. He wouldn't leave her there all night, would he?

Sixteen

A woman's dress and deportment should
enhance the gentleman on whose arm
she appears.
— Miss Abigail Jenkins, 1875

It didn't take long for news of Jenny's
incarceration to reach her sisters at the
hotel. They rushed to the jail and, for the
most part, exhibited the appropriate amount
of ladylike hysteria given the circumstances.
Jenny could hear their high-pitched voices
even before they stepped into the anteroom.

Brenda took one look at Jenny and
promptly burst into tears. Mary Lou stood
wringing her hands and glancing around
nervously as if she expected some creature
to jump out of a dark corner.

"Brenda, please don't cry," Jenny said
gently. She hated for her sisters to see her
in jail and was determined to ease their
minds. "You'll mess up your face. Do you

236

want Mr. Hampton to see you all red and blotchy?"

Mr. Hampton! Jenny groaned inwardly. If her being in jail cast an unfavorable light on either sister, she would never forgive herself.

"I'm not going carriage riding with Mr. Hampton," Brenda cried, tears rolling down her face.

"Of course you are," Jenny said. It wasn't like Brenda to be difficult, but lately she'd been nothing but. "Nothing's changed."

"How can you say that?" Mary Lou's eyes grew wide in astonishment. "You're in *jail.*"

"So I've noticed. However, it's only a temporary inconvenience." Rhett wouldn't — couldn't — leave her there overnight. "And it's for a good cause. I'll be out before you know it," she added brightly, though with considerably less confidence than she felt.

Her assurances did nothing to appease her sisters' concerns. Mary Lou looked uncommonly worried, and tears continued to roll down Brenda's cheeks.

"Marshal Armstrong didn't sound like it was only t–t–temporary," Brenda sobbed.

"Of course it is," Jenny insisted. Still, just to be on the safe side, she drew pencil and paper from her reticule and listed the things she needed. "Bring me a change of clothing. I also need my hand mirror and hairbrush. And perfume." Though she doubted anything could cover the stench left behind by the former occupants. "And don't forget my notebook."

Her sisters stared at her in disbelief while she scribbled her notes and issued orders. She knew from experience that action was the best way to handle their emotional outbursts. Keep them busy and they wouldn't have time to worry about her.

She reached through the bars and shoved her list into Mary Lou's hand. "I have three interviews scheduled for tomorrow. If perchance I'm not back, let the men know there's been a change of location."

Mary Lou gaped at her. "You're going to interview here?" She glanced around, her nose wrinkled in disgust. "In jail?"

"Of course." Unless the marshal sees the error of his ways, which she was beginning to doubt. "What choice do I have? We've already wasted enough time. Our money won't hold out forever."

Their small farm had sold for more than she hoped, considering the work that needed to be done on it. Even so, the money would have to last until she married off her sisters and could obtain employment.

"Now run along." They turned to leave, and she called after them. "Don't forget to act like ladies. And do bring me Miss Abigail Jenkins's book."

Jenny didn't sleep a wink that night, not a wink. Though she sprinkled perfume liberally around the cell, the air hung thick with the smell of alcohol, tobacco, and who knew what else.

She lay on her cot looking out the little square of window high above her head. A star winked back as if enjoying a joke at her expense. Loneliness welled up inside. Her heart squeezed in anguish.

Seldom did she succumb to emotions. She was always the strong one. The one her sisters depended on when things got tough. Never did she let them see her cry or even worry. Even now, she fought to control the tears that burned her eyes, fought them until she realized there was no need. No one was around to see her moment of weakness. She was utterly alone.

How she wished for a shoulder to lean on. Someone to help carry the load.

If only she and God . . .

She considered praying but quickly abandoned the idea. It was no good. She didn't deserve God's grace or forgiveness, so what was the point of wasting His time?

It had been a mistake coming to Rocky Creek. If it hadn't been for that newspaper article describing this horrid town in such glowing terms, she would have gone elsewhere. She'd probably have more luck finding eligible bachelors on the moon than in this decrepit town.

Two more weeks. If Brenda didn't change her mind about Mr. Hampton or she didn't find a suitable man for Mary Lou in two weeks' time, she and her sisters would pack up and leave.

What sounded like a squeaking floorboard startled her. Heart pounding, she lifted her head and strained her ears. Was someone in the marshal's office? Had someone come to do her harm? Senses alert, she sat up on her cot. Was that the jingling of keys she heard?

She felt beneath the cot for her parasol to use as a weapon. Gripping it tightly to her chest, she lay her head down.

The cot squeaked beneath her weight and she froze. For several minutes she didn't dare move. No other sound broke the silence.

Rhett stood in his darkened office, keys in hand. He thought he heard her moan or cry out, but now all that greeted him was silence.

Normally he had no qualms about leaving the jailhouse after a day's work. He simply locked up everything good and tight and never had any problems. Most of his prisoners were rowdies needing a couple of days to cool off or dry out.

Serious outlaws were now sent to the county jail, which was more secure. Jenny was a whole different problem. Stubborn as a mule she was. Independent as a wild Texas horse. Still, he sensed a vulnerability in her that brought out his protective nature. For that reason, he couldn't bring himself to leave her alone and unguarded.

He hated keeping her locked up, but she didn't give him much choice. Not only had she freed a prisoner, she put him in a difficult position with the townsfolk. If he let her get away with breaking the law, it would set a dangerous precedent and he couldn't take that chance.

Still, he longed to go to her. To comfort her and tell her she wasn't alone, but he didn't dare. Didn't trust himself. Not with the memory of her sweet lips so vivid in his mind. Not with the heat of desire flowing through his body.

His resolve to keep his distance and never

let anyone get too close had been wiped out in one thoughtless, reckless, moonlit moment. After that, it was almost impossible to stay away from her. Even in church, he couldn't seem to keep from seeking her out. Still, it wasn't until tonight that he realized how much trouble he was in. Now all he could do was try to undo the damage. That meant keeping his distance. Staying away. Forgetting the kiss. The eyes. The smile.

He replaced the keys on the hook ever so quietly then fell upon one knee to pray: "Lord, give me strength."

A man stood in the distance gesturing for her to come to him, promising to protect her. Joyfully, she ran to him and flung herself into his open arms. Smiling, she looked up. The smile died and she recoiled in horror. She tried to pull away but couldn't. Too late, she realized she had thrown herself into the arms of Horace Blackman III.

She woke with a start, not knowing where she was. Trembling, she gasped for air in an effort to still her erratic pulse. Then she remembered. It was her nightmare that woke her, woke her like it did every other night. Only tonight, Brenda wasn't there to comfort her and rub her back. No one was.

The arms that looked so welcoming from

a distance were like iron chains that continued to hold her prisoner long after the dream had faded away. Even after all this time, even after she paid back every last penny she owed him, the man named Blackman still held her captive, if only in her mind.

Shuddering, she forced the memory of him away.

The night sky slowly turned to silver. She got up and washed her face with water from the pitcher her sisters had brought her. Her body ached from lying on the thin lumpy mattress. She stretched to remove the kinks. It helped her back but her head still throbbed.

After changing into a fresh skirt and shirtwaist, she arranged her hair. No sooner had she finished dressing than Redd delivered breakfast.

"Made the coffee fresh just for you," he said. In the dim morning light, his hair was more rust-colored than red, and he looked even more downcast than usual. He obviously felt sorry for her.

She forced a smile in an effort to cheer him up. "Thank you."

He pushed the tray through the slot and shook his head. "This is no place for a lady."

"It won't be for much longer." She only

hoped that was true. The thought of spending another night in that cell was more than she could bear.

She wasn't hungry but forced herself to eat a couple of spoonfuls of cornmeal mush so as not to hurt Redd's feelings. Though the coffee was bitter and strong enough to bring tears to her eyes, she welcomed its warmth.

He watched her eat with approval. "You need anything else, ma'am, you just let me know, you hear?"

"Thank you, Redd."

After he left, she sat on the cot and waited. Surely Rhett would let her go now. The minutes turned to hours and, though she could hear him moving around in his office, he stayed away.

She'd almost given up when a rattle of keys made her heart leap. It was about time. The door to the anteroom opened and the preacher's wife, Sarah, walked in. The door closed behind her.

Not wanting to show her disappointment, Jenny welcomed her with a smile.

"I brought you wildflowers," Sarah said. "Give you somethin' purty to look at."

Though she had hoped that Rhett had come to set her free, she really liked Sarah and was grateful for the company. "The flowers are beautiful. Thank you."

Bending sideways to accommodate her expanding middle, Sarah set her basket on the floor next to the iron bars. The yellow-and-white flowers added a cheery note to the drabness.

She straightened and looked around. One hand on her back, she placed the other on her protruding stomach. In her usual disregard for style, she wore a man's black hat. Her red hair fell loose around her shoulders.

"I'm sorry I can't offer you tea or lemonade," Jenny said. "Or a place to sit."

"Don't you worry none about me, you hear?" Her gaze traveled past Jenny. "This ol' cell hasn't changed since I was here."

"You were here?" Jenny asked, surprised.

Sarah nodded. "Locked up tighter than a new corset, I was. Waitin' for my own hangin' party."

Jenny gaped at her. "They were going to *hang* you? What . . . what did you do?"

"It had nothin' to do with me. Briggs — he was the marshal before Armstrong — wanted to hang me on account of my outlaw brothers. If he got it in his mind to hang you, it didn't matter none if you were guilty, innocent, or betwixt. Praise the Lord for our new marshal."

Jenny scoffed. "He put a twelve-year-old

boy in jail." Not to mention what he did to her.

"Knowing Marshal Armstrong, he prob'ly had good reason," Sarah said. "Scooter and his brother have been given the run of the pasture since their poor mama died. Boys that age need to be corralled."

"What about their father?" Rhett had told her he was a drunk but hadn't said much else about the man.

"He's a good for nothin' —" Catching herself, Sarah raised her eyes to the watermarked ceiling. "Lord forgive me, but it's true. Since his wife's death, he's done nothin' but pickle his brain. The reverend keeps tryin' to talk to him, but God don't see fit to open the man's ears." She gave a nod of her head. "But He will. Mark my words. He will. I just pray it's soon."

She glanced past Jenny to the stack of books piled on the cot and the schedule hanging from a nail.

"I reckon you're still tryin' to find husbands for your sisters."

"I'm not having much luck, I'm afraid." Jenny picked up the dog-eared copy of Miss Abigail Jenkins's book. "I've done everything the book says to do."

Sarah glanced at the book with a frown. "I don't cotton much to instruction books.

I reckon the Good Book has all the advice a body needs."

Jenny tossed the book onto a cot. "Including how to find husbands?"

"The Bible says that no matter your plans, it's the Lord's plan that prevails. I reckon that includes matchmakin'."

"I doubt God is interested in helping me find husbands for my sisters," Jenny said. He didn't bother helping her when she needed help all those years ago after her parents died. What reason did she have to believe He would help her now?

"Oh, He's interested," Sarah said. "If He's interested in me, He's sure gonna be interested in you. Let me tell you how I know." She then told Jenny how she met her preacher husband.

"So there I was, handcuffed to a dying marshal in the middle of nowhere. I sure thought my goose was cooked. Then who should come along but this handsome preacher?" Her eyes clouded momentarily with visions of the past. A smile inched across her face. "Now if that wasn't God's plan, I don't know what to call it."

"Some people might say it was simply good luck," Jenny said cautiously, not wanting to offend.

Sarah waved a hand. "And some people

don't know a bean from a turnip."

Jenny couldn't help but laugh. She'd never met anyone quite like Sarah and couldn't imagine a less pretentious person. "Like I told you before, me and God —"

"That don't matter none. God the Father welcomes His children with open arms. It don't much matter how long we've been away. I'm livin' proof of that."

"I'm not the one who went away," Jenny said. "I was there all along. What kind of Father is He to desert you in time of need?"

"I reckon bein' a parent is the hardest job there is," Sarah said softly, caressing her belly with loving strokes. "Not many of us get it right. We're either overprotective like I am with Elizabeth or neglectful like Scooter's pa. Far as I know, God, the heavenly Father, is the only one who gets it right."

"Really?" Jenny crossed her arms in front to ward off a sudden chill. "After my parents died, I needed God, but He was nowhere to be found. We had no money." Her voice thick from painful memories, she forced herself to continue. "We had nothing. No food. No firewood. No medicine. I tried to sell my parents' farm, but the town was going through tough times. Nothing I did worked. Where was He then?"

"He was there," Sarah said with a conviction that Jenny could only envy. "All you had to do was call out to Him."

Jenny shook her head. "It wouldn't have done any good. He wasn't there. Otherwise I wouldn't have —" She clamped her mouth shut. She'd already said too much. Spending the night in jail had weakened her carefully constructed defenses, and it scared her.

Sarah's face softened. "I'm there for Elizabeth, but that don't mean she's always gonna do what's right. Do your sisters always do what you want?"

The idea seemed so absurd, Jenny couldn't help but laugh. "Don't I wish!"

"God made us human, and that means we're gonna make mistakes. All Elizabeth wants to do is climb." Sarah smiled to herself as if picturing the two-year-old. "I'm 'fraid she's goin' to fall, but Justin says if we don't let her try things, she'll never learn what she's capable of doin'."

Jenny's mind reeled with confusion. "So you're saying God wanted me to fall?"

"No, no." Sarah shook her head. "No parent wants a child to fall. We want them to learn and to grow. The only way they can do that is to find their own way."

Jenny still didn't understand. "Didn't you say a child needs to be corralled?"

"Yes, when they're young. The hardest

249

part is knowin' when to cut 'em loose and see where they 'light." She gave a determined nod of the head. "Looking at your sisters, I'd say you did a mighty fine job of carin' for them. Now you just have to trust them enough to cut them loose."

"By cutting them loose, are you saying I should let them find their own husbands?" Jenny asked.

"I'm sayin' that God has bigger plans for us than we can ever dream up for ourselves. You're gonna have to cut your sisters loose and let them run free. It's the only way they'll find out what plans God has for 'em."

Jenny mind boggled. *Cut them loose? Let them run free? God's plan?*

What kind of crazy talk was this?

Sarah laughed. "If that don't take the rag off the bush. I'm beginning to sound like a preacher's wife."

The astonishment on Sarah's face made Jenny laugh. "A very *nice* preacher's wife." At long last she had made a friend.

Keys rattled, and Jenny's first interview of the day walked through the door.

Sarah greeted the newcomer with a smile. "If it's not Jimmy Tucker. Haven't seen you at church lately."

"Been mighty busy, ma'am," Tucker said in a wheezy voice. He was dressed in canvas pants and a wrinkled plaid shirt. Holding his hat by the brim, he turned it like a wagon wheel.

"I didn't know you were lookin' to take a wife," Sarah said.

He made a strange grunting sound. "It don't seem right to keep some lucky woman from gettin' a fine husband," he said.

"I better be going and let you two get to work." Sarah gave Jenny a meaningful look before knocking on the door separating the marshal's office from the jail. "Maybe you oughta give that *other* instruction book a try."

SEVENTEEN

A husband-seeking woman is advised to
practice the passive art of silent suffering.
— MISS ABIGAIL JENKINS, 1875

Rhett felt like he'd been run over by a herd
of cattle. He'd spent the night in his office,
sitting in his hardback chair, feet on his
desk. Sleep, if it came at all, was anything
but restful.

He rubbed his aching head and took a
long swallow of Arbuckle's, his third cup of
the morning. Redd's coffee was bitter as
poison, but it opened the eyes and stirred
the blood.

Applegate and his bachelor friends were
happy, but that didn't make Rhett feel any
better. No matter how many times he told
himself that Jenny was where she deserved
to be, he felt guilty. More than that, her very
presence was a distraction. Though a wall
separated his office from the jail cells, he

could no more forget her presence had he found her in his bed.

Even if he could forget, the steady stream of visitors was a constant reminder. Never had he seen so many comings and goings. The parade started the moment he returned from his shave at the barbershop first thing that morning, and it hadn't stopped since. He finally left the anteroom door unlocked so he wouldn't have to keep jumping up and down to let the latest visitor inside.

First the pastor's wife, Sarah, stopped by, followed by that fool man Tucker. Jenny's two sisters made several trips yesterday and again this morning, carrying clothes and all matter of toiletries. Did women really need so many trappings?

Next came the townsfolk. Some dropped by out of curiosity, others from a sense of responsibility. Members of the Rocky Creek Quilting Bee came just to be nosy.

One by one they trotted by his desk. Leading the parade of quilters, Mrs. Emma Fields stalked by his desk like a broad-chested bird, a nestlike bun on top of her head.

Not ten minutes after she left, Mrs. Hitchcock arrived, the feathers on her hat fluttering as she shook her head. "Oh, dear. Oh, dear," she exclaimed. "We just wanted her to leave our men alone. We never wanted her in jail." She clucked her tongue and repeated herself before adding, "I can understand, understand Sarah Prescott being in jail, her being an outlaw and all. But Miss Higgins?"

Sarah Prescott's imprisonment was before his time, but people still talked about how the preacher's wife almost became the first woman hanged in Rocky Creek — not that any had been hanged since. It was hard to believe that the woman he had come to like and respect was the sister of the infamous Prescott brothers. The gang robbed stages in four states before disappearing. Sarah claimed not to have any knowledge of their whereabouts, and he believed her. But he was always on the lookout lest they pay their sister a visit.

The parade continued all morning. Rhett was relieved when the last of the Rocky Creek quilters left. Now maybe he could have some peace and quiet.

A fat lot!

No sooner had he settled down to do some work when the door swung open and in walked Archie Walbrook. "I have a one o'clock appointment," he announced in his high, reedy voice.

He had short legs, long arms, wide shoulders, and slender hips. His upper and lower halves were so out of proportion that he walked with apelike awkwardness. Even his high forehead seemed at odds with his chinless jaw.

"What business do you have with the prisoner?" Rhett asked out of habit. He knew very well that Walbrook was there for his interview.

"Marriage business," he said proudly.

Rhett waved him through the open door. By the time Stu Cotts entered the office, the umpteenth visitor to do so, Rhett was out of patience.

Rising from his chair, he said, "Wait here."

Enough was enough. Who ever heard of a prisoner carrying on so? This was a jail, not a church social.

Once he arrived in the back, he stopped and stared. Unaware of his presence, Jenny sat perched on the edge of a cot writing in her notebook. Books, notes, and paper were strewn upon two of the cots. Clothes and personal belongings were arranged neatly on the third. A schedule hung from a nail on the wall.

Dressed in a blue skirt and ruffled shirtwaist, she looked all efficient and businesslike. Her hair was pulled back in a tight bun at the back of her head with not a strand out of place. Except for the light shadows beneath her eyes, she looked none the worse for spending the night in jail. If anything, she looked mighty pleasing to the eye, and he felt something stir inside.

Irritated, he shook his head in an effort to chase the thought away. The woman was a nuisance and needed to be put in her place. Not only must the parade of visitors be stopped, Jenny must not treat jail like her own private office. Such foolishness would *not* be tolerated.

"Miss Higgins!"

Clearly startled, she glanced up, cold dignity settling on her face. She then closed her notebook and stood. "Marshal."

He walked toward the cell. Up close she looked more vulnerable than efficient, and his anger deserted him. "Don't you ever stop?" The question was as much of a surprise to him as it evidently was to her.

A shadow danced across her forehead. "What?"

His glanced at the books and papers scattered around the cell then stared straight at her. "What do you think would happen if you left something to chance? Or even to God?"

This time she stared at him as if he'd lost his mind. Maybe he had.

Her forehead creased. "I have no idea what you're talking about."

He took another step closer. Today her eyes reminded him of bluebonnets that bloomed in the spring. "What would happen if you lost control?" *If your hair fell loose as it did the night I knocked on your door . . . If you followed your heart instead of your head?* "Whatever it is you're running from —"

He spotted a glimpse of surprise, which she tried to hide behind a mask of indifference. "I'm not running from anything." What she couldn't hide was her trembling lips or the fear, maybe even panic, in her eyes.

She quickly regained control but her efforts were too late. He saw and he knew.

"I'm simply taking care of my sisters," she said.

"Who's taking care of you?"

The question seemed to disarm her. For the second time, she let down her guard, allowing a glimpse of the hurt and pain and maybe even loneliness she normally kept hidden. All too soon, the door slammed shut, and she resorted back to her usual cool, efficient self.

Bold eyes met his. "I don't need anyone taking care of me."

Repelled by the mask but not the woman, he backed away. He'd stripped her emotionally, but the pain on her face only made him more aware of his own inadequacies. He had no idea how to help her. Didn't know if anyone could. What he did know was that she had to stop doing what she was doing. She had to stop running. Stop racing like a train on a track. *That* he could make her do.

"There'll be no more visitors," he said.

She shook her head in protest. "I've got an appointment —"

"No more!" he said, and left.

For two more days he kept her locked up. Two long, torturous days. The only visitors she was allowed were her sisters, the preacher and his wife, and Redd.

Helping a prisoner to escape was a serious crime that required sentencing by Judge Fassbender. Rhett didn't have the heart to submit the necessary paperwork. This meant he couldn't legally hold her any longer. He'd either have to release her or formally charge her.

Keys in hand, he walked to the cells. Normally he kept the door to the anteroom locked, but during the last two days, he left the door ajar. This way he could stay close and still keep his distance.

Jenny sat on the cot staring into space. He

didn't know she could sit so still. Or look so sad.

Watching her was like watching a rare bird. He didn't want to move or even breathe for fear of losing her — or at least losing the part of her that was honest and real.

All too soon, she sensed his presence. She lifted her head but said nothing. She looked tired, pale, so unlike her usual lively self. This time she made no effort to pretend she was in control. He didn't know if that was a good thing or bad.

He moved closer to the cell. "What you did . . . Normally, you would be sentenced by a judge."

He could only hope that no irreparable damage was done to his reputation or credibility as a lawman.

She bit her lip. "I was wrong to intervene." Her voice was so soft, he had to strain to capture her every word.

For a moment they stared at each other.

"Is . . . is Scooter all right?" she asked.

He nodded. "I had a long talk with him." He also talked to Scooter's father, for all the good it did him. What would it take to get Matt Maxwell to see what he was doing to his boys? What damage had already been done?

"Scooter begged me to let you go."

She smiled, but said nothing.

After a moment, she looked away and cleared her throat. "How . . . how long do you plan to keep me here?" she asked.

"It's over, Jenny," he said, though he knew it was a lie. It wasn't over. Not by any means. She made him feel again. She made him care. How or why she managed to do that he couldn't say. All he knew was that nothing would ever be the same.

Without another word, he unlocked her cell. "You're free to go."

Mary Lou was in the worst possible mood.

Not once since kissing her nearly a week ago had Jeff Trevor spoken to her. The man hadn't even looked at her.

At worship, he sat at the back of the church as far away from her as possible, his eyes averted. It was the Sunday following Jenny's incarceration, and Jeff was the only one in the whole church who didn't stare at them.

No sooner had Reverend Wells given the benediction than Jeff quickly disappeared and was nowhere to be found. Not that Mary Lou looked for him, of course. Still, it was hard not to notice his absence.

Was she really that forgettable? Was she so

utterly ordinary that a man could walk away without a backward glance?

Other men didn't seem to think so. Since Jenny's release from jail, she was even more determined to accomplish her goal. Every day Mary Lou was obliged to go carriage or horseback riding or promenading with Jenny's latest pick, and the men had become progressively worse. One spent the entire time talking to his dead wife and asking her if she approved of Mary Lou. It was creepy.

To make matters even more intolerable, Jeff saw her riding by with another man and didn't so much as blink an eye. Not one single eye.

Drat! What if he meant what he said about never bothering her again? What if he really *was* a man of his word?

Oh, God, please don't let it be so. Men like that were the very worst kind.

Eighteen

Callow youth must be avoided in favor of
mature sophistication; a healthy bank
account trumps both.
— MISS ABIGAIL JENKINS, 1875

"Shh," Brenda cautioned. She and Mary
Lou knelt on hands and knees, peering
through the second-floor railing to the hotel
lobby below.

Jenny and Mr. Hampton sat at the small
table in front of the hotel fireplace. They
looked as stiff as boards and kept their
voices low.

Jenny was proper and businesslike, her
ever-present notes spread on the table in
front of her. Mr. Hampton sat opposite her,
his derby in his hands.

If Brenda didn't know better, she would
think they were discussing funeral arrange-
ments. Since she knew of no one's death,
she could think of only one other explana-

tion for their somber expressions; Mr. Hampton was asking Jenny's permission to propose marriage.

The thought made her feel sick. "Can you hear what they're saying?" Her whispered voice grated with anxiety.

"Something about *bob* wire," Mary Lou whispered back, pronouncing the word the way Mr. Hampton always did. "Maybe he'll give you a *bob* wire wedding ring."

Brenda poked Mary Lou with her elbow. "Be serious. What am I going to do? I can't stand the man. I've told Jenny that, but she won't listen."

Mary Lou grew serious. "Are you sure you're not in love with him?"

Brenda sat back on her heels. "Why in the world would you think such a thing?"

"You don't eat. You hardly sleep. Not to mention all those carriage rides. What else can I think?"

Brenda pressed her head against the railing. "Promise you won't say a word?"

Mary Lou made an X on her chest with her finger.

"I *am* in love."

Her sister gasped so loud Brenda feared she gave away their presence. A quick glance at the lobby set her mind at rest. Jenny never looked up.

"You *are* in love with Mr. Hampton. I knew it!" Mary Lou's surprise made her voice sound louder than it actually was.

Brenda made a face. "Not with Mr. Hampton, you silly mule. I'm in love with Mr. Barrel." It was the first time she'd spoken the words out loud, the first time she had ever admitted to loving a man, even to herself.

Mary Lou's jaw dropped. "The barber?" she gasped.

"The singer," Brenda said. The man whose heavenly voice had a way of burrowing into her heart. "You promised not to say anything."

"I told you I won't." Mary Lou gave her a shrewd look. "Does he love you?"

Brenda closed her eyes. Picturing him clearly, it was as almost as if she could reach out and touch him. The way he looked at her, the softness in his voice when he said her name had to mean something, didn't it? She opened her eyes and sighed. "I don't know. I think so."

Mary Lou shook her head. "Oh, wow."

Brenda suddenly had second thoughts about confessing her feelings for Kip. Mary Lou's ability to keep a secret was self-serving at best. If it benefitted her to reveal it, she would. "Don't forget, you promised not to say anything."

Mary Lou sat back against the railing and hugged her knees. "If you don't tell Jenny, she'll make you marry Mr. Hampton. You're going to have to tell her."

Brenda groaned. She couldn't bear the thought. "She'll never let me marry Mr. Barrel. You know she won't."

Mary Lou scrunched up her face. "I'm sick of Jenny bossing us around. She acts like we haven't got a brain in our heads."

"*Shh,* she'll hear you."

Mary Lou lowered her voice to a whisper but still managed to sound remarkably like Jenny. "Don't do this and don't do that. Act like ladies." She stuck out her lips. "All she cares about is how much money a man has in his bank account."

Brenda laid a steadying hand on her sister's arm. "Don't be angry with her. She just wants us to have a secure future and not go hungry again. If it wasn't for Jenny, we wouldn't have survived that awful winter."

Mary Lou lifted her chin in defiance. "That doesn't give her the right to tell us who we can and cannot marry."

"Papa made Jenny promise to take care of us, and we promised to let her."

"We didn't promise to let her run our

lives." The anger left Mary Lou's face as she pleaded with her. "If you don't tell her how you feel about marrying Mr. Hampton, you'll spend the rest of your days regretting it."

Brenda wrapped her hands around the posts and peered below. Jenny and Mr. Hampton were still talking.

She heaved a sigh. He had shown no romantic interest in her, none whatsoever. She in turn had done nothing to encourage him, had, indeed, hardly spoken during their carriage rides, though she had been honest about her feelings, or lack of them.

He assured her that he expected nothing and appreciated their outings as it allowed him time away from the rigors of running a ranch. He talked on and on about barbed wire, a rancher's life, and the pros and cons of shorthorns over long. His boring discourses made her wonder if he *really* wanted to get away from work or if that had simply been an excuse.

If only she hadn't agreed to those carriage rides, she wouldn't be in this predicament. But as boring as Mr. Hampton was, spending the day working on needlepoint and reading dull poetry was even more mind-numbing.

The truth was that she had no one to

blame but herself. She had prevailed upon Mr. Hampton's kindness to escape the hotel and had purposely refused to answer Jenny's questions. She left that up to Mr. Hampton. Another mistake.

"I've never met a more congenial conversationalist than Brenda," he told Jenny after one such outing.

She should have put a stop to their outings right then and there. She should have known that her very presence was encouragement enough for him.

"Meeting's over," Mary Lou whispered.

Brenda shook away her thoughts. Mr. Hampton had left and Jenny was briskly gathering up her notes.

"What do you think?" Brenda asked, her stomach tied in knots. She couldn't tell much from looking at her oldest sister, whose measured movements made her difficult, if not altogether impossible, to read.

"I think Jenny hears wedding bells," Mary Lou said.

Ever since leaving jail more than a week earlier, Jenny had been in a state of confusion. She even began to have doubts about her methods for finding suitable husbands for her sisters.

Mr. Hampton met every requirement

stated in *The Compleat and Authoritative Manual for Attracting and Procuring a Husband.* The unfortunate truth was that he was the only one in Rocky Creek who did. He was rich, educated, owned a great deal of land, attended church, dressed like a banker, and soundly denounced the habits of spitting and cussing. According to the book's author, he was the perfect candidate. According to his PHAT score, he was the answer to every woman's prayer.

Brenda denied being attracted to him, but Jenny suspected she was more interested in Mr. Hampton than she let on. Brenda had grown increasingly quiet over the last several days. Even more amazing, the girl had no appetite. She had hardly eaten a thing, and as unlikely as it seemed, Jenny found herself coaxing Brenda to eat.

Could it be? Dare she hope?

Was it possible that despite her protests to the contrary, Brenda had fallen in love with, or at least had feelings for, Mr. Hampton?

She raced to the desk and picked up Miss Jenkins's book. Turning to the chapter on "How To Know if You're in Love," she ran her finger down the "Signs of Undying Affection":

- Loss of appetite

Check.

- Staring into space

Check.

- Insomnia
- Anxiety
- Irritability

Check, check, and check.

She closed the book. Brenda could very well have feelings for Mr. Hampton.

Still, Jenny couldn't shake away the notion that something was amiss.

That belief started in jail and kept gnawing at her. After the marshal took away her visitor privileges, there was nothing left to do but pace the tiny cell and think. She thought about the things she wanted to forget, but mostly she thought about her sisters. She tried to imagine Mary Lou and Brenda having marriages like the one that Sarah and Reverend Wells had. A marriage filled with mutual love and respect.

She didn't dare hope to know that kind of love personally, but was she wrong to want it for her sisters? She tried to imagine

Brenda and Mr. Hampton having the kind of love that Justin and Sarah Wells had, and couldn't.

She rifled through the desk for Mr. Hampton's application. Everything was in order. He'd even listed the marshal as a reference. The latter made her think. Miss Jenkins *did* emphasize the importance of checking references. It might be interesting to know what Rhett had to say about him.

The thought brought an unexpected quickening of her pulse.

Since her release from jail, she'd purposely avoided Rhett. The truth was the entire jail episode embarrassed her. When she got something in her mind, she plunged ahead and nothing and no one could stop her. This had been the source of her trouble most of her life. She never learned to consider all the options before whirling into action. Nor had it ever occurred to her that God might have other ideas until Sarah brought it up.

The Bible says that no matter your plans, it's the Lord's plan that prevails.

Did that mean that God even had plans for her? She was afraid to hope that such a thing could be true. Pushing her thoughts aside, she grabbed her notebook.

Moments later, she entered the marshal's office only to find him gone. She waited for several minutes then turned to leave just as he walked in the door.

He looked surprised to see her. "Jenny."

Following his lead, she addressed him by his first name. "Hello, Rhett," she said. How she missed him, missed their lighthearted banter, missed everything about him.

"I had a couple of questions to ask you. That is . . . if you're not busy."

"What about?" He flung his hat on its hook and sat on the corner of his desk, arms folded.

Anxious to gain control of her racing pulse, she got right to the point of her visit. "Mr. Hampton has asked for Brenda's hand in marriage, and he named you as a reference."

He looked surprised. "I don't know anything about his marital qualifications. Perhaps you should talk to his banker."

With cool efficiency meant to hide her hurt, she opened up her notebook.

His words stung. Somehow he always managed to break down her defenses, but never more so than at that moment. Swallowing hard, she struggled to maintain control beneath his probing stare. Was that rancor in his voice? Reproach in his eyes? She was used to censure. Since her release from jail, the townsfolk seemed even more hostile toward her than before. Wherever she went, she heard the whispers, felt the stares, was confronted by the newly posted signs of The Society for the Protection and Preservation of Male Independence. For a town as humble as Rocky Creek, its citizens certainly had the nerve to criticize her.

Still, nothing anyone said or did disturbed her more than Rhett's disapproval. Not that she could do anything about it. Her primary consideration was her sisters' welfare. Nothing else mattered. Nothing else could.

"I believe he listed you as a *character* reference," she said with pointed emphasis.

"Ah. That I can easily confirm. Hampton is a character if I ever met one."

She leveled him with a look of disapproval. Unless he took her seriously, this was a waste of time. She cleared her throat and began again. "Would you say he is a man of integrity?"

He considered this a moment then shrugged. "He's an honest businessman. I'll say that much for him."

Gratified that he had dropped his derisive tone and turned serious, she made a notation in her notebook, but only as an excuse to break eye contact. "A good Christian?"

When he didn't answer she looked up to find him staring at her. "Reverend Wells would be a better judge of that than me," he said.

Cheeks burning beneath his heated scrutiny, she forced herself to continue. "A pillar of society?"

"I believe so. There's been talk about making him mayor. He'll probably fence in the town with barbed wire, but he's the best we've got so far." He chuckled.

She laughed too. Apparently, her sisters hadn't exaggerated Hampton's barbed wire obsession.

The moment of shared humor seemed as intimate as a kiss — and radiated similar pleasure. Heart pounding, she quickly recovered her usual businesslike demeanor.

"I guess that pretty much covers it," she said abruptly, closing her notebook. "Thank you for your comments."

Rhett gave Hampton a better recommendation than she expected. It should have put her mind at rest but, oddly enough, it didn't. Or maybe it was simply that she couldn't think straight in his presence.

His eyebrow arched slightly as if he expected more questions. "Glad to help." He stood. He was so close to her it was hard to think.

She stepped back. "I won't take up any more of your time."

He took a step closer. "If you need any other character references —"

"I think you told me everything I need to know about Mr. Hampton." She turned to leave.

"Actually, I was thinking about Kip Barrel."

Hand frozen on the doorknob, she looked over her shoulder. "You know what I think about Mr. Barrel."

"What about Brenda? Don't you care what she thinks?"

She bristled. "I care very much what my sister thinks. If I didn't believe she had feelings for Mr. Hampton, I wouldn't be here."

He assessed her frankly before turning away. "Before you go . . ." He reached across the desk for a folded newspaper. "There's a disclaimer here in the *Lone Star Tribune* that I'm sure you'll find interesting."

Turning, she glanced at the page he held up. "A disclaimer?"

"Yes. It seems that they misprinted the name of the town with the richest men per capita."

Her mouth went dry.

"It's not Rocky Creek after all," he said, his voice flat. "It's *Rockland* Creek." He dropped the paper on his desk. "They aren't the first to get the two towns confused."

She stared at him. "*Rockland* Creek?" She'd never heard of that town.

His gaze settled on her lips before he looked away. "Sometimes the best laid plans have a way of going astray."

"They certainly do." Without another word, she swept out of his office.

Her mind awhirl, she headed for the general store. Rockland Creek? She couldn't believe it. She had wasted all this time and money, and for what? She wasn't even in the right town.

Just as she reached the store, Sarah's little girl Elizabeth ran outside. Sarah, her arms filled with packages, followed close behind.

"Whoa, there." Welcoming the distraction, Jenny swooped the two-year-old into her arms and held her close. "Where are you going in such a hurry?"

Elizabeth giggled and wrapped her arms around Jenny's neck.

Jenny laughed. "*Mmm,* you smell like peppermint." She buried her nose against the child's smooth skin.

Elizabeth wore a blue gingham dress with a matching bonnet that all but hid her long blonde hair. A frilly white apron over her dress was tied in a wide bow in back.

Sarah placed her packages in the back of

her buckboard. "Either I'm gettin' slower or she's gettin' faster."

"I suspect it's a little of both," Jenny said. "How are you feeling?"

Sarah flashed a smile. "Never felt better in my life. What about you? Bet you're glad to be out of jail."

"I can't tell you how much. Your visit meant a lot to me. I really don't know how to thank you."

"I enjoyed it too." Sarah suddenly brightened. "I have a gift for you." She reached into the back of her wagon and pulled out a package wrapped in plain brown paper and tied with a blue ribbon.

"For me?" Jenny couldn't remember the last time anyone had given her a gift, and she was deeply touched. She lowered Elizabeth to the ground and took the offered package.

"May I open it now?" Without waiting for an answer, she tore away the paper and stared down at the book in her hand — a leather-bound Bible.

A million thoughts ricocheted through her mind, and she felt a twist of guilt. She hadn't opened a Bible for years. Her parents' copy was damaged when the roof blew off their farmhouse and she never thought to replace it. She looked up to find Sarah watching her.

"What a lovely gift. Thank you. I will treasure it always."

"I asked my husband to mark all the passages about marriage," Sarah said, and laughed. "I didn't know there were some five hundred of 'em."

"Oh, no!" Jenny laughed, too, then grew serious. "I had no idea that God —"

"Cares so much about marriage?" Sarah finished for her.

"I know marriage shouldn't be taken lightly. That's why I'm working so hard to find suitable husbands for my sisters."

"Have you prayed for God's help?" Sarah asked.

"Well I . . ." Her face tingled with heat, and she looked away. "I told you that God and me —"

Sarah touched her arm. "Open up your heart and give Him a chance," she said softly.

Elizabeth tugged on her mother's skirt. Sarah looked down at her daughter with a fond smile. "I reckon you're hungry." She looked up at Jenny. "We best be goin'."

Jenny gave Elizabeth a boost and she scrambled onto the wagon seat. Sarah climbed on from the opposite side and adjusted a homemade harness around the wiggling tot's waist.

"Have you seen Scooter?" Jenny asked.

"No, but I know the marshal's been out to the Maxwell house several times. He really cares for the boy. For both those boys."

"He said he hoped that by putting Scooter in jail, it would make their father see what he was doing to his sons."

Sarah made a face. "That man's not sober long enough to know what he's doin'." She tugged on a leather strap. "The marshal's a good man. One day he's going to make some lucky girl a fine husband."

Jenny held her breath. *But not me. It can never be me.*

Sarah finished buckling Elizabeth in her harness and handed her a handkerchief doll. "I don't reckon there are many men who would spend three nights guardin' a prisoner."

Jenny stared at her in bewilderment. "What are you talking about?"

"You don't know?" Sarah's eyebrows shot up. "The marshal slept at his desk every night you were in jail. He told Justin he wanted to keep you safe."

Jenny was barely able to control her gasp of surprise. "Keep me —" Her thoughts ran rampant. Was it really true? She'd convinced herself that the sounds she heard were merely the wind or the creaking building. Never once did it occur to her that it was Rhett.

"I–I didn't know," she managed at last.

Sarah gave her a penetrating look. Next to her, Elizabeth tried to wiggle free from her harness. "I better mosey on home." Sarah picked up the reins. "Say bye-bye, Elizabeth."

Holding her doll with one hand, Elizabeth waved with the other. "Bye-bye."

Jenny waved back. "Thank you for the gift," she called after them.

He wanted to keep you safe. Sarah's words filled Jenny's head until she could think of nothing else. Forgetting about the general store, forgetting about everything but the words that kept repeating in her mind, she walked back to the hotel in a daze.

She didn't know why it mattered. Why thoughts of Rhett keeping watch over her filled her with such yearning. All she knew was that it had been a very long time since anyone worried about wanting to keep her safe.

The hotel room was empty. Both girls were taking their daily walk. Grateful to have the place to herself, she sat down at the desk and opened the Bible to the first verse Reverend Wells had marked. *"And the Lord God said, It is not good that the man should be alone,"* she read.

She leaned back and closed her eyes. No, it wasn't good to be alone, but sometimes it seemed like there was no other way. *He wanted to keep you safe.*

All those nights in jail . . . She had been so alone. Had she known that Rhett was watching over her, it would have made all the difference in the world. Had she called out to him, would he have come to her? Comforted her? Somehow she knew he would have. She imagined his arms around her and her eyes filled with tears.

She thought about the dark days of her past. The day she buried her mother . . . the day she buried her father. She thought about the day the roof blew off their farmhouse and how she was so certain that Brenda was going to die. How utterly alone she'd felt then, how afraid.

Had God been watching over her all that time as Sarah insisted? If she had called out to Him, would He have come to her? Comforted her? Taken her into His arms? It was a question very much on her mind for the remainder of the day.

Nineteen

Weigh your options carefully and never make snap judgments, which will likely come back to haunt you.
— MISS ABIGAIL JENKINS, 1875

Brenda hurried past the barbershop on the way to the general store. She hadn't wanted to leave the hotel again after her walk, but Jenny had forgotten to stop at the general store to purchase soap. Though they took their outerwear to Lee Wong's laundry, Jenny insisted that ladies wash their own undergarments.

Honestly, she didn't know what was wrong with Jenny lately. It wasn't like her oldest sister to be forgetful.

It was hot and the air shimmered with heat. A wagon drove by, kicking up dust. Tethered horses eyed her as she walked by, their tails swishing back and forth to ward off flies.

During her earlier walk, she avoided the barbershop, but now she had no choice but to walk past it. She didn't dare look in the window for fear of seeing Kip. Even so, memories of the night they spent together flooded back, and it was all she could do to keep from bursting into tears.

She hurried inside Fairbanks General Merchandise only to find it crowded. Keeping her head low, she scurried past the counter where Mr. Fairbanks was weighing coffee beans and dodged a group of ladies from church, all belonging to the Rocky Creek Quilting Bee. She didn't stop until she found an empty spot at the back of the store.

It did no good. Just as she feared, Kip spotted her as she hurried by his shop. Now he rushed into the store, knocking a bolt of fabric off the counter in his haste to join her.

"What is this I hear about you marrying Hampton?" he demanded.

She stared at him openmouthed. She had no idea Mr. Hampton's proposal was common knowledge.

"Well?"

"*Shh.*" She glanced over his shoulder. Mr. Fairbanks was staring straight at them. She turned her back and pretended to be studying the pots and pans hanging from a rough-hewn rafter. "Keep your voice down."

He repeated his question in a hushed but by no means quiet voice.

"Nothing's been decided yet," she whispered.

Following her lead, he lifted a cast-iron frying pan off its hook and examined it. "I thought if I gave your sister time to calm down, I could talk to her."

"It wouldn't do any good," she said.

He replaced the pan. "You can't marry Hampton." He turned to look her straight in the eyes. "I love you, Brenda Higgins."

His sudden outburst shocked her but only for the moment it took for his words to sink in. Then her heart leaped with joy. Never had she heard anything sweeter.

"I love you too." The words slipped out so quickly and so easily, it was as if she'd rehearsed them for a lifetime.

An expression that could only be described as sunshine crossed his face. It was very much how he looked when he sang in church and lifted his eyes to heaven. "Do you mean that?"

"Of course I–I mean it," she stammered, her cheeks hot with excitement. "I wouldn't have said it if I didn't mean it."

Hands on his hips, he frowned. "Then

would you please explain why you're marrying someone else?"

"I–I told you, nothing's been decided."

"What's to be decided?" he demanded,
not bothering to lower his voice. "You love
me, and I love you. What more is there to
say?"

"It's — it's complicated. My sister . . . I
promised my father. I —" Her eyes burned
and she looked away.

He grabbed her by both arms, forcing her
to look at him. His expression etched into a
desperate plea that nearly broke her heart.
"After the night we spent together —"

A gasp sounded behind them. Pulling
away from him, she turned and saw the line
of shocked faces staring at them.

Mrs. Taylor looked like she was about to
faint. "Oh, my, what is the world coming
to? In my day, a woman wouldn't be caught
dead under the same roof with a man not
her father or husband."

Mrs. Hitchcock sniffed, the feathers on
her hat tickling the underbelly of the ham
hanging from the rafters. "I'm telling you,
it's that *Harper's Bazar, Harper's Bazar.* The
magazine encourages young women to don
those dreadful divided skirts." She sniffed
and repeated herself.

One of the other women, whose name

Brenda couldn't remember, crossed her arms and gave a nod. "The next thing you know, women will be wearing trousers. Is there any wonder that our young people have such loose morals?"

Mrs. Taylor clucked her tongue. "I told my Harry years ago that when women starting riding horses clothespin style, it was the start of civilization's downfall."

Brenda's face flamed. She didn't know what to say. Never had she felt so humiliated.

Kip stepped in front to protect her. "Ladies and" — he glanced at Timber Joe and Mr. Fairbanks — "gentlemen. If you don't mind, this is a private conversation."

Timber Joe stepped forward. "Don't go worryin' none about that. What's said in this here spot" — he pounded the floor with the barrel end of his rifle — "stays in this here spot."

Behind him, Mrs. Hitchcock nodded her head, the feathers of her hat waving like a flag at sea. "We heard about your betrothal to Mr. Hampton, Mr. Hampton, and we came to pick out fabric for a quilt for your wedding, your wedding."

Brenda covered her mouth with her hand. Her betrothal? "N–nothing's been decided," she stammered.

Mrs. Taylor looked confused. "But I'm sure that's what I heard. Are you saying there's *not* going to be a wedding?"

"There *is* going to be a wedding," Kip assured her. He stared at the bolt of brown fabric in Mrs. Hitchcock's arms. "And if it's all the same to you, ma'am, the bride and I prefer blue."

Brenda didn't go back to the hotel. Instead she walked. She had no idea where she was going, but she simply couldn't face Jenny. Not yet. Had Jenny really accepted Mr. Hampton's proposal on her behalf? *Please, God, don't let it be true.*

Jenny hadn't said anything about her talk with Mr. Hampton, not a word. Mr. Hampton was out of town on business, and Brenda assumed Jenny would broach the subject upon his return. That gave her a couple of days to think of a way to discourage Mr. Hampton, Jenny, or both. Only now it looked like she didn't have a couple of days. If Mrs. Hitchcock and all the rest were right about her upcoming marriage, she was already doomed.

She followed the road leading away from town. She shook so hard she could hardly think. The sun was hot and her corset pinched, but she hardly noticed. Kip Barrel commanded her every thought. Even now as she stared at the road ahead through a veil of tears, she imagined she could see his smile, see his soft eyes dance with joy. Even the warm breeze seemed to carry the sound of his rich velvet voice.

She'd never gone against Jenny's wishes. Nor had she ever disobeyed her parents. Mary Lou had always been the willful child. One of Brenda's earliest memories was her poor mama throwing up her arms in dismay at something Mary Lou had said or done.

"You're my little angel," her mother liked to say whenever she tucked Brenda in bed for the night. Her father called her his good little girl and Brenda did her best to live up to everyone's expectations.

She followed the winding road up the hill, not knowing where she was going. It wasn't until she spotted the church that she realized it had been her destination all along.

She walked up to the door. The sound of children's voices and laughter prevented her from entering, but she peered inside. Boys and girls sat on chairs facing a young woman who pointed to the ABCs written on a wooden board.

Disappointed that she couldn't sit inside and pray, she closed the door softly so as not to disturb the class and walked away.

No sooner had she reached the end of the footpath when she heard someone call to her.

"Miss Higgins?"

She turned to find Reverend Wells walking toward her. Dressed in black trousers and a white shirt rolled up at the sleeves, he looked less formal today than during Sunday worship, but every bit as friendly.

Upon reaching her, he touched the brim of his hat. "Is there something I can help you with?"

"No, I–I was just out for a walk," she said. "It's a beautiful day."

"Indeed it is." He studied her for a moment. "Do you mind if I join you?"

"Yes, please do," she said, though she really wanted to be alone.

Together they started down the hill. Children's voices followed from the distance.

"I didn't know that Rocky Creek had a school," she said. Jenny constantly complained about the lack of such civilities as a school and library.

"Not a school," he said quickly. "Bible study."

She frowned. "I didn't know they taught the alphabet in Bible study."

"Nothing in the church's rules of order

288

says we can't teach reading, writing, and arithmetic."

"Then why not just call it a school?" she asked.

"I'm afraid it will take a change in the Texas constitution before we can do that," Pastor Wells explained. "Right now it says that we must provide separate schools for white and colored students. I don't think the good Lord meant for us to separate His children from one another." He gave her a conspiratorial wink. "As long as Rocky Creek doesn't have an official school, we're not required to comply with the constitution."

Brenda smiled. So the town wasn't as uncivilized as Jenny thought. For some reason this pleased her. The more she knew about Rocky Creek and its people, the more she liked it.

Reverend Wells led the way to a bench beneath a sprawling shade tree.

He sat down and waited for her to join him. "I hope you don't mind me asking, but you look troubled. Is there something you wish to talk about?"

She stared down at the ground. "It's just that . . . my sister wants me to marry Mr. Hampton."

"He's a fine man," the pastor said. "He

talked to me about the need to find a good wife and start a family."

Brenda said nothing. Instead she stared down the hill to the town below and wondered what a certain barber was doing.

"But you're not here to talk about Mr. Hampton, are you?" he asked.

She turned her head in his direction. She welcomed the opening. She would never have been brave enough to bring up the subject otherwise. "I don't want to go against my sister's wishes. She's taken care of us since Papa's death."

"And you feel that you owe her?"

"It's not that. I promised Papa to obey her. But —"

His hands clasped as if in prayer, he tilted his head to one side. "But?"

"I no longer think she knows what's best for me." No sooner were the words out of her mouth than she regretted them.

She hastened to explain. "She's doing her best, but after Papa's death, she . . . changed. She's not the same person I promised to obey."

It was hard to explain, but the sister who had driven desperately into town to seek help all those years ago was not the same when she returned. Brenda burst into tears. She missed the old fun-loving Jenny. Missed

290

the times they once shared. Hated the rigid way she ran their lives now. Surprised and embarrassed to find herself overcome with emotion, Brenda palmed her wet cheeks.

Reverend Wells handed her a clean handkerchief but made no effort to stop her from crying. Instead, he waited until the tears stopped of their own accord. "So what do you think caused her to change?"

"I don't know." Oh, she knew, but she couldn't bring herself to tell him. She hadn't even told Mary Lou her suspicions that Jenny had given herself to a man. It was the only way she could think to explain their sudden rise from rags to riches.

She dabbed at her eyes then twisted the handkerchief in her lap. "She used to be such a joyful person, always laughing and teasing. Now —"

"Now all she can think about is finding husbands for you and your sister."

Brenda nodded. "She's not a gold digger like some people think. They don't know her like I know her. She hardly spends any money on herself. She just doesn't want us to go hungry again." She beseeched him. "I don't want you to think I'm ungrateful or anything. I'm honored that Mr. Hampton thinks me worthy enough to be his wife, but . . ."

"But he's not Kip Barrel," he finished for her.

She gaped at him.

He laughed. "My wife, Sarah, doesn't miss a thing. Apparently she noticed the way the two of you look at each other in church."

Brenda's cheeks flared. "I didn't know we were that obvious."

Reverend Wells brushed her concerns away with a wave of his hand. "Kip is a very talented singer. I keep praying that he finds the courage to use God's gift to the fullest extent and sing solo."

Brenda smiled. "He sings to me," she said. She looked up at the clear blue sky through the leafy canopy of the tree overhead. "When he sings, it's like hearing a voice from heaven."

"Ah, then God *has* answered my prayers."

"But I'm only one person," she protested.

"It's a start," Reverend Wells said. "It's a start."

They sat in silence for several moments before she noticed the sun was low and sinking fast. "It's getting late. I better go back."

Before she stood, he stayed her with his hand. "Brenda, I know your sister has big plans for you. And I understand you don't want to disappoint her. But you can't

292

discount God's plan for you."

She wrinkled her brow. "God's plan?"

He nodded. "Marriage is a sacred oath that a couple makes before God. The Bible says that a couple becomes one flesh. For this reason, marriage cannot be entered into lightly or for the wrong reasons."

"My marrying Mr. Hampton would be for the wrong reasons," she admitted. "But I don't know that I can go against Jenny's wishes. I promised my father."

"The Bible says that we are not to please men." Reverend Wells glanced at her sideways. "And that includes your sister and father. We are to please *God, who tests our hearts.*"

She stared at the ground. It had never occurred to her that her eagerness to please first her parents, then her teachers and Jenny, could be contrary to what God wanted her to do. Was He testing her now? Did He really mean for her to be with Kip? Her heart leaped at the very thought.

Her joy was short-lived. As much as she wanted to believe that she and Kip were meant to be together, she was overcome with doubts. She had always done what everyone wanted her to do. It was how she won approval.

The problem was that, deep down inside,

she knew the compliments and praises were not directed at her but, rather, at the person she tried to be. The person who, in reality, didn't exist. And that was the source of her emptiness. It wasn't until she met Kip that she learned the wondrous joy of being herself, being loved for who she was, not who she tried to be.

The question was, did she have the courage to stand up to Jenny and follow her own heart? Would Jenny still love her if she did?

The doors to the church burst open and children poured out, running in all directions. It was the end of the day for Rocky Creek's unofficial school.

Children laughed together and no one seemed to notice race or skin color. Boys chased each other, their young voices bouncing off the hills and trickling into the valleys below. The loose pants worn by Chinese and Mexican boys provided an odd yet pleasing contrast to the knee pantaloons worn by others.

Girls in ankle-length dresses or native costumes walked to the waiting carriages or stood in little knots to share the day's events.

Brenda envied the children. Envied the way they accepted each other. She never knew that kind of happiness as a child, that kind of acceptance. There was always someone trying to shape her into something she was not.

Kip wasn't like that. With him, she felt free and the world seemed like a brighter place.

"I better go," she said, rising. "Jenny will wonder where I am."

The pastor stood. "Think about what I said."

"I will," she promised. "I will."

Whether she could find the courage to act on his advice hung heavy on her mind all the way back to town.

TWENTY

A love letter should be written with
great dignity and reserve, especially
when written to a gentleman of
brief acquaintance.
— MISS ABIGAIL JENKINS, 1875

Mary Lou walked up and down Main
Street, her gaze swinging back and forth
like the pendulum on a clock.

She wasn't looking for Jeff Trevor; she
wasn't. Of course, if she should *inadvertently*
bump into him, she would have no choice
but to speak to him, particularly if he spoke
first.

Miss Jenkins devoted an entire chapter in
her book to the subject of conversing with a
man in public. She wrote that it would be
the height of rudeness not to speak when
addressed by a man — unless, of course, he
was inebriated or possessed criminal ten-
dencies.

296

Mary Lou never paid much attention to the endless rules of etiquette Miss Jenkins, and therefore Jenny, advocated unless it suited her purposes. This was one of those times that it did — or would, if only Jeff would show his face.

Spotting a man in cropped pants and a red cap, her heart skipped a beat. Hastening her step, she soon realized her error. Up close, the lumberman didn't even look like Jeff.

Mr. Applegate watched her pass by the general store for the umpteenth time. The old geezer did nothing but sit on his creaky old rocking chair and glare at her every time she walked by. It was all she could do to keep from sticking out her tongue at him.

She sighed. Everything irritated her lately, even an old man. He wasn't the only one. She snapped at Jenny, growled at Brenda, and scowled at everyone else. She was so on edge it was all she could do not to fall apart completely.

Ever since Jeff kissed her she'd hardly been able to think of anything else. The memory of his kiss was her first thought in the morning, the last thing she contemplated at night.

Sleep offered no escape. Dreams of being in his arms plagued her. Every night she woke in a tangled knot of bedding.

Brenda and Jenny complained that she was keeping them awake. By the third such restless night, they made her sleep on the floor.

Adding to her misery was the heat. Though it was only June, already the town sizzled beneath what everyone called a hot wave.

The sun felt like a torch on her back. She longed to find someplace cool and strip off her layers of clothing. Back home in Haswell, she loved nothing more than to swim naked in the nearby lake. Had she not gotten that awful sunburn, Jenny would never have found out her secret. Naturally, Jenny had a fit and insisted that in the future she wear suitable swimming attire. Modesty being more important than practicality, the swimsuit consisted of bloomers, stockings, and drawers. She almost drowned the first time she wore the blasted thing.

The memory only worsened her mood. She was hot, she was bored, and she was sick and tired of this awful town.

Adding to her irritation was Brenda. Where in the world did she go? It wasn't like her to take off without telling anyone.

Not knowing what else to do, Mary Lou returned to the hotel more depressed than she'd ever felt in her life.

The lobby offered relief from the sun but not from the stifling hot air or her dismal mood. Four men sat around a table playing whist, but otherwise the lobby was deserted.

As usual the hotel clerk was asleep, his head resting against his shoulder. She tiptoed past him on the way to the stairs. What she wouldn't do to see Jeff Trevor again.

A thought suddenly occurred to her, a thought so daring it made her tremble. Maybe there was a way. It took her a moment to work up the nerve, but she finally walked back to the reception desk and rang the bell for service.

Startled, the clerk's eyes flew open. He made swimming motions to regain his balance and rose from his chair. "Miss Higgins."

"Would it be possible to have a message delivered?"

He nodded and reached for a piece of hotel stationery and a pen. "I'll see that it reaches the right person," he said.

"Thank you." She hesitated. She picked up the pen, dipped the metal nib into the inkwell, and began to write. *Dear Mr. Trevor.*

That part was easy. Now for the rest. Jenny never wrote a letter without first consulting *The Worcester Letter Writer,* a book that showed the correct form for addressing everything from accepting a marriage proposal to discouraging an unwanted suitor. Mary Lou doubted a model letter existed that would apply to her current situation with Mr. Trevor. She was definitely on her own.

Since he couldn't read, he'd have to ask someone to read it to him. That made choosing tactful wording even more imperative.

After much thought, she wrote, *Perhaps I was a bit hasty in judging your —*

Was there another more discreet word for *kiss? Peck* or *buss* wouldn't do. Nor did such words describe what transpired the night Jeff took her in his arms. She racked her brain for more judicious verbiage. *Performance? Amorous act?* Oh, dear. Blushing, she glanced up, but the clerk had already resumed his nap.

In the end, she settled on the word *test.* An inadequate substitute to be sure, but a third party reading the letter would have no way of knowing what it meant.

She read the sentence under her breath. *Perhaps I was a bit hasty in judging your test.*

The rest of the letter came easier. *Would it be possible to try again?* She signed it, *Re-*

spectfully, Miss Mary Lou Higgins.

Heart pounding, she folded the paper in two, creasing it carefully, then palmed the bell again to wake the clerk. She handed him the letter and drew a coin out of her reticule.

"I'll see that it's delivered," he said.

No sooner had he taken the letter from her than she had second thoughts. Would Jeff think her forward and bold? Would he laugh at her? Before she could retrieve the letter, Brenda burst through the door of the hotel like she was being chased by a pack of wolves.

"Brenda, stop!"

Mary Lou hurried across the lobby to join her sister, who looked flushed and bothered. Her bonnet dangled down her back and the ringlets that Jenny had taken such pains to achieve were in wild disarray. The hem of her skirt and her high-button shoes were covered in dust.

"What's the matter with you? Where have you been? I looked all over for you. And why are you in such a hurry?"

Instead of answering her questions, Brenda blurted, "I'm not marrying Mr. Hampton. I'm not! I'm on my way upstairs to tell Jenny."

Shocked by Brenda's sudden assertive-

301

ness, Mary Lou eyed her with suspicion. "You've never stood up to Jenny before."

"I'm only doing what God wants me to do," Brenda said with a determined nod of the head.

Mary Lou looked her sister up and down. It was Brenda all right, but it sure didn't sound like her. "If you're bringing God into it, you *must* be serious."

"I've never been more serious in my life." Brenda glanced at the men playing cards and lowered her voice. "I'm marrying Kip instead."

Mary Lou gasped, hand on her chest. "The barber?"

For answer, Brenda turned and bounded up the stairs.

"The barber?" Mary Lou shouted after her, forgetting to lower her voice. Not wanting to miss the fireworks that were sure to occur, she picked up her skirts and hurried after Brenda as fast as her feet could carry her.

They reached the hotel room at the same time, but Mary Lou pushed through the door first. Jenny was on the floor kneeling over a trunk that looked woefully inadequate to accommodate the pile of clothes on the bed.

Mary Lou stared at her. "What are you doing?"

"Packing," Jenny replied without looking up. "We're leaving Rocky Creek."

Brenda let the door slam shut, rattling the window. "What do you mean, leaving?"

Jenny picked a hat off the bed and carefully placed it in a round hatbox. "There was a misprint in the article about Rocky Creek. It should have read *Rockland* Creek. That's why I've had so much trouble finding appropriate husbands. Other than Mr. Hampton, there simply have been so few to choose from. I should have known a mistake was made. I can't believe we've wasted all this time and money for nothing."

"But —"

Jenny cut Brenda off. "Just so you know, I already informed Mr. Hampton of our departure, and he accepted my decision with remarkable grace." She looked straight at Brenda. "I hope you're not too disappointed."

Brenda shook her head. "I —"

"Good." Jenny resumed stuffing clothes into the trunk.

"We can't leave," Brenda protested. She poked Mary Lou with her elbow. "Say something," she mouthed, her eyes round.

Mary Lou's mind spun. If they left town,

she would never see Jeff again and she wanted to, she wanted to so much it hurt. It was the first time she dared admit it, but she could no longer deny what she knew in her heart to be true.

"We . . . we like it here," she said, dismayed by the inadequacy of her words. *Think, think!*

"We *both* like it here," Brenda added.

Jenny reached for a lace chemise and stuffed it into the trunk without bothering to fold it. "You've done nothing but complain about this town since we arrived."

"I changed my mind." Mary Lou crossed her arms. "And I'm not leaving."

"Neither am I," Brenda said.

Jenny glanced up but appeared unmoved by her sisters' united stand. "We're leaving," she said firmly.

"What if Brenda agrees to marry Mr. Hampton?" Mary Lou blurted out.

Brenda's jaw dropped. "Why don't *you* marry him?"

"I'd rather die first," Mary Lou added with equal vehemence.

Jenny gave Brenda a sharp look and tossed a pair of stockings into the trunk. "You needn't worry. I decided Mr. Hampton isn't as qualified as I previously thought." She straightened and reached for her reticule.

"You two can finish packing. I'm going to the train station to inquire about tickets to Rockland Creek. I believe one leaves in the morning." Without another word, she hustled out the door.

"What are we going to do?" Brenda wailed. "We can't leave. We can't!" She flung herself across the bed, sending the hatbox flying.

Mary Lou covered her ears to drown out Brenda's wails. How was a person to think? It wasn't like Brenda to be so melodramatic. She was always the calm and reasonable one. Brenda really must be in love with her barber.

Brenda sat up and rocked back and forth. The wails subsided, but not the tears that continued to roll down her cheeks.

Hands on her waist, Mary Lou stood at the bottom of the bed, her thoughts spinning. "You've got to agree to marry Mr. Hampton."

"Never!"

"It's the only way."

"I won't do it." Brenda said. A sob shuddered through her. "Besides . . . you heard what Jenny said. He's no longer suitable."

Mary Lou paced back and forth. "She didn't mean that. How could she? He's rich. She was just saying that." She stopped at

305

the foot of the bed. "Come on, Brenda. I don't mean that you actually have to *marry* him. You just have to pretend like you're going to."

Brenda shook her head. "I'm not going to lie to Jenny. Besides, it wouldn't be fair to Mr. Hampton to make a promise of marriage I don't intend to keep." Another wave of sobs escaped and she dabbed at her eyes with a balled handkerchief. "You've got to come up with something else."

"I'm thinking, I'm thinking." Mary Lou held her head with both hands. Who or what would make Jenny stay in town? *God, please, please help us.*

She paced around the room then stopped to glance out the window at the marshal crossing the street toward his office. Turning away, she was struck by sudden inspiration.

"I have an idea. Quick, pull yourself together." She picked up her skirt with both hands and danced around the room. "I know how to make Jenny stay," she shouted, gaily. "I do!"

Rhett looked up, surprised to see Jenny's sisters walk through the door of his office. He greeted the girls with a nod of his head.

"Mary Lou. Brenda. What can I do for you?"

The secret glances the two exchanged told him it wasn't a social visit. Mary Lou gestured to her sister, who shook her head. There was obviously some disagreement as to which of them would speak first.

Finally, Mary Lou took the lead. "We're getting ready to leave town."

He stared at them. "You're . . . leaving? Already?"

Mary Lou nodded. "Jenny is at the train station purchasing tickets as we speak."

He narrowed his eyes. "I didn't know you'd be leaving so . . . What about Jenny's plan to find you both husbands?"

"Her plans haven't changed," Mary Lou said.

"She's very determined," Brenda added.

"She thinks she'll meet with more success in Rockland Creek."

He sat back. The news was like a bullet to his heart. Knowing Jenny, it should have come as no surprise. If it hadn't been for that misprint in the newspaper, she and her sisters would never have come to Rocky Creek in the first place. Still, he hadn't expected her to abandon the town so quickly. Especially since she had Hampton on a hook.

"When . . ." He cleared his voice and started again. "When are you leaving?"

"Soon," Brenda said. "Probably on the next train heading that way."

"The next —" Jenny sure didn't waste time. "That'll be tomorrow morning." He drummed on his desk. He regretted telling Jenny about the misprint, but it seemed like the right thing to do at the time. Now he wasn't so sure.

Since both women were staring at him as if they expected him to explode or something, he forced himself to sound happy for them. "It was nice meeting you both. I wish you the best." The words felt like rocks in his mouth.

Neither sister made a move to leave.

"Is there something else?" he asked.

Mary Lou moistened her lips. "Jenny would kill us if she knew we were here."

Brenda nodded and made a slicing motion across her neck with her hand.

He frowned. "Are you saying she doesn't want me to know you're leaving?" he asked, confused.

"It's not that," Mary Lou said quickly.

He lifted a newspaper and waved it once before letting it fall back on the desk. "I know about the misprint. I'm the one who told your sister." His voice grew husky. "I'm sure she'll find the men in Rockland Creek more . . . to her liking."

"That's just it," Mary Lou said. "Jenny likes the men here just fine."

"*Some* men," Brenda amended.

"*One* man," Mary Lou added.

Rhett scratched his head. "I'm not sure what you mean. Are you talking about Mr. Hampton?"

"No!" both women exclaimed in unison.

"Then who?" he asked, more confused than ever.

"She means that Jenny likes *you,*" Brenda blurted out with such force that even Mary Lou looked taken aback.

"*Likes* me?" he asked, aghast. Thinking he'd misinterpreted what they were saying, he decided to ask for clarification. "When you say she likes me, do you mean —"

They both nodded.

"That's exactly what we mean," Mary Lou assured him.

Rhett couldn't believe his ears. Jenny *liked* him? How could that be? Except to question him about Hampton's character, she'd all but ignored him since her release from jail. Liked him? Not possible. Was it?

Mixed feelings welled up inside. He didn't want to know this, he didn't. Still, some uncontrollable, rebellious part of him

309

wanted it to be true.

He regarded the women with narrowed eyes. "If Jenny . . ." He shook his head in disbelief. "How come I don't know about it?"

"Jenny would never admit such a thing," Mary Lou said.

"Never," Brenda concurred.

Mary Lou leaned forward. "She's really very shy."

Jenny, shy? What a laugh. Only he wasn't laughing. Not laughing at all. Instead he sat forward. He had to make certain there was no misunderstanding.

"How do you know she . . . *likes* me?"

"We just do," Mary Lou assured him in the mysterious tone women used whenever they discussed feminine matters.

"We just thought you'd like to know," Brenda added.

The two women stared at him.

Finally Mary Lou pushed her sister toward the door, and they walked in tandem like they were attached at the hips. "We won't take up any more of your time."

After they were gone, Rhett sat at his desk in a state of confusion. She *liked* him. He shook his head. Not possible.

He didn't meet her standards. His bank account was pitiful. What extra money he had, he sent to Leonard's elderly parents. It was the least he could do for killing their son.

Her sisters were simply . . . what? Confused? Misinformed? Imagining things!

And what did it matter if she liked him or not? She'd been nothing but trouble since blowing into town. Thumbing her nose at his profession. Stirring up the men. Riling up the women. Now that she was leaving, maybe the town could get back to normal, and he could concentrate on restoring order.

Yes, it really was for the best, Jenny leaving and all.

He stood and paced around his office. Of course, Rocky Creek would never be the same once she was gone. Big blue eyes that seemed to change color at the drop of a hat. Yellow hair that turned to liquid gold in the moonlight.

He shook the thought away. Maybe once she left town the annoying memory of her sweet lips would go away. Perhaps then he could concentrate on work instead of wasting time watching for her to pass by his office.

The last thought struck him like a bolt from the sky. He hadn't really thought about it, but that's exactly what he did. He stopped pacing. He smiled at the memory of her walking by in that determined way of hers, shoulders back, head held high. His smile faded away. No denying it; he waited for her to walk past his office. Now why would he do that? To make sure she stayed out of trouble? Or . . . ?

He shook his head. There was no other possibility. He was simply doing his job and that required him to watch her like a hawk.

It didn't matter that she was leaving town. Didn't matter at all. He didn't care if she stayed or left. Made no difference to him either way.

Oh, but it did. It did.

No matter how hard he tried to convince himself he wanted her to go, he couldn't ignore the pain that ripped through him. Mary Lou's words continued to claw at him and refused to go away. Jenny *liked* him.

And he *liked* her.

Blasted!

He'd denied it, ignored it, and pretended it wasn't true, but no matter how hard he fought his feelings for her, he couldn't get her out of his mind. It started with a simple kiss — a kiss meant to disarm her, nothing more. Instead, it broke through the guilt and grief that had encased his heart all these years. He had killed his best friend. He didn't deserve to love or be loved. He didn't.

And yet . . .

He couldn't bear the thought of her leaving town.

Leonard, will you ever forgive me, my friend? Will you ever, ever forgive me for wanting what you can no longer have?

With quick, determined movements, he plucked his hat off a nail and pressed it hard on his head. He had run his share of misfits and troublemakers out of town since taking over as marshal, but never had he wanted anyone to go as much as he wanted Jenny to stay.

Twenty-One

The trick to chasing a man is knowing
when to let him catch you.
— MISS ABIGAIL JENKINS, 1875

Jenny couldn't make heads or tails of the
railroad schedule posted outside the waiting
room. Why did timetables have to be so
downright complicated?

Sighing, she headed for the ticket booth
to ask for information only to find a dozen
people in line ahead of her. She took her
place behind an elderly woman. Though it
was late afternoon, it was still in the eight-
ies. Nevertheless the old woman was dressed
for winter in a gray wool gown and knitted
shawl. A walking stick in one hand, she held
up her lorgnette and gazed at Jenny through
tortoise-rimmed lenses.

"I got off the train too soon," the woman
muttered in a crackling voice. "I thought
this was Rainbow Springs."

314

Jenny gave her a sympathetic smile. The woman wasn't the only one who ended up in Rocky Creek by mistake.

The line grew longer, but the people ahead of her didn't seem to move. Fanning herself against the heat of the late afternoon sun, Jenny tapped her toe and glared at the man in front of the ticket booth who seemed to be holding up the line.

At this rate, she'd be there all night. She had so much to do. If she didn't get started, she'd never get everything done in time to board the morning train. She couldn't leave without saying good-bye to Sarah and giving her darling little girl one last hug. And Scooter. She wanted to see him one last time.

She caught a glimpse of Rhett from the corner of her eye. What was he doing here? She strained her neck to get a better look and followed his progress until he disappeared behind a knot of people. Losing track of him altogether, she turned her attention back to the ticket booth. Rhett suddenly appeared by her side and she cried out in surprise.

"You startled me," she said, her hand on her chest.

"Hey, Marshal," someone called from behind. "Get in line and wait your turn."

"I'm not staying," Rhett called back, his gaze never wavering from her face.

"What are you doing here?" she asked.

His eyes were dark beneath the brim of his hat, but no amount of shade could hide their intensity. "You're leaving town," he said, his voice thick.

Not sure how to decipher his tight expression, she frowned. "How did you know where to find me?"

"I have my ways." His flippant answer was at odds with the serious tone of his voice.

"So which one was it? Mary Lou or Brenda?" she asked lightly. As much as she hated to admit it, she would miss bantering with Rhett Armstrong. The truth was, she would miss everything about him.

"Both. How did you guess?" he asked.

She pressed her lips together. If her sisters were so readily spreading news of their departure, they must be more eager to leave Rocky Creek than they let on.

"It was either them or Mr. Hampton. No one else knew of my plans. So why *are* you here?" she asked. "Did you come to say good-bye or good riddance?"

He studied her face with such intensity, she found herself blushing. It was as if he were trying to look into her very soul. "The question is why are *you* here? What about

316

Hampton? I thought you'd settled on him."

"Neither Brenda nor Mary Lou wish to be courted by him."

"Your sisters show good judgment." She looked for teasing lights in his eyes, but none of his usual humor was evident. "Since I have been their sole caretaker these last several years, I'll take that as a compliment. You still haven't told me what you're doing here."

"I came to give you a reason to stay," he said his voice low.

Her mouth went dry. Her heart thudded. He wanted her to stay? He couldn't possibly. She must have misunderstood. To cover her confusion, she laughed.

"This should be interesting," she said, her voice deceptively calm and lighthearted. "Do you plan to put me in jail again?"

"I hope that won't be necessary." He took a step closer, forcing her to look up at him.

Without another word, he slipped his arms around her waist and crushed her to him. Too shocked to protest, she unwittingly melted against him. His lips gently brushed hers before completely covering her mouth. With a soft groan he deepened the kiss, and currents of desire raced through her.

Oblivious to the gasps from stunned spectators, she kissed him back, savoring the sweet passion that flowed like music between them. Time and place had no meaning. All that existed were his lips, his arms, his all-encompassing embrace.

He pulled away, looking nearly as surprised as she felt. Her mouth still burning from his touch, she gazed at him, not knowing what to say. Her legs trembled and she feared they would buckle beneath her.

He looked deep into her eyes. As if he was suddenly aware of his surroundings, he glanced around before turning back to her.

"Meet me at my office," he said softly. "I'll be waiting." Then quickly and, without further ado, he walked away.

Jenny couldn't move. Her senses wouldn't stop spinning. What in the world had possessed him to — ? Possessed her to — ?

The old woman in front of her let out a long lingering sigh, her eyes huge behind the lens of her lorgnette. A smile lit her weathered face, hinting at the pretty young girl who once resided there.

"That would make *me* want to stay," she said.

Jenny left the railroad station in a hurry, cheeks burning. She tried to ignore the stares but there was no way to ignore her quivering limbs. What *was* that? Rhett

Armstrong said he wanted to give her a reason to stay. He then kisses her and, without so much as an explanation, takes off?

She raced along the boardwalk, looking neither left nor right. Men scampered out of her way. Women stepped to the side. She hardly noticed any of them.

I came to give you a reason to stay.

But why? Because he was interested in Mary Lou? Isn't that what he once told her? Then why didn't he just say so?

Oooh. The nerve of the man. How dare he make a spectacle of her? Who did he think he was? And what was the matter with her, getting all weak-kneed and shivery just because a man kissed her.

Not just any man. Rhett.

I came to give you a reason to stay.

Her steps faltered. He sounded sincere. And the way he looked at her . . .

He wanted to protect you.

She shook her head and picked up speed. He was playing games with her.

But the kiss, the kiss . . . This time she came to a complete halt. She took a deep breath and willed her heart to stop pounding. The last thing she wanted to do was let him see how much his kiss affected her.

Could it be that he — ? No, no, she

wouldn't allow it. If perchance he had . . . feelings for her, it was because he didn't know who or what she was. If he knew the truth, knew how another man had had his way with her, Rhett would most certainly want nothing to do with her.

He's a good man.

Yes, yes, he was. But God knew she was not a good woman.

She shook her head. She couldn't go to him, see him. Not while his kiss still trembled on her lips. She had no choice but to go back to the train station, purchase her ticket and leave town tomorrow. Just as she planned.

She whirled around and almost ran headlong into Mr. Barrel.

"Miss Higgins," he said with a polite nod of his head. "I wish to speak to you, if you don't mind."

"I don't have time right now." She tried to step past him. She moved to the right, to the left, to the right again. Anticipating her every move, he effectively blocked her way no matter which way she turned.

Hands on her hips, her voice dripped with annoyance. "Mr. Barrel, I'm in a hurry. Now would you kindly step aside?"

"This won't take long, ma'am, I promise."

She sighed in resignation. Obviously he

was determined to prevent her from going anywhere until she heard him out. "What is it you wish to say, Mr. Barrel?"

He cleared his throat. "It's about Brenda."

"As I already explained," she said patiently, "I simply cannot permit my sister to associate with a man who has no concern for her reputation."

"I'm concerned about her reputation, ma'am." His face grew red, but he showed no signs of backing down. "I love her."

"You hardly know her," she said. The poor man was obviously not thinking straight. "One night is hardly enough time to fall in love."

"Oh, I didn't fall in love with her the night we spent together," he said. "I fell in love with her the moment I found her outside the boardinghouse sniffing Ma's pies."

Aghast, Jenny stared at him. "You caught her sniffing your mother's pies?"

"Oh, Ma's not my mother. She's the nice lady who runs the boardinghouse," he explained as if this lack of kinship somehow excused Brenda's unseemly behavior. "And don't go blaming Brenda for doing what any sane person would do. No one can resist Ma's pies."

"This is all very interesting, but —"

"Wait, hear me out," he pleaded, his eyes

filled with determination.

He looked so desperate she simply didn't have the heart to turn him away. "I'm listening," she said and she meant it.

He cleared his throat. An alarming red color crept up his neck and worked its way up his face like a rising high tide. He took so long to speak she thought he'd changed his mind.

But then he surprised her by blurting out, "I want to marry your sister."

Her mouth fell open. Did he say *marry?* Without her permission? And before a proper courting? She shook her head. Nothing about this town made sense. Men kissed women without invitation and proposed marriage with even less inducement. Obviously, the people in Rocky Creek had no knowledge of proper courting manners!

Of course, there was the very real possibility that things weren't as innocent as Brenda insisted. It was preposterous to think that a man could spend a night with a woman and do nothing more than talk about opera.

Jenny studied him. "If you think that offering to do the honorable thing will excuse your wanton behavior, you are sadly mistaken."

His eyes blazed with determination. "I'm not trying to be honorable, ma'am. I love her and she loves me. And that's the God-honest truth. You've got to believe me."

"Believe you, Mr. Barrel? After you insist that nothing happened the night you spent with my sister?" She watched for the slightest flicker of guilt but saw none. "Who, I might add, was dressed in her night attire."

"Lots of things happened," he said.

She knew it!

"But it all happened here." He thumped his fist against his chest.

She opened her mouth to object, but the words wouldn't come. He looked so earnest and sincere it was all she could do not to submit to his charms. Despite her best efforts she softened toward him.

"Mr. Barrel, I don't doubt for a moment that you have feelings for my sister. But how can you presume to know how she feels about you?"

"He knows because I told him," Brenda said.

Jenny whirled about to face her youngest sister. "I made it very clear that we're leaving town."

"I'm not leaving. I'm staying here with Kip." Brenda sidled up to Barrel, and the two of them stood side by side. They made a formidable pair and looked ready to take on the world.

Momentarily speechless, Jenny stared at them. Barrel was nothing like the man she hoped to find for Brenda. Nothing! And yet . . .

The softness in his eyes when he looked at Brenda — the way she gazed back at him — could not be denied. Jenny had seen a similar expression on Reverend Wells's face when he gazed at his wife, Sarah.

"It is not good that the man should be alone."

Surely God hadn't intended to bring Brenda and Mr. Barrel together. What could she possibly have in common with an opera-singing barber?

How could two people so wrong for each other look so perfectly right together?

Still, long-held dreams refused to die an easy death. She wasn't willing to let go of her aspirations for Brenda. Not yet.

"Brenda, there's no future here," she managed at last. "Look around you. This town . . . it doesn't even have a proper school or a library. I was wrong to bring you here. It was all a terrible mistake. As I told you, we're leaving."

Brenda's eyes blazed with determination. "I love this town. I love the people and the church and I hope they never get a proper school. At least not until they change the constitution."

Jenny was unnerved by the change in Brenda. Never had she seen her youngest sister show so much passion. But the crazy talk worried her. "What's the constitution —"

Brenda cut her off with a soft beseeching look. "Jenny, please . . . It wasn't a mistake to come here. I think God brought us here for a reason."

Jenny's head pounded. Nothing made sense. "You can't know that."

"I *do* know it." Brenda's brows drew together. "And I thought you knew it too. Didn't you talk to Marshal Armstrong?"

Jenny stiffened. He was the main reason she couldn't stay. Not after today. "What has . . . the marshal got to do with this?"

Brenda bit her lip and glanced away.

"Brenda! Answer me."

Brenda glanced at Barrel as if to brace herself. "Mary Lou and I . . . we told the marshal that you liked him. We hoped he would convince you to stay."

Jenny's mouth dropped open. "You did what?" she sputtered. His kiss had simply been a ploy to appease her sisters? Had he simply taken pity on the girls and agreed to do their bidding? Was that it?

"We didn't mean any harm." Brenda

looked close to tears. She reached out her hand but Jenny pulled away.

The kiss meant nothing. Nothing! Everything now made sense. Everything, that is, but the yearning that burned inside her. Wanting to be alone, she turned to leave, but Brenda grabbed her arm.

"Jenny, all my life I've tried to be the daughter Mama and Papa wanted me to be. What *you* wanted me to be. I can't be that person anymore. Now I've got to be what God wants me to be."

Jenny blinked in an effort to both hold back tears and better observe the stranger before her. When did this happen? When did her baby sister turn into a confident young woman? A woman clearly in love?

"Ma'am, you don't have to worry about Brenda's future," Barrel said. "I may not be a rich man, but I intend to spend the rest of my life making her happy."

Brenda moved her hand away from Jenny's arm. "I don't care about money. Kip is the first person to love me for who I am. When I'm around him, I don't feel fat or ugly."

Barrel turned and took both of Brenda's hands in his, his face dark with dismay. "Don't say such things. Don't even think it.

You're the most beautiful woman I ever knew."

Brenda blushed. "And you're the most handsome man," she said.

The two gazed at each other with such adoration that Jenny could no longer fight them. She had battled poverty, illness, hopelessness, and despair, but the love that flowed between her sister and Kip Barrel was stronger than any of those.

Feeling like an intruder, she glanced down the street toward the marshal's office. Rhett stood outside. He leaned against a post, watching her. She couldn't see his face, but she could feel the heat of his gaze.

He made no secret how much he liked Barrel and disapproved of Hampton. No doubt he would be happy at how things turned out. Certain he was enjoying himself at her expense, she started toward the hotel before anyone could see her tears.

"Jenny?" Brenda called after her. "Where are you going?"

"To the hotel," Jenny called back, her voice muffled. "I've got a wedding to plan."

He waited.

Rhett waited for the rest of the day and well into the night for Jenny to come to him. While he waited, he practiced the words he wanted to say to her out loud.

"Jenny Higgins, I like you." Not *like. Love. Say it, you fool!*

"I love you," he said, savoring the sound of it. That wasn't so hard. Now if he could just get his tongue to cooperate when the time came to tell her to her face how he felt.

He could tease, joke, and banter with the best of them, but when it came to talking about the things that mattered most, he was tongue-tied. It hadn't always been that way. Then Leonard died, and suddenly he couldn't talk about feelings.

Leonard Stanford.

The official cause of death was listed as fratricide — blue killing blue, gray killing gray. It happened all the time. Even Stonewall Jackson had been shot by his own troops. The army blamed such mishaps on the fog of war, an all-encompassing term for smoke, fatigue, weapon failure, confusion, miscommunication, or just plain carelessness. Any and all could lead to a comrade's death.

For someone who claims it was an accident, you don't seem the least bit remorseful. The memory was like a knife piercing his heart. He could still see the rigid face of his commanding officer firing questions at him, *bang, bang, bang. Where were you? Where was he? Who gave the order to fire?*

Remorseful? That was the least of it. Though the army eventually ruled in his favor, he would never forget that he had killed his best friend.

Rhett was a front-rank soldier, not Leonard. Leonard should never have been up front. He had taken Rhett's place as a favor. Why Leonard had chosen that particular moment to bob up from his trench — the exact moment Rhett pulled the trigger — he would never know.

After the war, Rhett didn't know what to do with himself. He went back to Missouri to face Leonard's family, and it was the hardest thing he'd ever had to do. They didn't blame him, which somehow made him feel worse. What they did was talk about Leonard's dream of going into law enforcement.

That's when Rhett decided to become a lawman. He couldn't bring Leonard back, but he could keep his friend's dream alive.

It had been a long, hard road back. If it hadn't been for his faith, he wouldn't have survived. He still had nightmares. Still suffered from a soldier's heart. Still hadn't been able to talk to anyone except Reverend Wells about it. But recently something had changed.

Not something. Jenny!

For the first time since the war he found himself looking forward instead of back. He wanted to live life to the fullest again. He didn't just want to live another man's dream; he wanted to pursue his own.

She *likes* you.

She certainly seemed to like his kiss, or was it only his imagination? Never in his wildest dreams could he have imagined her response. So where was she?

He could hardly tell her how he felt at the railroad station with all those people around. Nor did it seem like a good idea to meet her at the hotel. He asked that she come to him so he wouldn't have to talk in front of her sisters.

He pulled his watch from his vest pocket. It was almost nine o'clock. She might have already retired for the night.

So what if she had? This was no time to worry about proper etiquette. He grabbed his hat and hurried toward the hotel. He bumped into Mary Lou in the lobby, and she looked nervous and anxious. Obviously the girl was up to something.

"Everything okay?" he asked. "You're not still leaving Rocky Creek, are you?"

"Not now," Mary Lou said, sounding

strangely out of breath. "We're so grateful for your help. Brenda is going to marry Mr. Barrel."

So that's what Jenny and Kip had been discussing. He stared at her, his mouth dry. "Is that why you and your sister were so anxious to stay? Because Brenda's sweet on Barrel?"

Mary Lou's cheeks flared red, and she lowered her lashes. "Yes," she admitted.

Had someone physically trampled on his heart, he couldn't have felt any worse than it felt at that moment. So all that business about Jenny liking him was just a trick to get him to talk to her on their behalf. Lies, all of it?

"But that's not the only reason," she added as if to guess his thoughts, and his optimism soared.

A smile played at the corner of her mouth. "There's someone I'm interested in too," she said, as if that made everything right.

His hope dashed again, he couldn't even bring himself to say he was happy for her. So Mary Lou had taken a fancy to someone too. The girls had played him like a fool and he had let them.

Afraid of what he would do or say if he stayed a moment longer, he bade Mary Lou goodnight and walked away, crushed.

And no matter how many times he told himself that he was better off without Jenny, he couldn't make the pain go away.

Twenty-Two

Never show affection in public. Love may be blind but the townspeople are not.
— Miss Abigail Jenkins, 1875

The moment the marshal left, Mary Lou pulled the message from behind her back where she'd hidden it from his view and read it again. *Meet me tomorrow at 11 p.m.*

It was written in a childish scrawl with none of the bold flourishes she would expect from a man like Jeff Trevor. Since Jeff claimed he could neither read nor write, she suspected someone had written the note for him, perhaps the messenger.

Heart pounding, she stood staring at the note in her hand. The loud voices of three men sitting in the lobby arguing politics brought her out of her reverie. None of them paid attention to her.

Her world had suddenly done a flip-flop, yet everything around her looked and sounded amazingly the same.

She read the message again. Her hands shook and the words blurred, but the message was clear. Jeff had agreed to meet her. More than that, agreed to kiss her. The very thought took her breath away.

The last twenty-four hours had been crazy. First, there had been that business about leaving Rocky Creek, followed by news of Brenda's engagement. By the time she realized she had made a terrible mistake in sending that letter to Jeff, it was too late. It had already left the hotel. All she could do was wait.

She'd hardly slept a wink last night. That morning she rushed through her lessons without argument or complaint, earning Jenny's approval. Her sister would have been less delighted at Mary Lou's sudden interest in Mr. Wordsworth had she known the real motivation. The sooner Mary Lou could complete her lessons, the faster she could escape downstairs to check for a message from Jeff.

By the end of the day, she'd practically given up hope of hearing from him. He'd obviously lost interest in her. Perhaps he was never really serious about her and was just using her for sport. Still, she decided it wouldn't hurt to check at the reception desk one last time. Pretending to leave the room to attend to her nightly ablutions, she ran downstairs to the lobby.

At long last, the clerk thrust an envelope at her containing Mr. Trevor's message.

Reading the note again, she then paced around the lobby in an effort to calm down. She didn't dare return to her room in her present state. Jenny was bound to suspect something.

Having left her father's pocket watch upstairs, she stopped to ask the clerk the time.

He pulled a watch from his vest. "Nine forty five," he said.

"Thank you."

In a little more than twenty-four hours, she would be in Jeff's arms once again.

At noon the Rocky Creek Café buzzed with activity. Jenny, Brenda, and Mr. Barrel had to wait for a rowdy group of lumbermen to leave before they could be seated.

While they waited to be served, Jenny studied her list and chatted amicably about all the things that had to be done for the wedding. The list went on and on.

It suddenly occurred to her that she was talking to herself.

She'd asked Brenda and Mr. Barrel to join

her at the café, along with Mary Lou, for all the good it did. Mary Lou had still not shown up, but that wasn't the only problem. Jenny was doing all the work while Brenda and Mr. Barrel did nothing but gaze at each other. Neither showed any interest in the bill of fare.

Jenny laid her list down. "Do you know where your sister is?"

When Brenda didn't answer, she rapped the table. That got Brenda's attention.

"Your sister?" she asked again. "I asked her to join us."

Brenda shrugged. "I have no idea. She's been acting very strange lately."

Jenny arched a brow. "Talk about the pot calling the kettle black."

Brenda gave her a strange look. "What?"

"Nothing," Jenny said.

She tried to shake off the depression that colored everything gray. She loved watching Brenda and Mr. Barrel together, but her enjoyment wasn't without pain. Their love for each other was like a bright beam illuminating the emptiness of her life. It was an emptiness that no amount of list-making, organizing, or busyness could fill.

"Perhaps we should go ahead and order." Her cheerful voice belied her despair. She would sooner die than put a damper on

Brenda's happiness.

She looked around, but Redd had disappeared into the kitchen in back. With a sigh of impatience, she picked up her list again. Keep busy. Don't think about anything but the wedding. And whatever you do, don't think about Rhett.

"What about guests?" she asked, her voice strained. "Do you have any family you wish to invite, Mr. Barrel?"

He hesitated, a look of discomfort on his face. "You can call me Kip, ma'am," he said.

Jenny nodded and when he made no effort to answer her question, she asked it again.

"What about your cousin in Haswell?" Brenda asked.

Surprised, Jenny asked, "You have family in Haswell?"

"Not really, ma'am. My family owns property in Haswell, which means they travel there on occasion for business," he explained. "The truth is I don't have much contact with my family." It was obvious that it pained him to admit it. "They don't approve of my singing."

"That's ridiculous," Brenda exclaimed. "You're the best singer in the world."

Barrel blushed. "Don't tell my father that. He's still furious at me for not going into the family cattle business." He chuckled. "Every time I get close to a steer, I sneeze." He gazed at Brenda with a look of wonder. "What does a beautiful woman like you see in the likes of me? An audience makes me screech, and cattle give me hives."

Brenda gazed at him with a tender smile. "I see a beautiful soul and a loving heart."

He patted her hand and smiled back at her.

Brenda's forehead creased. "It would be a pity not to have your family share our happy day."

"I don't know." He glanced at Jenny, then back to Brenda. "I'll send them a telegram, but I doubt anyone will show up."

Jenny checked off guests. "I talked to Mrs. Taylor this morning, and she's coming to the hotel this afternoon to take measurements for your wedding dress. What about music?"

"We could ask the choir to sing," Kip suggested, his eyes never leaving Brenda's face.

"I want *you* to sing," Brenda said. "Just you. And I want you to sing something romantic, from an opera. A *happy* opera."

Kip shook his head. "I can't do that," he said, his voice thick. "Whenever I sing solo in front of an audience, even the chickens run for cover. I told you what happened the last time I was onstage."

"But you won't be singing for an audience," Brenda protested. "You'll be singing to me."

Kip looked taken aback for a moment. "I–I don't know. I . . ."

Brenda put her hand on his. "I know you can do it," she said. "It would please me so much."

Kip hesitated. "I–I don't want to ruin our wedding."

"Nothing could possibly ruin our wedding," Brenda said. She pointed to Jenny's list. "You can check off music."

Jenny doubted the wisdom of asking Kip to perform when he was so clearly uncomfortable with the idea, but she said nothing. "Let's see . . . Next."

Kip glanced at Brenda then turned to Jenny. "Ma'am, just so you know, the bank has agreed to give me a loan to purchase property outside of town. It's a couple of acres with a small house, but we can add more rooms."

Jenny took both their hands in hers and squeezed. "That's wonderful. I'm so happy for you both." She released their hands with a loving smile.

Kip grinned back. "We were talking and —" He glanced at Brenda, who jumped in.

"We want you and Mary Lou to move in with us until you find a place of your own."

Jenny was so touched that at first she couldn't find her voice. "That's very generous of you, but Mary Lou and I will be leaving town after the wedding. We're going to Rockland Creek."

Kip lifted his brows. "What's in Rockland Creek?"

Brenda explained how the newspaper had misprinted the name of the town. "So instead of going to Rockland Creek, we ended up here."

"People are always confusing the two towns," Kip said. "Just think, if it wasn't for that error, you and I might never have met. God sure does work in strange ways, doesn't He?"

Jenny frowned but didn't say a word. They were in Rocky Creek because of a simple misprint. God had nothing to do with it. Or did He?

Since she'd begun her daily Bible reading, she'd been questioning things she never questioned before. Looking back on the chaos of her life, she saw patterns. Things that had seemed accidental or random suddenly looked deliberate. Perhaps God really did bring them to Rocky Creek so Kip and Brenda could be together.

The door of the café opened and a grisly man stuck his head inside. "What does a man have to do 'round here to get hisself a shave and haircut?"

"I'm coming," Kip said, rising. "Please excuse me, ladies, but duty calls." With that he left.

In quick order, Brenda rose from her seat. "I'm going back to the hotel."

"But you haven't eaten."

"I'm not hungry," she said, then laughed. "I bet you never thought to hear those words come out of my mouth."

Jenny grinned back at her. It did her heart good to see Brenda looking so happy. "Don't forget, Mrs. Taylor and Mrs. Hitchcock are coming to talk about your wedding gown," she called after her.

No sooner had Brenda left than Timber Joe limped into the café. Spotting her, he hobbled over to her table, his rifle flung over his shoulder.

"Do you mind if I have a word with you, ma'am?" he asked politely.

"Not at all," she said. Obviously no one else wanted to keep her company.

He pulled the rifle strap from his shoulder and leaned his weapon against the table. He then pulled out a chair and sat down, stretching his wooden leg out in front of him.

He leaned forward in earnest. "I never heard back from you," he said. "You know, after our interview and all."

"I didn't know how to reach you," she said, which was true. The man didn't seem to have a permanent home, or at least none that anyone knew about.

"That's why I'm here. I wanted to save you the bother of tracking me down."

"That's very thoughtful of you." She didn't want to hurt his feelings. Neither did she wish to give him false hope. "I don't know if you heard, but my sister Brenda is betrothed to Mr. Barrel."

"That's all everyone's been talking about, ma'am. No one ever thought Barrel would pass muster. Kind of gives the rest of us hope, if you know what I mean."

"Yes . . . eh." She stirred uneasily in her chair.

"With your permission, I'd like to ask your other sister . . . Mary Lou . . . if she would accompany me on guard duty."

Jenny wasn't sure what that meant. "Guard duty?"

"I've got a post on yonder hill where I can keep an eye out for advancing Yankee troops. Someone has to protect this town from invading forces."

She took a deep breath. Timber Joe was in worse shape than she thought. She could well imagine what Mary Lou would have to say about such an odd proposition.

"My sister would be most . . . flattered," she said, choosing her words with care. "However, a fine soldier such as yourself deserves a more patient . . . uncomplaining, and compliant wife. Someone sympathetic to the Confederate cause."

He gave a hearty nod. "That's exactly what I need."

"Yes, well . . ." She hated to say anything unpleasant about her sister, but she didn't know how else to discourage him without hurting his feelings. "I'm afraid you'd find Mary Lou wanting on all accounts."

His eyes shimmered with surprise. "Is that so, ma'am? I would never have guessed it to look at her."

"Looks can be deceiving," she said.

"Kind of reminds me of the Moon sisters," he said.

"Who?"

"The Moon sisters. Ginnie and Lottie. Lottie was one of our best spies. Even fooled Stanton," he said, referring to Abraham Lincoln's wartime secretary of state.

"Nobody could have guessed by looking

343

at her that she was a Confederate spy. Just like no one would have guessed your sister was a Union spy."

Alarmed, Jenny covered her mouth with her fingertips. "I didn't mean to suggest she was a spy."

A rumor like that could hamper Mary Lou's chances for marriage by cutting the pool of eligible men in half. The war was over and had been for a long time, but for many people, the North-and-South divide still existed.

"Don't you worry, ma'am. Your shameful secret is safe with me." He picked up his cap and placed it on his head. "Sure do appreciate your honesty," he said. Gathering his rifle with one hand, he stood.

Despite his odd ways, she liked the man. "If you ever need company, I'd be happy to stand guard with you."

"No offense, ma'am, but guard duty requires long hours of standing and doing nothing. I can tell by looking at you that you're the restless type. But I appreciate the offer." With that he flung his rifle over his shoulder and left.

Snatching up her notebook, she left the café too. She was so focused on all she had to do that she didn't see Rhett until she plowed into him.

"Oomph," he groaned, looking as startled as she was.

He steadied her with a hand to her arm, his eyes full of concern. "Are you all right?"

She was anything but all right, but she tried to hide her misery from his probing stare. "I'm fine. I wasn't watching where I was going."

He gazed at her a moment before pulling his hand away and stooping to pick up her notebook. He straightened and handed it to her. His hand brushing hers sent warm shivers up her arms.

"I heard about Brenda's betrothal," he said. "Kip's a good man."

She swallowed hard and bit her lip. She debated how much or how little to say. She finally decided it was best to clear the air.

"I know that my sisters asked you to" — she searched for the right word — "help them keep me from leaving Rocky Creek."

He narrowed his eyes but said nothing.

"T–they had no right to tell you that I —"

"Had feelings for me?" he prompted, his eyes hooded.

Heat crept up her face. "They didn't mean any harm."

He stepped back. "And no harm was done." His voice was as remote as the look on his face.

"I do apologize."

He touched a finger to the brim of his hat. "Apology accepted."

She watched him walk away and her heart squeezed in anguish. She fought the impulse to chase after him and . . . do what? Admit to the lie? Admit that she did, indeed, have feelings for him? Feelings that she could never act upon? Feelings that would require her to confess the truth about her past?

Holding on to what little resolve she had left, she hurried to the hotel.

TWENTY-THREE

Never compare your escort unfavorably
with another. It will only give him an
inferiority complex.
— MISS ABIGAIL JENKINS, 1875

Jenny arrived back at the hotel just in time
to greet Mrs. Taylor and Mrs. Hitchcock
and show them to her room. She was grateful for the distraction.

For some odd reason, the members of the
Rocky Creek Quilting Bee seemed relieved
— overjoyed in fact — to hear of Brenda's
betrothal, and they all offered to help with
the wedding decorations, cake, and liquid
refreshment.

Sarah had assured Jenny that no finer
seamstresses could be found throughout
Texas than Mrs. Taylor and Mrs. Hitchcock.
That might be true, but judging by the
women's apparel, sewing skills were no
guarantee of fashion sense.

Mrs. Hitchcock's purple gown, with its exaggerated bustle and layers of ruffles, made her already generous proportions look twice the size.

In contrast, Mrs. Taylor looked almost mouselike in her plain gray dress and unadorned bonnet. Even Brenda, who had previously shown little or no interest in fashion, regarded the women with a skeptical eye.

Despite her reservations, Jenny spread one of Brenda's frocks across the bed. She hoped they could turn the plain cream poplin dress into a wedding gown. The color complemented Brenda's complexion, and redesigning the dress rather than starting from scratch would save an enormous amount of time and money.

Brenda anxiously watched the two seamstresses examine the seams of her dress.

"I think it will work perfectly," Mrs. Taylor exclaimed.

Mrs. Hitchcock looked less enthusiastic. "It *is* rather plain," she said then repeated herself as she tended to do.

Jenny agreed. "I know, but lace is so expensive."

"We don't need lace," Mrs. Hitchcock assured her. "Some ruching here, some ruffles there." She swept a hand up and down the length of the gown, describing an amazing array of flourishes and embellishments, some of which Jenny had never heard.

"Mark my words. When I get through, no one will notice the lack of lace, lack of lace."

Mrs. Taylor looked horrified. "Nor will anyone notice the bride."

"Oh, there you go again," Mrs. Hitchcock complained in a tone that suggested the two never agreed on such matters. "If you had your way, she would look as plain as a whitewashed wall, white-washed —"

"Indeed!" Mrs. Taylor threw up her hands. "Ever since the invention of the sewing machine, fashions have taken a turn for the worse. Just because one can whip up a thousand yards of ruching in a flash doesn't mean they must all be attached to a single gown."

Mrs. Hitchcock heaved, her ample bosom rising and falling like a loaf of overbaked bread. "It's the fashion."

"It's a disgrace!"

The argument escalated, with each woman trying to outshout the other. Brenda tried to say something, but neither paid her any heed.

Finally Jenny had enough. She gave a firm clap of her hands. "Ladies, ladies."

She waited until she had their attention.

"I believe we should let my sister decide what kind of dress she wishes to wear to her own wedding."

"An excellent idea." Mrs. Taylor turned to Brenda. "What Mrs. Hitchcock suggests would make you look like a lamp shade. Whereas I —"

"Will make you look like day-old cream," Mrs. Hitchcock stormed. She glared at Mrs. Taylor, but she addressed her comments to Brenda.

Mrs. Taylor glared back. "If it were up to you, she'd look like a ruffled rooster."

"That's better than looking like a plucked hen, plucked hen!"

Mrs. Taylor's eyes narrowed. "The last dress you made was mistaken for a feather duster."

Mrs. Hitchcock folded her arms across her chest, no easy task. "That christening dress you designed was as dull as a porcelain bedpan."

The women might have gone on indefinitely had Jenny not yelled, "Stop!" She took a deep breath, forcing herself to calm down. "All right," she began in a low but firm voice. "It's Brenda's turn."

The women turned in unison to face the bride-to-be. It was obvious by their expressions that each thought she had won Brenda over to her side.

Brenda looked from one to the other and promptly burst into tears.

Late that night, Mary Lou waited for Jeff Trevor in front of the hotel. *Please, God, don't let Jenny wake and find me missing.*

She'd been doing that a lot, lately. Talking to God. In the past, prayers had never come easy and her mind wandered whenever Jenny got it into her head to say a blessing before meals. Lately, though, since going to church, she found herself thinking about the sermons or humming one of the hymns to herself. Mostly, she talked to God.

She glanced up at the starlit sky. Would God approve or disapprove? It wasn't as if she hadn't snuck out before, back in Haswell. She once even slipped out of the house to go to a barn dance that Jenny had forbidden her to attend. Now, instead of feeling smug for getting away with something, she was overcome with guilt.

What a nuisance. Since attending church, she was turning into a Goody Two-shoes just like — *gasp* — Brenda. Or at least the Brenda she knew before Mr. Barrel entered the picture.

She had just about decided to do the right thing and return to the hotel when Jeff galloped up on horseback. At precisely the same moment, all thoughts of right and wrong went out of her mind.

Her heart beat so fast, she could hardly stand it. She had taken great pains with her appearance. Even so, she felt unsure of herself. Was her blue gingham skirt and white frilly shirtwaist too much or too little? Should she have added another handkerchief or two to her bosom? Perhaps wound her hair on top of her head rather than let it cascade down her back?

He dismounted and walked up the stairs to the boardwalk. A thin, waxing moon smiled down at them. Or maybe it was laughing at the preposterous situation she found herself in.

"Miss Higgins," he said, his voice smooth as satin. His gaze drifted down the length of her before returning to her face. The warm light of approval in his eyes banished any insecurities she felt earlier about her appearance. One look from him and she felt like the most beautiful woman in the world.

Trembling, she bit her lip. "You may call me Mary Lou."

A wagon drawn by two horses drove past the hotel. A group of drunken men staggered out of the saloon singing off-key.

"Would you care to walk a bit?" he asked.

She swallowed hard and nodded. Together they strolled along the boardwalk to a quieter part of town. In the distance came the whining sound of a fiddle. A dog barked. Laughter rose, then faded away.

"I heard about your sister's betrothal to Kip Barrel," he said, leaning against one of only two lampposts in town. Bathed in amber gaslight, he looked even more handsome than usual.

Grateful to talk about something, anything, she replied. "Yes, it's very exciting."

"A good man, Mr. Barrel."

"So I've heard," she said, hoping he wouldn't elaborate. Mr. Barrel was all Brenda could talk about. If Mary Lou heard about the man's fine qualities one more time, she'd scream.

"I didn't think he'd meet with your older sister's approval," he said.

She tossed her head. "Jenny doesn't have the final say over what we do."

"Really?" His voice was as dubious as his expression. "I would never have guessed it." He shook his head. "Your sister persuaded close to a hundred men to fill out one of her applications. I hadn't seen so much paper flying since the tornado blew the roof off the bank."

The memory of standing in front of all

those leering men brought a flush of embarrassment to her face. "Jenny worries about us."

She still couldn't believe Jenny had so willingly accepted Brenda's choice for a husband. Would Jenny be as accommodating to her? Somehow she didn't think so.

"It must be nice to have a sister like that." His comment surprised her, and she wondered if he was only saying it to be polite. "It can be a nuisance sometimes." She eyed him with curiosity. There was so much she wanted to know about him. "Have you any family?"

"A brother," he replied. "His name is Michael. Last I heard, he was stationed at Fort Bridger in Wyoming. Our parents died when we were young and our grandmother raised us. She runs the boardinghouse on the other side of town. Everyone calls her Ma." His voice warm with affection, he added, "That's because she has no qualms about dishing out opinions and advice."

"Sounds like Jenny," she said.

His gaze held hers. "I told her about you."

She stared at him. A man generally didn't talk to his family about a woman unless he was serious. "What . . . what did you tell her?"

"That you refuse to marry me."

She held her breath for a moment before replying. "I hardly know you."

"You know all the important stuff."

She laughed.

"What's so funny?"

"You. I know what . . . two things about you? Three? Let's see, I know you work at the sawmill. You said you can neither read nor write —"

"It's all true."

"Your grandmother runs a boardinghouse, and you have a brother. Oh, yes, and you go to church every Sunday."

He shrugged. "Like I said, the important things."

"So how about some of the *unimportant* things?" Her sudden interest in trivial matters surprised her. Maybe something good did come out of reading all those Wordsworth poems.

He gave a low laugh. "You'll be bored to tears."

"I'll take my chances," she said, though she couldn't imagine him boring her. "Let's start with . . . your favorite food? Favorite color? What do you do in your spare time?"

He grinned and shook his head as if he couldn't imagine anyone caring about such mundane matters. "If you insist." He then answered her questions one by one. "Let's see, my favorite food. That's easy. My grandma's pies. My favorite color is . . . the blue of your eyes." He lowered his voice. "In my spare time, I think about you."

A knot caught in her chest, making it hard to breathe.

"Your turn," he said.

She forced herself to inhale. Trust him to turn a few simple questions into a game. "I like roast beef. My favorite color is yellow." She thought a moment and decided to give him some of his own medicine. "In my spare time, I think about you."

His laugh held a wistful note. "If only that were true."

It *was* true, though she wasn't about to argue with him. Better to keep him guessing.

"Music," she said to hide her discomfort. "Let's talk about music. What is your favorite song?"

He thought for a moment. "A hymn I learned to sing while in the Union army. It's called 'The Battle Hymn of the Republic.' "

"I never heard of it," she said.

"More's the pity. It was written by a woman. She heard the men singing 'John Brown's Body' and rightly decided that such a strong marching beat deserved more

356

meaningful words." He sang the song right then and there. The words practically moved her to tears.

When he finished, he bowed at the waist and she clapped.

"It's your turn," he said. "Name your favorite song."

"All right, but don't expect me to sing it. I was going to say that new Christmas carol, 'O Little Town of Bethlehem.' " She'd heard it sung by a group of carolers a few years ago and never forgot it. "But I think I like yours better."

They whiled the time away, talking about anything and everything that occurred to them. She told him about growing up in Haswell. He told her about joining the Union army as a drummer boy at the tender age of fourteen.

"You were so young," she whispered, imagining him in uniform.

He shrugged. "It was a boy's war," he said. "Over a hundred thousand of us were fifteen or younger. One boy was only nine."

She folded her arms with a determined nod of the head. "No son of mine is going to fight in any old war."

"Let's hope and pray that no one ever has to fight another war," he said.

A rooster crowed and Jeff pulled out his

pocket watch. "Five thirty," he announced.

She stared at him in disbelief. It wasn't possible, was it? Never could she imagine having so much fun. "I better get back before Jenny wakes."

He stepped toward her. "We never did take care of that . . . little business between us."

The kiss.

No longer shy in front of him, she gazed into his eyes. She didn't need to kiss him to know that, not only was she in love with Jeff Trevor, but she wanted to be his wife.

On the outside chance she was being too hasty in making such an important life-changing decision, she rushed into his waiting arms to make absolutely certain.

TWENTY-FOUR

*When a man's on his knee proposing,
resist the urge to look triumphant.*
— MISS ABIGAIL JENKINS, 1875

Jenny was first to smell the smoke. Instantly awake, she shook Brenda and jumped out of bed. Running to the window, she threw up the sash and stuck her head outside. "Fire!" she yelled. "Fire!"

Smoke curled out of the window next to theirs. She brushed the smoke away from her face. "Wake up," she shouted, hoping to raise the occupants.

A movement in the distance caught her eye. Despite the early morning hour, a man and woman walked hand in hand. She waved her arms to get their attention and blinked. It looked like . . .

She glanced over her shoulder. Brenda sat up in bed rubbing her eyes. Next to her the bed was empty. Mary Lou was gone!

Forgetting about the fire, Jenny turned back to the window. It couldn't be . . . She squinted. Between the early morning light and the smoke, it was hard to know for sure. She coughed and waved the smoke away with her hand.

It *was* Mary Lou. But who was the man with her? And why were they holding hands? Anger swelled up inside. "Why that little —"

"Hurry!" Brenda shouted.

Reluctantly, Jenny pulled away from the window. There would be time enough later to deal with her wayward sister. Sliding her feet into her slippers, she grabbed her dressing gown. She followed Brenda into the hall, stuffing her arms into the sleeves as she ran.

She stopped in the hall. Smoke escaped from the room next to theirs, slithering from beneath the closed door like ghostly snakes. Was that a cough? Someone calling for help?

She motioned Brenda downstairs. "Quick, tell the desk clerk to sound the alarm."

She knocked on the door once before throwing it open. The room was filled with smoke and her throat closed in protest. The mattress smoldered, but so far no flames were visible. Hand over her mouth, she raced to the body on the floor by the bed and dropped to her knees.

"Sir, are you all right?" She shook him and he moaned.

The man opened his eyes, but his breathing was labored and rattled in his chest. An older man with a balding head, he had a long white beard. He coughed, spraying her with a whiff of stale alcohol.

"Let's get you out of here."

She slipped her hands beneath his arms and tried lifting him. He slumped over, a dead weight. She ran around to grab his feet and pulled him inch by inch across the floor.

A man she didn't recognize rushed to her side. He was as muscular as he was tall. "I have him," he said.

The man lifted the bulky body off the floor with remarkable ease and flung him over his shoulder.

No sooner had he left than Mary Lou rushed into the room. Flames now shot up from the mattress. In the distance came the tinny sound of metal upon metal as the hotel clerk sounded the fire alarm, but in the time it would take for the volunteer firemen to arrive, it could be too late.

"Quick, the blanket!" Jenny yelled. She glanced around and grabbed the first thing she could find. It was only a threadbare towel, but it would have to do. She brandished the towel over her head and flung it down on the flames. The butt of a smoldering cheroot fell to the floor and she stomped it out.

Mary Lou threw the blanket across the bed in an effort to smother the fire but the blanket was too small to cover the entire mattress. Flames shot up the headboard, licking the wallpaper with long, fiery tongues.

With her hand covering her nose and mouth, Mary Lou grabbed a wool shirt from the floor and slapped it against the wall.

Jenny ran around the bed, beating the mattress with frantic swipes. Her throat raw, she coughed and her eyes watered. Despite her discomfort, the memory of Mary Lou walking hand in hand with a stranger was as persistent as the flames.

"Where were you and who was that . . . that man you were with?" she rasped.

"Not now, Jenny," Mary Lou grated, smacking a flare-up with a well-aimed swat.

"I want to know this minute," Jenny demanded, her voice hoarse. She batted a glowing ember. "Who is he?"

"My fiancé," Mary Lou rasped. "Are you happy?"

Stiff with shock, Jenny lowered her arm.

"Y–your fiancé?" A spark flared on a nearby upholstered chair, bringing her back to her senses. Wielding the towel, she extinguished the flame and then turned her attention to another.

"Who is he?" she demanded while clobbering flare-ups. She coughed before continuing. "How do you know him?"

"It doesn't matter."

"It matters to me."

"I love him," Mary Lou croaked.

Jenny stared at her sister from the opposite side of the charred mattress. Dear God. Here they go again.

"H–how do you know him?" Jenny repeated.

Mary Lou opened her mouth to say something but her words were garbled by a coughing spell. Her face red, she glared at Jenny with open defiance before finding her voice again.

"I met him that first day . . . when you and the marshal were arguing."

Jenny frowned. "And you never said anything. Not a word?"

"How could I?" Mary Lou cried. "You expect a man to be perfect —"

"Not perfect," Jenny argued, smothering the last flame. "I just want to make sure your future is secure. I promised Papa —"

"Promised him what?" Mary Lou choked out. "That I wouldn't marry a failure like him?"

Her angry retort hardened her features, and Jenny barely recognized the glowering mask of rage in front of her.

"How dare you say such a thing!"

"It's true. You know it is. He dragged us all over the country, chasing the next dream. If we hadn't moved so much, maybe Mama would still be alive."

"We don't know that Mama would still —"

"Yes, we do, Jenny. Everyone knew it. Even Grandfather. She had a bad heart. Traveling put a strain on her. You tried to hide Papa's faults as if we would love him any less if we knew what he was really like."

Mary Lou's claims sliced through the last of Jenny's defenses. It was true, all of it. She lied about their father, making him seem like a responsible parent, but only because she was afraid to confront her anger at him for leaving them destitute. Now it shocked her to think that the lies and half-truths had inadvertently sent the wrong message about love to her sisters.

Jenny swatted a glowing ember. "Papa loved us all very much."

Mary Lou stared, her features contorted

with disbelief. "Why is it so hard to admit that no one is perfect? That Papa wasn't? You think a person has to be perfect to be loved. But that's not true."

"I'm not looking for perfection."

"Yes you are! You want Brenda and me to be perfect ladies and to marry perfect men."

Mary Lou's words stung. If Jenny demanded perfection from others it was only because she saw so little of it in herself.

"I was wrong to make you feel that you had to be perfect to be loved," Jenny said. "And I should never have lied about Papa. He was charming and fun and he loved us all dearly, but . . ."

What she didn't say, couldn't say, was that the constant moves probably *had* hastened their mother's death.

"He was a thoughtless, reckless man who cared more for following his dreams than providing for his family!" Mary Lou spit the words out with such force that even the walls seemed to shrink from her anger.

Jenny's first instinct was to defend her father as she had done so many times in the past. Instead, she held her tongue and smothered a burning ember, but the painful memories of the past could not be so easily stifled.

"I don't want to talk about Papa. I want

to talk about you and that . . . that . . . Does this man even have a profession?"

"He's a logger." Mary Lou's mouth twisted in defiance. "Yes, you heard me right. He cuts down trees for a living. And no, he can't read or write because the letters keep bouncing, whatever that means, but I don't care. I love him and he loves me."

Can't read? Can't write? Bouncing letters? What in the world?

As distressing as all this was, she was more concerned about Mary Lou's behavior than the man's abilities or lack of them. First Brenda had sneaked off in the middle of the night to be with a man, now Mary Lou. Hadn't Jenny taught them better? Had she expected too much from them? Too little?

Frustrated that her efforts had been in vain, Jenny swatted the bed with angry strokes even after the last of the flames had died down.

Mary Lou matched her lash by lash, glare by glare. Jenny smacked the towel across the headboard. Mary Lou wielded the shirt upon the wall.

Whack.

Smack.

Thwack.

Slap.

They might have continued that way indefinitely had Redd Reeder not rushed into the room with a bucket of water and thoroughly drenched them both.

Later that same day, Jenny drove out of town in a rented buckboard, forcing the gelding to pick up speed the moment the road veered toward the river.

Not only was it hot, the acrid smell of smoke clung to her body and no amount of bathing could get rid of it. The hot sun, humidity, and dust only added to her discomfort.

No matter. She had other things on her mind. Namely one Mr. Jeff Trevor.

What kind of man would propose to a young woman without consulting with her family? *Can't read. Can't write. No manners. Drat!*

She hadn't seen or spoken to Mary Lou since the fire. Not that she was worried. There would be time enough later to try and talk some sense into her. Still, the argument left her depressed. Both Mary Lou and Brenda had accused her of trying to change them rather than love them for who they were. It wasn't true, of course. She did love her sisters, would always love them no matter what they did or who they married.

As far as changing them . . . Maybe she *had* gone overboard, but only because of her anxiety about the future. About *their* future.

Perhaps if she let up a bit, Mary Lou would be less inclined to rebel by marrying the first man she fancied. Encouraged by the thought, she urged the horse to go faster. The sooner she confronted Mr. Trevor and told him exactly what she thought of him and his proposal, the sooner she could drive back to town and make amends with her sister.

She barreled along the wooden bridge leading to the other side of the river and followed the dirt road to the sawmill. On one side of the bridge, the water was thick with logs. On the opposite side, a man on a flat-bottomed bateau guided the logs toward the landing with long metal-tipped staffs.

Just as she cleared the bridge, she thought she caught a glimpse of Scooter. She glanced back over her shoulder to have another look, but he was gone. She shook her head with disapproval. She hated to see the boy's fine mind wasted. Too bad Rocky Creek didn't have a school. Brenda insisted it did, but Jenny had yet to see one.

The mill consisted of several buildings. She drove past the one that appeared to be the bunkhouse, then pulled up in front of a stone and wood building with a silo-shaped sawdust burner attached.

A young man dressed in stagged pants cut to his knees and steel-caulked river boots greeted her. She guessed he was in his late teens. His dark skin glistened in the sun.

"Wouldn't park there if I was you, ma'am," he said.

He nodded toward a heavy wagon piled high with freshly cut lumber attached to a team of mules. Her buckboard blocked its way, but since the mule driver was absent, she set the brake and jumped to the ground.

"I understand Mr. Trevor works here."

The youth's eyes grew wide with curiosity. "He's the manager, ma'am."

"The manager?" A man who can't read or write?

"Yes, ma'am."

"I wish to speak with him."

At first she thought he would deny her request, but then he shrugged and said, "Wait here."

He walked away and disappeared into the building. She paced back and forth in front of a boom of logs waiting to be sawed into lumber. The air was thick with the smell of sawdust.

Several minutes passed before a man she

guessed was Mr. Trevor walked out of the building. When he drew near, she recognized him as the same man who'd rushed into the smoky room that morning and carried the near-unconscious man to safety.

He pulled his red cap off and greeted her with a nod. "You're Mary Lou's sister. If you're worried about Chester, he's doing fine."

"Chester?"

"The man who set his bed afire. Doc Myers plans to keep him a day or two for observation."

Caught off guard, she was momentarily speechless. In all the confusion following the fire, it never occurred to her that the man who rushed into the smoke-filled room that morning was Mary Lou's so-called fiancé.

"I'm happy to hear that," she managed, and because it seemed liked the proper thing to do, she thanked him for his help.

"No problem, ma'am. It was just plain luck that I happened to be in the neighborhood."

Luck? She studied him with cool regard. He really was pleasing to the eye. She could almost understand why Mary Lou had lost her head. Still, that was no excuse for sneaking behind a person's back.

"I appreciate your help, Mr. Trevor. What I *don't* appreciate is your disregard for common courtesy."

He quirked a dark eyebrow but said nothing, and she continued, "You had no right to propose marriage to my sister."

"Oh, I didn't propose marriage, ma'am. To propose means to suggest. I told her loud and clear on the first day we met that we were going to be married."

His arrogance astonished her, but not nearly as much as her sister's submission. Mary Lou hated being told what to do. Yet she allowed herself to fall for a man who did exactly that.

Refusing to be sidetracked by semantics, she continued, "Whatever you choose to call it, it's customary to consult with a young woman's guardian. That would be me."

He rubbed his chin. "Didn't see any sense in that, ma'am. I already knew you'd say no. I couldn't even fill out the application. A hog would have a better chance of meeting your requirements than me."

"But . . . you're the manager," she said. She glanced around. The mill was no small enterprise. To successfully operate such a business would require many different skills, certainly math, and possibly even the capacity to read.

He wrinkled his brow as if he found her surprise amusing. "I don't read books. I read trees. I can look at a tree and tell you exactly how to make it fall the way I want it to fall, how much lumber it will yield, and how much it will bring at market.

"I can read people too. That's how I knew the first day I saw Mary Lou that I wanted to marry her. She struck me as a woman who's not afraid to look truth in the face. I figured she wouldn't cotton to a man who beats around the bush, so I made sure she knew where I stood from the start."

"You knew that about her so soon?" Jenny hadn't even known that about her sister until recently. If she had, she would have been more honest with Mary Lou about their father and not tried to hide his shortcomings.

"Yes, ma'am. And you needn't worry about my ability to support your sister, if that's what's worrying you. She'll always have a roof over her head, food on the table, and those pretty clothes she's so fond of."

Oh, yes, she could see how he managed to turn her sister's head. She doubted Mary Lou had looked much past his blue eyes and winning smile. Certainly she never considered what it meant to be a logger's wife.

Since Mary Lou obviously couldn't see past his good looks, it was up to Jenny to put a stop to this madness.

"Mr. Trevor, you cannot marry my sister. It simply would not be in her best interests —"

"I plan to give her all the love and protection I have to give," he said.

She didn't miss the intensity of his voice or the blazing determination on his face. Shocked to find herself wavering, she fought to maintain her earlier stance.

"I don't doubt your sincerity, but —"

Before she had a chance to finish her thought, a male voice yelled, "Logjam!"

Suddenly the place came alive. Men ran from every direction. Downstream logs flipped out of the water like the wooden jackstraws of a children's game. They fell with a thud, spraying water upward. Someone started beating on a metal triangle.

Every muscle in Trevor's body seemed to come alive. "Get the flyboom," he bellowed. No sooner were the words out of his mouth than several men ran behind a building. They reappeared almost instantaneously, pulling a series of logs chained together.

Trevor bolted past her in the opposite direction of the logjam.

She was so intent on watching the activity

that it took her a moment to realize that it wasn't only the shouts of men issuing orders that filled the air. Someone was screaming for help.

Her mouth went dry. Something about the high-pitched cries turned her blood icy cold. She whirled around. *Scooter!*

TWENTY-FIVE

Never criticize your beau. If it wasn't for
his faults he'd probably be courting
someone else.
— MISS ABIGAIL JENKINS, 1875

Jenny hiked up her skirts and raced to the
bridge. Heart pounding, she gasped for air.

Scooter leaned so far over the wooden
railing, she feared he would fall. She
grabbed him by the back of his shirt and
pulled him away.

"Scooter, what is it?"

He gripped the rail hard, his knuckles
white. "Jasooon!"

She scanned the surface of the water. In
the middle of the river, a boy clung to a log
floating downstream. Jenny stared at the
child in horror. The boy was in terrible
danger of being crushed in the logjam.

Trevor stood knee deep in water shouting
instructions. Further upstream, several pile

drivers ran along the water's edge. Men with long poles worked frantically to guide fast-moving logs away from the boy.

Jason's log hit another and whirled about, but he hung on tight.

"I told him not to ride the logs," Scooter sobbed. A shudder ran through his thin body. She hugged him with one arm. He stiffened beneath her touch but didn't pull away.

"It's all right," she said soothingly. "Mr. Trevor will save him." *Dear God, let that be true.*

"Hold on, Jason," she shouted. "Hold on." Hand on her mouth, she prayed — prayed like she hadn't prayed in years. *God, please, please, please don't let anything happen to Scooter's brother.*

Men frantically worked to push back the logs. Others ran to join them, dragging ropes and chains. Jason's log crashed against another and then another. It spun around in circles and headed for several logs bound together. Jason was perilously close to being crushed in between.

"Let go!" Trevor bellowed. "Let go of the log."

The boy held on.

Scooter pulled away from her. He cupped his hands around his mouth and yelled, "Jason, let go of the log. Swim!"

At the last possible moment, Jason let go and splashed around frantically in a dog paddle.

Trevor dove into the river, his arms and legs breaking the water with strong kicks and swift strokes. Never had she seen anyone swim so fast. Even so, the distance between him and the boy seemed insurmountable.

Jason struggled to swim ashore but he wasn't strong enough to fight the current. Visibly tiring, his arms slowed until they barely moved.

"Swim!" Scooter yelled.

Encouraged by his brother's voice, Jason made one last attempt to stay afloat before his head sank beneath the surface.

Jenny gasped then held her breath in horror.

Scooter let out a bloodcurdling scream. "Noooooooooo!" His arms shot up teepee style, but before he could dive into the water, she grabbed hold of him. "No, Scooter, no." The last thing Trevor needed was to have to rescue two boys.

He fought her but she held on tight. Digging his fingers into her arms, he crumbled down until he was on his knees, sobbing.

She scanned the water anxiously. Several

logs forged together, blocking Trevor's progress. He disappeared beneath the surface. Her gaze weaved in and out of logs but she saw no sign of him. Minutes passed. Hours. Or was it only seconds?

At last, Trevor's head bobbed up and he raised a single arm. Applause sounded from both sides of the river followed by whoops and hollers. It took a moment before Jenny realized that two heads were in the water.

She almost fainted with relief. "Look, Scooter, look!"

Scooter moved his hands away from his face. "Is Jason — ?"

"Yes, yes, he's safe." She lifted her eyes to heaven. "Thank you, thank you, God!"

Jenny tugged on Scooter's arm, helping him to his feet, and together they watched Trevor swim with the boy to the river's edge. Several men rushed to take Jason out of Trevor's arms and carry him to dry land.

"Let's go," she sang out. "Come on."

Scooter raced across the bridge ahead of her, his bare feet seeming to fly. Already a crowd had gathered around the younger boy.

"Jason, Jason!" Scooter pushed his way past the men and skidded on his knees to his brother's side.

Jason's blue lips trembled, but he was

awake and responsive. He coughed and a stream of water trickled from his mouth. Though Jason was four years younger than Scooter, the two boys were similar in appearance. They even had a similar sprinkle of freckles.

Trevor attempted to put Scooter's mind at rest with a wink. "He'll be fine." He then set to work pulling off Jason's wet clothes. Both Jason's arms were bruised and one side of his face scratched, but otherwise he seemed okay. After making certain there were no serious injuries, Trevor wrapped Jason in someone's dry shirt.

"That was some ride you took," Trevor said. "Bet you won't try that again."

"I'd say he's one lucky fella," said a tall, muscular man. He stuck out an iron hook. "See this, boy? Lost my hand while ridin' a log."

Jason stared at the hook with saucer-wide eyes.

Trevor called out to one of the men in the distance. "We need a blanket."

Someone held a canteen to Jason's lips and he took a swallow.

Jenny kneeled next to Scooter, her hand on his back. He was trembling and her heart went out to him.

Jenny backed away to give Trevor more

room to work. Something blue caught her eye next to the bushes that separated the river from the main road. It looked like . . .

She blinked. *No, no, it can't be. Please don't let that be Mary Lou's skirt.*

Trying not to seem obvious, she inched her way toward the row of bushes. A high-button shoe lay on its side next to a ruffled white petticoat. No doubt about it; Mary Lou was up to her old tricks again and had resumed her scandalous habit of swimming with nothing on.

Jenny seethed with anger. First, Mary Lou sneaks out of their hotel room to be with a man. Now this. Oh, the shame, the shame. What would the girl do next?

Jenny glanced at the men. They all stood facing Jason with their backs turned toward her. So far no one else had noticed the shocking display of woman's apparel spread out in plain sight. Nor did anyone suspect the nearby presence of her stark-naked sister.

She quickly scanned the nearby bushes. Mary Lou ducked, but not soon enough. "Stay down," Jenny hissed.

Keeping a watchful eye on Trevor and his men, she quickly gathered Mary Lou's clothes and tossed them into the bushes. That girl would be the death of her yet.

She moved back to Scooter's side just as someone came running up with a blanket. Trevor unfolded it and wrapped it around Jason. The boy had stopped shaking, but he still looked alarmingly pale.

Trevor made a funny face and Jason gave a wan smile. "I'm gonna take you to see Doc Myers. We want to make sure everything's okay."

Scooter wiped the tears from his cheeks with the palm of his hands. "We ain't got money for no doctor."

"Don't worry," Jenny said. She had every intention of paying whatever bills were incurred.

Trevor looked up at her. "It happened at the sawmill. I reckon that makes it my responsibility." Without further ado, he lifted Jason into his arms and carried him to the nearby horse and wagon one of his workers had supplied.

"All right, men. Get to work. We got ourselves a logjam."

The men picked up their equipment and raced away. The bridge shook and groaned beneath the hammering of caulked boots as the men hastened across to the other side.

After Trevor placed Jason into the back of the wagon, he swung into the driver's seat and picked up the reins with one hand. Waving at Jenny with the other, he called, "See you at my wedding."

"Your . . . ?" Jenny's mouth dropped open, but she couldn't help but smile. The nerve of the man. Despite her reservations, she liked him, liked the way he handled Jason, liked the way the other men seemed to respect him. She especially liked the way he looked upon mentioning Mary Lou's name.

She remembered something Reverend Wells had said. *Sometimes God brings couples together for His own purpose.*

It would be interesting to know God's purpose in bringing this particular couple together. Mr. Trevor had no idea what he was getting himself into. Surprised by the thought, she shook her head. A match made in heaven? Hardly.

She ran her hand across Scooter's back. "My wagon's next to the silo. Wait for me there and I'll drive you back to town. I don't know about you, but I'm hungry."

A sudden brightness flickered across his face, but he left without saying a word.

She waited for Scooter to cross the bridge before she turned toward the bushes where her sister still hid. "You can come out now."

Mary Lou stepped out, slapping branches away from her face. She was fully dressed.

Her wet hair hung in long limp strands down her back. She looked a mess but no less defiant.

"Why were you at the mill?" she fumed, hands on her waist.

"Me?" Jenny fought to control her anger. "Why are *you* here? Swimming like . . . like some common tramp. What if someone had seen you?"

Mary Lou showed no sign of backing down. "I was upset and hot and . . . The swimming hole is well hidden. No one saw me."

"*I* saw you."

"How was I supposed to know that you and everyone else would come running over to this side of the river?" Mary Lou covered her face with both hands. "You had no right to come here. No right at all."

"I talked to Mr. Trevor," Jenny said calmly.

Mary Lou dropped her hands to her side. "I don't care what you say, I love him and he loves me."

"That does not excuse your disgraceful behavior."

"Don't say it." Mary Lou covered both ears with her hands. "I don't want to hear it!" She stomped away and Jenny chased after her. She grabbed her by the shoulder and swung her around.

Mary Lou glared at her. "How could you? You've ruined everything!"

"We need to talk."

"I'm not talking to you. Not ever again."

Scooter drove up in the wagon. As if sensing the tension in the air, he stopped and his expression stilled.

"We'll discuss this later," Jenny said. She nodded toward Scooter, hoping her sister would take the hint.

Mary Lou opened her mouth to argue then changed her mind. She stormed to the wagon without another word.

Jenny was still furious with her, of course. Why wouldn't she be? Sneaking out in the middle of the night. Swimming in the altogether. As for the match, naturally she had reservations. Anyone who knew Mary Lou would have concerns.

Still, she couldn't help but think that something was at work here over which she had no control. God's plan?

Was that why she had such difficulty finding suitable husbands? Did God also have a hand in that misprint that brought her to Rocky Creek in the first place? Was it possible that Sarah was right? That God really did have a plan for bringing people together?

Dear God, please let it be true.

Startled to find herself talking to God

several times in the course of a single hour, she climbed onto the wagon seat and took over the reins.

Mary Lou didn't say a word on the way back to town. She sat with her arms folded and glowered. The moment they reached the livery stable, she jumped out of the wagon and ran to the hotel. That was just as well. Jenny was in no mood to deal with her. Not yet. At the moment, she was more interested in the welfare of the Maxwell brothers.

"Is she mad because you caught her swimmin' naked?" Scooter asked.

Alarmed, Jenny glanced around to make sure no one else heard. She then gave him a stern look. "How do you know . . . Never mind, don't answer that. I don't want to know." She stepped off the boardwalk and started across the street toward the café.

"Come along. Let's go and eat. I'm famished."

A short while later, Jenny sat watching Scooter gobble down everything Redd put in front of him.

"That boy eats more than a dozen cowhands," Redd said, looking pleased. He obviously considered the boy's ferocious appetite a compliment to his cooking.

Scooter didn't talk much, and when she

385

questioned him about his father, he clammed up completely.

This worried her. The boy was protecting his father, but from what? The two boys were neglected, that much was clear. The question was, were they also physically abused? Judging by the way Scooter tightened up when she hugged him earlier, she feared she already knew the answer.

"Come on, I'll take you home," she said. Maybe she could talk to his father, though she doubted it would do any good. If nothing else, perhaps she could get a better idea what kind of home life the boys had.

No sooner had they stepped outside than Scooter let out a strangled cry.

Alarmed, she touched his arm. "Scooter?"

All the blood had drained from his face. Following his gaze, she stared at a man staggering toward them.

"Where you been, boy?" the man demanded, his eyes hard as stone. It was obvious from his slurred words he'd been drinking, if he wasn't altogether drunk.

Before Scooter could answer, she stepped in front of him. "I'm Jenny Higgins." She held out her hand, but the man ignored it.

"Matt Maxwell," he spit out.

So this was Scooter's father. A tall thin man with a bushy beard and balding head, the only resemblance to his sons was the poor condition of his clothes.

"Git your butt home, boy. You got chores."

She grabbed on to Scooter's arm to prevent him from leaving.

"Your son Jason almost drowned today. He suffered some minor injuries and he's at the doctor's —"

Maxwell glared at Scooter. "What did you do now? I told you to stay out of trouble." He took an unsteady step forward, hand raised. Next to her, Scooter cowered.

The man's hand came down, but Jenny stayed it with a swing of her parasol. Caught off balance, Maxwell fell back. Surprise soon turned to rage, and his eyes glowered dangerously.

"What gives you the right to go interferin' in other people's bithness?"

Seething with anger, she glared back at him. "I just told you that your youngest son was injured, and you didn't so much as ask how he was. What kind of father are you?"

"You know nothin' 'bout me."

"I know that you neglect and mistreat your sons," she sputtered. "I don't need to know anything more."

His lip curled upward. "You're jus' like the rest of 'em. You fink it's eathy takin' care of two boyth? Let me tell you somfin', lady, it ain't eathy."

"No one ever said it *was*." Her voice thin with anger, she stared straight at him. A crowd had gathered around, but she didn't care. "You do what you have to do. You care for them; you love them. You don't always get it right. Sometimes you're so afraid to let them fail that you try to do too much." *Like telling them who they can and cannot wed.* Talking more to herself than to him, she added, "In the end, they've got to know that everything you did or tried to do was out of love."

"I think they know that." Rhett stood a few feet away, looking at her with an odd expression. How long he'd been standing there, she didn't know, but she was glad to see him.

"About t–time you got here, Marshal," Maxwell slurred. "Thith woman athalted me. Arrest her."

Rhett glanced at Scooter, then at the damaged parasol Jenny held at her side. He shrugged. "It looks like a clear case of self-defense to me," he said.

He held up a paper. "I have an order here signed by the honorable Judge Fassbender to remove Scooter and Jason Maxwell from your custody and place them with another family."

Tears stung Jenny's eyes. In the past, neglected or abused children were put in orphanages. It had only been in recent years that the Societies for the Prevention of Cruelty to Children advocated placement with families.

Maxwell's face turned white. "You can't take my boys away," he said. The news seemed to have a sobering effect as he hardly slurred his words.

"I just did," Rhett said. He folded the paper and turned to Scooter. "Reverend and Mrs. Wells have agreed to let you and your brother stay with them until your father has time to work things out."

Afraid to take her eyes off Maxwell, Jenny held her breath. She wasn't certain how he would react to the news, but he surprised her. Instead of turning violent, he gave his son a spiteful look.

"Good riddance," he said, wiping the back of his hand across his mouth.

Without another word, he turned and staggered toward the nearest saloon.

Jenny turned to Scooter. The boy's stricken face drove a nail in her heart. "He didn't mean that," she said. "It was the alcohol talking, not him."

"It don't matter none," Scooter said.

But it did. It did. She could tell by the

look on his face that it mattered more than he was willing to admit. He would never forget his father's hurtful words, but she prayed to God he would one day forgive them.

Rhett laid a hand on Scooter's shoulder. "Come on, son," he said.

Later that afternoon, after Rhett had fetched Jason from Doc Myers's, he drove both boys out to the pastor's house. Sarah Wells greeted them with a wide smile and ushered them into the cozy cabin they called home.

Holding his young daughter in one arm, Reverend Wells reached out to shake Rhett's hand with the other. "Welcome."

Sarah turned her attention to the two boys. Rhett had done his best to calm their fears, but Jason still looked pale and shaken by his earlier ordeal. Scooter just looked sullen. While Sarah tried to make Jason and Scooter feel at home, Rhett looked around.

He couldn't believe what they'd done to the place since he'd last stepped foot in it. Originally built with only two rooms, the cabin now had an additional bedroom that the boys would share.

A colorful rag rug centered in front of a woodstove provided a cheerful contrast to the dark wooden floor. The room was modestly furnished with table and chairs and a plain wooden bench. A small cot that appeared to be Elizabeth's bed was pushed against one wall.

Blue gingham curtains hung from the windows. Colorful flowers from Sarah's garden cascaded out of canning jars. A child's rocking horse stood next to a half-built woodblock tower. The bright cheery colors and scattered toys filled him with longing. His room at Ma's boardinghouse was adequate and, some might say, even cheerful, but it was lonely and stark and lacked the warmth of the preacher's home. Much to Rhett's surprise, he found himself wanting more.

"You can call me Mrs. Bumble Rumble," Sarah was saying to the boys. "Don't tell me your names. Let me guess." She tapped a finger on her chin while she studied Jason.

"I know. You must be Bronco Buster Picklepiper, and you . . ." She turned to Scooter, "You must be Chuckleberry Scooterdoodle."

Justin giggled and Elizabeth laughed. Scooter tried to maintain his serious expression, but even he couldn't suppress his smile for long.

Rhett relaxed. At first he hesitated to accept Sarah and Justin's generous offer to care for the boys. Not only did the preacher watch over Marshal Owen's widow and three children, but he and Sarah also had their hands full with Elizabeth and an infant on the way. Rhett couldn't imagine how they would manage two more. Since no other family offered to give the boys a home, he finally relented despite his reservations. Now he was glad that he had.

"Come along Mr. Picklepiper and Mr. Scooterdoodle," Sarah sang out. "I'll show you to your room." She winked at Rhett before herding the boys into the next room.

At Elizabeth's insistence, Justin set her down and she ran after them as fast as her little feet could carry her. "Wait for me."

Rhett was grateful for the opportunity to talk to the preacher in private. "I can't tell you how much I appreciate your help."

"It was Sarah's idea," Justin said. He pointed to the wooden bench. "Have a seat." He swung a chair away from the table and sat opposite Rhett. "What's going to happen to Maxwell?"

Rhett glanced toward the door of the bedroom to make certain the boys were out of hearing range. "I've got a warrant for his arrest for child neglect," he said, keeping his voice low. It took weeks of badgering the county sheriff and judge, but it was worth the effort. "I didn't want to arrest him in front of his sons."

Justin gave a grave nod. "I'd like to talk to him."

"It won't do any good until he's sober."

"I'll wait."

"What makes you think he'll listen?" Rhett asked. The preacher had talked to Maxwell many times before. They both had, and it had done no good.

"This time, there's more at stake."

How Rhett wished that were true. "When I informed him that I was taking his boys away, he showed no remorse." The memory of Maxwell's cruel words to his son sickened him.

Pastor Wells didn't look the least bit surprised. "Grief can separate us from God. It happened to the disciples Peter and John. If you recall, they didn't recognize Jesus after He rose from the dead. I believe it was because they were blinded by grief. Anything that keeps us from God keeps us from our loved ones." Justin looked Rhett square in the face. "Grief's not the only thing that keeps us from God. Guilt does that too."

They were no longer talking about Maxwell or even his sons. Rhett shifted uneasily in his seat. He now wished he hadn't been so forthright in telling the preacher he had accidentally caused his friend's death.

"God and I are on good terms," he said. "I go to church. I pray and read the Bible."

"A lot of people go to church and read the Bible. Doesn't mean they have a good relationship with God. Going through the motions doesn't mean it's coming from the heart."

The pastor's words sent a jolt through him. Is that what he was doing? Going through the motions? "I never blamed God for what happened. I blame myself."

"There are many ways to separate one's self from God," Pastor Wells said. "One way is to keep from loving and being loved by His people."

Rhett didn't know what to say. He hated to contradict the preacher but it just wasn't true. Okay, maybe it was in the past but no more. If it had been, he wouldn't have gotten so involved with the Maxwell boys.

Wells regarded him thoughtfully, not as a preacher but as a friend. "Sarah thinks you're in love with Jenny Higgins."

Jolted, Rhett was momentarily speechless. To hear it so plainly stated by another was a shock. He didn't know what to say.

Wells didn't let the silence last for long. "I hope you don't let your guilt for what happened to your friend keep you from acting on your feelings."

He shook his head. "It's not me. I've tried to get close to Jenny, but she keeps pushing me away."

"Are you sure about that?"

Rhett frowned. "What do you mean?"

"I sense that you still think yourself undeserving of love or forgiveness. That you're still hiding behind your guilt."

"That's not true."

Wells gave him a sharp look. "Isn't it?"

Rhett shook his head. "Now you sound like Ma."

"Oh?"

"She said there's a difference between godly sorrow and guilt."

Wells smiled fondly. "Sometimes I think Ma's a better preacher than I am."

Despite his earlier denial, Rhett wondered if what the pastor said was true. Maybe he *was* still hiding behind his guilt. Perhaps deep down he wanted Jenny to reject him as proof of his unworthiness.

He was still mulling that possibility when Sarah returned with the children. Shaken, he stood to leave. He suddenly needed to be alone.

"You're welcome to stay for dinner, Marshal," Sarah said.

"Thank you, but I . . . have some business to attend to." That was partially true as he intended to arrest Maxwell before the day was over.

Bidding the boys good-bye, he left. He drove the wagon slowly back to the livery stable. It was hard to know what weighed more heavily on his mind — the thought that he'd been holding back from Jenny and maybe even God, or the burden of having to arrest Jason and Scooter's father again, this time for child neglect.

TWENTY-SIX

Never fall victim to fashion's tyranny
unless it enhances, flatters, and, at the
very least, dazzles your intended.
— MISS ABIGAIL JENKINS, 1875

"My life is ruined!" Mary Lou wailed. She sat in the bathtub and covered her face with both hands. "Ruined, do you hear? Ruined!"

Jenny dumped a pitcher of water down her sister's back. "I'm sure the whole town heard," she muttered. Certainly everyone in the hotel did.

Covered from head to toe in poison ivy, Mary Lou hadn't stopped complaining since the first spot appeared following her ill-fated swim. One eye was swollen shut, and blisters oozed on her arms and legs. The toxic plant evidently surrounded the old swimming hole, which probably explained why no one swam there anymore.

Jenny did everything Doc Myers told her

to do, but nothing seemed to stop the itching —or Mary Lou's incessant complaints.

"My life is ruined," Mary Lou cried again.

One of the other hotel guests pounded on the wall and shouted a string of obscenities. "Can't a body git some sleep 'round here?"

Brenda lay on the bed, a pillow over her head.

It was nearly 1:00 a.m. and Jenny was exhausted. She set the pitcher on the stand and grabbed a towel. "Get out of the bath, and I'll put more salve on you."

"It won't do any good," Mary Lou blubbered. "My life is ruined."

"It's not ruined," Jenny said. Her voice thick with impatience, she stifled a yawn. "By your wedding day, you'll be as good as new."

Mary Lou pulled her hands away from her swollen face. "What wedding?"

Jenny sighed in resignation. She no longer had the strength or inclination to fight what she now believed to be inevitable. "*Your* wedding to Mr. Trevor, of course." Still angry at Mary Lou for sneaking behind her back, she nevertheless felt sorry for her. "I like him. I like him a lot."

Mary Lou's mouth dropped open. "You *like* him?" she asked aghast. "Even if he can't read or write?"

"One has nothing to do with the other," Jenny said. She made some inquiries around town, and everyone from Mr. Barrel to Mr. Fairbanks had nothing but good things to say about him. At this point, however, she was desperate enough to approve Mary Lou's marriage to that outlaw Jesse James in return for peace and quiet.

"He's a good man and I believe he loves you very much."

Mary Lou stared with her one good eye. "He loves *me?* Someone who's *not* perfect? Is such a thing possible?"

Jenny chose to ignore Mary Lou's sarcasm. "Of course it's possible. You're a beautiful woman. Your Mr. Trevor is a lucky man."

"But, but —" Mary Lou dropped her hands in the tub, splashing water on to the floor, and stared at Jenny in disbelief. "What about Miss Jenkins and those interviews and that silly test?"

Jenny twisted the towel in her hand. In retrospect, it all did seem rather silly. "It's come to my attention that there's another marriage expert I'd not considered."

Mary Lou groaned and drove her fist against the tub's tin side. "Not another instruction book."

"This one I think you'll approve," Jenny

said. "It's the Bible, and it does not demand perfection."

Mary Lou gaped at her. "You mean we don't have to act like ladies anymore?"

"You most definitely *do* have to act like ladies," Jenny said with mock gravity. "You just don't have to be *perfect*."

Mary Lou's face grew still. "What you said about Jeff . . ." She swiped at a tear with her fingertip. "Did you mean it? Do you really like him?"

"I like him a lot." Jenny glanced at Brenda, who had crawled to the foot of the bed to be closer to them. "I like *both* your young men."

Brenda rewarded her with a beautiful smile.

Jenny turned back to her poor sister, and her heart softened. Mary Lou looked so miserable Jenny could no longer hold on to her anger. "Will you ever forgive me for giving you such a hard time?"

Mary Lou stared at her for a moment before reaching for her hand and squeezing it. "Only if you forgive me for all the trouble I've caused you."

Surprised but, more than anything, touched by Mary Lou's apology, Jenny smiled. "Forgiven and forgotten." She held the towel up with both hands.

"You better get out before you catch your death of cold." Not that there was much chance of that in this heat.

Mary Lou stood, but before climbing out of the tub she caught sight of herself in the mirror. A look of horror crossed her face, followed by a piercing scream. "My life is ruined!"

Someone pounded on the wall and yelled out in a rough voice. "If you don't shut up, I'll personally see to it that your life is ruined for good!"

Jenny threw the towel around her sister and wrapped her in it. "Enough," she ordered, her patience spent. "Not another word or I'll take back every nice thing I said about your Mr. Trevor!"

It was nearly 3:00 a.m. before Mary Lou calmed down enough to fall asleep.

Though Jenny was tired, her mind remained active.

She sat at the desk and opened the Bible Sarah had given her. She read and reread several of the verses Reverend Wells had marked. *God is love,* she read, and the words washed over her like a warm tide.

She thumbed through the pages until she found the verse she studied daily. *The Lord's plan shall prevail.*

She closed the Bible and leaned her head

401

against the back of the chair. God certainly seemed to have a hand in planning her sisters' futures. There simply was no other way to explain the way things worked out.

But what about Scooter and Jason? What were God's plans for them? *And what plans do You have for me, Lord?*

So many questions. So many things she didn't know, didn't understand.

The acrid smell of smoke drifted through the open window. Fortunately, the fire damage was confined to only the one room. Jenny had no idea what they would have done had the hotel burned down.

Hands on her face, she sighed. It had been an exhausting yet oddly exhilarating day. True, nothing had worked out as she had hoped. Yet in some strange way, things had worked out beyond her wildest expectations.

Mr. Trevor was kindhearted and certainly pleasing to the eye. Mr. Barrel had a puppy-dog quality that was hard to resist. Both men were churchgoing Christians. Most important, both were obviously head over heels in love. Her sisters were in good hands.

Jenny was happy for them though she couldn't help but feel envious. How would it feel to be loved by a man? To be cherished and protected by him? A man willing to forgive the past. A man who loved her and wanted to care for her.

Tears burned her eyes. God loved her. That's what the Bible said. Even if she *was* far from perfect.

But no earthly being could be expected to forgive what she had done to protect and care for her sisters, not even Rhett Armstrong. Stunned by the thought, she shook her head. *Now where did that come from?*

Oh, she knew, she knew. She could deny it all she wanted, but she knew. She had fallen in love with the marshal. It was the only way to explain her throbbing pulse whenever he came near . . . the way her body trembled when he so much as walked past her window. She knew what time he left his office at night, what time he arrived in the morning. She'd gotten so good at tracking his comings and goings, she could pick out the sound of his horse's hooves passing the hotel.

She shook the thought away. Mustn't think about him. It wouldn't do any good and it only deepened her pain. Must concentrate on her sisters. She had a double wedding to plan. Yes, yes, that's what she must focus on.

When she was actively pursuing her plans, she didn't have time to think about the past or anything else. Idle hands not only led to bad memories, but thoughts of Rhett and all the things she could never have. As long as she made lists, as long as she filled every moment with preparations, as long as she maintained a tight schedule, then and only then could she keep thoughts of Rhett at bay.

At the first light of dawn, she rose from the bed and rushed to her desk to grab her notebook. She'd hardly slept a wink, but she was anxious to work on the wedding invitations.

She reached across the desk to grab her pen. In her haste, she knocked the copy of *The Compleat and Authoritative Manual for Attracting and Procuring a Husband* on the floor. She stooped to pick it up. The book was written by Miss — *Miss!* — Abigail Jenkins. Probably a spinster!

She leafed through the dog-eared volume. Definitely a spinster. All the rules for choosing a husband and not one of them correct. Not one! Sarah was absolutely right. Jenny had been referring to the wrong book.

With a disgusted sigh, she tossed the book across the room. Instead of landing in the wastebasket as she intended, it bounced on the sill and flew out the open window.

A voice cried out from the street below.

"Oh!" Fearing she'd caused injury, she

flung herself to the window.

Miss Emma Hogg stood directly below, looking none the worse for wear. Holding the book with one hand, she flipped the pages with the other.

Jenny leaned out of the window to apologize, but before she had a chance, the spinster stuffed the manual in her basket, looked around as if to make certain no one had seen her, and hurried away.

Jenny shook her head. Poor Miss Hogg. She probably thought the book was a gift from heaven.

She considered warning Redd, the spinster's likely target, but decided against it. He was in no danger of losing his membership in The Society for the Protection and Preservation of Male Independence. Not as long as Miss Hogg followed Miss Jenkins's advice.

Rhett swung open the door separating his office from the jail cells. Earlier he'd summoned Doc Myers to examine Maxwell and the doctor had spent an hour with the prisoner. Now he stepped into Rhett's office with a grave nod and set his leather bag on the desk. White shirt rolled up at the sleeves, he drew out a handkerchief and mopped his sweaty forehead. He was clean-shaven except for his muttonchop side-burns, his hair parted in the middle.

"What do you think?" Rhett asked.

Myers pocketed his handkerchief and leaned against the desk, arms folded. The town's doctor had two different colored eyes, one blue and the other brown, the result of a childhood carriage accident.

"I think it's going to take a long time for him to dry out."

It wasn't the answer Rhett wanted. "What about a cure?"

"For alcoholism?" The doctor raised a dubious brow.

Rhett knew as well anyone that no easy cures existed for dipsomania or alcoholism, as it was called since the war, but they had to try. "I read about a doctor who chloroforms his patients. He keeps them unconscious until they dry out."

The doctor shook his head, obviously disapproving of such methods. "There are all kinds of so-called cures," he said. "Colloidal gold is the end-all cure at the moment. Far as I know, success is mixed at best."

Rhett grimaced in frustration. "We've got to do something."

"Nothing we do medically or otherwise will work unless Maxwell wants it to."

"He hasn't got a choice," Rhett said, his voice brusque. The memory of Maxwell's hateful words still rang in his ears. "He's got two sons."

"He has to want the cure, and he has to want it with everything he's got," the doctor insisted. "That's the only way he's going to stop drinking." He reached for his bag and started for the door. "I'll check him again tomorrow. How long do you plan to keep him locked up?"

Rhett slammed a fist into his open palm. "For however long it takes him to want the cure with everything he's got."

The next week was a nightmare that left Jenny ready to scream. Mary Lou refused to see anyone, including Trevor. She wouldn't even leave the room for meals.

She moaned, groaned, and did nothing but complain. Even Brenda's usual good nature was pushed to the limits.

Jenny was so desperate, she even tried to rent an extra room so that she and Brenda could get a decent night's sleep, but no rooms were available.

One afternoon someone banged on their door. Before Jenny had a chance to open it, Jeff Trevor burst into the room. Too startled to offer an objection, Jenny could only stare as he stormed to the bed, which Mary Lou refused to leave.

"Get dressed!" he ordered.

Mary Lou tried to hide under the covers, but he yanked the blanket away.

"Don't look at me," she cried.

Jenny's mouth dropped open. How dare he bully her sister! "Mr. Trevor, you may be her fiancé, but that does not give you the right to —"

Brenda stopped her. "Let him take her."

Jenny started to protest, but Brenda grabbed her by the arm and pulled her away from the bed. "I need the rest," she pleaded. "We both do."

No further argument was necessary. Peace and quiet was too much of a temptation for Jenny to pass up.

Trevor sat on the bed by Mary Lou's side and gently pulled her hands away from her face.

"Don't," Mary Lou pleaded, turning her head away. "I look horrible."

"You look beautiful." Fingers curved beneath her chin, he forced her to look up at him. This time Mary Lou didn't fight him, but whether from surprise or surrender, Jenny didn't know.

Most of the swelling had gone down, but she was still covered with pink bumps.

"I'm going to look at you," he said, "and I plan to keep looking at you for the rest of my born days."

No sooner were the words out of his mouth than the most amazing transition occurred. Mary Lou's face brightened as if lit from an inner source, and her mouth curved in a wide, open smile. Jenny couldn't remember her ever looking more beautiful.

It was amazing. Not only was Trevor capable of managing sawmill emergencies, but he handled Mary Lou with the ease of a gentle breeze. Any lingering doubts Jenny had about the couple's suitability vanished along with Mary Lou's bad mood.

Brenda looked pleased with herself. "Aren't you glad you listened to me?"

Jenny smiled. Glad didn't begin to describe how she felt. Both sisters knew enough to follow their hearts and find God's plan for them. For that she would always be grateful.

As soon as Trevor left with Mary Lou, Jenny and Brenda fell into bed for some much-needed sleep.

In early July, Jenny woke to a shrill voice. "Extra, extra. Read all about it!"

Racing to the window, she lifted the sash and stuck her head outside. "What happened?"

Scooter gazed up at her, a canvas bag of newspapers slung on his back. Sarah and her husband had done a remarkable job in caring for him and his brother.

His shirt, trousers, and boots were obviously new and his hair neatly combed; he looked quite handsome. Grown-up, even. He and Jason were already attending Rocky Creek's unofficial school and nothing pleased Jenny more.

Now he called up to her. "President Garfield was shot."

"Oh, no!" Garfield had only been in office for four months. "Is he dead?"

Scooter shook his head. "No, but he's hurt bad."

"Save me a paper," she said. "I'll be right down." She then hurried to get dressed.

By the time she ran downstairs for a paper, the shocking news had spread through town like wildfire.

Garfield's condition was all anyone talked about for the next several days. Even Brenda and Mary Lou's upcoming double wedding played second fiddle to the president. He was still alive, the bullet lodged somewhere in his chest. No one knew where, exactly, and how to locate the slug without causing further damage was the subject of much debate.

One night Jenny lay in her bed staring at the ceiling. She envied her sisters the ability to sleep in the stifling heat.

Loud voices rose from the street below. Jenny grimaced. Not again. Since the president had been shot, everyone was suddenly an expert in human anatomy.

"Those White House doctors don't know beans," someone shouted. "They should take that bullet out!"

"I say leave it in," came another voice.

It was a growing controversy and everyone had an opinion. Even a man named Bell wanted to use his new telephone contraption to locate the bullet.

The argument escalated.

"Break it up!"

Hearing Rhett's voice, Jenny's breath caught in her chest. She slipped out of bed and ran to the window.

The men scattered, their voices fading in the distance. Only Rhett remained. He stood in the middle of the street, hands at his waist, looking up at her window. Though the room was dark and she was certain he couldn't see her, she backed away. Heart pounding, she pressed her body against the wall.

She closed her eyes, shutting in the hot tears that gathered there. She imagined herself going to him. She imagined him kissing her like he kissed her twice before. Only this time, the kiss would be for all the right reasons.

The Lord has a plan.

For me, God? For me? Even after everything I've done?

Wanting it so much to be true, she looked out the window again, thinking to call to him. Thinking to ask him to wait till she got dressed. Thinking to beg him to forgive her past sins enough to love her.

But he was already gone.

For the last couple of weeks Rhett had worked nonstop to help Maxwell, but to no avail. The stubborn fool refused to admit he had a drinking problem, let alone a need for a cure.

Reverend Wells had spent long hours at the jailhouse counseling Maxwell. He prayed for him and read from the Bible — all which seemed to fall on deaf ears. Even Doc Myers had lost hope that anything could be done for the man.

Late one afternoon Rhett was sitting at his desk when Scooter walked into his office. At first, Rhett didn't recognize the boy in his new clothes. He'd even put on some weight, or at least his face looked less gaunt. Rhett couldn't thank the preacher and his wife enough for the care and love they had shown the Maxwell boys.

"Is it okay if I see my pa?" he asked.

Rhett hesitated. No good would come out of such a visit. Maxwell's withdrawal symptoms had subsided in recent days, but he was still belligerent. Scooter was likely to end up more hurt than he already was.

"Give it a couple more days," Rhett said. "I'll let you know when he's ready."

Scooter's gaze flickered toward the door leading to the cells in back, but he said nothing. He simply nodded and left.

Rhett stared at the door long after Scooter was gone. He then grabbed a chair, reached for the cell keys, and walked through the door leading to the jail.

He placed the chair in front of Maxwell's cell and sat.

Maxwell lifted his head. "Get out of here. I want to be alone. I ain't listenin' to any more of your lectures."

Rhett remained seated and said nothing.

"Get out of here. Do you hear me?"

When that got no response, Maxwell shook the bars, yelling for him to leave at the top of his lungs. When that didn't work, he picked up a cot and threw it. It hit the bars and fell to the floor with a hollow clang. He kicked the mattress out of the way, screaming obscenities. The cussing went on for close to an hour before he crumbled to the floor, holding his head.

After a long silence, he looked up. "What do you know about it? You never buried a wife."

They were the first civil words out of Maxwell's mouth since he was jailed, and Rhett felt a flicker of hope. "You're right. I never did. But I did bury a friend."

"Not the same."

"No, I'm sure it's not. But the guilt is similar."

Maxwell studied him. "What do you know about guilt?"

"I know," Rhett said. "The friend I buried . . . my best friend . . . I'm the one who killed him." He found himself telling Maxwell the whole story. The words were slow in coming. Had to be, for they were coming from a very deep well. He talked for a solid hour. He described in detail the way it happened. For some reason, it seemed necessary to describe his friend's blood that even now he could see and smell, the sound of his shovel in the soil as he dug the grave, the nightmares, the aftermath.

He didn't know if Maxwell heard a word he said, nor did he care.

By the time he finished, Rhett felt sapped. Empty. Had someone turned him upside down like a burlap bag and dumped the contents of his body to the floor, he couldn't have felt emptier.

"So much blood," Maxwell murmured. Rhett nodded before he realized Maxwell was describing the night his wife died in childbirth. "I should have called the doctor, but everything seemed normal. She was in labor for more than eighteen hours with both boys. I thought we had plenty of time before . . ." His voice faded away.

It was a long time before he continued. He talked about the rest of that long-ago night, the stillborn child, his wife slipping away, his sons' cries.

But then he did something that surprised Rhett. He talked about the happy times he and his wife shared. He talked about her life rather than her death.

"She was a good mother," he said. "The best." An anguished expression crossed his face. His mouth twisted, his eyes dark with despair, he sobbed.

Rhett envied Maxwell's ability to talk about her life even if it did hurt. He never thought much about Leonard's life. About the fun times they had growing up in Missouri on adjacent farms. It was as if Rhett had blocked out everything but the day he died.

Not only had Rhett stolen Leonard's future, he'd robbed him of his past.

It was something else to feel guilty about, something else to grieve. This time, at least, his misery had company and somehow that made it more bearable.

Maxwell began rocking back and forth. Moving faster and faster he cried out, "What have I done, Lord? What have I done?"

And Rhett found himself echoing the very same prayer.

Morning came and Rhett hadn't slept a wink. He left his office, but instead of heading to the boardinghouse as he intended, he found himself riding up the hill to the church. He'd spent an entire night watching Maxwell, but what he really observed was himself. And he didn't like what he saw, not one bit. Didn't like the shadow of the man he'd become.

Reverend Wells greeted him on the steps of the church. Judging by the pastor's worried expression, Rhett figured he looked pretty bad. No matter.

"Rhett? What's wrong?"

"Me," Rhett said. "I'm what's wrong."

TWENTY-SEVEN

A smart, marriage-minded miss
never shows her hand until the
ring is on her finger.
— MISS ABIGAIL JENKINS, 1875

Miss Jenny Higgins requests the pleasure
of your company
at the marriages of
Miss Brenda Lynn Higgins
to
Mr. Kipland Robert Barrel
and
Miss Mary Lou Higgins
to
Mr. Jeffrey William Trevor
at two o'clock on Saturday, July 30, 1881
at the Rocky Creek Church

The door to Rhett's office flew open, and
Redd Reeder stuck in his head. "Looks like
trouble in front of Fairbanks," he called.

Rhett rose in one swift movement, plucked his hat off the hook, and followed Redd to Fairbanks General Merchandise. At least half the townsfolk gathered in front. Everyone talked at once, gesturing to the handwritten invitations in their hands. They were written on the back of the hotel stationery and had been delivered earlier by Scooter.

"I've never seen anything like it," Mrs. Taylor was saying. "Is it like a theater ticket?"

"They never sent out wedding invitations much before the war," Mrs. Cranston explained. "I heard they used to do that back east."

Mrs. Taylor sniffed and looked down her considerable nose. "If you ask me, that war has been nothing but trouble. Before the war, you never had to have a passport to travel abroad. Now look at us." *Sniff.* "Imagine having to pass out handbills just to get married."

Mrs. Hitchcock nodded, the feathers in her hat bopping up and down like a nervous actor onstage. "Before the war, ladies knew how to act, how to act." She glared at Mrs. Taylor. "They also knew how to dress." She repeated herself two times for good measure.

"I think we should go back to the way

things were," Mrs. Taylor said with a haughty toss of her head. "When Reverend Wells married Sarah, they simply put up signs all over town."

Mrs. Hitchcock wrinkled her nose. "A wedding calls for a bit more pageantry, don't you think?"

Before she could repeat herself, Mrs. Taylor scorned the idea. "A wedding should be sedate and dignified."

"If you had your way, a wedding would look like a funeral," Mrs. Hitchcock charged.

"Sounds right to me," Hank Applegate interjected.

Mrs. Taylor placed a gloved hand by her mouth as if confiding a secret, though she made no attempt to lower her voice. "Handbills are the least of it. Would you believe they actually *rehearsed* the wedding ceremony?"

A collective gasp rose from the group. "Nooo!"

"Just like a stage play," she continued. "With music, the preacher, and all."

Link Haskell, the town blacksmith, spat a stream of tobacco onto the dirt-packed street. "That's the most ridiculous thin' I ever did hear. Next they'll be rehearsin' the honeymoon."

Mrs. Hitchcock looked about to faint. "The very idea, idea."

Applegate clucked his tongue. "If you ask me, this whole marriage thin' is gittin' out of hand. Next they'll be sending out engraved invites."

"Are you going to the wedding, Marshal?" Mrs. Taylor asked.

Caught off guard by the question, Rhett took a moment to answer. "I haven't thought about it," he said, though in reality, he'd done little else but think about it since Scooter delivered his invitation . . . think about Jenny, that is, not the double wedding.

Since he kissed her at the railroad station, Jenny had avoided him. Once or twice he caught her staring at him from a distance only to turn away the moment he made eye contact. On several occasions, she crossed to the other side of the street to avoid him. Obviously she wanted nothing more to do with him.

And who can blame her, God? Who can blame her?

The day of the wedding dawned hot and humid. The month of July had seemed interminable. If Jenny had her way, the wedding would have taken place weeks ago, and she would now be far away from Rocky Creek.

Unfortunately things didn't work out as planned. Mary Lou insisted upon waiting until every last unsightly bit of poison ivy had disappeared.

It was worth the wait. Mary Lou and Brenda radiated so much happiness on their wedding day that their faces seemed to shine. Surprisingly, Mary Lou hadn't uttered one word of complaint during the last week's hectic preparations.

Equally amazing, the laces on Brenda's corset required only a minimum of tension. She hadn't stopped eating but neither was she stuffing herself. Kip Barrel had clearly replaced food as her main source of comfort.

Mrs. Hitchcock had delivered the wedding dresses the day before. She and Mrs. Taylor did an amazing job of turning two plain frocks into beautiful gowns that even *Harper's Bazar* would approve.

Mary Lou's gown had a soft pleated skirt. Strips of gathered fabric took the place of expensive lace. A carefully draped overskirt ended in a delicate bustle in back.

"Don't you think the neckline rather high?" Mary Lou asked. She stood in front of the mirror, turning this way and that.

Jenny straightened Mary Lou's skirt and fastened the row of bone buttons in back. "Remember what Reverend Wells said?"

"I know, I know." Mary Lou wrinkled her nose. "Marriage is a serious step." She sighed. "I can be just as serious in a lower neckline."

"You're not going to a ball. You're going to a religious ceremony." Jenny turned to examine Brenda's dress.

Brenda's dress had less trim, but the plain skirt and circular cape had a slimming effect.

"Perfect," Jenny said. "I'd say Mrs. Hitchcock and Mrs. Taylor achieved the perfect balance between a ruffled rooster and a plucked hen."

Brenda laughed. "At least I don't look like a porcelain chamber pot."

Jenny reached behind her neck and untied the cameo she wore. "I don't think even Mrs. Taylor and her disdain for ruffles and flourishes could manage that." After a moment, she added, "I have something special for both of you." The cameo belonged to their mother. She tied the white ribbon around Mary Lou's neck. "Something borrowed."

Mary Lou looked in the mirror and touched the delicately carved ivory with her fingers. "I wish Mama was here," she whispered. "Papa too."

"They are here," Jenny said. She was encouraged that Mary Lou wanted her father at her wedding. Maybe she'd forgiven him, or at least accepted his imperfections. Maybe they all had. She met her sister's eyes in the mirror. "I can feel them."

Fearing that Mary Lou would start to cry and mess up her face, Jenny picked up a crown of white orange blossoms tied with blue ribbons and set it on her head. "Something blue."

She then turned to button up Brenda's dress. Even leaving Brenda's corset lacings loose, Jenny was able to fasten the buttons without any difficulty.

"Has anyone seen Papa's watch?" Mary Lou asked. "Since I'm wearing something of Mama's, it seems only right that I carry something of his."

"It *was* on the desk," Brenda said.

"There." Jenny spun Brenda around so she could have a better look. "You make beautiful brides, both of you."

She reached over to her jewelry box and pulled out her mother's locket. Brenda cupped the locket to her throat while Jenny fastened it around her neck.

"What is this?" Mary Lou asked. She

picked up the railroad ticket from inside the desk where Jenny had hidden it.

Jenny crossed the room to snatch the ticket out of Mary Lou's hand and placed it back in the drawer. "What are you looking for?"

"I told you. Papa's watch." Mary Lou narrowed her eyes. "You didn't answer my question."

Since there was no way around it, Jenny explained her plans. "I'm leaving first thing tomorrow morning."

"Leaving?" both girls gasped in unison.

"Don't look so surprised. That was my plan all along. Surely you didn't expect me to stay here."

"Why not?" Mary Lou asked, her voice shrill. "We're still your family. Where else would you go? Back to Haswell?"

"Certainly not!" The very thought turned Jenny's stomach. "I want to check out San Antonio. Maybe even Austin."

"Why not stay here?" Brenda looked about to cry.

Jenny scoffed. "In Rocky Creek? What would I do here? The money from the sale of our farm won't last forever." The double wedding had saved money, but it still cost more than she planned. "Maybe I'll open up a women's ready-made emporium."

An article she'd read predicted that, one day, women's gowns would be produced in large quantities and sold in stores. Given the intricacies of design and the diversity of women's sizes and shapes, she doubted such a thing possible. However, corsets and cloaks came ready-made, along with gloves and other accessories, and she envisioned a shop where women could try such things on before purchasing.

"Why not open an emporium in Rocky Creek?" Mary Lou asked. "We certainly could use one."

"Here?" Jenny blinked. The idea was so absurd it was all she could do to keep from laughing out loud. "I'd probably sell more fashions on the moon than I could ever sell here."

"You could tutor," Brenda suggested.

"Maybe you could work at the café," Mary Lou added. "Mr. Reeder is looking for help."

Their concern touched her heart, but none of their suggestions seemed right. Staying in town would mean staying close to Rhett, and that was too painful to contemplate.

"I don't think pouring week-old coffee is what God has planned for me," she said.

Her sisters stared at her as if she had suddenly sprouted a beard, and she could well guess their thoughts. It wasn't like her to leave things in God's hands, but she was trying. She really was trying.

"Don't look so sad. We'll write to each other nearly every day and I'll visit you at least once a year."

Brenda looked close to tears. "That won't be the same."

"You'll both be married and busy with your new lives," Jenny said with a cheerfulness she didn't feel. "You won't have time to think about me."

Brenda's eyes watered and it was all Jenny could do to swallow the lump in her own throat. Her sisters had been a pain at times. Many were the days she resented having to care for them. Still, she never imagined how much it hurt to lose them, even to something as wonderful as marriage.

Refusing to give in to her emotions, she clapped her hands briskly. "Come along now. We don't want to be late."

Brenda wiped away her tears and Mary Lou looked relieved. Jenny was back to her old bossy ways.

Jenny peered out the window. Two carriages were parked out front. "Ah, our rides are here. Brenda, you come with me. Mary Lou, you take the second one."

She handed each girl a flower bouquet while she fired off instructions. It was the only way she could keep her emotions under control. "Stand tall. Take little steps. Act like ladies." She stared at Mary Lou's bodice. "Please tell me you're not wearing bosom enhancers." It was obvious, of course, that she was by the unnatural curves of her figure.

After confiscating Mary Lou's bosom pads, she led the way out the door and down the stairs. Jeff had arranged for their transportation to the church and had sent two of his workers to drive the open carriages.

Jenny took one more look at her sisters, and this time she couldn't hold back the tears.

Mary Lou took her time climbing onto the seat of the second carriage. She fiddled with her gown until the one carrying Brenda and Jenny left. What she wouldn't give to have her bosom enhancers back. Why, oh, why hadn't she sent away to Montgomery Ward's for two pairs instead of one?

She took her place in the passenger seat. No sooner had they started down Main Street than she ordered the driver to stop.

He pulled to the side of the road to allow

a wagon to pass in the other direction. He pushed his felt hat back. He was dressed in a lumberman's cropped pants but had traded the usual caulked boots for regular ones.

"Is everything all right, ma'am?" he asked. His ebony skin glistened beneath the hot afternoon sun.

Though she had her reservations, she nodded. "Please wait here. I'll be right back."

She handed the driver her bouquet then picked her way carefully down the carriage steps so as not to damage her gown. One hand holding the wreath of flowers on her head, she gathered her skirts in the other and dashed to the marshal's office.

He looked surprised to see her. "You make a mighty pretty bride," he said. "Jeff Trevor is a lucky man."

Ignoring his compliment, she stood in front of his desk. She had to do this quickly or not at all. "Jenny's leaving."

A muscle twitched at his jaw. "Leaving?" He frowned. "When?"

"Tomorrow."

He started to rise but then fell back in his chair. "So soon after your wedding?"

Mary Lou nodded. "You've got to stop her."

He rubbed a hand across his chin. "I don't

know that I can."

"If anyone can stop her, it's you." Hands on his desk, she leaned forward beseechingly. "I know you think I'm making this up, but I'm not. She cares for you. She really, really does. You have to believe me."

He brows knitted. "As much as I would like to believe you, I'm not sure it's true."

"It *is* true," she cried out. "There's a lot you don't know about her."

He looked tired, suddenly, his face drawn. "You better go or you'll be late for your wedding."

She stood her ground. "I'm not going until you hear me out."

His eyebrow rose in protest, but he indicated with a nod of his head that he would listen. As if he had a choice.

The more she knew about Jeff, the more she loved him. Maybe if the marshal knew more about Jenny, his love would grow so much he couldn't bear to let her go.

So she told him about that long-ago winter. "Jenny decided to walk the ten miles to town in the storm. She was gone for two days, and we thought we would never see her again.

"When she came back, she was driving a carriage filled with food, firewood, and medicine." Her voice choked with memories. "After that, Jenny was never the same. She even stopped laughing. We never knew what happened during those two days, but it changed her."

He scratched his temple, a puzzled look on his face. "This is all very interesting, but I still don't know why you think she has feelings for me."

"Because you made her laugh again," Mary Lou said. It was as simple as that. After that terrible time, Jenny became serious, her cheery disposition nothing more than a memory. "You were the only one able to do that."

Something like a low flame flickered in his eyes. His hand curved into a fist as if holding on to something he didn't want to let go.

The door opened and the driver poked his head inside. "Ma'am, if we don't get a move on, you'll be late for your own weddin' and my boss ain't gonna like that."

Mary Lou gave the marshal one last beseeching look. "Please, you're the only one who can make her stay."

With that she turned and followed the driver back to the carriage.

TWENTY-EIGHT

Once your vows are exchanged, devote
yourself to domestication — his.
— MISS ABIGAIL JENKINS, 1875

Jenny insisted Brenda wait in the carriage
until the last of the guests were ushered
inside the church and seated. Many clutched
their "wedding tickets" and almost all wore
their best bibs and tuckers.

Jenny stood on the steps of the church,
anxiously peering inside. Timber Joe was
the self-appointed sentinel. Rifle flung over
his shoulder and dressed in his usual Rebel
uniform, he looked over every guest before
allowing them inside.

Bouquets of wildflowers tucked in every
nook and cranny filled the church with an
array of bright colors. Brenda's favorite
bluebonnets were no longer in bloom, but
the golden waves and purple verbenas more
than made up for them. Red and yellow

coneflowers looked like high-crowned hats worn at Mexican fiestas. Yellow-tipped fire-wheels sprouted from knots and nail holes like little whirligigs waiting to spin at the slightest breath.

Both bridegrooms stood in the front of the church. Kip looked perfectly at ease in his dark trousers and frock coat. Dressed in a similar suit, Jeff moved like he was encased in plaster of Paris. The poor man was used to clothes that allowed him the freedom of movement necessary for his job. He kept fiddling with his collar and cuffs and pulling at the knees of his pants.

Ma, Jeff Trevor's grandmother and owner of the boardinghouse where Kip Barrel lived, took her place at the piano. She smiled at both bridegrooms like a proud mother hen. She then arranged the sheets of music before lowering her hands upon the yellowed keys.

Wondering what was keeping Mary Lou, Jenny motioned for Brenda to join her.

Not wanting to leave anything to chance, Jenny ran down her list. Everything was in tip-top order — everything except the last thing on her list. At the bottom of the page she had written *Rhett Armstrong.* She had no memory of writing his name, but there it was, clear as day. Her gaze swept over the seated guests one more time on the off chance she had missed his handsome dark head.

Sarah rushed up with little Elizabeth in tow. The child wore an ankle-length white dress layered in ruffles and tied at the waist with a big blue bow. Her hair fell down her back in a riot of curls. Copper toe caps on her black leather boots gleamed in the sun.

"Don't you look fancy," Jenny said, and the little girl beamed with pleasure. "Where are Jason and Scooter?"

Sarah gave a fond smile. "We're makin' progress with those boys, but gettin' 'em in their Sunday-go-to-meetin' clothes on a Saturday is pushin' our luck."

Jenny laughed. "I remember how hard it was to get Scooter to take a bath." It did her heart good to know that Scooter and his brother had found a good home. "How kind of you and the pastor to take care of them. You already have your hands full with Elizabeth. I'm not sure how you'll manage when the baby comes."

"We'll manage just fine," Sarah said. "The boys really aren't that much trouble, and I do have some good news." She could barely contain her joy. "Justin has been working with Matt Maxwell, and the Lord has seen fit to touch the man's heart. Losin' his boys hit him hard. He's gonna take the cure. Said he owes it to the memory of his wife."

"That's wonderful," Jenny said, adding a silent prayer of thanksgiving. *God, please let it work, for his sons' sake.*

Sarah gushed over Brenda. "I reckon there's never been a more beautiful bride." Sarah's middle had grown considerably in the last couple of weeks, but she glowed with an inner contentment that Jenny envied.

Jenny walked Sarah to the door of the church. "I've been reading the Bible you gave me."

Sarah looked pleased. "I hope it helped."

Jenny nodded. "I was just wondering . . ." Feeling foolish, she bit her lower lip before forcing herself to continue. "The Bible says God has a plan for us."

"He does," Sarah said. "Oh, Jenny, He does."

"How do you know? I mean, I don't know what God wants me to do." She couldn't make up her mind whether to stay in Texas or go somewhere else. Should she try to open her own business or tutor? None of her ideas seemed quite right.

"I feel like I'm caught in a crosscurrent. I don't know which way to turn." Jenny prayed for God's guidance, but so far, no answers had been forthcoming.

Sarah's mouth curved upward. "You'll know by the signs."

Jenny frowned. "Signs? What signs?"

"God's signs." Sarah leaned over and whispered in her ear. "You just have to open your eyes. God's leadin' the way." Smiling, Sarah took Elizabeth by the hand and ambled into the church.

Ignoring the heaviness in her heart, Jenny stepped back. She signaled for Timber Joe to close the doors of the church.

Signs? From God? Of all the foolish notions. Nevertheless, she looked around before catching herself. Shaking her head at the absurdity of it, she peered anxiously at the road leading up to the church.

"Where is she?" Jenny muttered. She paced back and forth, growing more worried by the minute. Both carriages had left the hotel at the same time. How was it possible that Mary Lou had not yet arrived?

"Maybe she's having second thoughts," Brenda suggested.

Second thoughts? About marrying Jeff Trevor? Jenny didn't believe that for a second. Not after the way she bemoaned every minute she and Jeff were apart during her bout with poison ivy.

The sound of wagon wheels lifted her

spirits until she realized a shay, not a carriage, raced up the hill toward them. The vehicle pulled up in front of the church and a well-dressed man stepped to the ground. He looked like an Easterner in his dark suit and high hat, and he carried a gold-tipped cane.

Ignoring him, Jenny attended to Brenda's veil, which didn't need fixing but gave her something to do to quiet her nerves. While she worked she kept one eye on the road.

She didn't pay any attention to the man until he spoke. "Hello, Jennifer."

The sound of his voice turned her blood cold. Only one person called her Jennifer. She straightened and stared at the face straight out of her nightmares. The face of Horace B. Blackman III.

Her jaw dropped. *Dear God, not now. Not today of all days.* "What . . . what are you doing here?" she stammered.

His tight-lipped smile failed to reach his eyes. Funny how she failed to miss that at the age of fifteen.

"I'm here for the wedding. Kip Barrel is my cousin. Unfortunately, the task of representing the family fell on my shoulders." His eyes slid down the length of her, a look of possessiveness in their depths. "It's been awhile."

Looking at him now, Jenny wondered how she ever imagined that he was a kind and caring man. How young she had been. How innocent. How utterly trusting.

Brenda glanced at Jenny, her expression dark with uncertainty. "You two know each other?"

"Yes, my family owns property in Haswell. I would say we know each other quite well, wouldn't you agree, Jennifer?" His voice thick with innuendo, his gaze bored into hers. "Very well, indeed."

Hands held tight by her side, Jenny could hardly hide her contempt. "We knew each other a long time ago," she said, her voice cold.

He shrugged as if the intervening years had not existed, and he gave Brenda a critical squint. "My cousin neglected to mention the name of his bride in his telegram. You are?"

"Brenda Higgins."

He bowed slightly. "Horace Blackman III, at your service." He stared at Timber Joe with a careful eye and glanced at the church with equal disdain.

"Hard to believe my cousin would settle in a town like this. A barber no less." He scoffed. "He always was the black sheep in the family. At least he's no longer making a fool of himself onstage."

Brenda's eyes flashed with anger. "He's a talented singer. Had his family been less critical and more supportive, maybe —"

Jenny stopped Brenda with a hand to her arm. Nothing, not even Horace Blackman, was going to spoil her sister's wedding day.

She wanted to shrink beneath his mocking gaze, but she forced herself to stand her ground. "Please go inside and find a seat."

"Very well." He tipped his hat. "Perhaps we can catch up on old times after the ceremony." With that, he gave the weathered church steps a tap with his cane, pushed past Timber Joe, and vanished inside.

Brenda practically shook with rage. "What an awful, awful man. Kip didn't want to let his family know about the wedding, but I insisted and . . ."

Tuning her sister out, Jenny fanned herself to hide her inner turmoil. *You'll know by the signs. God's signs.* After all, what were the chances that Horace Blackman — the man who ruined her life — was Kip's cousin? Could God possibly have been any clearer?

God wanted her to leave town. Not tomorrow as planned, but today. The realization left her shaken. She hadn't known until that moment how very much she wanted to stay.

Brenda touched Jenny's arm. "Are you all right?"

"Yes, yes, I'm fine. It's hot." Trembling, she slumped against the outer wall of the church to brace herself. Her stomach was tied in knots. Her mouth dry, she fought the suffocating sensation in her throat.

How could this happen? On this of all days. She'd thought that once she left Haswell she would be able to put the past behind her. That hadn't happened. If anything, the past haunted her more and the nightmares didn't stop. Still, this was the worst nightmare of all.

"What are we going to do about Mary Lou?" Brenda asked.

Mary Lou! She'd been so distressed at seeing Blackman she'd almost forgotten her missing sister.

Just then a horse and carriage raced up the hill so fast it almost didn't make the turn. No sooner had the carriage pulled up in front than Mary Lou jumped to the ground. Her skirt gathered in her hands, she ran toward them. By the time she reached the church, her crown was askew, her bouquet missing flowers, and her face flushed.

"Look at you," Jenny scolded. "Where have you been?"

Before Mary Lou could answer, a ghastly sound rose from the interior of the church.

"What in the world?" Had a sick cow somehow wandered inside to die? Jenny yanked open the door, ready to do whatever necessary to save the day. Kip Barrel's voice stopped her from charging inside the church.

He stood in front of the altar facing the crowd, his face a brilliant red. Whether from the heat or embarrassment at the awful sound he emitted, it was hard to know.

Jenny groaned. After all her hard work, Barrel had ruined everything.

Behind her, Brenda gasped in delight. "He's singing." She pushed Jenny out of the way. "Oh, I did so hope he would." Despite Jenny's protests, Brenda pulled the door all the way open, not caring who saw her in her wedding gown.

Barrel spotted her immediately. He fell silent and motioned for Ma to stop playing. A strained silence followed. Brenda smiled at him and blew him a kiss. He smiled back and wiggled his fingers at her. He then gestured for Ma to begin again.

Groans of protests rose from the wedding guests. Several clapped their hands over their ears.

Then the most amazing thing happened.

Kip's gaze riveted upon Brenda's face, he opened his mouth, and this time his rich tenor voice rolled over the crowd like warm honey. Singing in Italian, he shaped each phrase lovingly with his hands. His body moved with exquisite timing. No one could understand the words, but it didn't matter. His eyes, his voice, his every move expressed his utmost feelings for his bride.

When the last note faded away, he took his place at the altar next to Jeff. Women dabbed at their eyes with lace handkerchiefs and sniffled. Men cleared their throats.

"Wasn't that the most beautiful sound you ever heard?" Brenda said, tears rolling down her cheeks. Even Mary Lou's eyes held a suspicious sheen.

Jenny pulled the girls away from the door. "It was beautiful," she agreed. Kip never failed to amaze her, and never more so than today.

Brenda gave an indignant nod. "I wonder what his horrible cousin has to say now?"

Mary Lou wrinkled her nose. "What horrible cousin?"

"Never mind," Jenny said, her voice sharper than she meant. She quickly straightened Mary Lou's crown and checked Brenda's dress.

The piano music began again, and the

shuffling of feet announced that the guests had risen and were waiting for the brides to start down the aisle.

"This is it," Jenny whispered. A lump rose in her throat. "I really am going to miss you both."

"Not if you stay in Rocky Creek," Mary Lou said.

Brenda tugged Jenny's sleeve. "Please say you will."

"I —" Jenny didn't want to make promises she couldn't keep, but neither did she want to put a damper on their special day. "We'll see."

Mary Lou squeezed her hand. "The marshal —"

Jenny stopped her. She couldn't think about Rhett. Not now. Not ever. "Stand up tall," she said in a desperate attempt to put him out of her mind. "Take dainty steps. Act like ladies." She caught herself and laughed. "You better go before I really do turn you into ladies."

Her sisters laughed too. Then Mary Lou surprised her by throwing her arms around her. "I love you, Jenny. You're the best sister ever."

Brenda joined the hug. "Oh, you are, you are."

"I love you both too." Fighting back tears,

Jenny pushed her sisters toward the church door. "Go. Your bridegrooms are waiting."

Neither Mary Lou nor Brenda argued with her.

Brenda went first. She floated down the aisle, her skirt billowing around her like a soft, puffy cloud.

Mary Lou was prepared to follow, but Timber Joe refused to let her in the church. Instead he glared at her and said, "No spies allowed."

Mary Lou glanced helplessly at Jenny. "What's he talking about?"

Jenny touched him on the arm. "Let Mary Lou in. We don't want to keep the groom waiting." When appealing to his lucid side didn't work, she tried another tactic. "Timber Joe, open that door. Now." Her voice stern, she continued, "Or I will report you to your commanding officer."

This time her approach worked. Timber Joe stood at attention and saluted. He then pulled the door open and stepped aside.

Mary Lou started down the aisle, looking more beautiful than Jenny had ever seen her look. Both young women took their places in front of the altar next to their respective fiancés.

Reverend Wells stood in front of the two couples. "Dearly beloved . . ."

Jenny watched from the back of the church as both couples pledged to love and cherish each other forevermore. Tears rolled down her cheeks, tears of happiness and joy. Tears of sadness. Her sisters were in good hands. They no longer needed her. She never thought in a million years she would ever say it but . . . oh, did she need them!

"Ladies and gentlemen," Reverend Wells said, addressing the guests, "I present Mr. and Mrs. Barrel and Mr. and Mrs. Trevor."

"Be happy," Jenny mouthed, wiping away her tears. "God bless."

Whispering a final good-bye, she slipped away.

Twenty-Nine

Eschew secrets, for they are normally
discovered at the worst possible time. If
confronted, weep and deny everything.
— MISS ABIGAIL JENKINS, 1875

Rhett stared at the wedding invitation, then crumpled it into a ball and tossed it at the waste basket. He missed.

Jenny was leaving. He couldn't bear the thought, but there was nothing he could do. She'd made her feelings more than clear.

He stared at the stack of paper on his desk, mostly telegrams. He knew from experience that more than half would contain advertisements for products he had no use for or appeals from charitable organizations that didn't exist.

He pulled a letter off the pile and slit it with a wax-seal letter opener. With everyone at the church, maybe he could get some work done.

He unfolded the handbill. Another WANTED poster, this one for a James Witter for cattle rustling. He studied the sketch. Not recognizing the man, he tossed it aside.

Feeling restless, he stood and stretched then stepped outside. The town was deserted except for the horses tethered in front of the saloons. Some he recognized. Some he didn't. Most locals were at the church. His gaze drifted to the hotel at the end of the street.

Barrel's Barbershop, Fairbanks General Merchandise, and the Rocky Creek Café and Chinese Laundry were closed. The Wells Fargo stage thundered past on its way out of town, but he gave it no heed.

He stepped back into his office and slammed the door. Peace and quiet. Just what he needed. Maybe he'd clear the pile of papers off his desk and call it a day. He could go home, of course, but the thought of being alone in his room at the boarding-house seemed even less appealing than staying in town.

Fishing. Ah, now there was a thought. He could go fishing. He would have done that, too, had two blue eyes not gotten in the way. *Her* eyes. Jenny's.

He squeezed his fists tight. Ever since the war, he'd kept himself from feeling. It was the only way he could get through the years. It wasn't easy. It meant keeping his distance and never getting close to anyone. It meant being forever on guard. It was a lonely way to live, but the only way he *could* live.

Lately, however, everything conspired against him. Jenny. Scooter. Jason. Even Maxwell had gotten to him. Then there was Reverend Wells, who continued to believe Rhett's guilt and grief distanced him from God and everyone else.

Was it possible that the good preacher was right? Had his guilt for accidentally killing his best friend kept him from giving of himself completely to anyone, including God, and most assuredly, Jenny? Was that why he had so much trouble putting his feelings into words?

He didn't know the answer to that. What he did know was that somewhere along the line the hard shell around his heart had cracked and it hurt. It hurt real bad.

She cares for you.

He shook his head. Mary Lou didn't know what she was talking about.

You made her laugh again.

He swallowed hard. No argument there. He could make her laugh. He could make her angry. He could even get her to respond to his kisses. The question was, could he make her love him? He opened his eyes wide.

You can't make someone love you. You can't.

Of course he couldn't. But what if Mary Lou was right and Jenny already loved him? Was that even possible? He thought about the times he caught her staring at him only to turn away when he stared back. The times she crossed over to the other side of the street when she saw him coming. Was she really rejecting him, as it seemed, or was something else afoot?

And what earthly difference did it make? The thought made him groan. Even after all Reverend Wells's counseling these last few weeks, he still resisted any possible chance for his own happiness.

He paced back and forth, but no matter how hard he tried, he couldn't escape the simple and honest truth. He was hopelessly in love with Jenny and couldn't bear the thought of her leaving town.

Leonard, forgive me, but I can't do this anymore. I can't.

Having finally cut the bond that tied him to the past, he still felt no peace. She could easily reject him — reject him as she had so many times before.

He tightened his fists along with his

resolve. She wouldn't. Not this time. He wouldn't let her. Neither grief nor guilt would hold him back. This time he would go to her with everything he had.

He reached for his hat and left his office on the run. Seconds later he was astride his horse and galloping up the winding road to the church.

People stood in knots outside when he arrived. Ma and some of the ladies provided cake and lemonade for the guests. The newlyweds stood slightly away from the milling guests, posing for photographs on the church grounds.

He tethered his horse and pushed his way through the crowd. Where was Jenny?

"Want some cake, Marshal?" Timber Joe called.

He shook his head. "Have you seen Jenny?"

"Not for a while."

He glanced around before striding quickly toward Mrs. Hitchcock, who was arguing with Mrs. Taylor about hat styles.

"Have either of you seen Jenny?" Rhett interrupted.

"Not since before the wedding," Mrs. Taylor said. Without missing a beat, she continued her discourse. "No woman should be caught dead in a hat that defies the law of gravity."

Leaving the two squabbling women behind, he hurried over to Mary Lou, who was finished posing for her photograph. "Where's Jenny?" he asked.

Mary Lou looked worried. She glanced up at her new husband before answering. "I don't know. I just hope she hasn't already left town."

He took a step back. Left? Already? While the newlyweds and guests were still celebrating? "She wouldn't do that without saying good-bye." He frowned. *Would she?*

"Maybe she's at the hotel," Trevor said.

That was a thought. "I'll check it out." Rhett tried to sound confident for Mary Lou's sake.

Loud voices rose above the soft murmurings of wedding guests. Everyone stopped talking and turned to stare at Kip Barrel quarreling with a stranger.

Torn between looking for Jenny and stopping an escalating argument, Rhett hesitated a moment before rushing toward them.

Barrel's face was red with fury. Next to him, Brenda looked about to burst into tears.

The stranger's voice sliced through the air like a sword. "Her sister's a tramp. How do you know your wife's any less?"

Barrel drew back his fist, but before he could throw his punch, Rhett stepped in front of him.

"Break it up." Rhett gave Brenda a look of sympathy and glared at Barrel. "What's the matter with you? This is your wedding day."

Barrel didn't look the least bit apologetic. "He has no right to call Jenny a tramp."

Rhett stared at him. "Jenny?" He turned to the stranger and felt an instant dislike. "Who *are* you?"

"My name's Horace B. Blackman III. Kip Barrel and I are cousins."

"You're related?"

That was a surprise. The men were complete opposites in appearance. Blackman's compact body was no match for Barrel's impressive size, but what he lacked in height and width he made up for in fashion and arrogance.

"I suggest you and your cousin work out your differences some other time," Rhett said.

Blackman sneered. "It's too late for that. He already married the tramp's sister."

Cold fury pulsed through Rhett's veins. "You'd better leave. Now."

Blackman shifted his weight but stayed in place. "This is a family matter, Marshal."

Rhett waved his hand, indicating the wedding guests who stood watching with open curiosity. "Which *you* chose to make public." He placed his hand on his gun. "Now either you leave, or I'll make you leave."

"I'm leaving." Blackman glowered at Barrel. "I can hardly wait to see your father's face when he hears you married the sister of a harlot."

Rhett's arm struck like lightning. Something broke beneath his fist, and Blackman fell to the ground. His hat flew in one direction, his gold-tipped cane in another. A collective gasp rose from the guests, but no one moved.

His knuckles sore, Rhett shook out his hand.

Blackman sat up and rubbed his cheek. An ugly red mark replaced his earlier arrogance — a definite improvement.

Blackman took a moment to pull himself together before he stood and reached down for his hat and cane. Without another word, he turned and walked away.

Mary Lou came rushing over. "That awful man. What he said about Jenny . . . It's not true." She looked at Brenda for confirmation, but Brenda was too upset to speak.

Rhett felt sorry for her. For both women. "This is your wedding day. Go back to your guests."

"But we don't know where Jenny is," Mary Lou protested, her face dark with worry.

"I'll find her," Rhett said. "And that's a promise."

Mary Lou's eyes filled with tears of gratitude. "Thank you," she whispered.

Leaving both brides in the care of their new husbands, Rhett ran for his horse and raced back to town, his thoughts outpacing Lincoln's fast flying hooves. Where was she? Had she left the wedding because of Blackman? And why would the man make such disparaging remarks?

Pressing his legs hard against Lincoln's side, he galloped toward the hotel.

Scooter sat on the edge of the boardwalk, holding his head. Though he tried to hide it, it was obvious he'd been crying. Rhett leaped off his horse and rushed to the boy in alarm, rein in hand.

"Scooter, what's wrong?"

Scooter lifted his face, his eyes red. "Miss Jenny's gone."

A cold chill shot down his spine. "Did she take the train?" There was a 3:00 p.m. train that left for Dallas.

Scooter shook his head. "Stage."

Rhett squeezed the boy's shoulder. "Crying isn't doing any good. If you want to help bring her back, you best start to pray."

"It won't do no good," Scooter said. "I prayed for Pa, and that didn't work."

Rhett bent over and looked him in square in the face. "Son, your prayers *were* answered. Your pa's not well yet, but he's getting there."

Scooter stared at him as if he wasn't sure whether to believe him.

Rhett confirmed what he said with an emphatic nod. "As soon as I find Jenny, I'll let you see for yourself."

"Do . . . do you mean it?" Scooter palmed his wet cheeks. "I can see Pa?"

"You can see him." Rhett straightened. "Meanwhile, if we want to bring Jenny back, we both got a job to do." With that he left.

Jenny couldn't stop crying. Her heart was broken, no . . . shattered. How was it possible to feel such agonizing pain without a visible wound? Even her father's death hadn't caused this much suffering. At fifteen, she had been too overwhelmed with responsibility to give her grief full vent.

Now she was alone with nothing to distract her.

She hadn't wanted to leave Rocky Creek, but that's what God wanted her to do. He couldn't have made a sign clearer than

Blackman. She still couldn't believe it. It didn't seem possible that Kip Barrel could be related to such a man. No wonder he was reluctant to invite his family to the wedding.

Her handkerchief soaked, she reached into her reticule for a dry one.

She was the only passenger, and for this she was grateful. The driver told her to enjoy the luxury because the stage would fill with passengers at the next stop.

She dabbed at her eyes, but the tears kept coming. It wasn't that she worried about her sisters. They were in good hands. Jeff Trevor and Kip Barrel gave every indication that they would make kind and loving husbands. Still, she would miss them. Already missed them. Missed Mary Lou's complaints, Brenda's shy smiles, the late-night hugs. Even the arguments.

The teasing lights in his eyes.

Overwhelmed with fresh tears, she shook her head hard. She mustn't think of Rhett. Couldn't.

Got to do something. Got to keep my mind busy. It was the only way she could control her thoughts. More out of habit than need, she opened her notebook. The previous pages had been torn out and discarded. Only blank pages remained, and she had no idea what to fill them with. Without a project or plan, she felt lost, bereft. Her future looked as empty as the notebook on her lap.

Exhausted, she eventually dozed off. *He stood in the distance, waiting for her. She ran into his arms and looked up . . .*

She woke with a start. Her notebook flew to the floor, but she didn't care. With the dream still fresh in her mind, she tried to think what was different this time. Then she remembered. When she looked up in her dream it was Rhett looking down at her. It was Rhett's face she saw, not Blackman's. Her chest tightened with pain. It was the first time she realized that a person could be equally tortured by a good dream as by a bad one.

"Whoa," the driver yelled and the stagecoach rolled to a stop. She moved the leather curtain aside and peered out the window. Flat grassland stretched as far as she could see. In the distance, cattle grazed serenely beneath the wide expanse of clear blue sky. So why did they stop?

A robbery? She dropped the curtain in place and reached for her parasol. Since she'd struck Scooter's father it no longer opened, but it still made a good weapon. Ears straining, she sat frozen in place, afraid to move.

Without warning, the door ripped open. Startled, she pressed her back against the horsehair seat. She blinked, not sure she could believe her eyes. Was she still dreaming?

"Rhett?"

"Hello, Jenny," he said.

"What . . . what are you doing here?" Her mind raced. "Is everything all right? Brenda? Mary Lou?"

As an answer, he grabbed her by the hand and pulled her out of the stage. He then reached inside the coach for her ever-present notebook. Drawing a pencil from his shirt pocket, he scribbled something across the page. He held it up for her to read.

Will you marry me?

She raised her eyes and stared at him. "You must be joking," she whispered.

He tossed the notebook into the coach. Grabbing her by the hand, he led her away from the stage, away from the nosy driver.

He jerked her around to face him. "Do I look like I'm joking?"

No, he did not. "I —" She shook her head. This was a side of Rhett she'd never seen before, a more open, impassioned side.

"I'm no good with words," he said, his

458

eyes brimming with ardor. "My feelings tend to get all bottled up inside. All I know is that I love you and I want to marry you."

Hand on her mouth, she choked back a sob. They were the sweetest, most wonderful words anyone had ever said to her. And clearly the most painful.

"I–I can't," she whispered. She backed away, but he kept moving toward her.

"At first I thought you pushed me away because of my profession," he said. "Or because I didn't have enough money in the bank."

She shook her head. "It was never about you."

He arched a brow. "Suppose you tell me what it is about?"

She turned to move away, but he grabbed her arm and held on tight. "Tell me," he bellowed.

She didn't want to answer that question, but it was obvious he wouldn't leave her alone until she did.

"Let go," she whispered.

He released her but the determined look remained. "Tell me!"

She flung out her arms in despair. "I'm the one who is not worthy," she shouted. "Is that what you wanted to hear?"

He stiffened. "No, that's not what I

wanted to hear."

"Why not? It's true!"

"Try again," he said, advancing toward her.

She backed away, but he kept coming. She hoped and prayed this day would never come. She never meant to tell anyone what she was about to tell him. Even her sisters didn't know the full story.

She raised a hand in surrender. "All right. I'll tell you everything."

He stopped in his tracks and waited.

She took a deep breath, but filling her lungs with air did nothing to alleviate her shame. "My mother died when I was fourteen, and my father died a year later. I didn't know what to do. I was desperate. We were behind on taxes and mortgage. We had no money, no food, no medical supplies. Nothing." She told him about the cold winter, the roof blowing off the farm, Brenda's illness. She told him about the things she wanted to forget, the things she couldn't.

He stood still as she spoke. Never had she seen him so still, his gaze riveted onto her face. Even nature seemed to hold its breath as if waiting for her to disclose her revelation.

"Haswell was going through hard times,"

she continued. "The ranches had been wiped out by Texas fever. I couldn't sell the farm, though I tried. No one could find work, and I didn't know what to do. Then I met . . . someone. He offered to help. He gave me money for food and medicine. He paid the mortgage and taxes. In return, he demanded —" She looked away, the rest of the words a knot in her throat.

"Blackman," he said.

She stared at him, her mouth open. "You . . . you know him?"

"We met," he said and gave no further explanation. "Is that all?" he asked.

He moved another step closer. "Is that why you keep pushing me away? Because of Blackman?"

"I haven't told you everything."

"I don't care," he said.

"What he demanded of me —"

He moved closer. "I don't care."

She had to make him understand. "It wasn't just once. I was in his debt for three years." Three long, horrible years. By the time she was eighteen, the economy had improved, and she was finally able to sell half of her parents' property. With the money from the sale, she paid Blackman back in full and earned her freedom.

"I don't care." He closed the distance

between them and put his hands on her waist.

She pulled away. "Are you listening to me? Do you understand what I'm telling you?"

A shadow crossed his face. "We've all done things we're ashamed of. Everyone has reason to feel guilty for something."

"Not you," she said. "Not you."

"Yes, me," he said roughly. "I killed . . . my best friend."

For a moment, his words hung between them like an open wound neither wanted to touch.

Shock turned to disbelief. "I don't believe it," she said.

"Believe it," he said. His voice low, he told her how he accidentally shot and killed his childhood friend during the war. "They called it *fratricide,*" he said bitterly. "It was a fitting name, since I felt like I'd killed my brother."

"What you did . . . it's not the same," she protested. "It was an accident. It should never have happened, but it wasn't your fault."

"It *was* my fault." His voice broke. "It was my fault. I was supposed to be front rank, but I was going through a rough patch. I had cannon fever and fell back. Leonard took my place. He wasn't even supposed to be there."

"Rhett, you can't blame yourself."

"I do blame myself. I'll probably go to my grave blaming myself," he said. "But I'm through punishing myself. I've seen what guilt has done to others. To Maxwell. And I'm asking you . . . no, begging you . . . to stop punishing yourself for keeping your sisters safe."

"Don't," she whispered. "Don't try to make me sound heroic. I had other options. My grandfather offered to help, but I was too proud to accept his money. I thought I could do it all on my own."

Eventually, she had gone back to her grandfather, but by then it was too late; upon learning how she had prostituted herself with Blackman, he refused to help her. If she had it to do over, she would have turned to God in those dark days. Maybe then she wouldn't have felt so overwhelmed and alone.

"Jenny, I —" He hesitated as if struggling to find the right words. "For the first time in years, I've actually started to sleep through the night without nightmares. Instead of my friend's face, I see yours. I've resisted any sort of happiness. I didn't think I deserved it. Reverend Wells told me that my guilt kept me from God."

"Oh, Rhett . . ."

"And you," he added. "My guilt was keeping me from you. Whenever you backed away, I told myself it's what I deserved."

He could have been describing her life. She gazed at him through a veil of tears. Guilt was more isolating than prison bars, self-punishment the worst possible kind. She avoided making friends, avoided church, avoided even God, and the loneliness had taken a toll. It had been easier to avoid God than to face him. Easier to quell her anger at her father than confront it. Easier to deny her feelings for Rhett than to acknowledge them. She always opted for the easy way out, only to find out that no such way existed.

Guarding her secret shame with her life, she lived by a set of rules found in books. Rules that told her how to dress, what to say, how to act, what to write. It was the only way she knew how to survive. She feared that, if left to her own devices, she would say or do something that would give her terrible secret away.

Today, she needed no such contrivances to tell her what to do. With nothing left to hide, she was free to be herself and listen to her heart. That was something she hadn't done for a very long time.

"You're like him, you know," he said softly.

"What?"

"My friend. He was stubborn, independent, and fiercely loyal. He would have done anything to protect those he loved. That was the quality that first drew me to you from the beginning."

She blinked away her tears. "I–I thought you were interested in Mary Lou," she said. "When I asked you which one you'd choose, you said the oldest."

His eyes flickered with humor. "Unless I'm mistaken, I believe that's you."

"You mean all this time, it was me?" She couldn't believe it. Rhett loved her, even now, after knowing her shameful past.

He nodded. "All this time."

She didn't know what to say. Seeing herself through Rhett's eyes was like peering into a mirror that reflected only the good. He made her feel worthy.

Sometimes God brings couples together for His own purpose.

She knew why God brought Rhett into her life. He helped her feel whole again. She didn't know if she could fill the hole left in Rhett's heart, but she had to try.

"If I'm like your friend," she said softly, "then I know he wouldn't want you to spend another moment blaming yourself for the past."

He studied her. "What I said about Leonard . . . that was the first time I've been able to talk about his life rather than his death, and it felt good."

"Oh, Rhett . . ."

He extended his hand. It was like a bridge pulling her from the darkness into the light. *Look for the signs . . .*

She laid her hand in his to form a bridge that ran both ways.

Tears rolled down her cheeks. A heavy weight had been lifted from her shoulders. She felt light enough to fly. "I —"

He touched his finger to her lips. "I don't care."

"I was going to say I love you."

A smile spread across his face. "Now *that* I care about."

He pulled her into his arms and kissed her. His ran his warm lips over her forehead, her nose, her cheeks, and the hollow of her neck. By the time he found her mouth, she was putty in his arms.

When at last they walked back hand in hand, they found her baggage piled on the roadside, and the stagecoach gone.

"I don't see your notebook," he said, looking around.

"I don't care," she said, and laughed.

EPILOGUE

God's plan is the best plan of all.
— SIGN ON JENNY HIGGINS
ARMSTRONG'S DESK

Old man Hank Applegate rocked on his chair, happy as a lark. It was late September and already the oppressive heat of summer was a fading memory. Thunderheads peered over the distant hills and the air hung heavy with the threat of rain. No matter. It was still a day for rocking and ruminating.

President Garfield had died the week before. He died two months after he'd been shot and after only six months in office. Chester Arthur had taken office, the third president of the year to do so. Hank grimaced and spit out his tobacco. He knew it! They should never have tried to remove that blasted bullet.

People would do well to listen to him. He had been right about the president's treat-

467

ment. He was right about a lot of things. He'd warned them against lettin' that iron horse come to town. Now look at them. The town was growin' in leaps and bounds.

By thunder, he'd even been right about those Hussy sisters. Fortunately, he didn't have to worry about them anymore.

With all *three* sisters happily married, the little town of Rocky Creek was once again a safe place for confirmed bachelors like himself. No more being accosted in the barber chair or saloons. No more being ambushed by a feminine flutter of lashes or pretty smiles. Emma Hogg was still on the prowl, of course, but she only had eyes for Redd.

Yessiree, life was good again.

The peace and quiet didn't last long, for the Wells Fargo stagecoach came barreling into town, late as usual. Eyes half closed, Applegate watched it drive by then bolted upward in his chair.

Baggage was piled high on the roof and tied to the back. He hadn't seen so much luggage since the colonel and her sisters breezed into town all those weeks ago.

He stood and leaned over the side railing. The driver climbed down from his seat and opened the door of the coach. Not one, not two, not three, but four women climbed out chattering like a bunch of old hens.

He crept down the steps on rickety legs for a closer look-see.

One high pitched voice asked, "Are you sure this is the right town?"

One of the women, dressed to the hilt, waved a newspaper. "It says so right here." She read aloud. "Mothers looking to find husbands for their daughters might do well to follow in the footsteps of the legendary Higgins sisters, who hit a marital mother lode in the unlikely town of Rocky Creek, Texas."

She folded the paper and tucked it under her arm. "Come on ladies, we have work to do." With that she led the new troops in petticoats into the hotel.

Applegate shook his head in dismay. Once again the town was under siege. Now that the marshal had turned traitor to his sex and gone and married *Colonel* Jenny, it was up to Hank to save the men of the town.

DEAR READER

I'll let you in on a little secret. As a school-girl I hated history. Nothing seemed more torturous than memorizing dates, battles, and charters. It wasn't until my teens that I discovered historical novels. That's when I came to realize that history wasn't about dates; it was about people and how they reacted to the ever-changing world around them.

I especially like the nineteenth century, as it mirrors so much of what is happening in our lives today. The 1800s had its share of depressions, recessions, bank failures, and political scandals. Even back then they were talking about health reform. That's not all; almost every household was bombarded with scams, advertisements, and foreign princes asking for money.

Sound like your e-mail inbox? You're close. Only back then it was called the telegraph, and it changed the way Victorians lived, did business, and yes, even fell in love. Wire romances bloomed and one couple even married by telegraph. In 1886, *Electrical World* magazine ran an article titled, "The Dangers of Wired Romances." That same article would no doubt be just as timely today.

Speaking of magazines, *Harper's Bazar,* a style resource for the well-dressed woman and well-dressed mind, got its start in 1867. Its focus hasn't changed much through the years, but William Randolph Hearst did add that extra "a" to Bazar in the 1900s — so no, that wasn't a typo you saw in the book.

In the 1800s, Jeff Trevor might have been considered slow or dim-witted, but his learning difficulties are shared by many of today's schoolchildren. We now know that his bouncing-letter problem was dyslexia, a word coined in 1884 by Rudolf Berlin, a German ophthalmologist who combined the Greek words for *difficult* and *word.*

I could go on and on about the similarities between the 1800s and today's world, but I think I'll wait to tell you more in my next Rocky Creek book.

Since one of my hobbies is collecting unusual and little-known facts about the nineteenth century, I'd love for you to send me any you may have. Please include the reference for fact checking. If I use it in a story, I'll send you a free copy of my next book. You can reach me through my website: www.margaretbrownley.com.

Until next time,
Margaret

READING GROUP GUIDE

1. Jenny protected and, in some ways, overprotected her sisters. Does overprotecting children keep them from discovering God's plan for their lives?
2. During the dark years of her life, Jenny found it easier to avoid God than to face Him. Describe a time in your life when you felt separated from God.
3. Jenny's fear of poverty interfered with her ability to trust that God was leading the way. What other fears can keep us from putting our trust in God?
4. Brenda tried to live up to her reputation as the "good" girl. As a result, she felt that any approval she received was for the person she tried to be, not for the person she was. How did this affect her? In what ways does labeling a child do harm? What labels did you have to overcome?
5. Jenny consulted books, administered tests, and conducted interviews while

searching for husbands for her sisters. She thought she knew how to pick "perfect" men, but God proved her wrong. Name something in your life that seemed totally wrong at the time but turned out to be perfectly right. Do you think this was God-sent? Why or why not?

6. Rhett cut off his feelings as a way to handle his guilt and grief. Timber Joe lived in a world of make-believe so he wouldn't have to face his. Scooter's father turned to alcohol. What are some of the other ways that a person might try to ignore or mask feelings of guilt or grief? How did Jenny, Brenda, and Mary Lou cope with their feelings?

7. Rhett sometimes questioned God's will but never His existence. Was there ever a time when you questioned God's will? Did this have a positive or negative influence on your faith?

8. Rhett recognized himself in Scooter's father, and he didn't much like what he saw. Have you ever seen yourself in others? What was your first reaction? Did it affect your behavior?

9. Reverend Wells said God sometimes brought couples together for His own purposes. He called this a God-match. Name a relationship of yours that was a

God-match. Do you think it's possible that a negative relationship (such as Jenny's relationship with Mr. Blackman) can be a God-match? Why or why not?

10. Jenny's ne'er-do-well father provided an unstable home for his family. How do you think this influenced Jenny's search for suitors?

11. Jenny filled every moment with busy-work. There was simply no room in her life for God. Do you think modern technology has made spending time with God more difficult? Why or why not?

12. Ma, the owner of the boardinghouse where Rhett lived, said there was a difference between guilt and godly sorrow. What do you think that difference is?

13. Reverend Wells told Brenda her job was not to please Jenny but to please God. Did you ever do something you didn't want to do to please your family? Boss? Friends?

ACKNOWLEDGMENTS

Every gift and kindness requires
a thank-you note written from the
heart on the finest stationery. Banknotes
should be mentioned only as "your
generosity." Other gifts, no matter how
frivolous or nonessential, should be
mentioned by name.
— MISS ABIGAIL JENKINS, 1875

First, I would like to thank my readers for the kind letters and emails regarding the first book in my Rocky Creek series, *A Lady Like Sarah.* Just so you know, I printed your e-mails out on the finest stationery.

Now as always I wish to thank my fabulous agent, Natasha Kern, for her wisdom, knowledge, kindness and faith.

Words can't express my gratitude to the entire Thomas Nelson family and their support of me and my work. Andrea, Becky, Ami, Jennifer, Katie, Amanda, and all the

479

rest — what a great group! Jeane Wynn and Jennifer Stair too. Enough good things can't be said about my editor, Natalie Hanemann, who always knows how to make a story stronger, and makes work seem like fun.

Not a moment goes by that I don't thank God for the rather odd circumstances that brought my best friend, teacher, and adopted "sister" Lee Duran into my life. Also, special thanks to the talented Popfiction group who rallied behind me all the way.

Love and appreciation to my husband, George. Thank you for patiently putting up with a wife who spends most of her waking hours communicating with people who don't exist outside the pages of her book.

Last but not least, I would like to thank the neighborhood cat for the nonessential *delicacy* left on my porch.

In closing I want you to know that any banknotes — I mean generosity — you wish to bestow on me in the future will be greatly appreciated.

Blessings,
Margaret